'Jane Austen, or maybe Edith Wharton, goes to Singapore, turning in this lively, entertaining novel of manners. You've got to like any novel set in Asia that includes, among many splendid one-liners, this *amah*'s admonition: "Don't you know there are children starving in America?" . . . Kwan's characters are urban sophisticates par excellence, many of them familiar with the poshest districts of London, Paris, New York and Hong Kong . . . An elegant comedy and an auspicious debut.' *Kirkus* (starred review)

Welcome to the outrageously funny debut novel about three super-rich, pedigreed Chinese families and the gossip, backbiting, and scheming that occurs when the heir to one of the most massive fortunes in Asia brings home his ABC (American-born Chinese) girlfriend to the wedding of the season.

When Rachel Chu agrees to spend the summer in Singapore with her boyfriend, Nicholas Young, she envisions a humble family home, long drives to explore the island, and quality time with the man she might one day marry. What she doesn't know is that Nick's family home happens to look like a palace, that she'll ride in more private planes than cars, and that with one of Asia's most eligible bachelors on her arm, Rachel might as well have a target on her back. Initiated into a world of dynastic splendor beyond imagination, Rachel meets Astrid, the It Girl of Singapore society; Eddie, whose family practically lives in the pages of the Hong Kong socialite magazines; and Eleanor, Nick's formidable mother, a woman who has very strong feelings about who her son should—and should not—marry.

Uproarious, addictive, and filled with jaw-dropping opulence, *Crazy Rich Asians* is an insider's look at the Asian jet set; a perfect depiction of the clash between old money and new money and between Overseas Chinese and Mainland Chinese; and a fabulous novel about what it means to be young, in love, and gloriously, *crazily* rich.

'Kwan's debut is a scintillating fictional look into the opulent lives of fabulously wealthy Chinese expats . . . From its delightful opening scene onward, this sleek social satire offers up more than a few hilarious moments as it skewers the crafty, rich schemers who populate its pages.' Kristine Huntley, *Booklist*

PRAISE FOR *CRAZY RICH ASIANS*

'*Crazy Rich Asians* is this summer's *Bergdorf Blondes*, over-the-top funny and a novelty to boot. Mr Kwan delivers nonstop hoots about a whole new breed of rich, vulgar, brand-name-dropping conspicuous consumers, with its own delicacies, curses, vices, stereotypes and acronyms.' *New York Times*

'High-quality first-time fiction ... An instant favourite ... Opulence and zaniness reign when one of Singapore's richest bachelors invites his American-born girlfriend to travel from New York to vacation in his native country.' *O, The Oprah Magazine*

'Deliciously decadent ... Rachel, an American-born Chinese (ABC), has no idea what to expect when she visits Singapore to meet her boyfriend Nick's multibillionaire family. There, she discovers mind-blowing opulence—next season's couture, palatial properties, million-dollar shopping sprees—and the over-the-top bad behaviour that comes with it ... This 48 carat beach read is crazy fun.' *Entertainment Weekly*

'*Crazy Rich Asians* is both a deliciously satiric read and a Fodor's of sorts to the world of Singapore's fabulously monied, both new and old.' *NY Daily News*

'There's rich, there's filthy rich, and then there's crazy rich ... A *Pride and Prejudice*-like send-up about an heir bringing his Chinese-American girlfriend home to meet his ancestor-obsessed family, the book hilariously skewers imperial splendour and the conniving antics of the Asians jet set.' *People*

'With his debut novel, [Kwan] delivers an uproarious, comical satire about a jet set life that most of us can only imagine. It's a page-turner that will leave you wanting more.' *Hello! Magazine*

'Singapore native Kevin Kwan's debut plays out like an extravagant romcom. Get swept into a culture of Rolls-Royces and ruthless high society in this lively page-turner.' *Chatelaine*

'Merits a place on the must-read list of every development exec in town ... Aimed at *Bridget Jones* lovers and those who got the satire behind Psy's "Gangnam Style".' Andy Lewis, *Hollywood Reporter*

'Kwan's debut is a fun, over-the-top romp through the unbelievable world of the Asian jet set, where anything from this season is already passé and one's pedigree is everything ... A witty tongue-in-cheek frolic about what it means to be from really old money and what it's like to be crazy rich.' *Publishers Weekly* Pick of the Week

'One of the 10 beach reads of all time!' *Glo*

'Private jets with yoga studios! Wedding receptions featuring Cirque du Soleil! State-of-the-art closets that never let you wear the same outfit twice! Ogling the habits of the rich never gets old, and today there's no better place to wealthy watch than in the dazzling cosmopolitan cities of Asia. Born and raised in Singapore—where 17 percent of people are millionaires!—Kevin Kwan satirises the jet-setting, couture-buying, back-stabbing ways of three Chinese families in his debut novel, *Crazy Rich Asians.' Goodreads*

'Read Kevin Kwan's debut, *Crazy Rich Asians*, on an exotic beach in super-expensive sunglasses . . . [Rachel] encounters outré fashion, private jets, and a set of aristocratic values so antiquated they'd make the Dowager Countess proud.' *Entertainment Weekly* Summer Roundup

'A juicy, close anthropological read of Singapore high society and its social and mating rituals . . . Kwan's satirical portrayal rings so true, I fear he'll need to bring a bodyguard next time he lands at Changi Airport. He gets the idiosyncratic details right: the market-savvy wives who day-trade and invest in poverty; the encyclopedic fashion knowledge; the Bible-study get-togethers; the way the whole milieu is interrelated by blood or marriage. And he does a particularly good job of illustrating the divide . . . between mainland wealth and establishment money—an uneasy tension that is very real.' *Elle*

Crazy Rich Asians

Kevin Kwan

ALLEN&UNWIN

SYDNEY • MELBOURNE • AUCKLAND • LONDON

This edition published in 2014

First published in Australia and New Zealand by Allen & Unwin in 2014
First published in the United States in 2013 by Doubleday,
a division of Random House, Inc.

Allen & Unwin
83 Alexander Street
Crows Nest NSW 2065
Australia
Phone: (61 2) 8425 0100
Email: info@allenandunwin.com
Web: www.allenandunwin.com

Cataloguing-in-Publication details are available
from the National Library of Australia
www.trove.nla.gov.au

Grateful permission is made to Kurt Kaiser for permission to reprint an excerpt
from the song 'Pass It On' from *Tell It Like It* Is. Reprinted by permission of the
artist.

ISBN 978 1 76011 040 6

Internal design by Maria Carella
Part opening illustration by Alice Tait
Printed in Australia by SOS Print + Media Group

20 19 18 17 16

For my mother and father

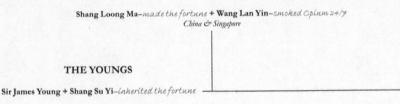

Shang Loong Ma–*made the fortune* + Wang Lan Yin–*smoked Opium 24/7*
China & Singapore

THE YOUNGS

Sir James Young + Shang Su Yi–*inherited the fortune*

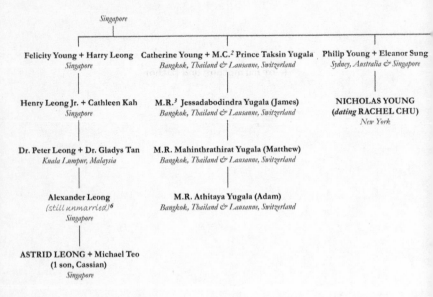

Singapore

Felicity Young + Harry Leong
Singapore

Catherine Young + M.C.[2] Prince Taksin Yugala
Bangkok, Thailand & Lausanne, Switzerland

Philip Young + Eleanor Sung
Sydney, Australia & Singapore

Henry Leong Jr. + Cathleen Kah
Singapore

M.R.[3] Jessadabodindra Yugala (James)
Bangkok, Thailand & Lausanne, Switzerland

NICHOLAS YOUNG
(*dating* RACHEL CHU)
New York

Dr. Peter Leong + Dr. Gladys Tan
Kuala Lumpur, Malaysia

M.R. Mahinthrathirat Yugala (Matthew)
Bangkok, Thailand & Lausanne, Switzerland

Alexander Leong
(*still unmarried*)[6]
Singapore

M.R. Athitaya Yugala (Adam)
Bangkok, Thailand & Lausanne, Switzerland

ASTRID LEONG + Michael Teo
(1 son, Cassian)
Singapore

---

[1] This is what happens when you get a face-lift in Argentina.

[2] M.C. is the abbreviation for Mom Chao, the title reserved for the grandsons of King Rama V of Thailand (1853 – 1910) and is the most junior class still considered royalty. In English this rank is translated as "His Serene Highness." Like many members of the extended Thai royal family, they spend part of the year in Switzerland. Better golf, better traffic.

[3] M.R. is the abbreviation for Mom Rajawongse, the title assumed by children of male Mom Chao. In English this rank is translated as "The Honorable." The three sons of Catherine Young and Prince Taksin all married Thai women of noble birth. Since these wives' names are all impressively long, unpronounceable to non-Thai speakers, and rather irrelevant to this story, they have been left out.

[4] Plotting to run away to Manila with his dear nanny so he can compete in the World Karaoke Championships.

[5] Her notorious gossip spreads faster than the BBC.

[6] But has fathered at least one child out of wedlock with a Malay woman (who now lives in a luxury condo in Beverly Hills).

[7] Hong Kong soap opera actress rumored to be the girl in the red wig from *Crouch My Tiger, Hide Your Dragon II.*

[8] But unfortunately takes after her mother's side of the family—the Chows.

[9] Sold his Singapore properties in the 1980s for many millions and moved to Hawaii but constantly laments that he would be a billionaire today "if he'd just waited a few more years."

THE YOUNG, T'SIEN & SHANG CLAN

(a simplified family tree)

THE SHANGS

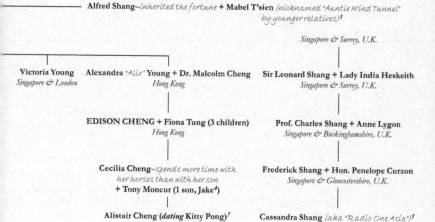

Alfred Shang–*inherited the fortune* **+ Mabel T'sien** *(nicknamed "Auntie Wind Tunnel" by younger relatives)[1]*

Singapore & Surrey, U.K.

Victoria Young
Singapore & London

Alexandra *"Alix"* **Young + Dr. Malcolm Cheng**
Hong Kong

Sir Leonard Shang + Lady India Heskeith
Singapore & Surrey, U.K.

EDISON CHENG + Fiona Tung (3 children)
Hong Kong

Prof. Charles Shang + Anne Lygon
Singapore & Buckinghamshire, U.K.

Cecilia Cheng–*spends more time with her horses than with her son* **+ Tony Moncur (1 son, Jake[4])**

Frederick Shang + Hon. Penelope Curzon
Singapore & Gloucestershire, U.K.

Alistair Cheng (*dating* Kitty Pong)[7]
Hong Kong

Cassandra Shang *(aka "Radio One Asia")[5]*
Singapore, London & Surrey, U.K.

THE T'SIENS

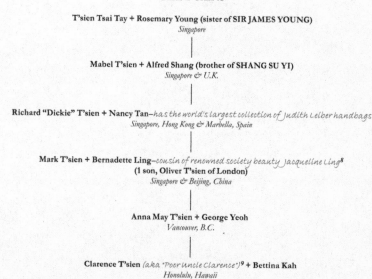

T'sien Tsai Tay + Rosemary Young (sister of SIR JAMES YOUNG)
Singapore

Mabel T'sien + Alfred Shang (brother of SHANG SU YI)
Singapore & U.K.

Richard "Dickie" T'sien + Nancy Tan–*has the world's largest collection of Judith Leiber handbags*
Singapore, Hong Kong & Marbella, Spain

Mark T'sien + Bernadette Ling–*cousin of renowned society beauty Jacqueline Ling[8]*
(1 son, Oliver T'sien of London)
Singapore & Beijing, China

Anna May T'sien + George Yeoh
Vancouver, B.C.

Clarence T'sien *(aka "Poor Uncle Clarence")[9]* **+ Bettina Kah**
Honolulu, Hawaii

Crazy Rich Asians

Prologue: The Cousins

LONDON, 1986

Nicholas Young slumped into the nearest seat in the hotel lobby, drained from the sixteen-hour flight from Singapore, the train ride from Heathrow Airport, and trudging through the rain-soaked streets. His cousin Astrid Leong shivered stoically next to him, all because her mother, Felicity, his *dai gu cheh*—or "big aunt" in Cantonese—said it was a sin to take a taxi nine blocks and forced everyone to walk all the way from Piccadilly Tube Station.

Anyone else happening upon the scene might have noticed an unusually composed eight-year-old boy and an ethereal wisp of a girl sitting quietly in a corner, but all Reginald Ormsby saw from his desk overlooking the lobby were two little Chinese children staining the damask settee with their sodden coats. And it only got worse from there. Three Chinese women stood nearby, frantically blotting themselves dry with tissues, while a teenager slid wildly across the lobby, his sneakers leaving muddy tracks on the black-and-white checkerboard marble.

Ormsby rushed downstairs from the mezzanine, knowing he could more efficiently dispatch these foreigners than his front-desk clerks. "Good evening, I am the general manager. Can I help you?" he said slowly, over-enunciating every word.

"Yes, good evening, we have a reservation," the woman replied in perfect English.

Ormsby peered at her in surprise. "What name is it under?"

"Eleanor Young and family."

Ormsby froze—he recognized the name, especially since the Young party had booked the Lancaster Suite. But who could have imagined that "Eleanor Young" would turn out to be *Chinese,* and how on earth did she end up here? The Dorchester or the Ritz might let this kind in, but this *was* the Calthorpe, owned by the Calthorpe-Cavendish-Gores since the reign of George IV and run for all intents and purposes like a private club for the sort of families that appeared in *Debrett's* or the *Almanach de Gotha.* Ormsby considered the bedraggled women and the dripping children. The Dowager Marchioness of Uckfield was staying through the weekend, and he could scarcely imagine what she would make of *these folk* appearing at breakfast tomorrow. He made a swift decision. "I'm terribly sorry, but I can't seem to find a booking under that name."

"Are you sure?" Eleanor asked in surprise.

"Quite sure." Ormsby grinned tightly.

Felicity Leong joined her sister-in-law at the front desk. "Is there a problem?" she asked impatiently, eager to get to the room to dry her hair.

"*Alamak,** they can't find our reservation," Eleanor sighed.

"How come? Maybe you booked it under another name?" Felicity inquired.

"No, *lah.* Why would I do that? It was always booked under my name," Eleanor replied irritatedly. Why did Felicity always assume she was incompetent? She turned back to the manager. "Sir, can you please check again? I reconfirmed our reservation just two days ago. We're supposed to be in your largest suite."

"Yes, I know you booked the Lancaster Suite, but I can't find your name anywhere," Ormsby insisted.

"Excuse me, but if you know we booked the Lancaster Suite, why don't we have the room?" Felicity asked, confused.

Bloody hell. Ormsby cursed at his own slip-up. "No, no, you mis-

---

* Malay slang used to express shock or exasperation like "oh dear" or "oh my God." *Alamak* and *lah* are the two most commonly used slang words in Singapore. (*Lah* is a suffix that can be used at the end of any phrase for emphasis, but there's no good explanation for why people use it, *lah.*)

understood. What I meant was that *you might think* you booked the Lancaster Suite, but I certainly can't find any record of it." He turned away for a moment, pretending to rummage through some other paperwork.

Felicity leaned over the polished oak counter and pulled the leather-bound reservations book toward her, flipping through pages. "Look! It says right here 'Mrs. Eleanor Young—Lancaster Suite for four nights.' Do you not see this?"

"Madam! That is PRIVATE!" Ormsby snapped in fury, startling his two junior clerks, who glanced uncomfortably at their manager.

Felicity peered at the balding, red-faced man, the situation suddenly becoming abundantly clear. She hadn't seen this particular brand of superior sneer since she was a child growing up in the waning days of colonial Singapore, and she thought this kind of overt racism had ceased to exist. "Sir," she said politely but firmly, "this hotel came highly recommended to us by Mrs. Mince, the wife of the Anglican Bishop of Singapore, and I *clearly* saw our name in your registry book. I don't know what sort of funny business is going on, but we have traveled a very long way and our children are tired and cold. I *insist* that you honor our reservation."

Ormsby was indignant. How *dare* this Chinese woman with the Thatcheresque perm and preposterous "English" accent speak to him in such a manner? "I'm afraid we simply do not have anything available," he declared.

"Are you telling me that there are no rooms left in this entire hotel?" Eleanor said incredulously.

"Yes," he replied curtly.

"Where are we supposed to go at this hour?" Eleanor asked.

"Perhaps someplace in Chinatown?" Ormsby sniffed. These foreigners had wasted enough of his time.

Felicity went back to where her younger sister Alexandra Cheng stood guarding the luggage. "Finally! I can't wait to take a hot bath," Alexandra said eagerly.

"Actually, this odious man is refusing to give us our room!" Felicity said, making no attempt to hide her fury.

"What? Why?" Alexandra asked, completely confused.

"I think it has something to do with us being Chinese," Felicity said, as if she didn't quite believe her own words.

"Gum suey ah!"[*] Alexandra exclaimed. "Let me talk to him. Living in Hong Kong, I have more experience dealing with these types."

"Alix, don't bother. He's a typical *ang mor gau sai!*"[†] Eleanor exclaimed.

"Even so, isn't this supposed to be one of London's top hotels? How can they get away with that sort of behavior?" Alexandra asked.

"Exactly!" Felicity raged on. "The English are normally so lovely, I have never been treated like this in all my years coming here."

Eleanor nodded in agreement, even though privately she felt that Felicity was partly to blame for this fiasco. If Felicity wasn't so *giam siap*[‡] and had let them take a taxi from Heathrow, they would have arrived looking far less disheveled. (Of course, it didn't help that her sisters-in-law always looked so dowdy, she had to dress down whenever she traveled with them, ever since that trip to Thailand when everyone mistook them for her maids.)

Edison Cheng, Alexandra's twelve-year-old son, approached the ladies nonchalantly, sipping soda from a tall glass.

"Aiyah, Eddie! Where did you get that?" Alexandra exclaimed.

"From the bartender, of course."

"How did you pay for it?"

"I didn't—I told him to charge it to our suite," Eddie replied breezily. "Can we go up now? I'm starving and I want to order from room service."

Felicity shook her head in disapproval—Hong Kong boys were notoriously pampered, but this nephew of hers was incorrigible. Good thing they were here to put him in boarding school, where he would have some sense knocked into him—cold morning showers and stale toast with Bovril was what he needed. "No, no, we're not staying here anymore. Go and watch Nicky and Astrid while we decide what to do," Felicity instructed.

Eddie walked over to his younger cousins, resuming the game

---

[*] Cantonese for "How rotten!"

[†] A charming Hokkien colloquialism that translates to "red-haired" (*ang mor*) "dog shit" (*gau sai*). Used in reference to all Westerners, it's usually shortened to a simple *"ang mor."*

[‡] Hokkien for "stingy," "miserly." (The vast majority of Singaporeans speak English, but it is a common practice to mash up words in Malay, Indian, and various Chinese dialects to form a local patois known as "Singlish.")

they had begun on the plane. "Off the sofa! Remember, I'm the *chairman*, so I'm the one who gets to sit," he commanded. "Here, Nicky, hold my glass while I sip from the straw. Astrid, you're my executive secretary, so you need to massage my shoulders."

"I don't know why you get to be the chairman, while Nicky is the vice president and I have to be the secretary," Astrid protested.

"Didn't I explain this already? I'm the chairman, because I am four years older than the both of you. You're the executive secretary, because you're the girl. I need a girl to massage my shoulders and to help choose jewelry for all my mistresses. My best friend Leo's father, Ming Kah-Ching, is the third-richest man in Hong Kong, and that's what his executive secretary does."

"Eddie, if you want me to be your vice president, I should be doing something more important than holding your glass," Nick argued. "We still haven't decided what our company makes."

"I've decided—we make custom limousines, like Rolls-Royces and Jags," Eddie declared.

"Can't we make something cooler, like a time machine?" Nick asked.

"Well, these are ultra-special limousines with features like Jacuzzis, secret compartments, and James Bond ejector seats," Eddie said, bouncing up from the settee so suddenly that he knocked the glass out of Nick's hand. Coca-Cola spilled everywhere, and the sound of smashing glass pierced the lobby. The bell captain, concierge, and front-desk clerks glared at the children. Alexandra rushed over, shaking a finger in dismay.

"Eddie! Look what you've done!"

"It wasn't my fault—Nicky was the one who dropped it," Eddie began.

"But it's *your* glass, and you hit it out of my hand!" Nick defended himself.

Ormsby approached Felicity and Eleanor. "I'm afraid I'm going to have to ask you to leave the premises."

"Can we just use your telephone?" Eleanor pleaded.

"I *do* think the children have done quite enough damage for one night, don't you?" he hissed.

It was still drizzling, and the group huddled under a green-and-white-striped awning on Brook Street while Felicity stood inside a phone booth frantically calling other hotels.

"*Dai gu cheh* looks like a soldier in a sentry box in that red booth," Nick observed, rather thrilled by the strange turn of events. "Mummy, what are we going to do if we can't find a place to stay tonight? Maybe we can sleep in Hyde Park. There's an amazing weeping beech in Hyde Park called the upside-down tree, and its branches hang down so low that it's almost like a cave. We can all sleep underneath and be protected—"

"Don't talk nonsense! No one is sleeping in the park. *Dai gu cheh* is calling other hotels right now," Eleanor said, thinking that her son was getting far too precocious for his own good.

"Oooh, I want to sleep in the park!" Astrid squealed in delight. "Nicky, remember how we moved that big iron bed at Ah Ma's house into the garden and slept under the stars one night?"

"Well, you two can sleep in the *loong kau** for all I care, but I'll take the big royal suite, where I can order club sandwiches with champagne and caviar," Eddie said.

"Don't be ridiculous, Eddie. When have you ever had caviar?" his mother asked.

"At Leo's house. Their butler always serves us caviar with little triangles of toasted bread. And it's always Iranian beluga, because Leo's mum says Iranian caviar is the *best*," Eddie declared.

"Connie Ming *would* say something like that," Alexandra muttered under her breath, glad her son was finally away from that family's influence.

Inside the telephone booth, Felicity was trying to explain the predicament to her husband over a crackly connection to Singapore.

"What nonsense, *lah*! You should have *demanded* the room!" Harry Leong fumed. "You are always too polite—these service people need to be put in their place. Did you tell them who we are? I'm going to call up the minister of trade and investment right now!"

"Come on, Harry, you're not helping. I've called more than ten hotels already. Who knew that today was Commonwealth Day? Every VIP is in town and everyone is booked solid. Poor Astrid is soaked through. We need to find someplace for tonight before your daughter catches her death of cold."

"Did you try calling your cousin Leonard? Maybe you could take a train straight to Surrey," Harry suggested.

* Cantonese for "gutter."

"I did. He's not in—he's grouse hunting in Scotland all week-end."

"What a bloody mess!" Harry sighed. "Let me call Tommy Toh over at the Singapore embassy. I'm sure they can sort things out. What is the name of this bloody racist hotel?"

"The Calthorpe," Felicity answered.

"*Alamak*, is this the place owned by Rupert Calthorpe-something-something?" Harry asked, suddenly perking up.

"I have no idea."

"Where is it located?"

"It's in Mayfair, close to Bond Street. It's actually a rather beauti-ful hotel, if it wasn't for this horrible manager."

"Yes, I think that's it! I played golf with Rupert what's his name and a few other Brits last month in California, and I remember him telling me all about his place. Felicity, I have an idea. I'm going to call this Rupert fellow. Just stay put and I'll call you back."

Ormsby stared in disbelief when the three Chinese children burst through the front door again, barely an hour after he had evicted the whole lot of them.

"Eddie, I'm getting *myself* a drink. If you want one, go get it your-self," Nick said firmly to his cousin as he walked toward the lounge.

"Remember what your mummy said. It's too late for us to drink Cokes," Astrid warned as she skipped through the lobby, trying to catch up with the boys.

"Well then, I'll get a rum and coke," Eddie said brazenly.

"What on God's green earth . . ." Ormsby bellowed, storming across the lobby to intercept the children. Before he could reach them, he suddenly caught sight of Lord Rupert Calthorpe-Cavendish-Gore ushering the Chinese women into the lobby, seemingly in the midst of conducting a tour. "And my grandfather brought over René Lalique in 1918 to do the glass murals you see here in the great hall. Needless to say, Lutyens, who supervised the restoration, did not approve of these art nouveau flourishes." The women laughed politely.

The staff quickly snapped to attention, surprised to see the old lord, who hadn't set foot inside the hotel in years. Lord Rupert turned toward the hotel manager. "Ah, Wormsby, isn't it?"

"Yes, m'lord," he said, too dazed to correct his boss.

"Would you kindly have some rooms readied for the lovely Mrs. Young, Mrs. Leong, and Mrs. Cheng?"

"But sir, I just—" Ormsby tried to protest.

"And Wormsby," Lord Rupert continued dismissively, "I am entrusting you to inform the staff of a very important announcement: as of this evening, my family's long history as custodians of the Calthorpe has come to an end."

Ormsby stared at him in utter disbelief. "M'lord, surely there's some mistake—"

"No, no mistake at all. I sold the Calthorpe a short while ago, lock, stock, and barrel. May I present the new mistress, Mrs. Felicity Leong."

"WHAT?"

"Yes, Mrs. Leong's husband, Harry Leong—a wonderful chap with a lethal right-arm swing, whom I met at Pebble Beach—called me up and made me a marvelous offer. I can now devote all my time to bonefishing in Eleuthera without having to worry about this Gothic pile."

Ormsby stared at the women, his mouth agape.

"Ladies, why don't we join your adorable children at the Long Bar for a toast?" Lord Rupert said merrily.

"That would be wonderful," Eleanor replied. "But first, Felicity, isn't there something you wanted to tell this man?"

Felicity turned to Ormsby, now looking as if he was about to faint. "Oh yes, I almost forgot," she began with a smile, "I'm afraid I'm going to have to ask you to leave the premises."

Part One

*Nowhere in the world are there to be found
people richer than the Chinese.*

IBN BATUTA (FOURTEENTH CENTURY)

Part One

1

Nicholas Young and Rachel Chu

"You sure about this?" Rachel asked again, blowing softly on the surface of her steaming cup of tea. They were sitting at their usual window table at Tea & Sympathy, and Nick had just invited her to spend the summer with him in Asia.

"Rachel, I'd love it if you came," Nick reassured her. "You weren't planning on teaching this summer, so what's your worry? Think you won't be able to handle the heat and humidity?"

"No, that's not it. I know you're going to be so busy with all your best-man duties, and I wouldn't want to distract you," Rachel said.

"What distraction? Colin's wedding is only going to take up the first week in Singapore, and then we can spend the rest of the summer just bumming around Asia. Come on, let me show you where I grew up. I want to take you to all my favorite haunts."

"Will you show me the sacred cave where you lost your virginity?" Rachel teased, arching an eyebrow playfully.

"Definitely! We can even stage a reenactment!" Nick laughed, slathering jam and clotted cream onto a scone still warm from the oven. "And doesn't a good friend of yours live in Singapore?"

"Yes, Peik Lin, my best friend from college," Rachel said. "She's been trying to get me to come visit for years."

"All the more reason. Rachel, you're going to love it, and I just know you're going to flip out over the food! You do realize Singapore is the most food-obsessed country on the planet?"

"Well, just watching the way you fawn over everything you eat, I figured it's pretty much the national sport."

"Remember Calvin Trillin's *New Yorker* piece on Singapore street foods? I'll take you to all the local dives even *he* doesn't know about." Nick took another bite of his fluffy scone and continued with his mouth full. "I know how much you love these scones. Just wait till you taste my Ah Ma's—"

"Your Ah Ma bakes scones?" Rachel tried to imagine a traditional Chinese grandmother preparing this quintessentially English confection.

"Well, she doesn't exactly bake them herself, but she has the best scones in the world—you'll see," Nick said, turning around reflexively to make sure no one in the cozy little spot had overheard him. He didn't want to become persona non grata at his favorite café for carelessly pledging allegiance to another scone, even if it was his grandmother's.

At a neighboring table, the girl huddled behind a three-tiered stand piled high with finger sandwiches was getting increasingly excited by the conversation she was overhearing. She suspected it might be him, but now she had absolute confirmation. It *was* Nicholas Young. Even though she was only fifteen at the time, Celine Lim never forgot the day Nicholas strolled past their table at Pulau Club* and flashed that devastating grin of his at her sister Charlotte.

"Is that one of the Leong brothers?" their mother had asked.

"No, that's Nicholas Young, a cousin of the Leongs," Charlotte replied.

"Philip Young's boy? Aiyah, when did he shoot up like that? He's so handsome now!" Mrs. Lim exclaimed.

"He's just back from Oxford. Double-majored in history and law," Charlotte added, anticipating her mother's next question.

"Why didn't you get up and talk to him?" Mrs. Lim said excitedly.

"Why should I bother, when you swat away every guy who dares come near," Charlotte answered curtly.

---

* Singapore's most prestigious country club (with membership practically harder to obtain than a knighthood).

"*Alamak,* stupid girl! I'm only trying to protect you from fortune hunters. This one you'd be lucky to have. This one you can *cheong!*"

Celine couldn't believe her mother was actually encouraging her big sister to *snatch* this boy. She stared curiously at Nicholas, now laughing animatedly with his friends at a table under a blue-and-white umbrella by the pool. Even from afar, he stood out in high relief. Unlike the other fellows with their regulation Indian barbershop haircuts, Nicholas had perfectly tousled black hair, chiseled Cantonese pop-idol features, and impossibly thick eyelashes. He was the cutest, dreamiest guy she'd ever seen.

"Charlotte, why don't you go over and invite him to your fundraiser on Saturday?" their mother kept on.

"Stop it, Mum." Charlotte smiled through gritted teeth. "I know what I'm doing."

As it turned out, Charlotte did not know what she was doing, since Nicholas never showed up at her fund-raiser, much to their mother's eternal disappointment. But that afternoon at Pulau Club left such an indelible mark on Celine's adolescent memory that six years later and on the other side of the planet, she still recognized him.

"Hannah, let me get a picture of you with that delicious sticky toffee pudding," Celine said, taking out her camera phone. She pointed it in the direction of her friend, but surreptitiously trained the lens on Nicholas. She snapped the photo and immediately e-mailed it to her sister, who now lived in Atherton, California. Her phone pinged minutes later.

BigSis: OMFG! THAT'S NICK YOUNG! WHERE ARE U?
Celine Lim: T&S.
BigSis: Who's the girl he's with?
Celine Lim: GF, I think. Looks ABC.*
BigSis: Hmm . . . do you see a ring?
Celine Lim: No ring.
BigSis: PLS spy for me!!!
Celine Lim: You owe me big-time!!!

Nick gazed out the café window, marveling at the people with tiny dogs parading along this stretch of Greenwich Avenue as if it

* American-born Chinese.

were a catwalk for the city's most fashionable breeds. A year ago, French bulldogs were all the rage, but now it looked like Italian greyhounds were giving the Frenchies a run for their money. He faced Rachel again, resuming his campaign. "The great thing about starting out in Singapore is that it's the perfect base. Malaysia is just across a bridge, and it's a quick hop to Hong Kong, Cambodia, Thailand. We can even go island-hopping off Indonesia—"

"It all sounds amazing, but *ten weeks* . . . I don't know if I want to be away that long," Rachel mused. She could sense Nick's eagerness, and the idea of visiting Asia again filled her with excitement. She had spent a year teaching in Chengdu between college and grad school but couldn't afford to travel anywhere beyond China's borders back then. As an economist, she certainly knew enough about Singapore—this tiny, intriguing island at the tip of the Malay Peninsula, which had transformed within a few short decades from a British colonial backwater into the country with the world's highest concentration of millionaires. It would be fascinating to see the place up close, especially with Nick as her guide.

Yet something about this trip made Rachel a little apprehensive, and she couldn't help but ponder the deeper implications. Nick made it seem so spontaneous, but knowing him, she was sure he had put far more thought into it than he let on. They had been together for almost two years, and now he was inviting her on an extended trip to visit his hometown, to attend his best friend's wedding, no less. Did this mean what she thought it did?

Rachel peered into her teacup, wishing she could divine something from the stray leaves pooled at the bottom of the deep golden Assam. She had never been the sort of girl who longed for fairytale endings. Being twenty-nine, she was by Chinese standards well into old-maid territory, and even though her busybody relatives were perpetually trying to set her up, she had spent the better part of her twenties focused on getting through grad school, finishing her dissertation, and jump-starting her career in academia. This surprise invitation, however, sparked some vestigial instinct within her. *He wants to take me home. He wants me to meet his family.* The long-dormant romantic in her was awakening, and she knew there was only one answer to give.

"I'll have to check with my dean to see when I'm needed back, but you know what? Let's do this!" Rachel declared. Nick leaned across the table, kissing her jubilantly.

Minutes later, before Rachel herself knew for certain her summer plans, the details of her conversation had already begun to spread far and wide, circling the globe like a virus set loose. After Celine Lim (Parsons School of Design fashion major) e-mailed her sister Charlotte Lim (recently engaged to venture capitalist Henry Chiu) in California, Charlotte called her best friend Daphne Ma (Sir Benedict Ma's youngest daughter) in Singapore and breathlessly filled her in. Daphne texted eight friends, including Carmen Kwek (granddaughter of Robert "Sugar King" Kwek) in Shanghai, whose cousin Amelia Kwek had gone to Oxford with Nicholas Young. Amelia simply *had* to IM her friend Justina Wei (the Instant Noodle heiress) in Hong Kong, and Justina, whose office at Hutchison Whampoa was right across the hall from Roderick Liang's (of the Liang Finance Group Liangs), simply *had* to interrupt his conference call to share this juicy tidbit. Roderick in turn Skyped his girlfriend Lauren Lee, who was holidaying at the Royal Mansour in Marrakech with her grandmother Mrs. Lee Yong Chien (no introductions necessary) and her aunt Patsy Teoh (Miss Taiwan 1979, now the ex-wife of telecom mogul Dickson Teoh). Patsy made a poolside call to Jacqueline Ling (granddaughter of philanthropist Ling Yin Chao) in London, knowing full well that Jacqueline would have a direct line to Cassandra Shang (Nicholas Young's second cousin), who spent every spring at her family's vast estate in Surrey. And so this exotic strain of gossip spread rapidly through the levantine networks of the Asian jet set, and within a few hours, almost everyone in this exclusive circle knew that Nicholas Young was bringing a girl home to Singapore.

And, *alamak*! This was big news.

2
Eleanor Young
•
SINGAPORE

Everyone knew that *Dato** Tai Toh Lui made his first fortune the dirty way by bringing down Loong Ha Bank in the early eighties, but in the two decades since, the efforts of his wife, *Datin* Carol Tai, on behalf of the right charities had burnished the Tai name into one of respectability. Every Thursday, for instance, the *datin* held a Bible study luncheon for her closest friends in her bedroom, and Eleanor Young was sure to attend.

Carol's palatial bedroom was not actually in the sprawling glass-and-steel structure everyone living along Kheam Hock Road nicknamed the "Star Trek House." Instead, on the advice of her husband's security team, the bedroom was hidden away in the pool pavilion, a white travertine fortress that spanned the swimming pool like a postmodern Taj Mahal. To get there, you either had to follow the footpath that wound along the coral rock gardens or take the shortcut through the service wing. Eleanor always preferred the quicker route, since she assiduously avoided the sun to maintain her porcelain-white complexion, and also, as Carol's oldest friend, she

---

* A highly regarded honorific title in Malaysia (similar to a British knighthood) conferred by a hereditary royal ruler of one of the nine Malay states. The title is often used by Malay royals to reward powerful businessmen, politicians, and philanthropists in Malaysia, Singapore, and Indonesia, and some people spend decades sucking up just to get the title. The wife of a *dato'* is called a *datin*.

considered herself exempt from the formalities of waiting at the front door, being announced by the butler, and all that nonsense.

Besides, Eleanor enjoyed passing through the kitchens. The old *amahs* squatting over enamel double boilers would always open the lids for Eleanor to sniff the smoky medicinal herbs being brewed for Carol's husband ("natural Viagra," as he called it), and the kitchen maids gutting fish in the courtyard would fawn over how youthful Mrs. Young still looked for sixty, what with her fashionably shagged chin-length hair and her unwrinkled face (before furiously debating, the moment she was out of earshot, what expensive new cosmetic procedure Mrs. Young must have endured).

By the time Eleanor arrived at Carol's bedroom, the Bible study regulars—Daisy Foo, Lorena Lim, and Nadine Shaw—would be assembled and waiting. Here, sheltered from the harsh equatorial heat, these longtime friends would sprawl languorously about the room, analyzing the Bible verses assigned in their study guides. The place of honor on Carol's Qing dynasty *Huanghuali** bed was always reserved for Eleanor, for even though this was Carol's house and she was the one married to the billionaire financier, Carol still deferred to her. This was the way things had been since their childhood as neighbors growing up on Serangoon Road, mainly because, coming from a Chinese-speaking family, Carol had always felt inferior to Eleanor, who was brought up speaking English *first*. (The others also kowtowed to her, because even among these exceedingly well-married ladies, Eleanor had trumped them all by becoming Mrs. Philip Young.)

Today's lunch started off with braised quail and abalone over hand-pulled noodles, and Daisy (married to the rubber magnate Q. T. Foo but born a Wong, of the Ipoh Wongs) fought to separate the starchy noodles while trying to find 1 Timothy in her King James Bible. With her bobbed perm and her rimless reading glasses perched at the tip of her nose, she looked like the principal of a girls' school. At sixty-four, she was the oldest of the ladies, and even though everyone else was on the New American Standard, Daisy always insisted on reading from her version, saying, "I went to convent school and

---

* Literally "yellow flowering pear," an exceedingly rare type of rosewood now virtually extinct. In recent decades, *Huanghuali* furniture has become highly sought after by discerning collectors. After all, it goes so well with mid-century modern.

was taught by nuns, you know, so it will always be King James for me." Tiny droplets of garlicky broth splattered onto the tissue-like page, but she managed to keep the good book open with one hand while deftly maneuvering her ivory chopsticks with the other.

Nadine, meanwhile, was busily flipping through *her* Bible—the latest issue of *Singapore Tattle*. Every month, she couldn't wait to see how many pictures of her daughter Francesca—the celebrated "Shaw Foods heiress"—were featured in the "Soirées" section of the magazine. Nadine herself was a fixture in the social pages, what with her Kabuki-esque makeup, tropical-fruit-size jewels, and over-teased hair. "Aiyah, Carol, *Tattle* devoted two full pages to your Christian Helpers fashion gala!" Nadine exclaimed.

"Already? I didn't realize it would come out so quickly," Carol remarked. Unlike Nadine, she was always a bit embarrassed to find herself in magazines, even though editors constantly fawned over her "classic Shanghainese songstress looks." Carol simply felt obligated to attend a few charity galas every week as any good born-again Christian should, and because her husband kept reminding her that "being Mother Teresa is good for business."

Nadine scanned the glossy pages up and down. "That Lena Teck has *really* put on weight since her Mediterranean cruise, hasn't she? It must be those all-you-can-eat buffets—you always feel like you have to eat more to get your money's worth. She better be careful—all those Teck women end up with fat ankles."

"I don't think she cares how fat her ankles get. Do you know how much she inherited when her father died? I heard she and her five brothers got seven hundred million *each*," Lorena said from her chaise lounge.

"Is that all? I thought Lena had at least a billion." Nadine sniffed. "Hey, so strange Elle, how come there's no picture of your pretty niece Astrid? I remember all the photographers swarming around her that day."

"Those photographers were wasting their time. Astrid's pictures are never published anywhere. Her mother made a deal with all the magazine editors back when she was a teenager," Eleanor explained.

"Why on earth would she do that?"

"Don't you know my husband's family by now? They would rather die than appear in print," Eleanor said.

"What, have they become too grand to be seen mingling with other Singaporeans?" Nadine said indignantly.

"Aiyah, Nadine, there's a difference between being grand and being discreet," Daisy commented, knowing full well that families like the Leongs and the Youngs guarded their privacy to the point of obsession.

"Grand or not, I think Astrid is wonderful," Carol chimed in. "You know, I'm not supposed to say, but Astrid wrote the biggest check at the fund-raiser. And she insisted that I keep it anonymous. But her donation was what made this year's gala a record-breaking success."

Eleanor eyed the pretty new Mainland Chinese maid entering the room, wondering if this was another one of the girls that the *dato'* had handpicked from that "employment agency" he frequented in Suzhou, the city reputed to have the most beautiful women in China. "What do we have today?" she asked Carol, as the maid placed a familiar bulky mother-of-pearl chest beside the bed.

"Oh, I wanted to show you what I bought on my Burma trip."

Eleanor flipped open the lid of the chest eagerly and began methodically taking out the stacked black velvet trays. One of her favorite parts of Thursday Bible study was looking at Carol's latest acquisitions. Soon the bed was lined with trays containing a blinding array of jewels. "What intricate crosses—I didn't realize they did such good setting work in Burma!"

"No, no, those crosses are Harry Winston," Carol corrected. "The rubies are from Burma."

Lorena got up from her lunch and headed straight for the bed, holding up one of the lychee-size rubies to the light. "Aiyah, you have to be careful in Burma because so many of their rubies are synthetically treated to boost the redness." Being the wife of Lawrence Lim (of the L'Orient Jewelry Lims), Lorena could speak on this topic with authority.

"I thought rubies from Burma were supposed to be the best," Eleanor remarked.

"Ladies, you need to stop calling it Burma. It's been called *Myanmar* for more than twenty years now," Daisy corrected.

"*Alamak!* You sound just like Nicky, always correcting me!" Eleanor said.

"Hey, speaking of Nick, when does he arrive from New York? Isn't he the best man at Colin Khoo's wedding?" Daisy asked.

"Yes, yes. But you know my son—I'm always the last to know anything!" Eleanor complained.

"Isn't he staying with you?"

"Of course. He always stays with us first, before heading to Old Lady's," Eleanor said, using her nickname for her mother-in-law.

"Well," Daisy continued, lowering her voice a bit, "what do you think Old Lady will do about his guest?"

"What do you mean? What *guest*?" Eleanor asked.

"The one . . . he's bringing . . . to the wedding," Daisy replied slowly, her eyes darting around at the other ladies mischievously, knowing they all knew to whom she was referring.

"What are you talking about? Who is he bringing?" Eleanor said, a little confused.

"His latest girlfriend, *lah*!" Lorena revealed.

"No such thing! No way Nicky has a girlfriend," Eleanor insisted.

"Why is it so hard for you to believe that your son has a girlfriend?" Lorena asked. She had always found Nick to be *the* most dashing young man of his generation, and with all that Young money, it was such a pity her good-for-nothing daughter Tiffany never managed to attract him.

"But surely you've heard about this girl? *The one from New York*," Daisy said in a whisper, relishing that she was the one breaking the news to Eleanor.

"An *American* girl? Nicky wouldn't *dare* do such a thing. Daisy, your information is always *ta pah kay*!"*

"What do you mean? My news is not *ta pah kay*—it comes from the most reliable source! Anyway, I hear she's Chinese," Daisy offered.

"Really? What's her name, and where is she from? Daisy, if you tell me she's from Mainland China, I think I'll have a stroke," Eleanor warned.

"I heard she's from Taiwan," Daisy said carefully.

"Oh my goodness, I hope she's not one of those Taiwanese tornadoes!" Nadine cackled.

"What do you mean by that?" Eleanor asked.

"You know how notorious those Taiwanese girls can be. They

* Malay for "not accurate."

swoop in unexpectedly, the men fall head over heels, and before you know it they are gone, but not before sucking up every last dollar, just like a tornado," Nadine explained. "I know so many men who have fallen prey—think about Mrs. K. C. Tang's son Gerald, whose wife cleaned him out and ran off with all the Tang heirlooms. Or poor Annie Sim, who lost her husband to that lounge singer from Taipei."

At this moment, Carol's husband entered the room. "Hello, hello, ladies. How is Jesus time today?" he said, puffing away on his cigar and swirling his goblet of Hennessy, looking every portly inch the caricature of an Asian tycoon.

"Hello, *Dato'*!" the ladies said in unison, hurriedly shifting themselves into more decorous positions.

"*Dato'*, Daisy here is trying to give me a stroke! She's telling everyone that Nicky has a new *Taiwanese* girlfriend!" Eleanor cried.

"Relax, Lealea. Taiwanese girls are *lovely*—they really know how to take care of a man, and maybe she'll be prettier than all those spoiled, inbred girls you try to matchmake him to." The *dato'* grinned. "Anyway," he continued, suddenly lowering his voice, "if I were you, I would be less worried about young Nicholas, and more worried about *Sina Land* right now."

"Why? What's happening to Sina Land?" Eleanor asked.

"Sina Land *toh tuew*. It's going to collapse," the *dato'* declared with a satisfied grin.

"But Sina Land is blue-chip. How can that be? My brother even told me they have all these new projects in western China," Lorena argued.

"The Chinese government, my source assures me, has pulled out of that huge new development in Xinjiang. I just unloaded my shares and I'm shorting a hundred thousand shares every hour until market closes." With that, the *dato'* expelled a big puff of smoke from his Cohiba and pressed a button next to the bed. The vast wall of glass facing the sparkling swimming pool began to tilt forty-five degrees like an enormous cantilevered garage door, and the *dato'* lumbered out into the garden toward the main house.

For a few seconds, the room went absolutely still. You could almost hear the wheels in each woman's head whirling into overdrive. Daisy suddenly jumped up from her chair, spilling the tray of noodles onto the floor. "Quick, quick! Where's my handbag? I need to call my broker!"

Eleanor and Lorena both scrambled for their cell phones as well. Nadine had her stockbroker on speed dial and was already screaming into her phone, "Dump all of it! SINA LAND. Yes. Dump it all! I just heard from the horse's mouth that it's *gone case!*"

Lorena was on the other end of the bed, cupping her phone close to her mouth. "Desmond, I don't care, please just start shorting it now."

Daisy began to hyperventilate. "*Sum toong, ah!*[*] I'm losing millions by the second! Where is my bloody broker? Don't tell me that moron is still at lunch!"

Carol calmly reached for the touch-screen panel by her bedside table. "Mei Mei, can you please come in and clean up a spill?" Then she closed her eyes, lifted her arms into the air, and began to pray aloud: "*Oh Jesus, our personal lord and savior, blessed be your name. We come to you humbly asking for your forgiveness today, as we have all sinned against you. Thank you for showering your blessings upon us. Thank you Lord Jesus for the fellowship that we shared today, for the nourishing food we enjoyed, for the power of your holy word. Please watch over dear Sister Eleanor, Sister Lorena, Sister Daisy, and Sister Nadine, as they try to sell their Sina Land shares . . .*"

Carol opened her eyes for a moment, noting with satisfaction that Eleanor at least was praying along with her. But of course, she couldn't know that behind those serene eyelids, Eleanor was praying for something else entirely. *A Taiwanese girl! Please God, let it not be true.*

---

[*] Cantonese for "my heart aches."

3

Rachel Chu

It would be just after dinnertime in Cupertino, and on the nights she wasn't at Nick's, it became Rachel's habit to call her mother right as she was getting into bed.

"Guess who just closed the deal on the big house on Laurel Glen Drive?" Kerry Chu boasted excitedly in Mandarin as soon as she picked up the phone.

"Wow, Mom, congratulations! Isn't that your third sale this month?" Rachel asked.

"Yes! I broke last year's office record! You see, I *knew* I made the right decision to join Mimi Shen at the Los Altos office," Kerry said with satisfaction.

"You're going to make Realtor of the Year again, I just know it," Rachel replied, re-fluffing the pillow under her head. "Well, I have some exciting news too . . . Nick invited me to come with him to Asia this summer."

"He *did*?" Kerry remarked, her voice lowering an octave.

"Mom, don't start getting any ideas," Rachel warned, knowing that tone of her mother's so well.

"Hiyah! What ideas? When you brought Nick home last Thanksgiving, everyone who saw you two lovebirds together said you were perfect for each other. Now it's his turn to introduce you to his family. Do you think he's going to propose?" Kerry gushed, unable to contain herself.

"Mom, we've never once talked about marriage," Rachel said, trying to downplay it. As excited as she was about all the possibilities that hung over the trip, she wasn't going to encourage her mom for the time being. Her mother was already far too invested in her happiness, and she didn't want to get her hopes up . . . too much.

Still, Kerry was brimming with anticipation. "Daughter, I know men like Nick. He can act the bohemian scholar all he wants, but I know deep down he is the marrying kind. He wants to settle down and have many children, so there is no more time to waste."

"Mom, just stop!"

"Besides, how many nights a week do you already spend at his place? I'm shocked you two haven't moved in together yet."

"You're the only Chinese mom I know who's actually encouraging her daughter to shack up with a guy." Rachel laughed.

"I'm the only Chinese mother with an unmarried daughter who's almost thirty! Do you know all the inquiries I get almost every day? I'm getting tired of defending you. Why, even yesterday, I ran into Min Chung at Peet's Coffee. 'I know you wanted your daughter to get her career established first, but isn't it time that girl got married?' she asked. You know her daughter Jessica is engaged to the number-seven guy at Facebook, right?"

"Yeah, yeah, yeah. I know the whole story. Instead of an engagement ring, he endowed a scholarship in her name at Stanford," Rachel said in a bored tone.

"And she's nowhere as pretty as you," Kerry said indignantly. "All your uncles and aunties gave up on you a long time ago, but I always knew you were waiting for the right one. Of course, you had to choose a professor just like yourself. At least your children will get a discount on tuition—that's the only way the two of you can afford to put them through college."

"Speaking of uncles and aunties, promise me you won't go telling everyone right away. Please?" Rachel pleaded.

"Hiyah! Okay, okay. I know you are always so cautious, and you don't want to be disappointed, but I just know in my heart what's going to happen," her mother said merrily.

"Well, until *something* happens, there's no point making a big deal out of it," Rachel insisted.

"So where will you be staying in Singapore?"

"At his parents' place, I guess."

"Do they live in a house or an apartment?" Kerry asked.

"I have no idea."

"You must find out these things!"

"Why does it matter? Are you going to try to sell them a house in Singapore?"

"I'll tell you why it matters—do you know what the sleeping arrangements will be?"

"Sleeping arrangements? What are you talking about, Mom?"

"Hiyah, do you know if you will be in a guest bedroom or sharing a bed with him?"

"It never occurred to me—"

"Daughter, that is the most important thing. You mustn't assume that Nick's parents are going to be as liberal-minded as I am. You are going to Singapore, and those Chinese Singaporeans are the most uptight of all the Chinese, you know! I don't want his parents to think I didn't raise you properly."

Rachel sighed. She knew her mother meant well, but as usual she had managed to stress her out about details Rachel never would have imagined.

"Now, we must plan what you will bring as a present for Nick's parents," Kerry continued eagerly. "Find out what Nick's father likes to drink. Scotch? Vodka? Whiskey? I have so many spare bottles of Johnny Walker Red left over from the office Christmas party, I can send you one."

"Mom, I'm not going to cart over a bottle of booze that they can get there. Let me think of the perfect present to bring them *from America*."

"Oh, I know just the thing for Nick's mother! You should go to Macy's and buy her one of those pretty gold powder compacts from Esteé Lauder. They are having a special offer right now, and it comes with a free gift—an expensive-looking leather pouch with lipstick and perfume and eye-cream samples. Trust me, every Asian woman loves those free gifts—"

"Don't worry, Mom, I'll take care of it."

Nicholas Young

•

Nick was slouched on his battered leather sofa grading term papers when Rachel casually brought it up. "So . . . what's the story when we're staying at your parents' place? Are we sharing a bedroom, or would they be scandalized?"

Nick cocked his head. "Hmm. I suppose we'll be in the same room—"

"You *suppose* or you know?"

"Don't worry, once we arrive everything will get sorted."

Get sorted. Normally Rachel found Nick's Britishy phrases so charming, but in this instance it was a tad frustrating. Sensing her unease, Nick got up, walked over to where she was sitting, and kissed the top of her head tenderly. "Relax—my parents aren't the kind of people who pay any attention to sleeping arrangements."

Rachel wondered if that was really true. She tried to go back to reading the State Department's Southeast Asia travel advisory website. As she sat there in the glow of the laptop, Nick couldn't help but marvel at how beautiful his girlfriend looked even at the end of a long day. How did he get so lucky? Everything about her—from the dewy just-back-from-a-morning-run-on-the-beach complexion to the obsidian-black hair that stopped just short of her collarbone—conveyed a natural, uncomplicated beauty so different from the red-carpet-ready girls he had grown up around.

Now Rachel was absentmindedly rubbing her index finger back and forth over her upper lip, her brow slightly furrowed. Nick knew that gesture well. What was she worrying about? Ever since he had invited Rachel to Asia a few days ago, the questions had been piling on steadily. Where were they staying? What gift should she bring for his parents? What had Nick told them about her? Nick wished he could stop that brilliant analytical mind of hers from overthinking every aspect of the trip. He was beginning to see that Astrid had been right. Astrid was not only his cousin, she was his closest female confidant, and he had first fielded the idea of inviting Rachel to Singapore during their phone conversation a week ago.

"First of all, you know you'll be instantly escalating things to the next level, don't you? Is this what you really want?" Astrid asked point-blank.

"No. Well . . . maybe. This is just a summer holiday."

"Come on, Nicky, this is not 'just a summer holiday.' That's not how women think, and you know it. You've been dating seriously for almost two years now. You're thirty-two, and up till now you have *never* brought anyone home. This *is* major. Everyone is going to assume that you're going to—"

"Please," Nick warned, "don't say the m-word."

"See—you know that is *precisely* what will be on everyone's mind. Most of all, I can guarantee you it's on Rachel's mind."

Nick sighed. Why did everything have to be so fraught with significance? This always happened whenever he sought the female perspective. Maybe calling Astrid was a bad idea. She was older than him by just six months, but sometimes she slipped into big-sister mode too much. He preferred the capricious, devil-may-care side of Astrid. "I just want to show Rachel my part of the world, that's all, no strings attached," he tried to explain. "And I guess part of me wants to see how she'll react to it."

"By 'it' you mean our family," Astrid said.

"No, not just our family. My friends, the island, everything. Can't I go on holiday with my girlfriend without it becoming a diplomatic incident?"

Astrid paused for a moment, trying to assess the situation. This was the most serious her cousin had ever gotten with anyone. Even if he wasn't ready to admit it to himself, she knew that on a subconscious level, at least, he was taking the next crucial step on the way to the altar. But that step needed to be handled with extreme care. Was Nicky truly prepared for all the land mines he would be setting off? He could be rather oblivious to the intricacies of the world he had been born into. Maybe he had always been shielded by their grandmother, since he was the apple of her eye. Or maybe Nick had just spent too many years living outside of Asia. In their world, you *did not* bring home some unknown girl unannounced.

"You know I think Rachel is lovely. I really do. But if you invite her to come home with you, it *will* change things between you, whether you like it or not. Now, I'm not concerned about whether your relationship can handle it—I know it can. My worry is more about how everyone else is going to react. You know how small the island is. You know how things can get with . . ." Astrid's voice was suddenly drowned out by the staccato scream of a police siren.

"That was a strange noise. Where are you right now?" Nick asked.

"I'm on the street," Astrid replied.

"In Singapore?"

"No, in Paris."

"What? Paris?" Nick was confused.

"Yep, I'm on rue de Berri, and two police cars just whizzed by."

"I thought you were in Singapore. Sorry for calling so late—I thought it was morning for you."

"No, no, it's fine. It's only one thirty. I'm just walking back to the hotel."

"Is Michael with you?"

"No, he's in China for work."

"What are you up to in Paris?"

"Just my annual spring trip, you know."

"Oh, right." Nick remembered that Astrid spent every April in Paris for her couture fittings. He had met her in Paris once before, and he could still recall the fascination and tedium he felt sitting in the Yves Saint Laurent atelier on avenue Marceau, watching three seamstresses buzz around Astrid as she stood Zen-like, swathed in an airy confection for what seemed like ten hours, guzzling down Diet Cokes to fight off her jet lag. She looked to him like a figure from a baroque painting, a Spanish *infanta* submitting to an archaic costuming ritual straight out of the seventeenth century. (It was a "particularly uninspired season," Astrid had told him, and she was buying "only" twelve pieces that spring, spending well over a million euros.) Nick didn't even want to imagine how much money she must be blowing on *this* trip with no one there to rein her in.

"I miss Paris. It's been ages since I've been. Remember our crazy trip there with Eddie?" he said.

"Aiyoh, please don't remind me! That's the last time I ever share a suite with that rascal!" Astrid shuddered, thinking she would never be able to erase the image of her Hong Kong cousin with that amputee stripper and those profiteroles.

"Are you staying in the Penthouse at the George V?"

"As always."

"You're such a creature of habit. It would be super-easy to assassinate you."

"Why don't you try?"

"Well, next time you're in Paris, let me know. I might just surprise you and hop the pond with my special assassin's kit."

"Are you going to knock me out, put me in a bathtub, and pour acid all over me?"

"No, for you there will be a far more elegant solution."

"Well, come and get me. I'll be here till early May. Don't you get some sort of spring break soon? Why not bring Rachel to Paris for a long weekend?"

"Wish I could. Spring break was last month, and we interim-adjunct-sub-associate professors don't get any extra vacation days. But Rachel and I have the whole summer off, which is why I want her to come home with me."

Astrid sighed. "You know what will happen the minute you land at Changi Airport with this girl on your arm, don't you? You know how brutal it was for Michael when we first started going out publicly. That was five years ago, and he's still getting used to it. Do you really think Rachel is ready for all that? Are *you* ready for it?"

Nick remained silent. He was taking in everything Astrid had to say, but his mind was already made up. He was ready. He was absolutely head over heels in love with Rachel, and it was time to show her off to the whole world.

"Nicky, how much does she know?" Astrid asked.

"About what?"

"About our family."

"Not much. You're the only one she's met. She thinks you've got great taste in shoes and that your husband spoils you rotten. That's about it."

"You probably want to prepare her a bit," Astrid said with a laugh.

"What is there to prepare her for?" Nick asked breezily.

"Listen, Nicky," Astrid said, her tone getting serious. "You can't just throw Rachel into the deep end like this. You *need* to prep her, do you hear me?"

5

Astrid Leong

Every May 1, the L'Herme-Pierres—one of France's great banking families—would host *Le Bal du Muguet*, a sumptuous ball that was the highlight of the spring social season. This year, as Astrid entered the arched passageway leading into the L'Herme-Pierres' splendid *hôtel particulier* on Île Saint-Louis, she was handed a delicate sprig of flowers by a footman in smart black-and-gold livery. "It's after Charles IX, you know. He would present lilies of the valley to all the ladies at Fontainebleau every May Day," a woman wearing a tiara explained to her as they emerged into the courtyard where hundreds of miniature eighteenth-century hot-air balloons floated among the topiaries.

Astrid barely had time to take in the delightful sight when the Vicomtesse Nathalie de L'Herme-Pierre pounced on her. "I'm so glad you could make it," Nathalie effused, greeting Astrid with quadruple cheek kisses. "My goodness, is that *linen*? Only *you* could get away with wearing a simple linen dress to a ball, Astrid!" The hostess laughed, admiring the delicate Grecian folds of Astrid's buttercup-yellow gown. "Wait a minute . . . is this an *original* Madame Grès?" Nathalie asked, realizing that she had seen a similar dress at the Musée Galliera.

"From her early period," Astrid replied, almost embarrassed to have been found out.

"But of course. My goodness, Astrid, you've outdone yourself once again. How on earth did you get your hands on an early Grès?" Nathalie asked in awe. Recovering herself, she whispered, "I hope you don't mind, but I have put you next to Grégoire. He is being a *beast* tonight, as he thinks I am still fucking the Croatian. You are the only person I can trust next to him at dinner. But at least you'll have Louis on your left."

"Don't worry about me. I always enjoy catching up with your husband, and it will be a treat to sit next to Louis—I just saw his new film the other day."

"Wasn't it a pretentious bore? Hated the black-and-white, but at least Louis looked edible with his clothes off. Anyway, thank you for being my savior. Are you sure you have to leave tomorrow?" the hostess asked with a pout.

"I've been gone almost a month! I'm afraid my son will forget who I am if I stay one more day," Astrid answered as she was ushered along into the grand foyer, where Nathalie's mother-in-law, the Comtesse Isabelle de L'Herme-Pierre, presided over the receiving line.

Isabelle let out a small gasp when she caught sight of Astrid. "Astrid, *quelle surprise!*"

"Well, I wasn't sure that I would be able to attend until the last minute," Astrid said apologetically, smiling at the stiff-looking grande dame standing beside Comtesse Isabelle. The woman did not smile back. Rather, she tilted her head ever so slightly as if appraising every inch of Astrid, the gigantic emerald earrings fastened to her long earlobes swaying precariously.

"Astrid Leong, permit me to present my dear friend Baronne Marie-Hélène de la Durée."

The baronne nodded curtly, before turning back to the comtesse and resuming their conversation. As soon as Astrid had moved on, Marie-Hélène said to Isabelle, *sotto voce,* "Did you notice that necklace she was wearing? I saw it at JAR last week. It's unbelievable what these girls can get their hands on nowadays. Tell me, Isabelle, *whom* does she belong to?"

"Marie-Hélène, Astrid is not a kept woman. We've known her family for years."

"Oh? Who is her family?" Marie-Hélène asked in astonishment.

"The Leongs are a Chinese family from Singapore."

"Ah yes, I've heard that the Chinese are getting quite rich these days. In fact, I read that there are now more millionaires in Asia than in all of Europe. Who would have ever imagined?"

"No, no, I'm afraid you don't quite understand. Astrid's people have been wealthy for generations. *Her father is one of Laurent's biggest clients*," Isabelle whispered.

"My dear, are you giving away all my secrets again?" Comte Laurent de L'Herme-Pierre remarked as he rejoined his wife in the receiving line.

"Not at all. Merely enlightening Marie-Hélène about the Leongs," Isabelle replied, flicking away a speck of lint on her husband's gros-grain lapel.

"Ah, the Leongs. Why? Is the ravishing Astrid here tonight?"

"You just missed her. But don't worry, you have all night to ogle her across the dinner table," Isabelle teased, explaining to Marie-Hélène, "Both my husband and my son have been obsessed with Astrid for years."

"Well, why not? A girl like Astrid only exists to feed obsession," Laurent remarked. Isabelle smacked her husband's arm in mock out-rage.

"Laurent, tell me, how is it possible that these Chinese have been rich for generations?" Marie-Hélène inquired. "I thought they were all penniless Communists in drab little Mao uniforms not too long ago."

"Well, first of all, you must understand that there are two kinds of Chinese. There are the Chinese from *Mainland China*, who made their fortunes in the past decade like all the Russians, but then there are the *Overseas Chinese*. These are the ones who left China long before the Communists came in, in many cases hundreds of years ago, and spread throughout the rest of Asia, quietly amassing great for-tunes over time. If you look at all the countries in Southeast Asia—especially Thailand, Indonesia, Malaysia—you'll see that virtually *all* the commerce is controlled by the Overseas Chinese. Like the Liems in Indonesia, the Tans in the Philippines, the Leongs in—"

His wife cut in. "Let me just say this: we visited Astrid's family a few years ago. You can't *imagine* how staggeringly rich these people are, Marie-Hélène. The houses, the servants, the style in which they live. It makes the Arnaults look like *peasants*. What's more, I've been told that Astrid is a double heiress—there's an even more enormous fortune on her *mother's* side."

"Is that so?" Marie-Hélène said in astonishment, staring across the room at the girl with renewed interest. "Well, she *is* rather *soignée*," she conceded.

"Oh, she's incredibly chic—one of the few from her generation who gets it right," the comtesse decreed. "François-Marie tells me Astrid has a couture collection that rivals the Sheikha of Qatar's. She never attends the shows, because she loathes to be photographed, but she goes straight to the ateliers and snaps up dozens of dresses every season as if they were *macarons*."

Astrid was in the salon admiring the Balthus portrait over the mantelpiece when someone behind her said, "That's Laurent's mother, you know." It was the Baronne Marie-Hélène de la Durée, this time attempting a smile on her tightly pulled face.

"I thought it might be," Astrid replied.

"*Chérie*, I must tell you how much I adore your necklace. In fact, I had admired it at Monsieur Rosenthal's a few weeks ago, but sadly, he informed me it was already spoken for," the baronne gushed. "I can see now that you were clearly meant to wear it."

"Thank you, but you've got the most magnificent earrings," Astrid replied sweetly, rather amused by the woman's sudden about-face.

"Isabelle tells me that you are from *Singapour*. I have heard so much about your country, about how it's become the Switzerland of Asia. My granddaughter is making a trip to Asia this summer. Perhaps you will be kind enough to give her some advice?"

"Of course," Astrid said politely, thinking to herself, *Wow—it took only five minutes for this lady to go from snooty to suck-up.* It was quite disappointing, really. Paris was her escape, and here she strove to be invisible, to be just another of the countless Asian tourists who crammed eagerly into the boutiques along the Faubourg-Saint-Honoré. It was this luxury of anonymity that made her love the City of Lights. But living here several years back had changed all that. Her parents, concerned that she was living alone in a foreign city with no proper chaperone, made the mistake of alerting friends in Paris, like the L'Herme-Pierres. Word had gotten out, and suddenly she was no longer just the *jeune fille* renting a loft in the Marais. She was *Harry Leong's daughter*, or *Shang Su Yi's granddaughter*. It was soooo frustrating. Of course, she should be used to this by now, to people talking about her as soon as she left the room. It had been going on practically since the day she was born.

To understand why, one had to first consider the obvious—her astonishing beauty. Astrid wasn't attractive in the typical almond-eyed Hong Kong starlet sort of way, nor was she the flawless celestial-maiden type. One could say that Astrid's eyes were set too far apart, and her jawline—so similar to the men on her mother's side—was too prominent for a girl. Yet somehow with her delicate nose, bee-stung lips, and long naturally wavy hair, it all came together to form an inexplicably alluring vision. She was always *that girl* stopped on the street by modeling scouts, though her mother fended them off brusquely. Astrid was not going to be modeling for anyone, and certainly not for *money*. Such things were far beneath her.

And that was the other, more essential detail about Astrid: she was born into the uppermost echelon of Asian wealth—a secretive, rarefied circle of families virtually unknown to outsiders who possessed immeasurably vast fortunes. For starters, her father hailed from the Penang Leongs, a venerable Straits Chinese* family that held a monopoly over the palm oil industry. But adding even more oomph, her mother was the eldest daughter of Sir James Young and the even more imperial Shang Su Yi. Astrid's aunt Catherine had married a minor Thai prince. Another was married to the renowned Hong Kong cardiologist Malcolm Cheng.

One could go on for hours diagramming all the dynastic links in Astrid's family tree, but from any angle you looked at it, Astrid's pedigree was nothing short of extraordinary. And as Astrid took her place at the candlelit banquet table in the L'Herme-Pierres' long gallery, surrounded by the gleaming Louis XV Sèvres and rose-period Picassos, she could not have suspected just how extraordinary life was about to become.

---

* The Straits Chinese, also known as the Peranakans, are the descendants of late-fifteenth- and sixteenth-century Chinese immigrants to the Malaya region during the colonial era. They were the elites of Singapore, English-educated and more loyal to the British than to China. Often intermarried with the native Malays, the Straits Chinese created a unique culture that is a hybrid of Chinese, Malay, English, Dutch, and Indian influences. Peranakan cuisine, long the cornerstone of Singaporean and Malaysian cooking, has become all the rage with foodies in the West, although visiting Asians are dumbstruck by the outrageous prices charged in trendy restaurants.

6

The Chengs

•

Most people driving past the squat grayish-brown building on a busy intersection of Causeway Bay would likely assume it was some sort of government health office, but the Chinese Athletic Association was actually one of Hong Kong's most exclusive private clubs. Despite its rather perfunctory name, it was the first Chinese-founded sports facility in the former British Crown colony. It boasted the legendary gambling tycoon Stanley Lo as its honorary president, and its restrictive membership had an eight-year waiting list open only to the most established families.

The CAA's public rooms were still firmly entrenched in late-seventies chrome-and-leather decor, since members voted to spend all the money on updating the sports facilities. Only the acclaimed restaurant had been revamped in the last few years into a plush dining room with pale-rose brocade walls and windows overlooking the main tennis courts. The round tables were strategically aligned so that everyone was seated with a view of the restaurant's main door, allowing its esteemed members to make a grand entrance in their après-sport outfits and making mealtimes a prime spectator sport.

Every Sunday afternoon, the Cheng family would come together without fail for lunch at the CAA. No matter how busy or hectic the week had been, everyone knew that Sunday dim sum at the

Clubhouse, as they called it, was mandatory attendance by all family members who were in town. Dr. Malcolm Cheng was Asia's most esteemed heart surgeon. So prized were his skilled hands that he was famous for always wearing lambskin gloves—made specially for him by Dunhill—to protect his precious hands whenever he ventured out in public, and he took additional measures to safeguard them from the wear and tear of driving, opting instead to be chauffeured in his Rolls-Royce Silver Spirit.

This was something his well-brought-up wife, the former Alexandra "Alix" Young of Singapore, felt to be overly ostentatious, so she preferred to call for a taxi wherever possible and allow her husband the exclusive use of his car and driver. "After all," she was keen to say, "he's saving people's lives every day and I'm just a housewife." This self-deprecation was standard behavior for Alexandra, even though she was the true architect of their fortune.

As a bored doctor's wife, Alexandra began channeling every cent of her husband's considerable earnings into properties just as the Hong Kong housing boom was taking off. She found that she had a preternatural talent for timing the market, so beginning in the oil-recession days of the seventies, through the Communist-panic sell-off of the mid-eighties and the Asian financial crisis of 1997, Alexandra was always snapping up properties when they hit rock bottom and selling at the peak. By the middle of the first decade of the new century, with Hong Kong property going for more money per square foot than anywhere else in the world, the Chengs found themselves sitting on one of the largest privately held real estate portfolios on the island.

Sunday lunch gave Malcolm and his wife a chance to inspect their children and grandchildren on a weekly basis, and it was a duty they undertook with utter seriousness. For in spite of all the advantages the Cheng children had growing up, Malcolm and Alexandra were constantly worrying about them. (Actually, Alexandra was the one doing most of the worrying.)

Their youngest son, Alistair, "the hopeless one," was the pampered ne'er-do-well who had just barely scraped through Sydney University and was now doing something or other in the Hong Kong film industry. He had recently become involved with Kitty Pong, a soap-opera star who claimed she was from "a good Taiwanese family," even though everyone else in the Cheng family doubted it, since her spoken Mandarin took on a distinctive northern China accent rather than the more cutesy inflections of Taiwanese Mandarin.

Their daughter, Cecilia, "the horsey one," had developed a passion for dressage at an early age and was constantly dealing with her temperamental horse or her temperamental husband, Tony, an Australian commodities trader whom Malcolm and Alexandra secretly nicknamed "the Convict." A "full-time mother," Cecilia actually spent more time on the international equestrian circuit than raising their son, Jake. (Due to all the hours he spent with their Filipino maids, Jake was becoming fluent in Tagalog; he could also do a brilliant impression of Sinatra's "My Way.")

And then there was Eddie, their firstborn. To all appearances, Edison Cheng was "the perfect one." He had breezed through Cambridge Judge Business School with distinction, done a stint at Cazenove in London, and was now a rising star in Hong Kong's private banking world. He had married Fiona Tung, who hailed from a politically connected family, and they had three very studious, well-behaved children. But privately, Alexandra worried the most about Eddie. In the last few years, he was spending far too much time hanging around with these dubious Mainland Chinese billionaires, flying all over Asia every week to attend parties, and she worried how this might be affecting his health and his family life.

Today's lunch was especially important since Alexandra wanted to plan the logistics of the family trip next month to Singapore for the Khoo wedding. It was the first time the entire family—parents, children, grandchildren, servants, and nannies included—was traveling together, and Alexandra wanted to make sure everything went off perfectly. At one o'clock, the family began filtering in from all corners: Malcolm from a mixed-doubles tennis match; Alexandra from church with Cecilia, Tony, and Jake; Fiona and her children from their weekend tutors; and Alistair from rolling out of bed fifteen minutes ago.

Eddie was the last to arrive, and as usual he was on his phone, coming to the table and ignoring everyone, chattering loudly in Cantonese on his Bluetooth earpiece. When he finally finished his call, he flashed his family a self-satisfied grin. "It's all sorted! I just spoke with Leo, and he wants us to use his family jet," Eddie declared, referring to his best friend Leo Ming.

"For all of us to fly to Singapore?" Alexandra asked, a bit confused.

"Yes, of course!"

Fiona raised an immediate objection. "I'm not sure that's such a good idea. First, I really don't think the entire family should be traveling together on the same plane. What would happen if there was an accident? Second, we shouldn't be asking such a favor of Leo."

"I knew you were going to say that, Fi," Eddie began. "That's why I came up with this plan: Daddy and Mummy should go a day earlier with Alistair; Cecilia, Tony, and Jake can fly with us the next day; and later in the day, the nannies can bring our children."

"That's outrageous. How can you even think of taking advantage of Leo's plane like that?" Fiona exclaimed.

"Fi, he's my best friend and he couldn't care less how much we use the plane," Eddie retorted.

"What kind of jet is it? A Gulfstream? A Falcon?" Tony asked.

Cecilia dug her nails into her husband's arm, annoyed at his eagerness, and cut in. "Why do *your* kids get to fly separately while my son has to travel with us?"

"What about Kitty? She's coming too," Alistair asked quietly.

Everyone at the table glared at Alistair in horror. "*Nay chee seen, ah!*"* Eddie snapped.

Alistair was indignant. "I already RSVP'd for her. And Colin told me that he couldn't *wait* to meet her. She's a big star, and I—"

"In the *New Territories* maybe a couple of idiots watching trashy soap operas might know who she is, but trust me, nobody in Singapore has ever heard of her," Eddie cut in.

"That's not true—she's one of Asia's fastest-rising stars. And that's beside the point—I want all our relatives in Singapore to meet her," Alistair said.

Alexandra considered the implications of his declaration quietly, but decided to pick her battles one at a time. "Fiona is right. We can't possibly borrow the Ming family plane two days in a row! In fact, I think it would look very inappropriate for us to fly in a private plane at all. I mean, who do we think we are?"

"Daddy's one of the most famous heart surgeons in the world! You are Singaporean royalty! What's wrong with flying on a private

---

* Cantonese for "You're out of your mind!"

plane?" Eddie shouted in frustration, his hands gesticulating so wildly that he almost hit the waiter behind him, who was about to place a huge stack of bamboo steamers on the table.

"Uncle Eddie, look out! There's food right behind you!" his nephew Jake shouted.

Eddie glanced around for a second and continued on his tirade. "Why are you always like this, Mummy? Why do you always behave so provincial? You are filthy rich! Why can't you be a little less cheap for once and have more a sense of your own self-worth?" His three children looked up momentarily from their math practice test books. They were used to his rages at home but had rarely seen him so upset in front of *Gong Gong* and Ah Ma. Fiona pulled at his sleeve, whispering, "Lower your voice! Please don't talk about money in front of the children."

His mother shook her head calmly. "Eddie, this has nothing to do with self-worth. I just feel this sort of extravagance is completely unnecessary. And I am not Singaporean royalty. Singapore has no royalty. What a ridiculous thing to say."

"This is so typical of you, Eddie. You just want all of Singapore to know that you flew in on Ming Kah-Ching's plane," Cecilia interjected, reaching for one of the plump roast-pork buns. "If it was *your* own plane, that would be one thing, but to have the audacity to *borrow* a plane for three trips in two days is just unheard of. I personally would rather pay for my own tickets."

"Kitty flies private all the time," Alistair said, though no one at the table paid him any attention.

"Well, we *should* get our own jet. I've been saying it for years. Dad, you spend practically half the month in the Beijing clinic, and since I plan to expand my presence into China in a big way in the coming year—" Eddie began.

"Eddie, I have to agree with your mother and sister on this one. I just would not want to be indebted to the Ming family in this way," Malcolm finally said. As much as he enjoyed flying private, he could not stomach the thought of borrowing the Ming jet.

"Why do I keep trying to do this ungrateful family so many favors?" Eddie huffed in disgust. "Okay, you all do what you want. Squeeze into economy on China Airlines for all I care. *My* family and I are taking Leo's plane. And it's a Bombardier Global Express. It's huge, state-of-the-art. There's even a Matisse in the cabin. It's going to be *amazing*."

Fiona gave him a disapproving look, but he glared at her so forcefully that she retreated from any further objection. Eddie shoveled down a few rolls of shrimp *cheong fun*, got up, and announced imperiously, "I'm off. I have important clients to attend to!" And with that, Eddie stormed out, leaving a rather relieved family in his wake.

Tony, mouth full of food, whispered to Cecilia, "Let's see their entire family plunge into the South China Sea on Leo Ming's fancy-ass plane."

As much as she tried to, Cecilia couldn't stifle her laugh.

7

Eleanor

•

SINGAPORE

After a few days of strategically placed phone calls, Eleanor finally nailed down the source of the disturbing rumor involving her son. Daisy confessed hearing it from her daughter-in-law's best friend Rebecca Tang, who in turn revealed that she'd heard it from her brother Moses Tang, who had been at Cambridge with Leonard Shang. And Moses had this to report to Eleanor:

"I was in London for a conference. At the last minute, Leonard invites me down to dinner at his country estate in Surrey. Have you been there, Mrs. Young? Aiyoh, what a palace! I didn't realize it was designed by Gabriel-Hippolyte Destailleur, the architect who built Waddesdon Manor for the English Rothschilds. Anyway, we were dining with all these *ang mor** VIPS and MPs† visiting from Singapore and as usual Cassandra Shang is holding court. And then out of nowhere Cassandra says loudly across the table to your sister-in-law Victoria Young, 'You'll never guess what I heard . . . Nicky has been dating a Taiwanese girl in New York, and now he's bringing her to Singapore for the Khoo wedding!' And Victoria says, 'Are you sure? *Taiwanese?* Good grief, did he fall for some gold digger?' And then

---

* In this instance, *ang mor* is used in reference to British politicians, most likely Tories.

† Abbreviation for "members of Parliament," used in this instance to refer to Singapore MPs, most definitely from the People's Action Party.

Cassandra says something like, 'Well, it might not be as bad as you think. I have it on good authority that she's one of the Chu girls. You know, of the Taipei Plastics Chus. Not exactly old money, but at least they are one of the most solid families in Taiwan."

Had it been anyone else, Eleanor would have dismissed all this as nothing but idle talk among her husband's bored relatives. But this came from Cassandra, who was usually dead accurate. She hadn't earned the nickname "Radio One Asia" for nothing. Eleanor wondered how Cassandra obtained this latest scoop. Nicky's big-mouthed second cousin was the last person he would ever confide in. Cassandra must have gotten the intel from one of her spies in New York. She had spies everywhere, all hoping to *sah kah** her by passing along some hot tip.

It did not come as a surprise to Eleanor that her son might have a new girlfriend. What surprised her (or, more accurately, annoyed her) was the fact that it had taken her until now to find out. Anyone could see that he was prime target number one, and over the years there had been plenty of girls Nicky *thought* he had kept hidden from his mother. All of them had been inconsequential in Eleanor's eyes, since she knew her son wasn't ready to marry yet. But this time was different.

Eleanor had a long-held theory about men. She truly believed that for most men, all that talk of "being in love" or "finding the right one" was absolute nonsense. Marriage was purely a matter of timing, and whenever a man was finally done sowing his wild oats and ready to settle down, whichever girl happened to be there at the time would be *the right one*. She had seen the theory proven time and again; indeed she had caught Philip Young at precisely the right moment. All the men in that clan tended to marry in their early thirties, and Nicky was now ripe for the plucking. If someone in New York already knew so much about Nicky's relationship, and if he was actually bringing this girl home to attend his best friend's wedding, things must be getting serious. Serious enough that he *purposely* hadn't mentioned her existence. Serious enough to derail Eleanor's meticulously laid plans.

---

* A Hokkien term that literally means "three legs" and comes from a rude hand gesture made by holding up three fingers as if supporting someone's genitals. This is the Chinese version of a practice more commonly known to Westerners as "sucking up."

The setting sun refracted its rays through the floor-to-ceiling windows of the recently completed penthouse apartment atop Cairnhill Road, bathing the atrium-like living room in a deep orange glow. Eleanor gazed at the early-evening sky, taking in the colonnade of buildings clustering around Scotts Road and the expansive views all the way past the Singapore River to the Keppel Shipyard, the world's busiest commercial port. Even after thirty-four years of marriage, she did not take for granted all that it meant for her to be sitting here with one of the most sought-after views on the island.

To Eleanor, every single person occupied a specific space in the elaborately constructed social universe in her mind. Like most of the women in her crowd, Eleanor could meet another Asian anywhere in the world—say, over dim sum at Royal China in London, or shopping in the lingerie department of David Jones in Sydney—and within thirty seconds of learning their name and where they lived, she would implement her social algorithm and calculate precisely where they stood in her constellation based on who their family was, who else they were related to, what their approximate net worth might be, how the fortune was derived, and what family scandals might have occurred within the past fifty years.

The Taipei Plastics Chus were very new money, made in the seventies and eighties, most likely. Knowing next to nothing about this family made Eleanor particularly anxious. How established were they in Taipei society? Who exactly were this girl's parents, and how much did she stand to inherit? She needed to know what she was up against. It was 6:45 a.m. in New York. *High time to wake Nicky up.* She picked up the telephone with one hand, and with the other she held at arm's length the long-distance discount calling card* that she always used, squinting at the row of tiny numbers. She dialed a complicated series of codes and waited for several beeping signals before finally entering the telephone number. The phone rang four times before Nick's voice mail picked up: *"Hey, I can't come to the phone right now, so leave a message and I'll get back to you as soon as I can."*

Eleanor was always a little taken aback whenever she heard her

---

* Old-money Chinese absolutely loathe wasting money on long-distance telephone calls, almost as much as they hate wasting money on fluffy towels, bottled water, hotel rooms, expensive Western food, taking taxis, tipping waiters, and flying anything other than economy class.

son's "American" accent. She much preferred the normal Queen's English he would revert to whenever he was back in Singapore. She spoke haltingly into the phone: "Nicky, where are you? Call me tonight and let me know your flight information, *lah*. Everyone in the world except me knows when you're coming home. Also, are you staying with us first or with Ah Ma? Please call me back. But don't call tonight if it's after midnight. I am going to take an Ambien now, so I can't be disturbed for at least eight hours."

She put down the phone, and then almost immediately picked it up again; this time dialing a cell-phone number. "Astrid, ah? Is that you?"

"Oh, hi, Auntie Elle," Astrid said.

"Are you okay? You sound a bit funny."

"No, I'm fine, I was just asleep," Astrid said, clearing her throat.

"Oh. Why are you sleeping so early? Are you sick?"

"No, I'm in Paris, Auntie Elle."

"*Alamak,* I forgot you were away! Sorry to wake you, *lah*. How is Paris?"

"Lovely."

"Doing lots of shopping?"

"Not too much," Astrid replied as patiently as possible. Did her auntie really call just to discuss shopping?

"Do they still have those lines at Louis Vuitton that they make all the Asian customers wait in?"

"I'm not sure. I haven't been inside a Louis Vuitton in decades, Auntie Elle."

"Good for you. Those lines are terrible, and then they only allow Asians to buy one item. Reminds me of the Japanese occupation, when they forced all the Chinese to wait in line for scraps of rotten food."

"Yes, but I can sort of understand why they need these rules, Auntie Elle. You should see the Asian tourists buying up all the luxury goods, not just at Louis Vuitton. They are everywhere, buying everything in sight. If there's a designer label, they want it. It's absolutely mad. And you know some of them are just bringing it back home to resell at a profit."

"Yah *lah*, it's those fresh-off-the-boat tourists that give us a bad name. But I've been shopping in Paris since the seventies—I would never wait in any line and be told what I can buy! Anyway Astrid, I wanted to ask . . . have you spoken to Nicky recently?"

Astrid paused for a moment. "Um, he called me a couple of weeks ago."

"Did he tell you when he was coming to Singapore?"

"No, he didn't mention the exact date. But I'm sure he'll be there a few days before Colin's wedding, don't you think?"

"You know *lah*, Nicky doesn't tell me anything!" Eleanor paused, and then continued cautiously. "Hey, I'm thinking of throwing him and his girlfriend a surprise party. Just a small party at the new flat, to welcome her to Singapore. Do you think that's a good idea?"

"Sure, Auntie Elle. I think they would love that." Astrid was quite taken aback that her aunt was being so welcoming to Rachel. *Nick must have really worked his charm overtime.*

"But I don't really know what she would like, so I don't know how to plan this party properly. Can you give me some ideas? Did you meet her when you were in New York last year?"

"I did."

Eleanor seethed quietly. *Astrid was in New York last March, which meant this girl had been in the picture for at least a year now.*

"What's she like? Is she very Taiwanese?" she asked.

"Taiwanese? Not at all. She seems completely Americanized to me," Astrid offered, before regretting what she'd said.

How horrible, Eleanor thought. She had always found Asian girls with American accents to be quite ridiculous. *They all sounded like they were faking it, trying to sound so* ang mor.

"So even though the family is from Taiwan, she was raised in America?"

"I didn't even know she was from Taiwan, to tell you the truth."

"Really? She didn't talk about her family back in Taipei?"

"Not at all." *What was Auntie Elle getting at?* Astrid knew that her aunt was prying, so she felt like she had to present Rachel in the best possible light. "She's very smart and accomplished, Auntie Elle. I think you'll like her."

"Oh, so she's the brainy type, like Nicky."

"Yes, definitely. I'm told she's one of the up-and-coming professors in her field."

Eleanor was nonplussed. *A professor! Nicky was dating a professor! Oh my, was this woman older than him?* "Nicky didn't tell me what her specialty was."

"Oh, economic development."

A cunning, calculating older woman. Alamak. *This was sounding worse and worse.* "Did she go to university in New York?" Eleanor pressed on.

"No, she went to Stanford, in California."

"Yes, yes, I know Stanford," Eleanor said, sounding unimpressed. *It's that school in California for those people who can't get into Harvard.*

"It's a top school, Auntie Elle," Astrid said, knowing exactly what her aunt was thinking.

"Well, I suppose if you are forced to go to an *American* university—"

"Come on, Auntie Elle. Stanford is a great university for anywhere. I believe she also went to Northwestern for her master's. Rachel is very intelligent and capable, and completely down-to-earth. I think you'll like her very much."

"Oh, I'm sure I will," Eleanor replied. *So, her name was Rachel.* Eleanor paused. She just needed one more piece of information—the correct spelling of the girl's surname. But how was she going to get it without Astrid getting suspicious? Suddenly she had a thought. "I think I'm going to get one of those nice cakes from Awfully Chocolate and put her name on it. Do you know how she spells her surname? Is it C-H-U, C-H-O-O, or C-H-I-U?"

"I think it's just C-H-U."

"Thank you. You've been so helpful," Eleanor said. *More than you'll ever know.*

"Of course, Auntie Elle. Let me know if there's anything I can do to help out for your party. I can't wait to see your spectacular new flat."

"Oh, you haven't seen it yet? I thought your mother bought a unit here as well."

"She may have, but I haven't seen it. I can't keep up with all of my parents' property juggling."

"Of course, of course. Your parents have so many properties around the world, unlike your poor uncle Philip and me. We just have the house in Sydney and this small little pigeonhole."

"Oh, I'm sure it's anything but small, Auntie Elle. Isn't it supposed to be the most luxurious condo ever built in Singapore?" Astrid wondered for the millionth time why all her relatives constantly tried to outdo each other in proclaiming their poverty.

"No, *lah*. It's just a simple flat—nothing like your father's house.

Anyway, I'm sorry to wake you. Do you need something to get back to sleep? I take fifty milligrams of amitriptyline every night, and then an extra ten milligrams of Ambien if I really want to sleep through the night. Sometimes I add a Lunesta, and if that doesn't work, I get out the Valium——"

"I'll be fine, Auntie Elle."

"Okay then, bye-bye!" With that, Eleanor hung up the phone. Her gamble had paid off. Those two cousins were thick as thieves. Why didn't she think of calling Astrid sooner?

8

Rachel
.

Nick brought it up so nonchalantly, as he was sorting the laundry on the Sunday afternoon before their big trip. Apparently Nick's parents had only just been informed that Rachel was coming with him to Singapore. And oh, by the way, they had just been made aware of her existence too.

"I don't quite understand . . . *you mean your parents never knew about me in all this time?*" Rachel asked in astonishment.

"Yes. I mean, no, they didn't. But you need to know this has absolutely nothing to do with you—" Nick began.

"Well, it's a little hard not to take it personally."

"Please don't. I'm sorry if it seems that way. It's just that . . ." Nick swallowed nervously. "It's just that I've always tried to keep clear boundaries between my personal life and my family life, that's all."

"But shouldn't your personal life be the same as your family life?"

"Not in my case. Rachel, you *know* how overbearing Chinese parents can be."

"Well, yeah, but it still wouldn't keep me from telling my mom about something as important as my boyfriend. I mean, my mom knew about you five minutes after our first date, and you were sitting down to dinner with her—enjoying her winter melon soup—like, two months later."

"Well, you have a very special thing with your mum, you know that. It's not that easy for most other people. And with my parents, it's just . . ." Nick paused, struggling for the right words. "We're just different. We're much more formal with each other, and we don't really discuss our emotional lives at all."

"What, are they cold and emotionally shut down or something? Did they live through the Great Depression?"

Nick laughed, shaking his head. "No, nothing like that. I just think you'll understand when you meet them."

Rachel didn't know what to think. Sometimes Nick could be so cryptic, and his explanation made no sense to her. Still, she didn't want to overreact. "Anything else you want to tell me about your family before I get on a plane and spend the whole summer with you?"

"No. Not really. Well . . ." Nick paused for a bit, trying to decide if he should mention the housing situation. He knew he had screwed things up royally with his mother. He had waited too long, and when he called to break the news officially about his relationship with Rachel, his mother had been silent. Ominously silent. All she asked was, "So where will you be staying, and where will *she* be staying?" It suddenly dawned on Nick that it would *not* be a good idea for the both of them to stay with his parents—not initially, at least. Nor would it be appropriate for Rachel to stay at his grandmother's house without her explicit invitation. They could stay with one of his aunts or uncles, but that might incite his mother's wrath and create even more of an internecine war within his family.

Not sure how to get out of this quagmire, Nick sought the counsel of his great-aunt, who was always so good at sorting out these sorts of matters. Great-aunt Rosemary advised him to book into a hotel first, but emphasized that he must arrange to introduce Rachel to his parents on the day of his arrival. "The very first day. Don't wait until the next day," she cautioned. Perhaps he should invite his parents out to a meal with Rachel, so they could meet on neutral territory. Someplace low-key like the Colonial Club, and better to make it lunch instead of dinner. "Everyone is more relaxed at lunchtime," she advised.

Nick was then to proceed to his grandmother's by himself and formally request permission to invite Rachel to the customary Friday-night dinner that Ah Ma hosted for the extended family. Only after

Rachel had been properly received at Friday-night dinner should the topic of where they might stay be broached. "Of course your grandmother will have you to stay, once she meets Rachel. But if worse comes to worst, *I* will invite you to stay with me, and no one will be able to say anything then," Great-aunt Rosemary assured him.

Nick decided to keep these delicate arrangements from Rachel. He didn't want to give her any excuse to back out of the trip. He wanted Rachel to be prepared to meet his family, but he also wanted her to create her own impressions when the time came. Still, Astrid was right. Rachel needed some sort of primer on his family. But how exactly could he explain his family to her, especially when he had been conditioned his whole life never to speak about them?

Nick sat on the floor, leaning against the exposed-brick wall and putting his hands on his knees. "Well, you probably should know that I come from a very big family."

"I thought you were an only child."

"Yes, but I have lots of extended relatives, and you'll be meeting lots of them. There are three intermarried branches, and to outsiders it can seem a bit overwhelming at first." He wished he hadn't used the word *outsiders* as soon as he said it, but Rachel seemed not to notice, so he continued. "It's like any big family. I have loudmouth uncles, eccentric aunts, obnoxious cousins, the whole nine yards. But I'm sure you'll get a kick out of meeting them. You met Astrid, and you liked her, didn't you?"

"Astrid is awesome."

"Well, she adores you. *Everyone* will adore you, Rachel. I just know it."

Rachel sat quietly on the bed beside the pile of towels still warm from the dryer, trying to soak in everything Nick had said. This was the most he had ever talked about his family, and it made her feel a little more assured. She still couldn't quite fathom the deal with his parents, but she had to admit that she had seen her fair share of distant families—especially among her Asian friends. Back in high school, she had endured dreary meals in the fluorescent-lit dining rooms of her classmates, dinners where not more than five words were exchanged between parent and child. She had noticed the stunned reactions from her friends whenever she randomly hugged her mother or said "I love you" at the end of a phone call. And several years ago, she had been e-mailed a humorous list entitled "Twenty

Ways You Can Tell You Have Asian Parents." Number one on the list: *Your parents never, ever call you "just to say hello."* She didn't get many of the jokes on the list, since her own experience growing up had been entirely different.

"We're so fortunate, you know. Not many mothers and daughters have what we have," Kerry said when they caught up on the phone later that evening.

"I realize that, Mom. I know it's different because you were a single mom, and you took me everywhere," Rachel mused. Back when she was a child, it seemed like every year or so her mother would answer a classified ad in *World Journal*, the Chinese-American newspaper, and off they would go to a new job in some random Chinese restaurant in some random town. Images of all those tiny boardinghouse rooms and makeshift beds in cities like East Lansing, Phoenix, and Tallahassee flashed through her head.

"You can't expect other families to be like us. I was so young when I had you—nineteen—we were able to be like sisters. Don't be so hard on Nick. Sad to say, but I was never very close to my parents either. In China, there was no time to be close—my mother and father worked from morning till night, seven days a week, and I was at school all the time."

"Still, how can he hide something as important as this from his parents? It's not like Nick and I have only been going out for a couple of months."

"Daughter, once again you are judging the situation with your American eyes. You have to look at this the Chinese way. In Asia, there is a proper time for everything, a proper etiquette. Like I said before, you have to realize that these Overseas Chinese families can be even more traditional than we Mainland Chinese. You don't know anything about Nick's background. Has it occurred to you that they might be quite poor? Not everyone is rich in Asia, you know. Maybe Nick has a duty to work hard and send money back to his family, and they wouldn't approve if they thought he was wasting money on girlfriends. Or maybe he didn't want his family to know that the two of you spend half the week living together. They could be devout Buddhists, you know."

"That's just it, Mom. It's dawning on me that Nick knows everything there is to know about me, about us, but I know almost nothing about his family."

"Don't be scared, daughter. You know Nick. You know he is a decent man, and though he may have kept you secret for a while, he is doing things the honorable way now. At last he feels ready to introduce you to his family—properly—and that is the most important thing," Kerry said.

Rachel lay in bed, calmed as always by her mother's soothing Mandarin tones. Maybe she was being too hard on Nick. She had let her insecurities get the better of her, and her knee-jerk reaction was to assume that Nick waited so long to tell his parents because he was somehow embarrassed about her. But could it be the other way around? Was he embarrassed of *them*? Rachel remembered what her Singaporean friend Peik Lin had said when she Skyped her and excitedly announced that she was dating one of her fellow countrymen. Peik Lin came from one of the island's wealthiest families, and she had never heard of the Youngs. "Obviously, if he comes from a rich or prominent family, we would know them. Young isn't a very common name here—are you sure they're not Korean?"

"Yeah, I'm sure they're from Singapore. But you know I couldn't care less how much money they have."

"Yes, that's the problem with you," Peik Lin cracked. "Well, I'm sure if he passed the Rachel Chu test, his family's perfectly normal."

9

Astrid

SINGAPORE

Astrid arrived home from her Paris sojourn in the late afternoon, early enough to give three-year-old Cassian his bath while Evangeline, his French au pair, looked on disapprovingly (*Maman* was scrubbing his hair too forcefully, and wasting too much baby shampoo). After tucking Cassian into bed and reading him *Bonsoir Lune*, Astrid resumed the ritual of carefully unpacking her new couture acquisitions and hiding them away in the spare bedroom before Michael got home. (She was careful never to let her husband see the full extent of her purchases every season.) Poor Michael seemed so stressed out by work lately. Everyone in the tech world seemed to work such long hours, and Michael and his partner at Cloud Nine Solutions were trying so hard to get this company off the ground. He was flying to China almost every other week these days to supervise new projects, and she knew he would be tired tonight, since he had gone straight to work from the airport. She wanted everything to be perfect for him when he walked through the door.

Astrid popped into the kitchen to chat with her cook about the menu, and decided they should set up dinner on the balcony tonight. She lit some fig-apricot-scented candles and set a bottle of the new Sauternes she had brought back from France in the wine chiller. Michael had a sweet tooth when it came to wines, and he had taken a liking to late-harvest Sauternes. She knew he was going to love this bottle, which had been specially recommended to her by Manuel, the brilliant sommelier at Taillevent.

To the majority of Singaporeans, it would seem that Astrid was in store for a lovely evening at home. But to her friends and family, Astrid's current domestic situation was a perplexing one. Why was she popping into kitchens talking to cooks, unpacking luggage by herself, or worrying about her husband's workload? This was certainly not how anyone would have imagined Astrid's life to be. Astrid Leong was meant to be the chatelaine of a great house. Her head housekeeper should be anticipating every one of her needs, while she should be getting dressed up to go out with her powerful and influential husband to any one of the exclusive parties being thrown around the island that night. But Astrid always confounded everyone's expectations.

For the small group of girls growing up within Singapore's most elite milieu, life followed a prescribed order: Beginning at age six, you were enrolled at Methodist Girls' School (MGS), Singapore Chinese Girls' School (SCGS), or the Convent of the Holy Infant Jesus (CHIJ). After-school hours were consumed by a team of tutors preparing you for the avalanche of weekly exams (usually in classical Mandarin literature, multivariable calculus, and molecular biology), followed on the weekends by piano, violin, flute, ballet, or riding, and some sort of Christian Youth Fellowship activity. If you did well enough, you entered the National University of Singapore (NUS) and if you did not, you were sent abroad to England (American colleges were deemed substandard). The *only* acceptable majors were medicine or law (unless you were truly dumb, in which case you settled for accounting). After graduating with honors (anything less would bring shame to the family), you practiced your vocation (for not more than three years) before marrying a boy from a suitable family at the age of twenty-five (twenty-eight if you went to med school). At this point, you gave up your career to have children (three or more were officially encouraged by the government for women of your background, and at least two should be boys), and life would consist of a gentle rotation of galas, country clubs, Bible study groups, light volunteer work, contract bridge, mah-jongg, traveling, and spending time with your grandchildren (dozens and dozens, hopefully) until your quiet and uneventful death.

Astrid changed all this. She wasn't a rebel, because to call her one would imply that she was breaking the rules. Astrid simply made her own rules, and through the confluence of her particular circumstances—a substantial private income, overindulgent parents, and her own savoir faire—every move she made became breathlessly talked about and scrutinized within that claustrophobic circle.

In her childhood days, Astrid always disappeared from Singapore during the school holidays, and though Felicity had trained her daughter never to boast about her trips, a schoolmate invited over had discovered a framed photo of Astrid astride a white horse with a palatial country manor as a backdrop. Thus began the rumor that Astrid's uncle owned a castle in France, where she spent all her holidays riding a white stallion. (Actually, it was a manor in England, the stallion was a pony, and the schoolmate was never invited again.)

In her teen years, the chatter spread even more feverishly when Celeste Ting, whose daughter was in the same Methodist Youth Fellowship group as Astrid, picked up a copy of *Point de Vue* at Charles de Gaulle Airport and came upon a paparazzi photograph of Astrid doing cannonballs off a yacht in Porto Ercole with some young European princes. Astrid returned from school holidays that year with a precociously sophisticated sense of style. While other girls in her set became mad for head-to-toe designer brands, Astrid was the first to pair a vintage Saint Laurent *Le Smoking* jacket with three-dollar batik shorts bought off a beach vendor in Bali, the first to wear the Antwerp Six, and the first to bring home a pair of red-heeled stilettos from some Parisian shoemaker named Christian. Her classmates at Methodist Girls' School strove to imitate her every look, while their brothers nicknamed Astrid "the Goddess" and anointed her the chief object of their masturbatory fantasies.

After famously and unabashedly flunking every one of her A levels (*how could that girl concentrate on her studies when she was jet-setting all the time?*), Astrid was shipped off to a preparatory college in London for revision courses. Everyone knew the story of how eighteen-year-old Charlie Wu—the eldest son of the tech billionaire Wu Hao Lian—bade a tearful goodbye to her at Changi Airport and promptly chartered his own jet, ordering the pilot to race her plane to Heathrow. When Astrid arrived, she was astonished to find a besotted Charlie awaiting her at the arrival gate with three hundred red roses. They were inseparable for the next few years, and Charlie's parents purchased a flat for him in Knightsbridge (for the sake of appearances), even though the cognoscenti suspected Charlie and Astrid were probably "living in sin" at her private quarters in the Calthorpe Hotel.

At age twenty-two, Charlie proposed on a ski lift in Verbier, and though Astrid accepted, she supposedly refused the thirty-nine-carat diamond solitaire he presented as far too vulgar, flinging it onto the slopes (Charlie did not even attempt to search for the ring). Social Singapore was atwitter over the impending nuptials, while her parents were aghast at the prospect of becoming connected to a family of no particular lineage and such shameless new money. But it all came to a shocking end nine days before the most lavish wedding Asia had ever seen when Astrid and Charlie were sighted having a screaming match in broad daylight. Astrid, it was famously said, "chucked him like she chucked that diamond outside Wendy's on Orchard Road, throwing a Frosty in his face," and took off for Paris the next day.

Her parents supported the idea of Astrid having a "cooling-off period" away, but try as she might to maintain a low profile, Astrid effortlessly enchanted *le tout Paris* with her smoldering beauty. Back in Singapore, the wagging tongues resumed: Astrid was making a spectacle of herself. She was supposedly spotted in the front row at the Valentino show, seated between Joan Collins and Princess Rosario of Bulgaria. She was said to be having long, intimate lunches at Le Voltaire with a married philosopher playboy. And perhaps most sensational, rumor had it that she had become involved with one of the sons of the Aga Khan and was preparing to convert to Islam so that they could marry. (The Bishop of Singapore was said to have flown to Paris on a moment's notice to intervene.)

All these rumors came to naught when Astrid surprised everyone again by announcing her engagement to Michael Teo. The first question on everyone's lips was "Michael *who*?" He was a complete unknown, the son of schoolteachers from the then middle-class neighborhood of Toa Payoh. At first her parents were aghast and mystified by how she could have come into contact with someone from "that kind of background," but in the end they realized that Astrid had made something of a catch—she had chosen a fiercely handsome Armed Forces Elite Commando who was a National Merit Scholar *and* a Caltech-trained computer systems specialist. It could have been much worse.

The couple married in a very private, very small ceremony (only three hundred guests at her grandmother's house) that garnered a pictureless fifty-one-word announcement in the *Straits Times*, even though there were anonymous reports that Sir Paul McCartney flew in to serenade the bride at a ceremony that was "exquisite beyond belief." Within a year, Michael left his military post to start his own tech firm and the couple had their first child, a boy they named Cassian. In this cocoon of domestic bliss one might have thought that all the stories involving Astrid would simmer down. But the stories were not about to end.

A little after nine, Michael arrived home, and Astrid rushed to the door, greeting him with a long embrace. They had been married for more than four years now, but the sight of him still sent an electric spark through her, especially after they had been apart for a while. He was just so startlingly attractive, especially today with his stubble and the rumpled shirt that she wanted to bury her face in— secretly, she loved the way he smelled after a long day.

They had a light supper of steamed whole pomfret in a ginger-wine sauce and clay-pot rice, and stretched out on the sofa afterward, buzzed from the two bottles of wine they had polished off. Astrid continued to recount her adventures in Paris while Michael stared zombielike at the sports channel on mute.

"Did you buy many of those thousand-dollar dresses this time?" Michael inquired.

"No . . . just one or two," Astrid said breezily, wondering what would happen if he ever realized that two hundred thousand per dress was more like it.

"You're *such* a bad liar," Michael grunted. Astrid nestled her head on his chest, slowly stroking his right leg. She brushed the tips of her fingers in one continuous line, tracing his calf, up the curve of his knee, and along the front of his thigh. She felt him get hard against the nape of her neck, and she kept stroking his leg in a gentle continuous rhythm, moving closer and closer toward the soft part of his inner thigh. When Michael could stand it no longer, he scooped her up in one abrupt motion and carried her into the bedroom.

After a frenzied session of lovemaking, Michael got out of bed and headed for the shower. Astrid lay on his side of the bed, deliriously spent. Reunion sex was always the best. Her iPhone let out a soft ping. Who could be texting her at this hour? She reached for the phone, squinting at the bright glare of the text message. It read:

MISS U NSIDE ME.

Makes no sense at all. Who sent me this? Astrid wondered, gazing in half amusement at the unfamiliar number. It looked like a Hong Kong number—was this one of Eddie's pranks? She peered at the text message again, realizing all of a sudden that she was holding her husband's phone.

10

Edison Cheng

•

SHANGHAI

It was the mirror in the closet that did it. The closet in Leo Ming's brand-new triplex penthouse in the Huangpu district really put Eddie over the edge. Ever since Shanghai became Asia's party capital, Leo had been spending more time here with his latest mistress, a Beijing-born starlet whose contract he had to "buy over" from a Chinese film company at the cost of nineteen million (one million for every year of her life). Leo and Eddie had flown up for the day to inspect Leo's new super-luxe apartment, and they were standing in a hangar-like two-thousand-square-foot closet that boasted an entire wall of floor-to-ceiling windows, Macassar ebony cupboards, and banks of mirrored doors that parted automatically to reveal cedar-lined suit racks.

"It's all climate controlled," Leo noted. "The closets on this end are maintained at fifty-five degrees specifically for my Italian cashmere, houndstooth, and fur. But the shoe-display cabinets are kept at seventy degrees, which is optimal for leather, and the humidity is regulated to a constant thirty-five percent, so my Berlutis and Corthays never break a sweat. You gotta treat those babies right, *hei mai?*"*

Eddie nodded, thinking that it was time to redo his own closet.

---

* Cantonese for "isn't that right?"

"Now let me show you the pièce de résistance," Leo said, pronouncing "pièce" like "peace." With a flourish, he glided his thumb over a mirrored panel and its surface instantly transformed into a high-definition screen that projected the life-size image of a male model in a double-breasted suit. Above his right shoulder hovered the brand names of each item of clothing, followed by the dates and locations where the outfit was previously worn. Leo waved a finger in front of the screen as if he were flicking a page, and the man now appeared in corduroy pants and a cable-knit sweater. "There's a camera embedded in this mirror that takes a picture of you and stores it, so you can see every single thing you've ever worn, organized by date and place. This way you'll never repeat an outfit!"

Eddie stared at the mirror in amazement. "Oh, I've seen that before," he said rather unconvincingly as the envy began to coarse through his veins. He felt the sudden urge to shove his friend's bloated face into the pristine mirrored wall. Once again, Leo was showing off another shiny new toy he did fuck-all to deserve. It had been like this since they were little. When Leo turned seven, his father gave him a titanium bicycle custom-designed for his pudgy frame by former NASA engineers (it was stolen within three days). At sixteen, when Leo aspired to become a Canto hip-hop singer, his father built him a state-of-the-art recording studio and bankrolled his first album (the CD can still be found on eBay). Then in 1999, he funded Leo's Internet start-up, which managed to lose more than ninety million dollars and go belly-up at the height of the Internet boom. And now this—the latest in a countless collection of homes around the globe showered upon him by his adoring father. Yes, Leo Ming, charter member of Hong Kong's Lucky Sperm Club, got everything handed to him on a diamond-encrusted platter. It was just Eddie's shitty luck to have been born to parents who never gave him a cent.

In what is arguably the most materialistic city on earth, a city where the key mantra is *prestige*, the tongue-waggers within Hong Kong's most prestigious chattering circles would agree that Edison Cheng lived a life to be envied. They would acknowledge that Eddie was born into a prestigious family (even though his Cheng lineage was, frankly, a bit common), had attended all the prestigious schools (nothing tops Cambridge, well . . . except Oxford), and now worked for Hong Kong's most prestigious investment bank (though it was a pity he didn't follow in his father's footsteps and become a doctor).

At thirty-six, Eddie still retained his boyish features (getting a bit plump, but never mind—it made him look more prosperous); had chosen well by marrying pretty Fiona Tung (Hong Kong old money, but what a shame about that stock-manipulation scandal her father had gotten into with *Dato'* Tai Toh Lui); and his children, Constantine, Augustine, and Kalliste, were always so well-dressed and well-behaved (but that younger son, was he a bit autistic or something?).

Edison and Fiona lived in the duplex penthouse of Triumph Towers, one of the most sought-after buildings high on Victoria Peak (five bedrooms, six baths, more than four thousand square feet, not including the eight-hundred-square-foot terrace), where they employed two Filipino and two Mainland Chinese maids (the Chinese were better at cleaning, while the Filipinos were great with the kids). Their Biedermeier-filled apartment, decorated by the celebrated Hong Kong–based Austro-German decorator Kaspar von Morgenlatte to evoke a Hapsburg hunting schloss, had recently been featured in *Hong Kong Tattle* (Eddie was photographed preening at the bottom of his marble spiral staircase in a forest-green Tyrolean jacket, his hair slicked back, while Fiona, sprawled uncomfortably at his feet, wore a claret-colored gown by Oscar de la Renta).

In the parking garage of their building, they owned five parking spots (valued at two hundred and fifty thousand each), where their fleet consisted of a Bentley Continental GT (Eddie's weekday car), an Aston Martin Vanquish (Eddie's weekend car), a Volvo S40 (Fiona's car), a Mercedes S550 (the family car), and a Porsche Cayenne (the family sport-utility vehicle). At Aberdeen Marina, there was his sixty-four-foot yacht, *Kaiser.* Then there was the holiday condo in Whistler, British Columbia (the only place to be seen skiing, since there was semi-decent Cantonese food an hour away in Vancouver).

Eddie was a member of the Chinese Athletic Association, the Hong Kong Golf Club, the China Club, the Hong Kong Club, the Cricket Club, the Dynasty Club, the American Club, the Jockey Club, the Royal Hong Kong Yacht Club, and too many private dining clubs to recount. Like most upper-crust Hong Kongers, Eddie also possessed what was perhaps the ultimate membership card—Canadian Permanent Resident Cards for his entire family (a safe haven in case the powers that be in Beijing ever pulled a *Tiananmen* again). He collected watches, and now possessed more than seventy timepieces from the most esteemed watchmakers (all Swiss, of course, except for a few vintage Cartiers), which he installed in a custom-designed bird's-eye maple display console in his private dressing room (his wife did not have her own dressing room). He had made *Hong Kong Tattle*'s "Most Invited" list four years in a row, and befitting a man of his status, he had already gone through three mistresses since marrying Fiona thirteen years ago.

Despite this embarrassment of riches, Eddie felt extremely deprived compared to most of his friends. He didn't have a house on the Peak. He didn't have his own plane. He didn't have a full-time crew for his yacht, which was much too small to host more than ten guests for brunch comfortably. He didn't have any Rothkos or Pollocks or the other dead American artists one was required to hang on the wall in order to be considered truly rich these days. And unlike Leo, Eddie's parents were the old-fashioned type—insisting from the moment Eddie graduated that he learn to live off his earnings.

It was so bloody unfair. His parents were loaded, and his mother was set to inherit another obscene bundle if his Singapore grandmother would ever kick the bucket. (Ah Ma had already suffered two heart attacks in the past decade, but now she had a defibrillator installed and could go on ticking for God only knows how long.) Unfortunately his parents were also in the pink of health, so by the time they keeled over and the money was split up between himself, his bitchy sister, and his good-for-nothing brother, it wouldn't be nearly enough. Eddie was always trying to guesstimate his parents' net worth, much of which was gleaned from information his real estate friends leaked to him. It became an obsession of his, and he kept a spreadsheet on his home computer, diligently updating it every week based on property valuations and then calculating his potential future share. No matter how he ran the numbers, he realized he would most likely never make *Fortune Asia*'s list of "Hong Kong's Top Ten Richest" with the way his parents were handling things.

But then his parents were always so selfish. Sure, they raised him and paid for his education and bought him his first apartment, but they failed him when it came to what was truly important—they didn't know how to flaunt their wealth properly. His father, for all his fame and celebrated skill, had grown up middle class, with solidly middle-class tastes. He was happy enough being the revered doctor, driven around in that shamefully outdated Rolls-Royce, wearing that rusty Audemars Piguet watch, and going to his clubs. And then there was his mother. She was so cheap, forever counting her pennies. She could have been one of the queens of society if she would just play up her aristocratic background, wear some designer dresses, or move out of that flat in the Mid-Levels. That goddamn flat.

Eddie hated going over to his parents' place. He hated the lobby, with its cheap-looking Mongolian granite floors and the old-lady security guard who was forever eating stinky tofu out of a plastic bag. Inside the flat, he hated the peach-colored leather sectional sofa and white lacquered consoles (bought when the old Lane Crawford on Queen's Road was having a clearance sale in the mid-1980s), the glass pebbles at the bottom of every vase of fake flowers, the random collection of Chinese calligraphy paintings (all presents from his father's patients) clustering the walls, and the medical honors and plaques lined up on the overhead shelf that ran around the perimeter of the living room. He hated walking past his old bedroom, which he had been forced to share with his little brother, with its nautical-themed twin beds and navy blue Ikea wall unit, still there after all these years. Most of all, he hated the large walnut-framed family portrait peeking out from behind the big-screen television, forever taunting him with its smoky brown portrait-studio backdrop and the gold-embossed SAMMY PHOTO STUDIO in the bottom right corner. He hated how he looked in that photograph—he was nineteen, just back from his first year at Cambridge, with shoulder-length feathered hair, wearing a Paul Smith tweed blazer he thought was so cool at the time, his elbow arranged jauntily on his mother's shoulder. And how could his mother, born to a family of such exquisite breeding, be completely devoid of taste? Over the years, he had begged her to redecorate or move, but she had refused, claiming that she "could never part with all the happy memories of my children growing up here." What happy memories? His only memories were of a childhood spent being too embarrassed to invite any friends over (unless he knew they lived in less prestigious buildings), and teen years spent in the cramped toilet, masturbating practically underneath the bathroom sink with two feet against the door at all times (there was no lock).

As Eddie stood in Leo's new closet in Shanghai, looking out through the floor-to-ceiling windows at the Pudong financial district

65

shimmering across the river like Xanadu, he vowed that he would one day have a closet so cool, it would make this one look like a fucky little pigsty. Until then, he still had one thing that even Leo's crisp new money could not buy—a thick, embossed invitation to Colin Khoo's wedding in Singapore.

11

Rachel

•

NEW YORK TO SINGAPORE

"You're kidding, right?" Rachel said, thinking Nick was pulling a prank when he steered her onto the plush red carpet of the Singapore Airlines first-class counter at JFK.

Nick flashed a conspiratorial grin, relishing her reaction. "I figured if you were going to go halfway around the world with me, I should at least try to make it as comfy as possible."

"But this must have cost a fortune! You didn't have to sell a kidney, did you?"

"No worries, I had about a million frequent-flier miles saved up."

Still, Rachel couldn't help feeling a little guilty about the millions of frequent-flier points that Nick must have sacrificed for these tickets. Who even flew first class anymore? The second surprise for Rachel came when they boarded the hulking two-story Airbus A380 and were promptly greeted by a beautiful stewardess who looked as if she had materialized straight out of a soft-focus ad from a travel magazine. "Mr. Young, Ms. Chu, welcome aboard. Please allow me to show you to your suite." The stewardess sashayed down the aisle in an elegant, figure-hugging long dress,* ushering them to the front section of the plane, which consisted of twelve private suites.

---

* Designed by Pierre Balmain, the signature uniform worn by Singapore Airlines flight attendants was inspired by the Malay *kebaya* (and which has long inspired many a business traveler).

Rachel felt as if she was entering the screening room of a luxurious TriBeCa loft. The cabin consisted of two of the widest armchairs she had ever seen—upholstered in buttery hand-stitched Poltrona Frau leather—two huge flat-screen televisions placed side by side, and a full-length wardrobe ingeniously hidden behind a sliding burled-walnut panel. A Givenchy cashmere throw was artfully draped over the seats, beckoning them to snuggle up and get cozy.

The stewardess gestured to the cocktails awaiting them on the center console. "An aperitif before takeoff? Mr. Young, your usual gin and tonic. Ms. Chu, a Kir Royale to get you settled in." She handed Rachel a long-stemmed glass with chilled bubbly that looked like it had been poured just seconds ago. *Of course* they would already know her favorite cocktail. "Would you like to enjoy your lounge chairs until dinner, or would you prefer us to convert your suite into a bedroom right after takeoff?"

"I think we'll enjoy this screening-room setup for a while," Nick replied.

As soon as the stewardess was out of earshot, Rachel declared, "Sweet Jesus, I've lived in apartments smaller than this!"

"I hope you don't mind roughing it—this is all rather lowbrow by Asian hospitality standards," Nick teased.

"Um . . . I think I can make do." Rachel curled up on her sumptuous armchair and began fiddling with her remote control. "Okay, there are more channels than I can count. Are you going to watch one of your bleak Swedish crime thrillers? Oooh, *The English Patient*. I want to see that. Wait a minute. Is it bad to watch a film about a plane crash while you're flying?"

"That was a tiny single-engine plane, and wasn't it shot down by Nazis? I think it should be just fine," Nick said, placing his hand over hers.

The enormous plane began to taxi toward the runway, and Rachel looked out the window at the planes lined up on the tarmac, lights flashing on the tips of their wings, each one awaiting their turn to hurtle skyward. "You know, it's finally sinking in that we're going on this trip."

"You excited?"

"Just a bit. I think sleeping on an actual *bed* on a plane is probably the most exciting part!"

"It's all downhill from here, isn't it?"

"Definitely. It's all been downhill since the day we met," Rachel said with a wink, entwining her fingers with Nick's.

NEW YORK CITY, AUTUMN 2008

For the record, Rachel Chu did not feel the proverbial lightning-bolt strike when she first laid eyes on Nicholas Young in the garden of La Lanterna di Vittorio. Sure, he was terribly good-looking, but she had always been suspicious of good-looking men, especially ones with quasi-British accents. She spent the first few minutes silently sizing him up, wondering what Sylvia had gotten her into this time.

When Sylvia Wong-Swartz, Rachel's colleague at New York University's Department of Economics, walked into their faculty suite one afternoon and declared, "Rachel, I just spent the morning with your future husband," she dismissed the declaration as another of Sylvia's silly schemes and didn't even bother to look up from her laptop.

"No, seriously, I've found your future husband. He was at a student governance meeting with me. It's the third time I've met him, and I'm convinced he's *the one* for you."

"So my future husband is a student? Thanks—you know how much I like jailbait."

"No, no—he's the brilliant new prof in the history department. He's also the faculty adviser to the History Organization."

"You know I don't go for professor types. Especially from the history department."

"Yeah, but this guy is different, I'm telling you. He's the most impressive guy I've met in years. So charming. And HOT. I would be after him in a second if I wasn't already married."

"What's his name? Maybe I already know him."

"Nicholas Young. He just started this semester, a transfer from Oxford."

"A Brit?" Rachel looked up, her curiosity piqued.

"No, no." Sylvia put her files down and took a seat, inhaling deeply. "Okay, I'm going to tell you something, but before you write him off, promise you'll hear me out."

Rachel couldn't wait for the other shoe to drop. What fabulously dysfunctional detail had Sylvia left out?

"He's . . . Asian."

"Oh God, Sylvia." Rachel rolled her eyes, turning back to her computer screen.

"I *knew* you were going to react like this! Hear me out. This guy is the total package, I swear—"

"*I'm sure*," Rachel said, dripping with sarcasm.

"He has the most seductive, slightly British accent. And he's a terrific dresser. He had the most perfect jacket on today, rumpled in all the right places—"

"Not. Interested. Sylvia."

"And he looks a bit like that Japanese actor from those Wong Kar-wai movies."

"Is he Japanese or Chinese?"

"What does it matter? Every single time any Asian guy so much as looks in your direction, you give them the famous Rachel Chu Asian freeze-out and they wither away before you give them a chance."

"I do not!"

"Yes, you do! I've seen you do it so many times. Remember that guy we met at Yanira's brunch last weekend?"

"I was perfectly nice to him."

"You treated him as if he had 'HERPES' tattooed on his forehead. Honestly, you are the most self-loathing Asian I've ever met!"

"What do you mean? I'm not self-loathing at all. How about you? *You're* the one who married the white guy."

"Mark's not white, he's Jewish—that's basically Asian! But that's beside the point—at least *I* dated plenty of Asians in my time."

"Well, so have I."

"When have you actually *ever* dated an Asian?" Sylvia arched her eyebrows in surprise.

"Sylvia, you have *no idea* how many Asian guys I've been set up with over the years. Let's see, there was the MIT quantum-physics geek who was more interested in having me as a twenty-four-hour on-call cleaning lady, the Taiwanese frat-boy jock with pecs bigger than my chest, the Harvard-MBA Chuppie* who was obsessed with Gordon Gekko. Should I go on?"

---

* Chinese + yuppie = Chuppie.

"I'm sure they weren't as bad as you make it sound."

"Well, it was bad enough for me to institute a 'no Asian guys' policy about five years ago," Rachel insisted.

Sylvia sighed. "Let's face it. The real reason you treat Asian men the way you do is because they represent the type of man your family *wishes* you would bring home, and you are simply rebelling by refusing to date one."

"You are so far off base." Rachel laughed, shaking her head.

"Either that, or growing up as a racial minority in America, you feel that the ultimate act of assimilation is to marry into the dominant race. Which is why you only ever date WASPs . . . or Eurotrash."

"Have you ever been to Cupertino, where I spent all my teenage years? Because you would see that Asians are the *dominant race* in Cupertino. Stop projecting your own issues onto me."

"Well, take my challenge and try to be color-blind just one more time."

"Okay, I'll prove you wrong. How would you like me to present myself to this Oxford Asian charmer?"

"You don't have to. I already arranged for us to have coffee with him at La Lanterna after work," Sylvia said gleefully.

By the time the gruff Estonian waitress at La Lanterna came to take Nicholas's drink order, Sylvia was whispering angrily into Rachel's ear, "Hey, are you mute or something? Enough with the Asian freeze-out!"

Rachel decided to play along and join in the conversation, but it soon became apparent to her that Nicholas had no idea that this was a set-up and, more disturbingly, seemed far more interested in her colleague. He was fascinated by Sylvia's interdisciplinary background and peppered her with questions about how the economics department was organized. Sylvia basked in the glow of his attention, laughing coquettishly and twirling her hair with her fingers as they bantered. Rachel glared at him. *Is this dude completely clueless? Doesn't he notice Sylvia's wedding ring?*

It was only after twenty minutes that Rachel was able to step outside of her long-held prejudices and consider the situation at hand. It was true—in recent years, she hadn't given Asian guys much of a chance. Her mother had even said, "Rachel, I know it's hard for you to relate properly to Asian men, since you never knew your father."

Rachel found this sort of armchair analysis much too simplistic. If only it were that easy.

For Rachel, the problem began practically the day she hit puberty. She began to notice a phenomenon that occurred whenever an Asian of the opposite sex entered the room. The Asian male would be perfectly nice and normal to all the other girls, but *special treatment* would be reserved for her. First, there was the optical scan: the boy would assess her physical attributes in the most blatant way—quantifying every inch of her body by a completely different set of standards than he would use for non-Asian girls. How big were her eyes? Were they double-lidded naturally, or did she have that eyelid surgery? How light was her skin? How straight and glossy was her hair? Did she have good child-birthing hips? Did she have an accent? And how tall was she really, without heels on? (At five foot seven, Rachel was on the tall side, and Asian guys would sooner shoot themselves in the groin than date a taller girl.)

If she happened to pass this initial hurdle, the *real* test would begin. Her Asian girlfriends all knew this test. They called it the "SATs." The Asian male would begin a not so covert interrogation focused on the Asian female's social, academic, and talent aptitudes in order to determine whether she was possible "wife and bearer of my sons" material. This happened while the Asian male not so subtly flaunted his own SAT stats—how many generations his family had been in America; what kind of doctors his parents were; how many musical instruments he played; the number of tennis camps he went to; which Ivy League scholarships he turned down; what model BMW, Audi, or Lexus he drove; and the approximate number of years before he became (pick one) chief executive officer, chief financial officer, chief technology officer, chief law partner, or chief surgeon.

Rachel had become so accustomed to enduring the SATs that its absence tonight was strangely disconcerting. This guy didn't seem to have the same MO, and he wasn't relentlessly dropping names. It was baffling, and she didn't quite know how to deal with him. He was just enjoying his Irish coffee, soaking in the atmosphere, and being perfectly charming. Sitting in the enclosed garden lit by colorful, whimsically painted lampshades, Rachel gradually began to see, in a whole new light, the person her friend had been so eager for her to meet.

She couldn't quite put her finger on it, but there was something curiously exotic about Nicholas Young. For starters, his slightly disheveled canvas jacket, white linen shirt, and faded black jeans were reminiscent of some adventurer just returned from mapping the Western Sahara. Then there was his self-deprecating wit, the sort that all those British-educated boys were so well known for. But underlying all this was a quiet masculinity and a relaxed ease that was proving to be infectious. Rachel found herself being pulled into his conversational orbit, and before she even realized it, they were yakking away like old friends.

At a certain point, Sylvia got up from the table and announced that it was high time she went home, before her husband starved to death. Rachel and Nick decided to stay for one more drink. Which led to another drink. Which led to dinner at the bistro around the corner. Which led to gelato in Father Demo Square. Which led to a walk through Washington Square Park (since Nick insisted on escorting her back to her faculty apartment). *He's the perfect gentleman*, Rachel thought, as they strolled past the fountain and the blond-dreadlocked guitarist wailing a plaintive ballad.

And you're standing here beside me, I love the passing of time, the boy sang plaintively.

"Isn't this Talking Heads?" Nick asked. "Listen . . ."

"Oh my God, it totally is! He's singing 'This Must Be the Place,'" Rachel said in surprise. She loved that Nick knew the song well enough to recognize this bastardized version.

"He's not half bad," Nick said, taking out his wallet and tossing a few dollars into the kid's open guitar case.

Rachel noticed that Nick was mouthing along to the song. *He's scoring some major bonus points right now*, she thought, and then she realized with a start that Sylvia had been right—this guy who she'd just spent six straight hours engrossed in conversation with, who knew all the lyrics to one of her favorite songs, this guy standing here beside her was the first man she could truly imagine as her husband.

12

The Leongs
•

SINGAPORE

"At last, the golden couple!" Mavis Oon proclaimed as Astrid and Michael made their entrance into the Colonial Club's formal dining room. With Michael in his crisp navy Richard James suit and Astrid in a long, flapper-style silk voile dress the color of persimmon, they made an exceedingly striking pair, and the room rippled with the usual hushed excitement from the ladies, who covertly scrutinized Astrid from hair to heels, and the men, who gazed at Michael with a mixture of envy and derision.

"Aiyah, Astrid, why so late?" Felicity Leong scolded her daughter as she arrived at the long banquet table by the trophy wall where members of the extended Leong family and their honored guests from Kuala Lumpur—*Tan Sri** Gordon Oon and *Puan Sri* Mavis Oon—were already seated.

"So sorry. Michael's flight back from China was delayed," Astrid apologized. "I hope you didn't wait for us to order? The food always takes ages here."

"Astrid, come, come, let me look at you," Mavis commanded.

---

* The second most senior federal honorific title in Malaysia (similar to a British duke), conferred by a hereditary royal ruler of one of the nine Malay states; his wife is called a *puan sri*. (A *tan sri* is usually richer than a *dato'*, and has likely spent far more time sucking up to the Malay royals.)

The imperious lady, who could easily have won an Imelda Marcos look-alike contest with her dramatically rouged cheeks and fat chignon, patted Astrid's face as if she were a little girl and launched into her trademark gushing. "Aiyah you haven't aged one bit since I last saw you how's little Cassian when are you going to have another one don't wait too long *lah* you need a little girl now you know my ten-year-old granddaughter Bella absolutely worships you ever since her last trip to Singapore she's always saying '*Ah Ma,* when I grow up I want to be just like Astrid' I asked why and she says 'Because she always dresses like a movie star and that Michael is such a hunk!'" Everyone at the table roared with laughter.

"Yes, don't we *all* wish we could have Astrid's clothing budget and Michael's eight-pack!" Astrid's brother Alexander quipped.

Harry Leong looked up from his menu and, catching sight of Michael, beckoned him over. With his silvery hair and dark tan, Harry was a leonine presence at the head of the table, and as always, Michael approached his father-in-law with no small amount of trepidation. Harry handed him a large padded envelope. "Here's my MacBook Air. There's something wrong with the Wi-Fi connection."

"What exactly is the problem? Is it not finding the right networks, or are you having log-in problems?" Michael asked.

Harry had already turned his attention back to the menu. "What? Oh, it just doesn't seem to work anywhere. You're the one who set it up, and I haven't changed any of the settings. Thank you *so much* for taking a look at it. Felicity, did I have the rack of lamb here the last time? Is this where they always overcook the meat?"

Michael dutifully took the laptop with him, and as he made his way back to his seat at the other end of the table, Astrid's eldest brother, Henry, grabbed him by his jacket sleeve. "Hey, Mike, hate to bother you with this, but can you stop by the house this weekend? There's something wrong with Zachary's Xbox. I hope you can fix it—it's too *mah fan** to send it back to the factory in Japan for repair."

"I might have to go away this weekend, but if not, I'll try to stop by," Michael said flatly.

"Oh thank you, thank you," Cathleen, Henry's wife, cut in. "Zachary has been driving us absolutely crazy without his Xbox."

---

* Cantonese for "troublesome."

"Is Michael good with gadgets or something?" Mavis inquired.

"Oh, he's an absolute *genius*, Mavis, a *genius*! He's the perfect son-in-law to have around—he can fix anything!" Harry proclaimed.

Michael smiled uncomfortably as Mavis fixed her gaze on him. "Now why did I think he was in the army?"

"Auntie Mavis, Michael used to work for the Ministry of Defense. He helped to program all the high-tech weapon systems," Astrid said.

"Yes, the fate of our country's ballistics defense is in Michael's hands. You know, in case we get invaded by the two hundred and fifty million Muslims surrounding us on all sides, we can put up a fight for about ten minutes," Alexander chuckled.

Michael tried to hide his grimace and opened up his heavy leather-bound menu. This month's culinary theme was "Taste of the Amalfi," and most of the dishes were in Italian. *Vongole*. That was clams, he knew. But what the heck was *Paccheri alla Ravello*, and would it have killed them to include an English translation? This was par for the course at one of the island's oldest sporting clubs, a place so pretentious and buttoned-up in Edwardian-era tradition that women were not even allowed to *peek* into the Men's Bar until 2007.

As a teenager, Michael had played soccer every week at the *Padang*, the immense green field in front of city hall that was used for all the national parades, and he often stared curiously at the august Victorian structure at the eastern edge of the *Padang*. From the goalie post, he could see the glittering chandeliers within, the silver-domed dishes set on crisp white tablecloths, the waiters in their black tuxedo jackets scurrying around. He would observe the important-looking people enjoying their dinners and wonder who they were. He longed to walk into the club, just once, to be able to look at the soccer field from the other side of those windows. On a dare, he had asked a couple of his friends to sneak into the club with him. They would go one day before soccer, when they were still dressed in their St. Andrew's school uniforms. They could just stroll in casually, as if they were members, and who would stop them from ordering a drink at the bar? "Don't even dream, Teo, don't you know what this place is? It's the Colonial Club! You either have to be *ang mor*, or you have to be born into one of those ultrarich families to get inside," one of his buddies commented.

"Gordon and I sold our Pulau Club memberships because I realized I was only going there to eat their *ice kacang*,"* Michael overheard Mavis telling his mother-in-law. What he wouldn't give to be back out on the field with his friends right now. They could play soccer until the sun went down, and then head to the nearest *kopi tiam*† for cold beers and some *nasi goreng*‡ or *char bee hoon*.§ It would be so much better than sitting here in this tie that choked him half to death, eating unpronounceable food that was insanely overpriced. Not that anyone at this table ever noticed the prices—the Oons owned practically half of Malaysia, and as for Astrid and her brothers, Michael had never once witnessed any of them pick up a dinner check. They were all adults with children of their own, but Papa Leong always signed for everything. (In the Teo family, none of his brothers or sisters would even consider letting their parents pick up the check.)

How long would this dinner take? They were eating European style, so it would be four courses, and here that meant one course per hour. Michael stared at his menu again. *Gan ni na!*¶ There was some stupid salad course. Who ever heard of serving salad *after* the main course? This meant five courses, because Mavis liked her desserts, even though all she ever did was complain about her gout. And then his mother-in-law would complain about her heel spurs, and the ladies would volley chronic health complaints back and forth, trying to outdo each other. Then it would be time for the toasts—those long-winded toasts where his father-in-law would toast the Oons for their brilliance in having been born into the right family, and then Gordon Oon would turn around and toast the Leongs for their genius in having been born into the right family as well. And then Henry Leong Jr. would make a toast to Gordon's son Gordon Jr., the wonderful chap who was caught with the fifteen-year-old schoolgirl in Langkawi last year. It would be a miracle if dinner ended before eleven thirty.

Astrid glanced across the table at her husband. That ramrod-

---

* A Malay dessert made of shaved ice, colorful sugar syrup, and a variety of toppings such as red beans, sweet corn, agar-agar jelly, palm seed, and ice cream.

† Hokkien for "coffee shop."

‡ Indonesian fried rice, an immensely popular dish in Singapore.

§ Fried vermicelli, another local favorite.

¶ A Hokkien term that could mean "fuck your mother," or, as in this case, "fuck me."

straight posture and tense half smile he was forcing himself to make as he spoke to Bishop See Bei Sien's wife was a look she knew well— she had seen it the first time they were invited to tea at her grand-mother's, and when they had dinner with the president at Istana.* Michael clearly wished he were somewhere else right now. Or was it *with someone* else? Who was that someone else? Since the night she had discovered *that* text message, she couldn't stop asking herself these questions.

MISS U NSIDE ME. For the first few days, Astrid tried to con-vince herself that there must be some rational explanation. It was an innocent mistake, a text to the wrong number, some sort of prank or private joke she didn't understand. The text message had been erased by the next morning, and she wished it could just as simply be erased from her mind. But her mind would not let it go. Her life could not go on until she solved the mystery behind these words. She began calling Michael at work every day at odd times, inventing some silly question or excuse to make sure he was where he said he would be. She started checking his cell phone at every fleeting opportunity, feverishly scrolling through all the text messages in the precious few minutes that he was away from his phone. There were no more incriminating text messages. Was he covering his tracks, or was she just being paranoid? For weeks now, she had been deconstructing every look, every word, every move of Michael's, searching for some sign, some evidence to confirm what she could not bring herself to put into words. But there had been nothing. Everything was seem-ingly normal in their beautiful life.

Until this afternoon.

Michael had just returned from the airport, and when he com-plained of being sore from cramming into a middle seat in the last, non-reclining row of an older China Eastern Airlines plane, Astrid suggested that he take a warm soak in the tub with Epsom salts. While he was out of commission, Astrid went snooping through his

---

* "Palace" in Malay; here it refers to the official residence of the president of Singa-pore. Completed in 1869 on the orders of Sir Harry Saint George Ord, Singapore's first colonial governor, it was formerly known as Government House and occupies 106 acres of land adjacent to the Orchard Road area.

luggage, aimlessly looking for something, anything. Rifling through his wallet, she came upon a folded piece of paper hidden underneath the plastic flap that held his Singapore Identity Card. It was a receipt for dinner from the night before. A receipt from Petrus. For HK$3,812. Pretty much the price of dinner for two.

What was her husband doing having dinner at Hong Kong's fanciest French restaurant when he was supposed to be working on some cloud-sourcing project in Chongqing in southwest China? And especially *this* restaurant, the sort of place he normally would have been dragged to kicking and screaming. There was no way his cash-strapped partners would approve this sort of expense, even for their top clients. (And besides, no Chinese clients would ever want to eat French nouvelle cuisine if they could possibly help it.)

Astrid looked at the receipt for a long time, staring at the bold strokes of his dark-blue signature against the crisp white paper. He had signed it with the Caran d'Ache fountain pen she had given him on his last birthday. Her heart was beating so fast it felt like it was going to jump out of her chest, and yet she felt completely paralyzed. She imagined Michael sitting in the candlelit room perched atop the Island Shangri-La hotel, staring out at the sparkling lights of Victoria Harbour, enjoying a romantic dinner with the girl who had sent the text message. They started off with a splendid Burgundy from the Côte d'Or and finished with the warm bitter-chocolate soufflé for two (with frosted lemon cream).

She wanted to burst into the bathroom and hold the receipt in his face while he was soaking in the tub. She wanted to scream and claw at his skin. But of course, she did no such thing. She breathed in deeply. She regained her composure. The composure that had been ingrained since the day she was born. She would do the sensible thing. She knew that there was no point making a scene, demanding an explanation. Any sort of explanation that could cause even the tiniest scratch on their picture-perfect life. She folded the receipt carefully and tucked it back into its hiding place, willing it to disappear from his wallet and from her mind. Just disappear.

13

Philip and Eleanor Young

SYDNEY, AUSTRALIA, AND SINGAPORE

Philip sat in his favorite metal folding chair on the dock that stretched out from his waterfront lawn, keeping one watchful eye on the fishing line that went straight into Watson's Bay and the other eye on the latest issue of *Popular Mechanics*. His cell phone began to vibrate in the pocket of his cargo pants, disrupting the serenity of his morning. He knew it would be his wife on the line; she was practically the only person who ever called his cell. (Eleanor insisted that he keep the phone on his body at all times, in case she needed him in an emergency, although he doubted he could be of any help since he spent much of the year here in Sydney while she was constantly traveling between Singapore, Hong Kong, Bangkok, Shanghai, and God knows where else.)

He answered the phone and immediately the hysterical torrent from his wife began. "Calm down and speak slower, *lah*. I can't understand a word you're saying. Now, why do you want to jump off a building?" Philip asked in his usual laconic manner.

"I just got the dossier on Rachel Chu from that private investigator in Beverly Hills who Mabel Kwok recommended. Do you want to know what it says." It wasn't a question; it sounded like more of a threat.

"Er . . . who is Rachel Chu?" Philip asked.

"Don't be so senile, *lah*! Don't you remember what I told you last week? Your son has been dating some girl *in secret* for more than a year, and he had the cheek to tell us about it just *days* before he brings her to Singapore!"

"You hired a private investigator to check up on this girl?"

"Of course I did. We know nothing about this girl, and everyone is already talking about her and Nicky—"

Philip looked down at his fishing pole, which was beginning to vibrate a hair. He knew where this conversation was leading, and he wanted no part in it. "I'm afraid I can't talk right now, darling, I'm in the middle of something urgent."

"Stop it, *lah*! *This* is urgent! The report is even worse than my worst nightmare! Your stupid cousin Cassandra got it wrong—it turns out the girl is *not* one of the Chus from that Taipei Plastics family!"

"I always tell you not to believe a word out of Cassandra's mouth. But what difference does it make?"

"What difference? This girl is being *deceitful*—she is pretending to be a Chu."

"Well, if her last name happens to be Chu, how can you accuse her of pretending to be a Chu?" Philip said with a chuckle.

"Aiyah—don't contradict me! I'll tell you how she's being deceitful. At first, the private investigator told me she was ABC, but then after more digging he found out that she's not even *truly* American-born Chinese. She was born in Mainland China and went to America when she was six months old."

"So?"

"Did you hear me? *Mainland China!*"

Philip was baffled. "Doesn't everybody's family ultimately originate from Mainland China? Where would you rather her be from? Iceland?"

"Don't be funny with me! Her family comes from some *ulu ulu**
village in China that nobody has ever heard of. The investigator thinks that they were most likely working class. In other words, they are PEASANTS!"

"I think if you go back far enough, darling, *all* our families were peasants. And don't you know that in ancient China, the peasant class was actually revered? They were the backbone of the economy, and—"

---

* Malay for "remote," "far from civilization."

"Stop talking nonsense, *lah*! You haven't heard the worst yet—this girl came to America as a baby with her mother. But where's the father? There's no record of the father, so they must have divorced. Can you believe it? *Alamak*, a child from some divorced *no-name ulu* family! I'm going to *tiao lau*!"*

"What's wrong with that? There are plenty of people these days who come from broken homes and go on to have happy marriages. Just look at the divorce rate here in Australia." Philip was trying to reason with his wife.

Eleanor sighed deeply. "These Aussies are all descended from criminals, what do you expect?"

"This is why you're so popular down here, darling," Philip joked.

"You are not seeing the big picture. This girl is obviously a cunning, deceitful GOLD DIGGER! You know as well as I do that your son can never marry someone like that. Can you imagine how *your* family is going to react when he brings this gold digger home?"

"Actually, I couldn't care less what they think."

"But don't you see how this will affect Nicky? And *of course* your mother is going to blame me for this, *lah*. I *always* get blamed for *everything*. *Alamak*, surely you know how this will end."

Philip sighed deeply. This was the reason he spent as much time as he possibly could *away* from Singapore.

"I've already asked Lorena Lim to use all her Beijing contacts to investigate the girl's family in China. We need to know everything. I don't want to leave a single stone unturned. We need to be prepared for every possibility," Eleanor said.

"Don't you think you're going a bit overboard?"

"Absolutely not! We must put a stop to all this nonsense before it goes any further. Do you want to know what Daisy Foo thinks?"

"Not really."

"Daisy thinks that Nicky is going to propose to the girl while they're in Singapore!"

"If he hasn't already," Philip teased.

"*Alamak!* Do you know something I don't? Has Nicky told you—"

"No, no, no, don't panic. Darling, you are letting your silly girlfriends work you up for nothing. You just need to trust our son's

* Hokkien for "jump off a building."

good judgment. I'm sure this girl is going to turn out just fine." The fish was really tugging at the line now. Maybe it was a barramundi. He could ask his chef to grill it for lunch. Philip just wanted to get off the phone.

———

That Thursday, at Carol Tai's Bible study, Eleanor decided that it was time to call in her ground troops. As the ladies sat around enjoying homemade *bobo chacha* and helping Carol organize her collection of Tahitian black pearls by color grade, Eleanor began her lament as she savored her chilled coconut-and-sago pudding.

"Nicky doesn't realize what a terrible thing he is doing to us. Now he tells me he's not even going to stay at our new flat when he arrives. He's going to stay at Kingsford Hotel with that girl! As if he needs to hide her from us! *Alamak*, how is this going to look?" Eleanor sighed dramatically.

"So disgraceful! Sharing a hotel room when they aren't even married! You know, some people might think they eloped and are coming here for their honeymoon!" Nadine Shaw chimed in, though secretly the thought of any potential scandal that might bring those high-and-mighty Youngs down a peg filled her with glee. She continued to fan Eleanor's flames, not that they needed any further stoking. "How dare this girl think she can just waltz right into Singapore on Nicky's arm and attend the social event of the year without your approval? She obviously has no clue how things work here."

"Aiyah, children these days don't know how to behave," Daisy Foo said quietly, shaking her head. "My sons are just the same. You're lucky that Nicky even *told* you he was bringing someone home. I would never be able to expect that from my boys. I have to find out in the newspapers what they're doing! What to do, *lah*? This is what happens when you educate your children overseas. They become too Westernized and *aksi borak** when they return. Can you imagine—my daughter-in-law Danielle forces me to make an appointment two weeks in advance just to see my grandchildren! She thinks that because she graduated from *Amherst* she knows better than me how to raise my own grandchildren!"

———

* A Malay slang term that means "to act like a show-off or know-it-all" (basically, a pompous ass).

"Better than *you*? Everyone knows these ABCs are descended from all the peasants that were too stupid to survive in China!" Nadine cackled.

"Hey, Nadine, don't underestimate them. These ABC girls can be *tzeen lee hai*,"* Lorena Lim warned. "Now that America is broke, all these ABCs want to come to Asia and sink their claws into our men. They are even worse that the Taiwanese tornadoes because they are Westernized, sophisticated, and worst of all, *college educated*. Do you remember Mrs. Hsu Tsen Ta's son? That Ivy League–degreed ex-wife of his *purposely* introduced him to the girl who would become his mistress, and then used that silly excuse to get a huge divorce settlement. The Hsus had to sell so many properties just to pay her off. So *sayang!*"†

"My Danielle was so *kwai kwai*‡ at first, so dutiful and modest," Daisy recalled. "Hiyah—the minute that thirty-carat diamond was on her finger, she transformed into the bloody Queen of Sheba! Nowadays she wears nothing but Prada, Prada, Prada, and have you seen how she makes my son waste money by hiring that whole security team to escort her everywhere she goes, as if she is some big shot? Who wants to kidnap her? My son and my grandchildren are the ones who should have the bodyguards, not this girl with the flat nose! *Suey doh say!*"§

"I don't know what I would do if my son brought home a girl like that." Eleanor moaned and put on her saddest expression.

"Come, come, Lealea, have some more *bobo chacha*," Carol said, trying to soothe her friend as she ladled more of the fragrant dessert into Eleanor's bowl. "Nicky is a good boy. You should thank the Lord that he isn't like my Bernard. I gave up trying to get Bernard to listen to me long ago. His father lets him get away with everything. What to do? His father just pays and pays, while I just pray and pray. The Bible tells us we must accept what we cannot change."

Lorena looked at Eleanor, wondering whether this was the right time to drop her bombshell. She decided to go for it. "Eleanor, you asked me to do a little investigating for you about this Chu girl's

* Hokkien for "very sharp" or "dangerous."

† Malay for "what a waste."

‡ Hokkien for "goody-goody."

§ Cantonese for "so atrocious I could die!"

family in China, and I don't want you to get *too* excited, but I've just received the most intriguing tidbit."

"So fast? What did you find out?" Eleanor perked up.

"Well, there's a fellow who claims to have 'very valuable' info on Rachel," Lorena continued.

"*Alamak*, what, what?" Eleanor asked, getting alarmed.

"I don't know exactly, but it comes from a source in Shenzhen," Lorena said.

"Shenzhen? Did they say what kind of information?"

"Well, they just said it was 'very valuable,' and they won't talk over the phone. They will only give you the information in person, and it's going to cost you."

"How did you find these people?" Eleanor asked excitedly.

"*Wah ooh kang tao, mah*,"* Lorena said mysteriously. "I think you should go to Shenzhen next week."

"That won't be possible. Nicky and that girl will be here," Eleanor replied.

"Elle, I think you should go *precisely* when Nicky and that girl arrive," Daisy suggested. "Think about it—they are not even staying with you, so you have the perfect excuse not to be here. And if you are not here, you have all the advantage. You will show everyone that you are NOT rolling out the red carpet for this girl, and you won't lose face if she turns out to be a total nightmare."

"Plus you'll have gained some vital new information," Nadine added. "Maybe she's already married. Maybe she already has a child. Maybe she's running some huge scam and—"

"Aiyah, I need a Xanax," Eleanor cried, reaching into her purse.

"Lorena, stop scaring Lealea!" Carol interjected. "We don't know this girl's story, maybe it's nothing at all. Maybe God will bless Eleanor with a dutiful God-fearing daughter-in-law. *'Judge not lest ye be judged.'* Matthew 7:1."

Eleanor considered everything that her friends had to say. "Daisy, you're always so smart. Lorena, can I stay at your beautiful flat in Shenzhen?"

"Of course. I was going to come with you. Also, I've been dying to go on another shopping marathon in Shenzhen."

"Who else wants to come to Shenzhen this weekend? Carol, are

---

* Hokkien for "I have my secret contacts, of course."

you in?" Eleanor asked, hoping that Carol could be roped in and they would get to use her plane.

Carol leaned over from her bed and said, "I'll check, but I think we can take the plane if we leave before the weekend. I know my husband has to fly to Beijing to take over some Internet company called Ali Baibai earlier in the week. And Bernard's using the plane for Colin Khoo's bachelor party on Saturday."

"Let's all go to Shenzhen for a ladies' spa weekend!" Nadine declared. "I want to go to that place where they soak your feet in those wooden buckets and then massage them for an hour."

Eleanor was beginning to get excited. "This is a good plan. Let's go shop till we drop in Shenzhen. We'll let Nicky and this girl manage on their own, and then I will return with my valuable information."

"Your valuable *ammunition*," Lorena corrected.

"Haha, that's right," Nadine cheered, digging into her handbag and beginning to text her stockbroker covertly. "Now Carol, what was the name of that Internet company the *dato'* is planning to take over?"

14

Rachel and Nicholas

SINGAPORE

The plane banked sharply to the left, breaking out of the clouds as Rachel caught sight of the island for the first time. They had departed New York twenty-one hours ago, and after one refueling stop in Frankfurt, she was in Southeast Asia now, in the realm her ancestors called the *Nanyang*.* But the view she could glimpse from the plane did not resemble some romantic terrain swathed in mist—rather, it was a dense metropolis of skyscrapers glittering in the evening sky, and from six thousand feet Rachel could already feel the pulsating energy that was one of the world's financial powerhouses.

As the electronic doors of the customs area slid open to reveal the tropical oasis that was the arrival hall of Terminal Three, the first thing Nick saw was his friend Colin Khoo holding up a large placard with BEST MAN printed on it. Beside him stood an exceedingly tan, willowy girl clutching a bunch of silver balloons.

Nick and Rachel rolled their luggage carts toward them. "What are you doing here?" Nick exclaimed in surprise as Colin squeezed him into a bear hug.

---

* Not to be confused with the Singapore academy where students are taught in—horrors—Mandarin, *Nanyang* is Mandarin for "Southern Sea." The word also became a common reference for the large ethnic Chinese migrant population in Southeast Asia.

"Come on! Of course I had to welcome my best man properly! This is full service, man," Colin beamed.

"My turn!" the girl beside him declared, leaning over and giving Nick a hug followed by a quick peck on the cheek. She turned next to Rachel, stretched out her hand, and said, "You must be Rachel. I'm Araminta."

"Oh sorry, let me make proper introductions—Rachel Chu, meet Araminta Lee, Colin's fiancée. And this, of course, is Colin Khoo," Nick said.

"So nice to finally meet you." Rachel smiled, shaking their hands vigorously. She wasn't prepared for this welcoming party, and after all those hours on the plane, she could only imagine how she must look. She studied the cheery couple for a bit. People always looked so different from their pictures. Colin was taller than she imagined, roguishly handsome with dark freckles and an unruly shock of hair that made him look a bit like a Polynesian surfer. Behind her wire-frame spectacles, Araminta had a very pretty face, even without a stitch of makeup. Her long black hair was pulled into a rubber-banded ponytail that reached down to the small of her back, and she looked far too skinny for her tall frame. She was wearing what appeared to be a pair of plaid pajama pants, a pale orange tank top, and flip-flops. Though she was probably in her mid-twenties, she looked more like a schoolgirl than someone about to walk down the aisle. They were an unusually exotic couple, and Rachel wondered how their children might end up looking.

Colin began texting away on his cell phone. "The drivers have been circling around for a while. Let me just make sure they know we're ready."

"I can't believe this airport—it makes JFK look like Mogadishu," Rachel remarked. She stared up in wonder at the soaring ultramodern structure, the indoor palm trees, and the immense, lush vertical hanging garden that seemed to make up an entire length of the terminal. A fine mist of water began to spread over the cascading greenery. "Are they misting the entire wall? I feel like I'm at some upscale tropical resort."

"This whole country is an upscale tropical resort," Colin quipped as he led them toward the exit. Waiting at the curb were two matching silver Land Rovers. "Here, pile all your luggage into this one, it's going straight to the hotel. We can all ride in the other one without being cramped." The driver in the first car got out, nodded to Colin, and went to join the other driver, leaving an empty car for them. In her jet-lagged fog, Rachel didn't know what to make of all this and just climbed into the backseat of the SUV.

"What a treat! I don't think I've been welcomed at the airport like this since I was a little kid," Nick said, recalling the times in his childhood when a large group of family members would gather at the airport. A visit to the airport back then was a thrilling event, since it also meant that his father would take him for a hot fudge sundae at the Swensen's Ice Cream Parlor in the old terminal. People seemed to go away on longer trips back then, and there were always tears from the women saying goodbye to relatives heading overseas or welcoming home children who had spent the school year abroad. He once even overheard his older cousin Alex whisper to his father just before Harry Leong was about to board a plane, "Be sure to pick me up the latest *Penthouse* on your layover in Los Angeles."

Colin settled behind the wheel and began adjusting the mirrors to fit his sightlines. "Where to? Straight to the hotel, or *makan*?"*

"I can definitely eat," Nick said. He turned around to look at Rachel, knowing she probably wanted to go straight to the hotel and collapse into bed. "Feeling okay, Rachel?"

"I'm great," Rachel replied. "Actually, I'm kinda hungry too."

"It's breakfast time back in New York, that's why," Colin noted.

"Did you have a good flight? Did you watch a lot of movies?" Araminta asked.

"Rachel went on a Colin Firth binge," Nick announced.

Araminta squealed. "OMG—I *love* him! He'll always be the one and only Mr. Darcy for me!"

"Okay, I think we can be friends now," Rachel declared. She looked out the window, amazed by the swaying palm trees and profusion of bougainvillea that lined the sides of the brightly lit highway. It was almost ten o'clock at night, but everything about this city seemed unnaturally bright—effervescent, almost.

"Nicky, where should we take Rachel for her first local meal?" Colin asked.

"Hmm . . . should we welcome Rachel with a feast of Hainanese chicken rice at Chatterbox? Or should we head straight for chili

* Malay for "eat."

crab at East Coast?" Nick asked, feeling excited and torn at the same time—there were about a hundred different eating places he wanted Rachel to experience *right now*.

"How about some satay?" Rachel suggested. "Nick is always going on and on about how you've never tasted decent satay until you've had it in Singapore."

"That settles it—we're going to Lau Pa Sat," Colin announced. "Rachel, you'll get to experience your first true hawker center. And they have the best satay."

"You think so? I like that place in Sembawang better," Araminta said.

"NOOOO! What are you talking about, *lah*? The fellow from the original Satay Club is still at Lau Pa Sat," Colin said insistently.

"You're wrong," Araminta replied firmly. "That original Satay Club guy moved to Sembawang."

"Lies! That was his cousin. An imposter!" Colin was adamant.

"Personally, I've always liked the satay at Newton," Nick cut in.

"*Newton?* You've lost your mind, Nicky. Newton is only for expats and tourists—there aren't any good satay stalls left," Colin said.

"Welcome to Singapore, Rachel—where arguing about food is the national pastime," Araminta declared. "This is probably the only country in the world where *grown men* can get into fistfights over which specific food stall in some godforsaken shopping center has the best rendition of some obscure fried noodle dish. It's like a pissing contest!"

Rachel giggled. Araminta and Colin were so funny and down-to-earth, she liked them both instantly.

Soon they were on Robinson Road, in the heart of the downtown financial district. Nestled in the shadows of massive towers was Lau Pa Sat—or "old market" in the Hokkien dialect—an octagonal open-air pavilion that housed a bustling hive of food stalls. Walking from the car park across the street, Rachel could already smell the delicious spice-filled aromas wafting through the balmy air. As they were about to enter the great food hall, Nick turned to Rachel and said, "You're going to go nuts for this place—it's the oldest Victorian structure in all of Southeast Asia."

Rachel stared up at the soaring cast-iron filigree arches that radiated out across the vaulted ceilings. "Looks like the inside of a cathedral," she said.

"Where the masses come to worship food," Nick quipped.

Sure enough, even though it was past ten, the place teemed with hundreds of fervent diners. Rows and rows of brightly lit food stalls offered up a greater array of dishes than Rachel had ever witnessed under one roof. As they walked around, peering at the various stalls where men and women were frenziedly cooking their delicacies, Rachel shook her head in awe. "There's just so much to take in, I don't know where to start."

"Just point to whatever looks interesting and I'll order it," Colin offered. "The beauty of the hawker center is that each vendor basically sells just one dish, so whether it's fried pork dumplings or fish-ball soup, they've spent a lifetime perfecting it."

"More than one lifetime. A lot of these people are second- and third-generation hawkers, cooking old family recipes," Nick chimed in.

A few minutes later, the four of them were seated just outside the main hall under a huge tree strung with yellow lights, every inch of their table covered with colorful plastic plates piled high with the greatest hits of Singaporean street cuisine. There was the famous *char kuay teow*, a fried omelet with oysters called *orh luak*, Malay *rojak* salad bursting with chunks of pineapple and cucumber, Hokkien-style noodles in a thick garlicky gravy, a fish cake smoked in coconut leaves called *otah otah*, and a hundred sticks of chicken and beef satay.

Rachel had never seen anything like this feast. "This is insane! Every dish looks like it came from a different part of Asia."

"That's Singapore for you—the true originators of fusion cuisine," Nick boasted. "You know, because of all the ships passing through from Europe, the Middle East, and India in the nineteenth century, all these amazing flavors and textures could intermingle."

As Rachel tasted the *char kuay teow*, her eyes widened in delight at the rice noodles flash-fried with seafood, egg, and bean sprouts in a dark soy sauce. "Why doesn't it ever taste like this at home?"

"Gotta love that burned-wok flavor," Nick remarked.

"I bet you'll love this," Araminta said, handing Rachel a plate of *roti paratha*. Rachel tore off some of the doughy golden pastry and dipped it into the rich curry sauce.

"Mmmm . . . heaven!"

Then it was time for the satay. Rachel bit into the succulent grilled chicken, savoring its smoky sweetness carefully. The rest of them watched her intently. "Okay Nick, you were right. I've never had decent satay until now."

"To think you doubted me," Nick tut-tutted with a smile.

"I can't believe we're pigging out at this hour!" Rachel giggled, reaching for another stick of satay.

"Get used to it. I know you probably want to go straight to bed, but we have to keep you up for a few more hours so that you'll adjust better to the time change," Colin said.

"Aiyah, Colin just wants to monopolize Nick for as long as possible," Araminta declared. "These two are inseparable whenever Nick's in town."

"Hey, I have to make the most out of this time, especially since mommie dearest is away," Colin said in his own defense. "Rachel—you're in luck, not having to deal with Nicky's mum the minute you arrive."

"Colin, don't you start scaring her," Nick chided.

"Oh Nick, I almost forgot—I ran into your mum the other day at Churchill Club," Araminta began. "She grabbed me by the arm and said, 'Aramintaaaaa! Aiyoh, you're too dark! You better stop going into the sun so much, otherwise on your wedding day you will be so black people will think you are Malay!'"

Everyone roared with laughter, except Rachel. "She *was* kidding, I hope?"

"Of course not. Nick's mum doesn't kid," Araminta said, continuing to laugh.

"Rachel, you'll understand once you meet Nicky's mum. I love her like my own mother, but she's one of a kind," Colin explained, trying to put her at ease. "Anyway, it's perfect that your parents are gone, Nick, because *this* weekend your presence is required at my bachelor party."

"Rachel, you'll have to come to *my* bachelorette party," Araminta declared. "Let's show the boys how it's *really* done!"

"You bet," Rachel said, clinking her beer with Araminta's.

Nick gazed at his girlfriend, thrilled that she had so effortlessly charmed his friends. He could still hardly believe that she was actually here with him, and that they had the whole summer ahead of them. "Welcome to Singapore, Rachel," he joyously declared, lifting up his bottle of Tiger beer in a toast. Rachel gazed into Nick's sparkling eyes. She had never seen him as happy as he was tonight, and she wondered how she could possibly have been worried about coming on this trip.

"How does it feel to be here?" Colin asked.

"Well," Rachel mused, "an hour ago we landed in the most beautiful, modern airport I've ever seen, and now we're sitting under these huge tropical trees by a nineteenth-century food hall, having the most glorious feast. I don't ever want to leave!"

Nick grinned broadly, not noticing the look Araminta had just given Colin.

15

Astrid

•

Whenever Astrid felt in need of a pick-me-up, she would pay a visit to her friend Stephen. Stephen had a small jewelry shop on one of the upper levels of the Paragon shopping center, tucked away from all the other high-end boutiques in a back hallway. While it lacked the visibility of high-profile local jewelers like L'Orient or Larry Jewelry, with their gleaming flagship stores, Stephen Chia Jewels was highly regarded by the island's most discerning collectors.

Not to disregard his studied eye for spectacular gemstones, but what Stephen truly offered was absolute discretion. His was the sort of niche operation where, for instance, a society matron in need of a quick cash infusion to pay off her idiot son's bad margin calls might go to dispose of an heirloom bauble without anyone finding out, or where a "very important piece" about to go on the block in Geneva or New York might be flown in for private inspection by a VIP client, away from the eyes of gossipy auction-house staffers. Stephen's shop was said to be a particular favorite of the wives of Persian Gulf sheikhs, Malay sultans, and the Indonesian Chinese oligarchs, who had no need to be seen buying up millions of dollars's worth of jewelry at the tony Orchard Road boutiques.

The shop consisted of a very small, rather stark front room where three French Empire vitrines displayed a small collection of moderately priced pieces, mainly by emerging artists from Europe.

The mirrored door behind the Boulle desk, however, hid a vestibule where another security door opened to reveal a narrow corridor of individual chambers. It was here that Astrid liked to hide out, in the tuberose-scented private salon lined from floor to ceiling in pale blue velvet, with its plush velvet Récamier settee where she could curl up her feet, sip a soda with lemon, and gossip with Stephen as he came in and out of the room bearing trays and trays of glorious gems.

Stephen and Astrid had met years ago in Paris, when she wandered into the jewelry shop on rue de la Paix where he was doing his apprenticeship. Back then it was as rare to meet a teenage Singapore girl interested in eighteenth-century cameos as it was to see a young Chinese man behind the counter at a *joaillier* as distinguished as Mellerio dits Meller, so an immediate bond was struck. Astrid was grateful to find someone in Paris who understood her exacting tastes and was willing to indulge her capricious hunt for rare pieces that might have once belonged to the Princesse de Lamballe. Stephen, however, knew immediately that this girl had to be the daughter of *some big shot*, though it took him another three years of careful cultivating to figure out exactly who she was.

Like many of the world's greatest jewelry dealers, from Gianni Bulgari to Laurence Graff, Stephen had over the years honed his skills in being perfectly attuned to the whims of the very rich. He had become a consummate soothsayer to the Asian billionaire set, and he had become an expert in recognizing Astrid's many-faceted moods. He could tell, simply by observing her reactions to the types of pieces he would present to her, what sort of day she was having. Today he was seeing a side to Astrid he had never witnessed in fifteen years of knowing her. Something was clearly wrong, and her mood had worsened dramatically while he was showing her a new series of bracelets by Carnet.

"Aren't these the most intricately detailed bracelets you've ever seen? They look like they could have been inspired by the botanical drawings of Alexander von Humboldt. Speaking of bracelets, did you like the charm bracelet your husband bought you?"

Astrid looked up at Stephen, confused by his question. "The charm bracelet?"

"Yes, the one Michael got you for your birthday last month. Wait a minute, didn't you know he got it from me?"

Astrid averted her gaze, not wanting to look surprised. She had not received any sort of gift from her husband. Her birthday wasn't until August, and Michael knew better than to ever buy her jewelry. She could feel all the blood rush to her face. "Oh yes, I forgot—it's *adorable*," she said lightly. "Did you help him pick it out?"

"Yes. He came in one night, all in a hurry. He had such a hard time making up his mind—I think he was afraid you wouldn't like it."

"Well, of course I do. Thanks so much for helping him out," Astrid said, keeping her face completely calm. *Oh God oh God oh God. Was Michael actually stupid enough to buy jewelry for someone else from her close friend Stephen Chia?*

Stephen wished he hadn't brought up the bracelet. He suspected that Astrid had not been impressed with the gift from her husband. Truth be told, he wasn't sure Astrid would ever wear something as quotidian as a bracelet with multicolored pavé diamond teddy bear charms, but it was one of the least expensive things he had in the shop, and he knew that Michael, a typically clueless husband, was making a great effort to find something within his budget. It was quite a sweet gesture really. But now, within twenty minutes of being at his shop, Astrid had already bought an extremely rare three-carat blue diamond set on a diamond eternity band that had just arrived from Antwerp, art deco cuff links that had once belonged to Clark Gable, a signed vintage Cartier platinum-and-diamond link bracelet, and she was seriously considering a fantastical pair of VBH earrings. It was a piece he had brought in to show her for the sheer folly of it, and he would never have imagined her to be interested.

"The pear-shaped stones are kunzites weighing forty-nine carats, and these remarkable sparkling disks are twenty-three-carat ice diamonds. A highly original treatment. Are you thinking of wearing something new to the Khoo wedding next weekend?" he asked, trying to make conversation with his unusually focused shopper.

"Um . . . maybe," Astrid replied, staring into the mirror and scrutinizing the multicolored gemstones dangling off the enormous earrings, the bottoms of which were brushing against her shoulders. The piece reminded her of a Native American dream catcher.

"It's such a dramatic look, isn't it? Very Millicent Rogers, I think. What kind of dress are you planning to wear?"

"I haven't really decided yet," she said, almost mumbling to herself. She wasn't really looking at the earrings. In her mind, all she could picture was a piece of jewelry from her husband hanging off some other woman's wrist. *First came the text message. Then the receipt from Petrus. Now there was an expensive charm bracelet. Three's a charm.*

"Well, I think you'd want to go with something dead simple if you wear these earrings," Stephen added. He was getting a bit concerned. The girl was not being herself today. Usually she would breeze in and they would spend the first hour chatting and munching on the delicious homemade pineapple tarts she always brought before he took out anything to show her. After another hour or so of looking at pieces, she might hand one thing over to him and say, "Okay, I'm going to think about this one," before blowing a kiss goodbye. She was not the sort of client who spent a million dollars in ten minutes.

And yet Stephen always cherished her visits. He loved her sweet nature, her impeccable manners, and her complete lack of pretension. It was so refreshing, not like the sort of ladies he usually had to deal with, the egos that required constant stroking. He enjoyed reminiscing with Astrid about their crazy younger days in Paris, and he admired the originality of her taste. She cared about the quality of the stones, of course, but she couldn't have cared less about the size and was never interested in the ostentatious pieces. Why would she need to be, when her mother already had one of the grandest jewelry collections in Singapore, while her grandmother Shang Su Yi possessed a trove of jewels so legendary he had only ever heard them mentioned in hushed whispers. *"Ming dynasty jade like you've never seen before, jewels from the czars that Shang Loong Ma cunningly bought from the grand duchesses fleeing into Shanghai during the Bolshevik Revolution. Wait till the old lady dies—your friend Astrid is the favorite granddaughter, and she's going to inherit some of the most unparalleled pieces in the world,"* Stephen had been told by the acclaimed art historian Huang Peng Fan, one of the few people who had ever witnessed the splendor of the Shang collection.

"You know what? I must have these earrings too," Astrid declared, standing up and smoothing out her short pleated skirt.

"Are you leaving already? Don't you want a Diet Coke?" Stephen asked in surprise.

"No, thank you, not today. I think I need to hurry off. So many errands. Do you mind if I take the cuff links now? Promise I'll have the funds transferred to your account by the end of day."

"My dear, don't be silly, you can have everything now. Let me just get you some nice boxes." Stephen left the room, thinking that the last time Astrid had been impulsive like this was after her breakup with Charlie Wu. *Hmm . . . was there trouble in paradise?*

Astrid walked back to her car in the parking garage of the mall. She unlocked the door, got in, and placed the black-and-cream-colored parchment shopping bag subtly embossed with STEPHEN CHIA JEWELS on the passenger seat beside her. She sat in the airless vehicle, which was getting more stifling by the second. She could feel her heart pounding so quickly. She had just bought a three hundred and fifty thousand dollar diamond ring she didn't much care for, a twenty-eight thousand dollar bracelet she quite liked, and a seven hundred and eighty-four thousand dollar pair of earrings that made her look like Pocahontas. For the first time in weeks, she felt bloody fantastic.

Then she remembered the cuff links. She rummaged through the bag, searching for the box that contained the art deco cuff links she had purchased for Michael. They were in a blue velvet vintage box, and she stared at the pair of little silver-and-cobalt cuff links fastened against a satin lining that had long since become mottled with pale yellow spots.

These had once brushed against Clark Gable's wrists, Astrid thought. *The gorgeous, romantic Clark Gable. Hadn't he been married several times? Surely he must have romanced many women in his time. Surely he must have cheated on his wives, even Carole Lombard. How could anyone ever want to cheat on a woman as beautiful as Carole Lombard? But sooner or later, it was bound to happen. Every man cheats. This is Asia. Every guy has mistresses, girlfriends, flings on the side. It's a normal thing. A status thing. Get used to it. Great-grandpa had dozens of concubines. Uncle Freddie had that whole other family in Taiwan. And how many mistresses has cousin Eddie had by now? I've lost count. It was all meaningless. Guys just need a cheap thrill, a quick shag. They need to go on the hunt. It's a primal thing. They need to spread their seed. They need to put their pricks inside things. MISS U NSIDE ME. No no no. It was nothing serious. Probably some girl he met on his work trip. A fancy dinner. A one-night stand. And he bought her off with a bracelet. A silly charm bracelet. So cliché. At least he was discreet. At least he went and screwed the girl in Hong Kong, not Singapore. Many wives have to put up with so much more. Think of some of my friends. Think of what Fiona Tung has to go through with Eddie. The humiliation. I am lucky. I am so lucky. Don't be so bourgeois. It's just a fling. Don't make this a big deal. Remember, grace under pressure. Grace under pres-*

sure. *Grace Kelly slept with Clark Gable while they were filming* Mogambo. *Michael is as handsome as Clark Gable. And now he will have Gable's cuff links. And he will love them. They weren't too expensive. He won't get mad. He will love me. He still loves me. He hasn't been that distant. He's just stressed out. All that work pressure. We'll be married five years this October. Oh my God. Not even five years and he is already cheating. He isn't attracted to me anymore. I'm getting too old for him. He's tired of me. Poor Cassian. What's going to happen to Cassian? My life is over. It's all over. This isn't happening. I can't believe this is happening.* To me.

16

The Gohs

·

SINGAPORE

Rachel peered at the clock and figured that she'd only slept about five hours, but it was dawn and she was too excited to go back to sleep. Nick was snoring softly beside her. She looked around at the room, wondering how much this hotel must be costing Nick per night. It was an elegant suite decorated in understated pale wood, the only burst of color coming from the fuchsia orchids on the console table against the mirrored wall. Rachel got out of bed, put on a plush pair of terrycloth slippers, and padded quietly into the bathroom to splash some water on her face. Then she walked over to the window and peeked through the curtains.

Outside was a perfectly manicured garden with a large, inviting swimming pool lined with deck chairs. A man in a white-and-teal uniform was walking around the pool with a long pole and net, meditatively fishing out the stray leaves that had settled on the surface of the water during the night. The garden was set within a quadrangle of poolside rooms, and just beyond the serenity of the low-rise Victorian structure rose a cluster of high-rise buildings, reminding her that they were in the heart of Singapore's fashionable Orchard Road district. Rachel could already feel the early-morning heat permeating through the double-pane windows. She closed the curtains and went into the sitting room to rummage for her laptop. After logging on, she began to draft an e-mail to her friend Peik Lin. Seconds later, an instant message popped up on her screen:

> GohPL: You're awake! Are you really here?
>
> me: Sure am!
>
> GohPL: Yippeeee!!!!
>
> me: It's not even 7 and already SO HOT!
>
> GohPL: This is nothing! Are you staying @Nick's parents?
>
> me: No. We're @Kingsford Hotel.
>
> GohPL: Nice. Very central. But why are you at a hotel?
>
> me: Nick's parents are out of town, and he wanted to be at a hotel during wedding week.
>
> GohPL: . . .
>
> me: But secretly, I think he didn't want to show up at parents' house with me on the very first night. LOL!
>
> GohPL: Smart guy. So can I see you today?
>
> me: Today's great. Nick's busy helping the groom.
>
> GohPL: Is he the wedding planner? LOL! Meet up at noon @ your lobby?
>
> me: Perfect. Can't wait to see you!!!
>
> GohPL: XOXO

At noon sharp, Goh Peik Lin came walking up the wide staircase of the Kingsford Hotel, and heads turned as she entered the grand lobby. With her broad nose, round face, and slightly squinty eyes, she was not a natural-born raving beauty, but she was one of those girls who really knew how to make the most out of what she had. And what she had was a voluptuous body and the confidence to pull off bold fashion choices. Today she was wearing a very short white shift dress that hinted at her curves and a pair of strappy gold gladiator sandals. Her long black hair was pulled into a tight, high ponytail and a pair of gold-rimmed sunglasses were clamped on her forehead like a headband. On her earlobes were three-carat diamond solitaire studs, and on her wrist a chunky gold-and-diamond watch. She finished off the look with a gold mesh tote bag, flung casually on her shoulder. She looked like she was ready for the beach club in Saint-Tropez.

"Peik Lin!" Rachel cried, running toward her with her arms outstretched. Peik Lin squealed loudly upon seeing her, and the friends hugged tightly. "Look at you! You look terrific!" Rachel exclaimed, before turning to introduce Nick.

"Great to meet you," Peik Lin said in a voice that was surprisingly loud for her tiny frame. She gave Nick the once-over. "So, it took a local boy to finally get her out here."

"Glad to be of service," Nick said.

"I know you're playing wedding planner today, but when do I get to do my CIA debriefing on you? You better promise I'll see you soon," Peik Lin said.

"I promise." Nick laughed and kissed Rachel goodbye. As soon as he was out of earshot, Peik Lin turned to Rachel and raised her eyebrows. "Well *he* was easy on the eyes. No wonder he managed to get you to stop working and take a holiday for once in your life."

Rachel just giggled.

"Really, you have no right to poach one of our endangered species! So tall, so fit, and *that accent*—I normally find Singapore boys with posh English accents to be incredibly pretentious, but on him it just works."

As they walked down the long flight of red-carpeted stairs, Rachel asked, "Where are we going for lunch?"

"My parents have invited you to our house. They are so excited to see you, and I think you'll enjoy some traditional home cooking."

"That sounds great! But if I'm going to be seeing your parents, should I change?" Rachel asked. She was wearing a white cotton blouse with a pair of khaki slacks.

"Oh, you're fine. My parents are so casual, and they know you are traveling."

Waiting for them at the entrance was a large metallic-gold BMW with tinted windows. The driver quickly got out and opened the door for them. As the car left the hotel grounds and turned onto a busy street, Peik Lin began to point out the sights. "This is the famous Orchard Road—tourist central. It's our version of Fifth Avenue."

"It's Fifth Avenue on steroids . . . I've never seen so many boutiques and shopping malls, lined up as far as the eye can see!"

"Yes, but I prefer the shopping in New York or LA."

"You always did, Peik Lin," Rachel teased, remembering her

friend's frequent shopping jaunts when she was supposed to be in class.

Rachel always knew that Peik Lin came from money. They met during freshman orientation at Stanford, and Peik Lin was the girl who showed up to 8:00 a.m. classes looking as if she had just come from a shopping spree on Rodeo Drive. As a newly arrived international student from Singapore, one of the first things she did was buy herself a Porsche 911 convertible, claiming that since Porsches were such a bargain in America "it's an *absolute crime* not to have one." She soon found Palo Alto to be too provincial, and tried at every opportunity to lure Rachel into skipping class and driving up to San Francisco with her (the Neiman Marcus there was *so* much better than the one at Stanford Shopping Center). She was generous to a fault, and Rachel spent most of her college years being showered with gifts, enjoying glorious meals at culinary destinations like Chez Panisse and Post Ranch Inn, and going on weekend spa trips all along the California coast courtesy of Peik Lin's handy American Express black card.

Part of Peik Lin's charm was that she made no apologies for being loaded—she was completely unabashed when it came to spending money or talking about it. When *Fortune Asia* magazine did a cover profile on her family's property development and construction company, she proudly forwarded Rachel a link to the article. She threw lavish parties catered by the Plumed Horse at the town house she rented off campus. At Stanford, this did not exactly make her the most popular girl on campus. The East Coast set ignored her, and the low-key Bay Area types found her much too SoCal. Rachel always thought Peik Lin would have fit in better at Princeton or Brown, but she was glad that fate had sent her this way. Having grown up under far more modest circumstances, Rachel was intrigued by this free-spending girl, who, while being filthy rich, was never a snob about it.

"Has Nick filled you in on the real estate insanity here in Singapore?" Peik Lin asked as the car zipped around Newton Circus.

"He hasn't."

"The market is really hot at the moment—everyone's flipping properties left and right. It's practically become the national sport. See that building under construction on the left? I just bought two new flats there last week. I got them at an insider price of two point one each."

"Do you mean two-point-one *million*?" Rachel asked. It always took her a while to get used to the way Peik Lin spoke about money—the numbers just seemed so unreal.

"Yes, of course. I got them at the insider price, since our company did the construction. The flats are actually worth three million, and by the time the building is completed at the end of the year I can sell each of them for three-point-five, four mil easy."

"Now why would the prices shoot up so quickly? Isn't that a sign that the market is in a speculative bubble?" Rachel inquired.

"We're not in a bubble because the demand is real. All the HNWIs want to be in real estate these days."

"Um, what are *Henwees*?" Rachel asked.

"Oh, sorry, I forgot you're not up on the lingo. HNWI stands for 'High Net Worth Individuals.' We Singaporeans love to abbreviate everything."

"Yeah, I've noticed that."

"As you may know, there's been an explosion of HNWIs from Mainland China, and they are the ones really driving up the prices. They are flocking here in droves, buying up properties with golf bags stuffed full of hard cash."

"Really? I thought it was the other way around. Doesn't everyone want to move to China for work?"

"Some, yes, but the *super-rich* Chinese all want to be here. We're the most stable country in the region, and Mainlanders feel that their money is far safer here than in Shanghai, or even Switzerland."

At this point, the car turned off a main thoroughfare and drove into a neighborhood of tightly packed houses. "So there actually *are* houses in Singapore," Rachel said.

"Very few. Only about five percent of us are lucky enough to live in houses. This neighborhood is actually one of the first 'suburban-style' developments in Singapore, begun in the seventies, and my family helped to build it," Peik Lin explained. The car drove past a high white wall, over which peeked tall thick bushes of bougainvillea. A large gold plaque on the wall was engraved VILLA D'ORO, and as the car pulled up to the entrance, a pair of ornate golden gates parted to reveal an imposing façade that bore a not so accidental resemblance to the Petit Trianon at Versailles, except that the house itself took up most of the lot, and the front portico was dominated by a massive four-tiered marble fountain with a golden swan spouting water from its long upturned beak.

"Welcome to my home," Peik Lin said.

"My God, Peik Lin!" Rachel gasped in awe. "Is this where you grew up?"

"This was the property, but my parents tore down the old house and built this mansion about six years ago."

"No wonder you thought your town house in Palo Alto was so cramped."

"You know, when I was growing up, I thought that everyone lived like this. In the States, this house is probably worth only about three million. Can you guess how much it's worth here?"

"I won't even try to guess."

"Thirty million, easy. And that's just for the land—the house itself would be a teardown."

"Well, I can only imagine how valuable land must be on an island with, what, four million people?"

"More like five million now."

The cathedral-size front door was opened by an Indonesian girl in a frilly black-and-white French maid's uniform. Rachel found herself standing in a circular entrance foyer with white-and-rose marble floors radiating out in a sunburst pattern. To the right, an enormous staircase with gold balustrades wound its way to the upper floors. The entire curved wall going up the staircase was a frescoed replica of Fragonard's *The Swing*, except that this re-creation was blown up to fill a forty-foot rotunda.

"A team of artists from Prague camped out for three months to paint the frescos," Peik Lin said as she led Rachel up a short flight of steps into the formal living room. "This is my mother's re-creation of the Hall of Mirrors at Versailles. Get ready," she warned. Rachel ascended the steps and entered the room, her eyes widening a little. Aside from the red velvet brocade sofas, every single object in the cavernous formal living room appeared to be made of gold. The vaulted ceiling was composed of layers upon layers of gold leaf. The baroque console tables were gilt gold. The Venetian mirrors and candelabra lining the walls were gold. The elaborate tassels on the gold damask curtains were yet a deeper shade of gold. Even the tchotchkes scattered around every available surface were golden. Rachel was completely dumbstruck.

To make matters even more surreal, the middle of the room was dominated by an enormous oval pond-cum-aquarium sunken into the gold-flecked marble floor. The pond was brightly lit, and for a second Rachel thought she could make out baby sharks swimming in the bubbling water. Before she could process the scene fully, three golden-haired Pekingese ran into the room, their high-pitched yaps echoing loudly against the marble.

Peik Lin's mother, a short, plumpish woman in her early fifties with a shoulder-length bouffant perm entered the room. She wore a tight shocking-pink silk blouse that stretched against her ample cleavage, belted with a chain of interlinked gold medusa heads and a tight pair of black trousers. The only thing incongruous about the outfit was the pair of cushioned pink slippers on her feet. "Astor, Trump, Vanderbilt, naw-tee naw-tee boys, stop barking!" she admonished. "Rachel Chu! Wel-kum, wel-kum!" she cried in her heavy Chinese-accented English. Rachel found herself crushed into a fleshy hug, the heady scent of Eau d'Hadrien filling her nose. *"Aiyah! So long I haven't seen you. Bien kar ah nee swee, ah!"* she exclaimed in Hokkien, cupping Rachel's cheeks with both hands.

"She thinks you've become very pretty," Peik Lin translated, knowing that Rachel only spoke Mandarin.

"Thank you, Mrs. Goh. It's so nice to see you again," Rachel said, feeling rather overwhelmed. She never knew what to say when someone complimented her looks.

"Whaaat?" the woman said in mock horror. "Don't call me Mrs. Goh. Mrs. Goh is my hor-eee-ble mah-der-in-law! Call me Auntie Neena."

"Okay, Auntie Neena."

"Come, come to the keet-chen. *Makan* time." She clamped her bronze fingernails onto Rachel's wrist, leading her down a long marble-columned hallway toward the dining room. Rachel couldn't help but notice the enormous canary diamond flashing on her hand like a translucent egg yolk, and the pair of three-carat solitaires in her earlobes, identical to Peik Lin's. *Like mother, like daughter—maybe they got a two-for-one deal.*

The baronial dining hall was somewhat of a respite after the rococo hell of the living room, with its wood boiserie walls and windows overlooking the lawn where a large oval swimming pool was encircled by Grecian sculptures. Rachel quickly registered two versions of the *Venus de Milo*, one in white marble, another in gold, of course. There was a huge round dining table that seated eighteen comfortably covered with a heavy Battenberg lace tablecloth and high-backed Louis Quatorze chairs that were, thankfully, upholstered in a royal blue brocade. Assembled in the dining room was the entire Goh family.

"Rachel, you remember my father. This is my brother Peik Wing and his wife, Sheryl, and my younger brother, Peik Ting, whom we call P.T. And these are my nieces Alyssa and Camylla." Everyone went around shaking hands with Rachel, who couldn't help but notice that not one of them happened to be over five foot five. The brothers were both much darker complexioned than Peik Lin, but they all shared the same pixieish features. Both were dressed in almost identical outfits of pale blue button-down dress shirts and dark gray slacks, as if they had adhered exactly to a company manual on how to dress for casual Fridays. Sheryl, who was much paler, stuck out from the rest of the family. She wore a pink floral tank top and a short denim skirt, looking rather frazzled as she fussed over her two young daughters, who were both being fed Chicken McNuggets, the paper boxes placed on heavy gold-rimmed Limoges plates along with the packets of sweet-and-sour dipping sauce.

Peik Lin's father gestured for Rachel to take the seat next to him. He was a stocky, barrel-chested man in khaki trousers and a red Ralph Lauren shirt, the kind with the oversize Polo-player logo in dark navy emblazened across the front. His clothes, coupled with his short stature, made him appear incongruously boyish for a man in his late fifties. On his small wrist was a chunky Franck Muller watch, and he too was wearing a pair of cushioned slippers over his socks.

"Rachel Chu, long time no see! We are so very grateful for all the help you gave Peik Lin back in her uni days. Without you, she would have been gone case at Stanford," he said.

"Oh, that's not true! Peik Lin was a great help to *me*. I am so honored to be invited to your . . . incredible . . . house for lunch, Mr. Goh," Rachel said graciously.

"Uncle Wye Mun, please call me Uncle Wye Mun," he said.

Three maids entered, adding plates of steaming food to a table already laden with dishes. Rachel counted a total of thirteen different dishes laid out on the table.

"Ok, everybody *ziak, ziak*.* Don't stand on ce-ree-moh-ny Rachel Chu, this is simple lunch, simple food *lah*," Neena said. Rachel stared down at the heaving platters that looked anything but simple. "Our new cook is from Ipoh, so today you are getting some ty-pee-cal Malaysian dishes and Singapore dishes," Neena continued, dishing a heaping portion of beef Rendang curry onto Rachel's gold-rimmed plate.

"Mama, we are done eating. Can we go to the playroom now?" one of the little girls asked Sheryl.

"You are not done. I still see a few chicken nuggets left," their mother said.

Neena looked over and scolded, "Aiyooooooh, finish everything on your plate, girls! Don't you know there are children starving in America?"

Rachel grinned at the girls with their adorable twin ponytails and said, "I'm so happy to meet the whole family at last. Does nobody have to work today?"

"This is the advantage of working for your own company—we can take long lunch breaks," P.T. said.

"Hey, not too long," Wye Mun growled jovially.

"So all your children work for your company, Mr. Goh . . . I mean, Uncle Wye Mun?" Rachel asked.

"Yes, yes. This is a true family business. My father is still active as the chairman, and I'm the CEO. All my children have different management roles. Peik Wing is the VP in charge of project development, P.T. is VP in charge of construction, and Peik Lin is VP in charge of new business. Of course, we also have about six thousand full-time employees between all our offices."

"And where are your offices?" Rachel inquired.

"Our main hubs are Singapore, Hong Kong, Beijing, and Chongqing, but we're starting satellite offices in Hanoi, and very soon, Yangon."

"Sounds like you're really pushing into all the high-growth regions," Rachel commented, impressed.

"For sure, for sure," Wye Mun said. "Aiyah, you're so smart—

* Hokkien for "eat."

Peik Lin told me you are doing very well at NYU. Are you single? P.T., P.T., why aren't you paying more attention to Rachel? We can add one more family member to the payroll!" Everyone at the table laughed.

"Papa, you're so forgetful. I told you she was here with her boyfriend," Peik Lin chided.

"*Ang mor, ah?*" he asked, looking at Peik Lin.

"No, Singapore boy. I met him earlier today," Peik Lin said.

"Aiyaaaah, why isn't he here?" Neena admonished.

"Nick wanted to meet you, but he had to help his friend with some last-minute errands. We're actually here for his friend's wedding. He's going to be the best man," Rachel explained.

"Who's getting married?" Wye Mun asked.

"His name's Colin Khoo," Rachel replied.

Everyone abruptly stopped eating and stared at her. "Colin Khoo . . . and Araminta Lee?" Sheryl asked, trying to clarify.

"Yes," Rachel said in surprise. "Do you know them?"

Neena slammed her chopsticks down on the table and stared at Rachel. "Whaaaaaat? You're going to COLIN KHOO'S wedding?" she screeched, her mouth full of food.

"Yes, yes . . . are you going too?"

"Rachel! You didn't tell me you were coming for *Colin Khoo's wedding*," Peik Lin said in a hushed tone.

"Um, you didn't ask," Rachel said uncomfortably. "I don't understand . . . is there a problem?" She suddenly feared that the Gohs might be mortal enemies of the Khoos.

"Nooooo!" Peik Lin cried, suddenly getting very excited. "Don't you know? It's the wedding of the year! It's been covered on every channel, in every magazine, and in about a million blogs!"

"Why? Are they famous?" Rachel asked, completely baffled.

"*AH-LA-MAAAK!* Colin Khoo is Khoo Teck Fong's grandson! He comes from one of the reeee-chest families in the world! And Araminta Lee—she's the supa-model daughter of Peter Lee, one of China's reeee-chest men, and Annabel Lee, the luxury hotel queen. This is like *royal weddeeeng*!" Neena gushed.

"I had no idea," Rachel said in astonishment. "I just met them last night."

"You met them? You met Araminta Lee? Is she as beautiful

in person? What was she wearing?" Sheryl asked, seemingly star-struck.

"She was very pretty, yes. But so simple—she was literally wearing pajamas when I met her. She looked like a schoolgirl. Is she Eurasian?"

"No. But her mum is from Xinjiang, so she has Uighur blood, so they say," Neena said.

"Araminta is our most celebrated fashion icon! She has modeled for all the magazines, and she was one of Alexander McQueen's favorite models," Sheryl continued breathlessly.

"She's a total babe," P.T. chimed in.

"When did you meet her?" Peik Lin asked.

"She was with Colin. They picked us up at the airport."

"*They picked you up at the airport!*" P.T. exclaimed in disbelief, laughing hysterically. "Was there an army of bodyguards?"

"Not at all. They came in an SUV. Actually, there were *two* SUVs. One took the luggage straight to the hotel. No wonder," Rachel recalled.

"Rachel, Colin Khoo's family owns the Kingsford Hotel! *That's* why you're staying there," Peik Lin said, jabbing her arm excitedly.

Rachel didn't quite know what to say. She found herself amused and a little embarrassed by all the excitement.

"Your boyfriend is Colin Khoo's best man? What's his name?" Peik Lin's father demanded.

"Nicholas Young," Rachel replied.

"Nicholas Young . . . how old is he?"

"Thirty-two."

"That's one year above Peik Wing," Neena said. She looked up at the ceiling, as if racking through her mental Rolodex to see if she could recall a Nicholas Young.

"Peik Wing—ever heard of Nicholas Young?" Wye Mun asked his eldest son.

"Nope. Do you know which school he went to?" Peik Wing asked Rachel.

"Balliol College, Oxford," she replied, hesitantly. She wasn't sure why they were suddenly so interested in every minute detail.

"No, no—I mean which primary school," Peik Wing said.

"Elementary school," Peik Lin clarified.

"Oh, I have no idea."

"Nicholas Young . . . sounds like an ACS* boy," P.T. chimed in. "All those ACS boys have Christian names."

"Colin Khoo went to ACS. Daddy, I already tried to check Nick out when Rachel first started dating him, but no one I know has ever heard of him," Peik Lin added.

"Nick and Colin went to elementary school together. They have been best friends since childhood," Rachel said.

"What is his father's name?" Wye Mun asked.

"I don't know."

"Well, if you find out the parents' names, we can tell you whether he comes from a good family or not," Wye Mun said.

"*Alamaaaaak*, of course he's from good family, if he's best friends with Colin Khoo," Neena said. "Young . . . Young . . . Sheryl, isn't there a gyney named Richard Young? The one who practices with Dr. Toh?"

"No, no, Nick's father is an engineer. I think he works in Australia part of the year," Rachel offered.

"Well, see if you can find out more about his background, and we can help you," Wye Mun finally said.

"Oh, you really don't have to do that. It's not important to me what sort of family he comes from," Rachel said.

"Nonsense, *lah*! Of course it's important!" Wye Mun was adamant. "If he's Singaporean, I have a responsibility to make sure he's good enough for you!"

---

* Among Singapore's upper crust, only two boys' schools matter: Anglo-Chinese School (ACS) and Raffles Institution (RI). Both are consistently ranked among the top schools in the world and have enjoyed a long, heated rivalry. RI, established in 1823, is known to attract the brainy crowd, while ACS, established in 1886, is popular with the more fashionable set and somewhat perceived to be a breeding ground for snobs. Much of this has to do with the 1980 article in the *Sunday Nation* entitled "The Little Horrors of ACS," which exposed the rampant snobbery among its pampered students. This led to a shamed principal announcing to stunned students (including this author) the very next morning during assembly that, henceforth, students were no longer allowed to be dropped off at the front entrance by their chauffeurs. (They had to walk up the short driveway all by themselves, unless it was raining.) Expensive watches, eyeglasses, fountain pens, briefcases, satchels, pencil boxes, stationery, combs, electronic gadgets, comic books, and any other luxury items would also be banned from school property. (But within a few months, Lincoln Lee started wearing his Fila socks again and no one seemed to notice.)

17

Nicholas and Colin

•

SINGAPORE

Perhaps out of nostalgia, Nick and Colin liked to meet up at the coffee shop of their old alma mater on Barker Road. Located in the sports complex between the main pool and the basketball courts, the Anglo-Chinese School coffee shop served a motley selection of Thai and Singaporean dishes as well as such oddities as British beef pies, which Nick loved. Back when the two of them were on the swim team, they would always grab a bite after practice at the "tuck shop," as they called it. The original cooks had long since retired, the legendary *mee siam* was no longer on the menu, and the coffee shop itself wasn't even in the original space—having long since been torn down during the redevelopment of the sports center. But for Nick and Colin, it was still the place to meet whenever they were both in town.

Colin had already ordered his lunch by the time Nick arrived. "Sorry I'm late," Nick said, patting him on the back as he got to the table. "I had to swing by my grandmother's."

Colin did not look up from his plate of salted fried chicken, so Nick continued. "So what else do we have to do today? The tuxes are in from London, and I'm just waiting to hear back from some of the last-minute people about the rehearsal next week."

Colin clamped his eyes shut and grimaced. "Can we please talk about something besides this fucking wedding?"

"Okay then. What do you want to talk about?" Nick asked calmly, realizing that Colin had hit one of his down days. The cheerful, life-of-the-party Colin of the night before had vanished.

Colin didn't respond.

"Did you get any sleep last night?" Nick asked.

Colin remained silent. There was no one else in the place, and the only sounds were the occasional muffled shouts of players on the basketball court next door and the clatter of dishes being washed every time the lone waiter walked in and out of the kitchen. Nick leaned back into his seat, patiently waiting for Colin to make the next move.

To the society pages, Colin was known as Asia's billionaire bachelor jock. Famed not only for being the scion of one of Asia's great fortunes but also as one of Singapore's top-ranked swimmers back in his college days. He was celebrated for his exotic good looks and debonair style, his string of romances with local starlets, and his ever-expanding collection of contemporary art.

With Nick, however, Colin had the freedom to be his true self. Nick, who had known him since childhood, was probably the only person on the planet who didn't give a damn about his money, and more important, the only one who was there during what they both referred to as "the war years." For beneath the wide grin and the charismatic personality, Colin struggled with a severe anxiety disorder and crippling depression, and Nick was one of the few people allowed to witness this side of him. It was as if Colin bottled up all of his pain and anguish for months at a time, unleashing it on Nick whenever he was in town. To anyone else, this would have been an intolerable situation, but Nick was so used to this by now, he almost didn't recall a time when Colin wasn't swinging between the highest of highs and the lowest of lows. This was just a prerequisite of being Colin's best friend.

The waiter, a sweaty teenager in a soccer T-shirt who didn't look old enough to pass child labor laws, approached the table to take Nick's order.

"I'll have the beef curry pie, please. And a Coke, extra ice."

Colin finally broke his silence. "As always, beef curry pie and Coke, extra ice. You never change, do you?"

"What can I tell you? I know what I like," Nick said simply.

"Even though you always like the exact same thing, you can always change your mind whenever you wish. That's the difference between us—you still have choices."

"Come on, that's not true. You *can* choose."

"Nicky, I haven't been in the position to make a single choice since I was born, and you know that," Colin said matter-of-factly. "It's a good thing I actually want to marry Araminta. I just don't know how I'll make it through the Broadway production, that's all. I have this perverse fantasy of kidnapping her, jumping on a plane, and marrying her at some little twenty-four-hour chapel in the middle of nowhere Nevada."

"So why not do it? The wedding isn't until next week, but if you're already this miserable, why not call it off?"

"You know this merger has been choreographed down to the most minute detail, and this is how it's going to be. It's good for business, and anything that's good for business is good for the family," Colin said bitterly. "Anyway, I don't want to dwell on the inevitable anymore. Let's talk about last night. How was I? Sufficiently cheery for Rachel, I hope?"

"Rachel loved you. It was a nice surprise to be welcomed like that, but you know, you don't ever have to put on a show for her."

"I don't? What have you told her about me?" Colin asked warily.

"I haven't told her anything, besides the fact that you once had an unhealthy obsession with Kristin Scott Thomas."

Colin laughed. Nick was relieved—it was a sign that the clouds were dissipating.

"You didn't tell her about how I tried to stalk Kristin in Paris, did you?" Colin continued.

"Er, no. I wasn't going to give her any more opportunities to back out of this trip by giving her full insight into my weird friends."

"Speaking of weird, could you believe how nice Araminta was being to Rachel?"

"I think you're underestimating Araminta's ability to be nice."

"Well, you know how she normally is with new people. But I think she wants to keep you on her side. And she could see that I liked Rachel instantly."

"I'm so glad." Nick smiled.

"To be quite honest, I thought I might be slightly jealous of her at first, but I think she's great. She's not clingy, and she's so refreshingly . . . American. You do realize that everyone is talking about you and Rachel, right? Everyone is already taking bets on the wedding date."

Nick sighed. "Colin, I'm not thinking about my wedding right now. I'm thinking about *yours*. I'm just trying to live in the here and now."

"So speaking of the here and now, when are you going to introduce Rachel to your grandmother?"

"I was thinking tonight. That's why I went to see my grandmother—to get Rachel invited to dinner."

"I'll say a little prayer," Colin quipped as he finished his last chicken wing. He knew how momentous it was for Nick's famously reclusive grandmother to invite a virtual stranger into her house. "You do realize that everything's going to change the minute you take Rachel into that house, don't you?"

"Funny, Astrid said the same thing. You know, Rachel is not expecting anything—she's never put any pressure on me when it comes to marriage. In fact, we've never even discussed it."

"No, no, that's not what I mean." Colin tried to clarify. "It's just that the two of you have been living this idyllic fantasy, this simple 'young lovers in Greenwich Village' life. Up until now, you've been the guy struggling to get tenure. Don't you think she's in for quite a shock tonight?"

"What do you mean? I *am* struggling to get tenure, and I don't see how Rachel meeting my grandmother will change things."

"Come on, Nicky, don't be naïve. The minute she walks into that house, it *will* affect your relationship. I'm not saying that things are going to be bad, necessarily, but an innocence will be lost. You won't be able to go back to the way it was before, that's for sure. No matter what, you'll forever be transformed in her eyes, just like all my former girlfriends the minute they found out I was *that* Colin Khoo. I'm only trying to prepare you a bit."

Nick pondered what Colin had just said for a while. "I think you're wrong, Colin. First of all, our situations are so completely different. My family isn't like yours. You've been groomed since day one to be the future CEO of the Khoo Organization, but nothing of the sort exists in my family. We don't even *have* a family business. And yes, I might have well-to-do cousins and all that, but you know my situation isn't like theirs. I'm not like Astrid, who inherited all her great-aunt's money, or my Shang cousins."

Colin shook his head. "Nicky, Nicky, this is why I love you. You are the only person in all of Asia who doesn't realize how rich you are, or should I say, how rich you will be one day. Here, hand over your wallet."

Nick was puzzled, but he took his well-worn brown leather wallet out of his back pocket and handed it to Colin. "You'll see I have about fifty dollars inside."

Colin fished out Nick's New York State driver's license and held it in front of his face. "Tell me what this says."

Nick rolled his eyes but played along. "Nicholas A. Young."

"Yes, that's it. YOUNG. Now, out of your entire family, are there any other male cousins with this surname?"

"No."

"My point exactly. Besides your father, you are the only *Young* left in the line. You *are* the heir apparent, whether you choose to believe it or not. What's more, your grandmother adores you. And everyone knows your grandmother controls *both* the Shang and Young fortunes."

Nick shook his head, partly in disbelief at Colin's presumption, but more because speaking of such things—even with his best friend—made him rather uneasy. It was something that had been conditioned into him since an early age. (He could still remember the time when he was seven, coming home from school and asking his grandmother at teatime, "My classmate Bernard Tai says that his father is very very rich, and that we're very very rich too. Is that true?" His aunt Victoria, immersed in her *London Times*, suddenly put her paper down and launched into him, "Nicky, boys with proper manners do not *ever* ask questions like that. You do not ever ask people if they are rich or discuss matters concerning money. We are not rich—we are simply well-off. Now, apologize to your Ah Ma.")

Colin continued. "Why do you think my grandfather, who treats everyone so dismissively, treats you like a visiting prince every time he sees you?"

"And here I thought your grandfather just liked me."

"My grandfather is an *asshole*. He only cares about power and prestige and expanding the fucking Khoo empire. That's why he encouraged this whole thing with Araminta to begin with, and that's why he's always dictated whom I could be friends with. Even when we were kids, I remember him saying, 'You be nice to that Nicholas. Remember, we are nothing compared to the Youngs.'"

"Your grandfather is going senile, I think. Anyway, all this inheritance nonsense is really beside the point, because, as you'll soon see, Rachel is not the sort of girl who cares about any of that. She may be an economist, but she's the least materialistic person I know."

"Well, then, I wish you the best. But you do realize that even in the here and now, dark forces are at work plotting against you?"

"What is this, *Harry Potter*?" Nick sniggered. "That's what you just sounded like. Yes, I am aware that even now dark forces are trying to sabotage me, as you put it. Astrid's already warned me, my mother inexplicably decided to go to China right when I arrived, and I had to enlist my great-aunt to persuade my grandmother into inviting Rachel tonight. But you know what? I don't really give a damn."

"I don't think it's your mother you have to worry about."

"Then whom should I be worried about, exactly? Tell me who is bored enough to waste their time trying to ruin my relationship, and why?"

"Practically every girl of marriageable age on the island *and* their mothers."

Nick laughed. "Wait a minute—why me? Aren't you Asia's most eligible bachelor?"

"I'm a lame duck. Everyone knows that nothing in the world is going to stop Araminta from walking down that aisle next week. I hereby pass the crown on to you." Colin chuckled, folding his paper napkin into a pyramid and placing it on Nick's head. "Now you are a marked man."

18

Rachel and Peik Lin

SINGAPORE

After they had finished lunch, Neena insisted on giving Rachel a complete tour of Villa d'Oro's other wing (which, not surprisingly, was done up in the baroque-on-crack style Rachel had gotten a whiff of earlier). Neena also proudly showed off her rose garden and the Canova sculpture they had recently installed there (thankfully spared the gold treatment). With the tour finally over, Peik Lin suggested that they head back to the hotel to relax over afternoon tea, since Rachel was still feeling a bit jet-lagged. "Your hotel serves a terrific high tea, with fabulous *nyonya kueh*."*

"But I'm still full from lunch," Rachel protested.

"Well, you'll just have to get used to the Singaporean eating schedule. We eat five times a day here—breakfast, lunch, tea, dinner, and late-night supper."

"God, I'm going to put on so much weight while I'm here."

"No you won't. That's the one good thing about this heat—you'll sweat it all out!"

"You might be right about that—I don't know how you guys deal

---

* Peranakan dessert cakes. These addictive, delicately flavored, and colorful *kuehs*, or cakes, usually made of rice flour and the distinctive pandan-leaf flavoring, are a beloved teatime staple in Singapore.

with this weather," Rachel said. "I'll have tea, but let's find the coldest spot inside."

They made themselves comfortable in the terrace café, which had a view of the pool but was blessedly air-conditioned. Smartly uniformed waiters walked by with trays bearing a selection of tea cakes, pastries, and *nyonya* delicacies.

"Mmmm . . . you need to try this *kueh*," Peik Lin said, putting a slice of glutinous rice-and-coconut custard on Rachel's plate. Rachel took a bite, finding the juxtaposition of subtly sweet custard with almost-savory sticky rice to be surprisingly addictive. She looked around at the bucolic garden, most of the deck chairs now occupied by guests asleep in the late-afternoon sun.

"I still can't believe Colin's family owns this hotel," Rachel said, taking another bite of the *kueh*.

"Believe it, Rachel. And they own a lot more besides—hotels all over the world, commercial properties, banks, mining companies. The list goes on and on."

"Colin seems *so* modest. I mean, we went to one of those outdoor food markets for dinner."

"There's nothing unusual about that. Everyone here loves the hawker centers. Remember, this is Asia, and first impressions can be deceiving. You know how most Asians hoard their money. The rich are even more extreme. Many of the wealthiest people here make an effort not to stand out, and most of the time, you would never know you were standing next to a billionaire."

"Don't take this the wrong way, but *your* family seems to enjoy their wealth."

"My grandfather came over from China and started out as a bricklayer. He is a self-made man, and he's instilled the same 'work hard, play hard' ethic in all of us. But come on, we're not in the same league as the Khoos. The Khoos are *crazy rich*. They are always at the top of the *Forbes* 'Asia Rich List.' And you know that's just the tip of the iceberg with these families. *Forbes* only reports on the assets they can verify, and these rich Asians are so secretive about their holdings. The richest families are always richer by billions than what *Forbes* estimates."

A piercing electronic melody began to play. "What's that sound?" Rachel asked, before realizing it was her new Singapore cell phone.

It was Nick calling. "Hey you," she answered with a smile.

"Hey yourself! Having a nice afternoon catching up with your friend?"

"Absolutely. We're back at the hotel enjoying high tea. What are you up to?"

"I'm standing here staring at Colin in his underwear."

"WHAT did you say?"

Nick laughed. "I'm over at Colin's. The tuxes just came in, and we're having the tailor make some final adjustments."

"Oh. How does yours look? Is it powder blue with ruffles?"

"You wish. No, it's all rhinestones with gold piping. Hey, I completely forgot to tell you, but my grandmother always has the family over for dinner on Friday night. I know you're still jet-lagged, but do you think you might be up for going?"

"Oh wow. Dinner at your grandmother's?"

Peik Lin cocked her head at Rachel.

"Who all is going to be there?" Rachel asked.

"Probably just a handful of relatives. Most of my family are still out of the country. But Astrid will be there."

Rachel was a little unsure. "Um, what do you think? Would you like me to come, or would you rather spend some time alone with your family first?"

"Of course not. I'd love you to come, but only if you're up for it—I know it's pretty short notice."

Rachel looked at Peik Lin, deliberating. Was she ready to meet the family?

"Say yes!" Peik Lin prompted eagerly.

"I'd love to go. What time do we have to be there?"

"Seven thirty-ish is fine. Here's the thing . . . I'm at Colin's place in Sentosa Cove. The Friday-evening traffic is going to be horrible going back into town, so it's much easier for me to meet you there. Would you mind taking a taxi to my grandmother's? I'll give you the address, and I'll be at the door waiting for you when you arrive."

"Take a taxi?"

Peik Lin shook her head, mouthing, "I'll take you."

"Okay, just tell me where it is," Rachel said.

"Tyersall Park."

"Tyersall Park." She wrote it down on a piece of paper from her purse. "That's it? What's the number?"

"There's no number. Look out for two white pillars, and just tell the driver it's off Tyersall Avenue, right behind the Botanic Gardens. Call me if you have any problems finding it."

"Okay, see you in about an hour."

As soon as Rachel hung up, Peik Lin snatched the piece of paper from her. "Let's see where Grandma lives." She scrutinized the address. "No number, so Tyersall Park must be an apartment complex. Hmm . . . I thought I knew every condo on the island. I've never even heard of Tyersall Avenue. I think it's probably somewhere on the West Coast."

"Nick said it was right by the Botanic Gardens."

"Really? That's very close. Anyway, my driver can figure it out. We have much more important things to deal with—like what you're going to wear."

"Oh God, I have no idea!"

"Well, you want to be casual, but you also want to make a good impression, don't you? Will Colin and Araminta be there tonight?"

"I don't think so. He said it was just his family."

"God, I wish I knew more about Nick's family."

"You Singaporeans crack me up. All this nosing around!"

"You have to understand. This is one big village—everyone is always in everybody's business. Plus, you have to admit it's become much more intriguing now that we know that he's Colin's best friend. Anyway, you need to look fabulous tonight!"

"Hmmm . . . I don't know. I don't want to make the wrong impression, like I'm high maintenance or something."

"Rachel, trust me, *no one* would ever accuse you of being high maintenance. I recognize the blouse you're wearing—you bought that in college, didn't you? Show me what else you brought. It's your first time meeting the family, so we need to be *really* strategic about this."

"Peik Lin, you're beginning to stress me out! I'm sure his family will be just fine, and they won't care what I'm wearing as long as I don't show up naked."

After multiple costume changes supervised by Peik Lin, Rachel decided to wear what she had been planning to wear in the first place—a long, sleeveless chocolate-colored linen dress with buttons down the front, a simple cinched belt made out of the same fabric, and a pair of low-heeled sandals. She put on a fun silver bracelet that wrapped around her wrist several times and wore the only expensive piece of jewelry she owned—Mikimoto pearl studs that her mother had given her when she got her doctorate.

"You look a bit like Katharine Hepburn on safari," Peik Lin said. "Elegant, proper, but not trying too hard."

"Hair up or down?" Rachel asked.

"Just leave it down. It's a little sexier," Peik Lin replied. "Come on, let's go or you'll be late."

The girls soon found themselves winding along the leafy back roads behind the Botanic Gardens, searching for Tyersall Avenue. The driver said he had driven past the street before but now could not seem to find it. "It's strange that the street doesn't show up on the GPS," Peik Lin said. "This is a very confusing area because it's one of the few neighborhoods with these narrow lanes."

The neighborhood took Rachel completely by surprise, as it was the first time she had seen such large, old houses on sprawling lawns. "Most of these street names sound so British. Napier Road, Cluny Road, Gallop Road . . ." Rachel commented.

"Well, this is where all the colonial British officials lived—it isn't really a residential area. Most of these houses are government-owned and many are embassies, like that gray behemoth with the columns over there—that's the Russian embassy. You know, Nick's grandma must live in a government housing complex—that's why I've never heard of it."

The driver suddenly slowed down, and veered left at a fork in the road, heading down an even narrower lane. "Look, this is Tyersall Avenue, so the building must be off this road," Peik Lin said. Huge trees with ancient, serpentine trunks rose up on both sides of the road, layered with the dense undergrowth of ferns belonging to the primeval rain forest that once covered the island. The road began to dip and curve to the right, and they suddenly noticed two white hexagonal pillars framing a low iron gate that had been painted pale gray. Tucked into the side of the road, almost hidden by the wild foliage, was a rusty sign that read TYERSALL PARK.

"I have never been down this street in my life. It's so strange to have apartments here," was all Peik Lin could say. "What do we do now? Do you want to call Nick?"

Before Rachel could answer, an Indian guard with a fierce-looking beard, wearing a crisp olive-green uniform and a bulky turban, appeared at the gates. Peik Lin's driver slowly inched forward, lowering his window as the man approached. The guard peered into the car and said in perfect Queen's English, "Miss Rachel Chu?"

"Yes, that's me," Rachel answered, waving from the backseat.

"Welcome, Miss Chu," the guard said with a smile. "Keep following the road, and stay to your right," he instructed the driver before he proceeded to open the gates and wave them along.

"*Alamak*, do you know who that man was?" Peik Lin's Malay driver said, turning around with a slightly awed expression.

"Who?" Peik Lin asked.

"That was a Gurkha! They are the deadliest soldiers in the world. I used to see them all the time in Brunei. The Sultan of Brunei only uses Gurkhas as his private protection force. What is a Gurkha doing here?" The car continued on the road and wound up a slight hill, both sides of the driveway a dense wall of clipped hedges. As it turned up a gentle curve, they came upon another gate. This time it was a reinforced steel gate, with a modern guardhouse attached. Rachel could see two other Gurkha guards staring out the window as the imposing gate silently rolled to the side, revealing yet another long driveway, this one paved in gravel. As the car rolled along, its tires crunching against the loose gray pebbles, the thick greenery gave way to a handsome avenue of tall palms that bisected rolling parklands. There were perhaps thirty palm trees perfectly lined up along both sides of the driveway, and someone had carefully placed tall rectangular lanterns lit with candles under each palm, like glowing sentinels leading the way.

As the car headed up the driveway, Rachel looked out in wonder at the flickering lanterns and the vast manicured grounds around her. "What park is this?" she asked Peik Lin.

"I have no idea."

"Is this all one housing development? It looks like we're entering a Club Med resort."

"I'm not sure. I've never seen a place like this in all of Singapore. It doesn't even feel like we're in Singapore anymore," Peik Lin said in amazement. The whole landscape reminded her of the stately country estates she had visited in England, like Chatsworth or Blenheim Palace. As the car rounded one last curve, Rachel suddenly let out a gasp, grabbing Peik Lin's arm. In the distance, a great house had come into view, ablaze with lights. As they got closer, the enormity of the place truly became evident. It wasn't a house. It was more like a palace. The front driveway was lined with cars, almost all of which were large and European—Mercedes, Jaguars, Citroëns, Rolls-Royces, many with diplomatic medallions and flags. A cluster of chauffeurs loitered in a circle behind the cars, smoking. Waiting by the massive front doors in a white linen shirt and tan slacks, hair perfectly tousled and hands pensively shoved into his pockets, stood Nick.

"I feel like I'm dreaming. This can't be real," Peik Lin said.

"Oh Peik Lin, who are these people?" Rachel asked nervously.

For the first time in her life, Peik Lin was at a loss for words. She stared at Rachel with a sudden intensity, and then she said, almost in a whisper, "I have no idea who these people are. But I can tell you one thing—*these people are richer than God.*"

Part Two

I did not tell half of what I saw,
for no one would have believed me.

MARCO POLO, 1324

1

Astrid
·

SINGAPORE

Cassian was just being buttoned into his smart new Prussian-blue sailor suit when Astrid got a call from her husband.

"I have to work late and won't make it in time for dinner at Ah Ma's."

"Really? Michael, you've worked late every single night this week," Astrid said, trying to maintain a neutral tone.

"The whole team is staying late."

"On a Friday night?" She didn't mean to give away any indications of doubt, but the words came out before she could stop herself. Now that her eyes were wide open, the signs were all there—he had canceled on almost every family occasion over the past few months.

"Yes. I've told you before, this is how it is at a start-up," Michael added warily.

Astrid wanted to call his bluff. "Well, why don't you join us whenever you get off work? It's probably going to be a late night. Ah Ma's *tan hua* flowers are going to bloom tonight, and she's invited some people over."

"Even more reason for me not to be there. I'm going to be much too worn out."

"Come on, it's going to be a special occasion. You know it's awfully good luck to witness the flowers bloom, and it will be so much fun," Astrid said, struggling to keep the tone light.

"I was there the last time they bloomed three years ago, and I just don't think I can deal with a big crowd tonight."

"Oh, I don't think it's going to be that big a crowd."

"You always say that and then we get there and it turns out to be a sit-down dinner for fifty, and some bloody MP is there, or there's some other sideshow distraction," Michael complained.

"That's not true."

"Come on *lah*, you know it's true. Last time we had to sit through a whole piano recital by that Ling Ling guy."

"Michael, it's Lang Lang, and you're probably the only person in the world who doesn't appreciate a private concert by one of the world's top pianists."

"Well, it was damn *lay chay*,* especially on a Friday night when I'm exhausted from the long week."

Astrid decided that it wasn't worth pushing him any further. He obviously had a thousand ready excuses not to be at dinner. *What was he really up to? Was the texting slut from Hong Kong suddenly in town? Was he going to hook up with her?*

"Okay, I'll tell the cook to make you something when you get home. What do you feel like eating?" she offered cheerily.

"No, no, don't bother. I'm sure we'll be ordering food here."

A likely story. Astrid hung up the phone reluctantly. *Where was he going to order the food? From room service at some cheap hotel in Geylang? There was no way he could meet this girl at a decent hotel—someone was bound to recognize him.* She remembered a time not long ago when Michael would be so sweetly apologetic for missing any family occasion. He would say soothing things like, "Honey, I'm soooo sorry I can't make it. Are you sure you'll be okay going on your own?" But that gentler side of him had dissipated. When exactly did that happen? And why had it taken her so long to notice the signals?

Ever since that day at Stephen Chia Jewels, Astrid had experienced a catharsis of sorts. In some perverse way, she was relieved to have proof of her husband's unfaithfulness. It was the uncertainty of it all—the cloak-and-dagger suspicions—that had been killing her. Now she could, as a psychologist might say, "learn to accept and learn to adapt." She could concentrate on the bigger picture. Sooner or later the fling would be over and life would go on, as it did for the

* Hokkien for "tedious."

millions of wives who quietly endured their husbands' infidelities since time immemorial.

There would be no need for fights, no hysterical confrontations. That would be much too cliché, even though every silly thing her husband had done could have come straight out of one of those "Is My Husband Cheating on Me?" quizzes from some cheesy women's magazine: *Has your husband been going on more business trips lately?* Check. *Are you making love less frequently?* Check. *Has your husband incurred mysterious expenses with no explanation?* Double check. She could add a new line to the quiz: *Is your husband getting text messages late at night from some girl proclaiming to miss his fat cock?* CHECK. Astrid's head was beginning to spin again. She could feel her blood pressure rise. She needed to sit down for a minute and take a few deep breaths. Why had she missed yoga all week, when she so badly needed to release the tension that had been building up? Stop. Stop. Stop. She needed to put all this out of her mind and just be in the moment. Right now, in this moment, she needed to get ready for Ah Ma's party.

Astrid noticed her reflection in the glass coffee table and decided to change her outfit. She was wearing an old favorite—a gauzy black tunic dress by Ann Demeulemeester, but she felt like she needed to turn up the volume tonight. She was not going to let Michael's absence ruin her night. She was not going to spend one more second thinking about where he could possibly be going, what he might or might not be doing. She was determined that this would be a magical night of wild blooming flowers under the stars, and that only good things would happen. *Good things always happened at Ah Ma's.*

She went into the spare bedroom, which had basically become an extra closet for her overflow of clothes (and this didn't even include the rooms upon rooms of clothes she still kept at her parents' house). The space was filled with metal rolling racks on which garment bags of outfits had been meticulously organized by season and color, and Astrid had to move one of the racks into the hallway in order to fit comfortably into the room. This apartment was much too tiny for the family of three (four if you counted the nanny, Evangeline, who slept in Cassian's room), but she had made the best of it for the sake of her husband.

Most of Astrid's friends would have been utterly horrified to discover the conditions in which she lived. To the majority of Singaporeans, a spacious two-thousand-square-foot, three-bedroom condo with two and a half baths and a private balcony in District Nine would be a cherished luxury, but for Astrid, who had grown up in such palatial surroundings as her father's stately house on Nassim Road, the modernist weekend beach bungalow in Tanah Merah, the vast family plantation in Kuantan, and her grandmother's Tyersall Park estate, it was totally unfathomable.

As a wedding gift, her father had planned to commission an up-and-coming Brazilian architect to build the newlyweds a house in Bukit Timah on land that had already been deeded to Astrid, but Michael would have none of that. He was a proud man and insisted on living in a place that he could afford to purchase. "I am capable of providing for your daughter and our future family," he had informed his stunned future father-in-law, who instead of being impressed by the gesture, found it rather foolhardy. How was this fellow ever going to afford the kind of place his daughter was accustomed to on his salary? Michael's meager savings would barely even get them a down payment on a private flat, and Harry found it inconceivable that his daughter might live in government-subsidized housing. Why couldn't they at the very least just move into one of the houses or luxury apartments that she already owned? But Michael was adamant that he and his wife begin their life on neutral territory. In the end, a compromise was struck and Michael agreed to let both Astrid and her father match what he was able to put in as a down payment. The combined amount allowed them a thirty-year fixed mortgage on this condo in an eighties-era apartment complex off Clemenceau Avenue.

As Astrid sifted through the racks, it suddenly, rather comically, occurred to her that the money she had spent on the couture outfits in this room alone could have paid for a house three times the size of this one. She wondered what Michael might think if he knew actually how many properties she already owned. Astrid's parents bought their children houses in a way that other parents might buy theirs candy bars. Over the years, they had purchased so many houses for her that by the time she became Mrs. Michael Teo, she was already in possession of a staggering real estate portfolio. There was the bungalow off Dunearn Road, the house in Clementi and the semidetached on Chancery Lane, a row of historic Peranakan shop houses on Emerald Hill left to her by a great-aunt on the Leong side, and numerous other luxury condominiums scattered throughout the island.

And that was just in Singapore. There were land holdings in Malaysia; a flat in London that Charlie Wu had secretly bought for her; a house in Sydney's exclusive Point Piper and another in Diamond Head, Honolulu; and recently, her mother had mentioned picking up a penthouse in some new tower in Shanghai under her name. ("I saw the special computer mirror in the closet that remembers everything you wear and immediately *knew* this place was for you," Felicity had excitedly informed her.) Quite frankly, Astrid didn't even bother trying to remember all of it; there were too many properties to keep track of.

It was all quite meaningless anyway, since aside from the shop houses on Emerald Hill and the London flat, none of the properties were truly hers—yet. This was all part of her parents' wealth-succession strategy, and Astrid knew that as long as her parents were alive, she had no real control over the properties, though she benefited from the income derived from them. Twice a year, when the family sat down with their business managers at Leong Holdings, she would notice that her personal accounts always increased in value, sometimes to an absurd degree, no matter how many couture dresses she had splurged on the previous season.

So what should she wear? Maybe it was time to bring out one of her latest Paris treats. She was going to wear her new embroidered Alexis Mabille white peasant blouse with the pearl-gray Lanvin cigarette pants and her new VBH earrings. The thing about those earrings was that they looked so over the top, everyone would think they were costume jewelry. They actually dressed *down* the whole outfit. Yes, she deserved to look this good. And now maybe she should also change Cassian's outfit to complement hers.

"Evangeline, Evangeline," she called out. "I want to change Cassian's clothes. Let's put him in that dove-gray jumper from Marie-Chantal."

2

Rachel and Nick

·

TYERSALL PARK

As Peik Lin's car approached the porte cochere of Tyersall Park, Nick bounded down the front steps toward them. "I was worried you'd gotten lost," he said, opening the car door.

"We did get a bit lost, actually," Rachel replied, getting out of the car and staring up at the majestic façade before her. Her stomach felt like it had been twisted in a vise, and she smoothed out the creases on her dress nervously. "Am I really late?"

"No, it's okay. I'm sorry, were my directions confusing?" Nick asked, peering into the car and smiling at Peik Lin. "Peik Lin—thanks so much for giving Rachel a lift."

"Of course," Peik Lin murmured, still rather stunned by her surroundings. She longed to get out of the car and explore this colossal estate, but something told her to remain in her seat. She paused for a moment, thinking Nick might invite her in for a drink, but no invitation seemed to be forthcoming. Finally she said as nonchalantly as possible, "This is quite a place—is it your grandmother's?"

"Yes," Nick replied.

"Has she lived here a long time?" Peik Lin couldn't resist trying to find out more as she craned her neck, trying to get a better look.

"Since she was a young girl," Nick said.

Nick's answer surprised Peik Lin, as she assumed that the house would have belonged to his grandfather. Now what she really wanted to ask was, *Who on earth is your grandmother?* But she didn't want to risk seeming too nosy. "Well, you two have a great time," Peik Lin said, winking at Rachel and mouthing the words *Call me later!* Rachel gave her friend a quick smile.

"Good night, and get home safe," Nick said, patting the roof of the car.

As Peik Lin's car drove off, Nick turned to Rachel, looking a little sheepish. "I hope it's okay . . . but it's not just the family. My grandmother decided to have a small party, all arranged at the last minute, apparently, because her *tan hua* flowers are going to bloom tonight."

"She's throwing a party because her flowers are in bloom?" Rachel asked, not quite following.

"Well, these are very rare flowers that bloom extremely infrequently, sometimes once every decade, sometimes even longer than that. They only bloom at night, and the whole thing only lasts for a few hours. It's quite something to witness."

"Sounds cool, but now I'm feeling *really* underdressed for the occasion," Rachel said pensively, eyeing the fleet of limousines that lined the driveway.

"Not at all—you look absolutely perfect," Nick told her. He could sense her trepidation and tried to reassure her, placing his hand on the small of her back and guiding her toward the front doors. Rachel felt the warm, radiating energy from his muscled arm and instantly felt better. Her knight in shining armor was at her side, and everything would be just fine.

As they entered the house, the first thing that caught Rachel's eye was the dazzling mosaic tiles in the grand foyer. She stood transfixed for a few moments by the intricate black, blue, and coral pattern before realizing that they were not alone. A tall, spindly Indian man stood silently in the middle of the foyer next to a circular stone table clustered with pots of enormous white-and-purple phalaenopsis orchids. The man bowed ceremoniously to Rachel and presented her with a hammered silver bowl filled with water and pale pink rose petals. "For your refreshment, miss," he said.

"Do I drink this?" Rachel whispered to Nick.

"No, no, it's for washing your hands," Nick instructed. Rachel dipped her fingers into the cool scented water before wiping them on the soft terry cloth that was proffered, feeling awed (and a little silly) by the ritual.

"Everyone's upstairs in the living room," Nick said, leading her toward the carved stone staircase. Rachel saw something out of the corner of her eye and let out a quick gasp. By the side of the staircase lurked a huge tiger.

"It's stuffed, Rachel." Nick laughed. The tiger stood as if about to pounce, mouth open in a ferocious growl.

"I'm sorry, it looked so real," Rachel said, recovering herself.

"It *was* real. It's a native Singaporean tiger. They used to roam this area until the late nineteenth century, but they were hunted into extinction. My great-grandfather shot this one when it ran into the house and hid under the billiard table, or so the story goes."

"Poor guy," Rachel said, reaching out to stroke the tiger's head gingerly. Its fur felt surprisingly brittle, as if a patch might fall off at any minute.

"It used to scare the hell out of me when I was little. I never dared go near the foyer at night, and I had dreams that it would come alive and attack me while I was sleeping," Nick said.

"You grew up here?" Rachel asked in surprise.

"Yes, until I was about seven."

"You never told me you lived in a palace."

"This isn't a palace. It's just a big house."

"Nick, where I come from, this is a palace," Rachel said, gazing up at the cast-iron and glass cupola soaring above them. As they climbed the stairs, the murmur of party chatter and piano keys wafted down toward them. When they reached the landing to the second floor, Rachel almost had to rub her eyes in disbelief. *Sweet Jesus.* She felt momentarily giddy, as if she had been transported back in time to another era, to the grand lounge of a twenties ocean liner en route from Venice to Istanbul, perhaps.

The "living room," as Nick so modestly called it, was a gallery that ran along the entire northern end of the house, with art deco divans, wicker club chairs, and ottomans casually grouped into intimate seating areas. A row of tall plantation doors opened onto the wraparound veranda, inviting the view of verdant parklands and the scent of night-blooming jasmine into the room, while at the far end a young man in a tuxedo played on the Bösendorfer grand piano. As Nick led her into the space, Rachel found herself reflexively trying to ignore her surroundings, even though all she wanted to do was study every exquisite detail: the exotic potted palms in massive *Qian-*

long dragon jardinieres that anchored the space, the scarlet-shaded opaline glass lamps that cast an amber glow over the lacquered teak surfaces, the silver- and lapis lazuli–filigreed walls that shimmered as she moved about the room. Every single object seemed imbued with a patina of timeless elegance, as if it had been there for more than a hundred years, and Rachel didn't dare to touch anything. The glamorous guests, however, appeared completely at ease lounging on the shantung silk ottomans or mingling on the veranda while a retinue of white-gloved servants in deep-olive batik uniforms circulated with trays of cocktails.

"Here comes Astrid's mother," Nick muttered. Before Rachel had a moment to collect herself, a stately-looking lady approached them, wagging a finger at Nick.

"Nicky, you naughty boy, why didn't you tell us you were back? We thought you weren't coming till next week, and you just missed Uncle Harry's birthday dinner at Command House!" The woman looked like a middle-aged Chinese matron, but she spoke in the sort of clipped English accent straight out of a Merchant Ivory film. Rachel couldn't help but notice how her tightly permed black hair fittingly resembled the Queen of England's.

"So sorry, I thought you and Uncle Harry would be in London at this time of the year. *Dai gu cheh*, this is my girlfriend Rachel Chu. Rachel, this is my auntie Felicity Leong."

Felicity nodded at Rachel, boldly scanning her up and down.

"So nice to meet you," Rachel said, trying not to be unnerved by her hawklike gaze.

"Yes of course," Felicity said, turning quickly to Nick and asking, almost sternly, "Do you know when your daddy gets in?"

"Not a clue," he replied. "Is Astrid here yet?"

"Aiyah, you know that girl is always late!" At that moment, his aunt noticed an elderly Indian woman in a gold and peacock-blue sari being helped up the stairs. "Dear Mrs. Singh, when did you get back from Udaipur?" she screeched, pouncing on the woman as Nick guided Rachel out of the way.

"Who is that lady?" Rachel asked.

"That's Mrs. Singh, a family friend who used to live down the street. She's the daughter of a maharaja, and one of the most fascinating people I know. She was great friends with Nehru. I'll introduce you later, when my aunt isn't breathing down our necks."

"Her sari is absolutely stunning," Rachel remarked, gazing at the elaborate gold stitching.

"Yes, isn't it? I hear she flies all her saris back to New Delhi to be specially cleaned," Nick said as he tried to escort Rachel toward the bar, unwittingly steering straight into the path of a very posh-looking middle-aged couple. The man had a pompadour of Bryl-creemed black hair and thick, oversize tortoiseshell glasses, while his wife wore a classic gold-buttoned red-and-white Chanel suit.

"Uncle Dickie, Auntie Nancy, meet my girlfriend Rachel Chu," Nick said. "Rachel, this is my uncle and his wife, from the T'sien side of the family," he explained.

"Ah Rachel, I've met your grandfather in Taipei . . . Chu Yang Chung, isn't it?" Uncle Dickie asked.

"Er . . . actually, no. My family isn't from Taipei," Rachel stammered.

"Oh. Where are they from, then?"

"Guangdong originally, and nowadays California."

Uncle Dickie looked a bit taken aback, while his well-coiffed wife grasped his arm tightly and continued. "Oh, we know California very well. Northern California, actually."

"Yes, that's where I'm from," Rachel replied politely.

"Ah, well then, you must know the Gettys? Ann is a great friend of mine," Nancy effused.

"Um, are you referring to the Getty Oil family?"

"Is there any other?" Nancy asked, perplexed.

"Rachel's from Cupertino, not San Francisco, Auntie Nancy. And that's why I need to introduce her to Francis Leong over there, who I hear is going to Stanford this fall," Nick cut in, quickly moving Rachel along. The next thirty minutes became a blur of nonstop greetings, as Rachel was introduced to assorted family and friends. There were aunties and uncles and cousins aplenty, there was the distinguished though diminutive Thai ambassador, there was a man Nick introduced as the sultan of some unpronounceable Malay state, along with his two wives in elaborately bejeweled head scarves.

All this time, Rachel had noticed one woman who seemed to command the attention of the room. She was very slim and aristocratic-looking with snow-white hair and ramrod-straight posture, dressed in a long white silk cheongsam with deep purple piping along the collar, sleeves, and hemline. Most of the guests orbited around her paying tribute, and when she at last came toward them, Rachel noticed for the first time Nick's resemblance to her. Nick had earlier informed Rachel that while his grandmother spoke English perfectly well, she preferred to speak in Chinese and was fluent in four dialects—Mandarin, Cantonese, Hokkien, and Teochew. Rachel decided to greet her in Mandarin, the only dialect she spoke, but before Nick could make proper introductions, she bowed her head nervously at the stately lady and said, "It is such a pleasure to meet you. Thank you for inviting me to your beautiful home."

The woman looked at her quizzically and replied slowly in Mandarin, "It is a pleasure to meet you too, but you are mistaken, this is not my house."

"Rachel, this is my great-aunt Rosemary," Nick explained hurriedly.

"And you'll have to forgive me, my Mandarin is really quite rusty," Great-aunt Rosemary added in her Vanessa Redgrave English.

"Oh, I'm so sorry," Rachel said, her cheeks flushing bright red. She could feel all eyes in the room upon her, amused by her faux pas.

"No need to apologize." Great-aunt Rosemary smiled graciously. "Nick has told me quite a bit about you, and I was so looking forward to meeting you."

"He has?" Rachel said, still flustered.

Nick put his arm around Rachel and said, "Here, come meet my grandmother." They walked across the room, and on the sofa closest to the veranda, flanked by a spectacled man smartly attired in a white linen suit and a strikingly beautiful lady, sat a shrunken woman. Shang Su Yi had steel-gray hair held in place by an ivory headband, and she was dressed simply in a rose-colored silk blouse, tailored cream trousers, and brown loafers. She was older and frailer than Rachel had expected, and though her features were partially obscured by a thick pair of tinted bifocals, her regal countenance was unmistakable. Standing completely still behind Nick's grandmother were two ladies in immaculate matching gowns of iridescent silk.

Nick addressed his grandmother in Cantonese. "Ah Ma, I'd like you to meet my friend Rachel Chu, from America."

"So nice to meet you!" Rachel blurted in English, completely forgetting her Mandarin.

Nick's grandmother peered up at Rachel for a moment. "Thank

you for coming," she replied haltingly, in English, before turning swiftly to resume her conversation in Hokkien with the lady at her side. The man in the white linen suit smiled quickly at Rachel, but then he too turned away. The two ladies swathed in silk stared inscrutably at Rachel, and she smiled back at them tensely.

"Let's get some punch," Nick said, steering Rachel toward a table where a uniformed waiter wearing white cotton gloves was serving punch out of a huge Venetian glass punch bowl.

"Oh my God, that had to be the most awkward moment of my life! I think I really annoyed your grandmother," Rachel whispered.

"Nonsense. She was just in the middle of another conversation, that's all," Nick said soothingly.

"Who were those two women in matching silk dresses standing like statues behind her?" Rachel asked.

"Oh, those are her lady's maids."

"Excuse me?"

"Her lady's maids. They never leave her side."

"Like ladies-in-waiting? They look so elegant."

"Yes, they're from Thailand, and they were trained to serve in the royal court."

"Is this a common thing in Singapore? Importing royal maids from Thailand?" Rachel asked incredulously.

"I don't believe so. This service was a special lifetime gift to my grandmother."

"A gift? From whom?"

"The King of Thailand. Though it was the last one, not Bhumibol the current king. Or was it the one before that? Anyway, he was apparently a great friend of my grandmother's. He decreed that she must only be waited on by court-trained ladies. So there has been a constant rotation ever since my grandmother was a young woman."

"Oh," Rachel said, stupefied. She took the glass of punch from Nick and noticed that the fine etching on the Venetian glassware perfectly matched the intricate fretwork pattern on the ceiling. She leaned against the back of a sofa for support, suddenly feeling overwhelmed. There was too much for her to take in—the army of white-gloved servants hovering about, the confusion of new faces, the mind-blowing opulence. Who knew that Nick's family would turn out to be these extremely grand people? And why didn't he prepare her for all this a little more?

Rachel felt a gentle tap on her shoulder. She turned around to see Nick's cousin holding a sleepy toddler. "Astrid!" she cried, delighted to see a friendly face at last. Astrid was adorned in the chicest outfit Rachel had ever seen, quite different from how she had remembered her in New York. So this was Astrid in her natural habitat.

"Hello, hello!" Astrid said cheerily. "Cassian, this is Auntie Rachel. Say hi to Auntie Rachel?" Astrid gestured. The child stared at Rachel for a moment, before burying his head shyly into his mother's shoulder.

"Here, let me take this big boy out of your hands!" Nick grinned, lifting a squirming Cassian out of Astrid's arms, and then deftly handing her a glass of punch.

"Thanks, Nicky," Astrid said as she turned to Rachel. "How are you finding Singapore so far? Having a good time?"

"A great time! Although tonight's been a bit . . . overwhelming."

"I can only imagine," Astrid said with a knowing glint in her eye.

"No, I'm not sure you can," Rachel said.

A melodious peel rang through the room. Rachel turned to see an elderly woman in a white cheongsam top and black silk trousers playing a small silver xylophone by the stairs.*

"Ah, the dinner gong," Astrid said. "Come, let's eat."

"Astrid, how is it that you always seem to arrive *just* when the food is ready?" Nick remarked.

"Choco-cake!" little Cassian muttered.

"No, Cassian, you already had your dessert," Astrid replied firmly.

The crowd began to make a beeline for the stairs, passing the woman with the xylophone. As they approached her, Nick gave the woman a big bear hug and exchanged a few words in Cantonese. "This is Ling Cheh, the woman who pretty much raised me from birth," he explained. "She has been with our family since 1948."

"*Wah, nay gor nuay pang yau gum laeng, ah! Faai di git fun!*" Ling Cheh commented, grasping Rachel's hand gently. Nick grinned, blushing a

---

* These "black and white amahs," nowadays a fast-disappearing group in Singapore, are professional domestic servants who hailed from China. They were usually confirmed spinsters who took vows of chastity and spent their entire lives caring for the families they served. (Quite often, they were the ones who actually raised the children.) They were known for their trademark uniform of white blouse and black pants, and their long hair that was always worn in a neat bun at the nape of the neck.

little. Rachel didn't understand Cantonese, so she just smiled, while Astrid quickly translated. "Ling Cheh just teased Nick about how pretty his lady friend is." As they proceeded down the stairs, she whispered to Rachel, "She also ordered him to marry you soon!" Rachel simply giggled.

A buffet supper had been set up in the conservatory, an elliptical-shaped room with dramatic frescoed walls of what appeared from a distance to be a dreamy, muted Oriental scene. On closer inspection, Rachel noticed that while the mural did evoke classical Chinese mountainscapes, the details seemed to be pure Hieronymus Bosch, with strange, lurid flowers climbing up the walls and iridescent phoenixes and other fantastical creatures hiding in the shadows. Three enormous round tables gleamed with silver chafing dishes, and arched doorways opened onto a curved colonnaded terrace where white wrought-iron bistro tables lit with tall votives awaited the diners. Cassian continued to squirm in Nick's arms, wailing even louder, "I want choco-cake!"

"I think what he really wants is S-L-E-E-P," his mother commented. She tried to take her son back from Nick, but the child began to whimper.

"I sense a crying fit on the way. Let's take him to the nursery," Nick offered. "Rachel, why don't you get started? We'll be back in a minute."

Rachel marveled at the sheer variety of food that had been laid out. One table was filled with Thai delicacies, another with Malaysian cuisine, and the last with classic Chinese dishes. As usual, she was a bit at a loss when confronted with a huge buffet. She decided to start one cuisine at a time and began at the Chinese table with a small helping of E-fu noodles and seared scallops in ginger sauce. She came upon a tray of exotic-looking golden wafers folded into little top hats. "What in the world are these?" she wondered aloud.

"That's *kueh pie tee*, a *nyonya* dish. Little tarts filled with jicama, carrots, and shrimp. Try one," a voice behind her said. Rachel looked around and saw the dapper man in the white linen suit who had been sitting next to Nick's grandmother. He bowed in a courtly manner and introduced himself. "We never met properly. I'm Oliver T'sien, Nick's cousin." Yet another Chinese relative with a British accent, but his sounded even plummier than the rest.

"Nice to meet you. I'm Rachel—"

"Yes, I know. Rachel Chu, of Cupertino, Palo Alto, Chicago, and Manhattan. You see, your reputation precedes you."

"Does it?" Rachel asked, trying not to sound too surprised.

"It certainly does, and I must say you're much more fetching than I was led to believe."

"Really, by whom?"

"Oh, you know, the whispering gallery. Don't you know how much the tongues have been wagging since you've arrived?" he said mischievously.

"I had no clue," Rachel said a little uneasily, walking out onto the terrace with her plate, looking for Nick or Astrid but not seeing them anywhere. She noticed one of Nick's aunties—the lady in the Chanel suit—looking toward her expectantly.

"There's Dickie and Nancy," Oliver said. "Don't look now—I think they're waving to you. God help us. Let's start our own table, shall we?" Before Rachel could answer, Oliver grabbed her plate from her hand and walked it over to a table at the far end of the terrace.

"Why are you avoiding them?" Rachel asked.

"I'm not avoiding them. I'm helping *you* avoid them. You can thank me later."

"Why?" Rachel pressed on.

"Well, first of all, they are insufferable name-droppers, always going on and on about their latest cruise on Rupert and Wendi's yacht or their lunch with some deposed European royal, and second, they aren't exactly on your team."

"What team? I didn't realize I was on any team."

"Well, like it or not, you *are*, and Dickie and Nancy are here tonight precisely to spy for the opposition."

"Spying?"

"Yes. They mean to pick you apart like a rotting carcass and serve you up as an *amuse-bouche* the next time they're invited to dine in the Home Counties."

Rachel had no idea what to make of his outlandish statement. This Oliver seemed like a character straight out of an Oscar Wilde play. "I'm not sure I follow," she finally said.

"Don't worry, you will. Just give it another week—I'd peg you for a quick study."

Rachel assessed Oliver for a minute. He looked to be in his mid-thirties, with short, meticulously combed hair and small round tortoiseshell glasses that only accentuated his longish face. "So how exactly are you related to Nick?" she asked. "There seem to be so many different branches of the family."

"It's really quite simple, actually. There are three branches—the T'siens, the Youngs, and the Shangs. Nick's grandfather James Young and my grandmother Rosemary T'sien are brother and sister. You met her earlier tonight, if you recall? You mistook her for Nick's grandmother."

"Yes, of course. But that would mean that you and Nick are second cousins."

"Right. But here in Singapore, since extended families abound, we all just say we're 'cousins' to avoid confusion. None of that 'third cousins twice removed' rubbish."

"So Dickie and Nancy are your uncle and aunt."

"Correct. Dickie is my father's older brother. But you do know that in Singapore, anyone you're introduced to who's one generation older should be called 'Uncle or Auntie,' even though they might not be related at all. It's considered the polite thing."

"Well, shouldn't you be calling your relatives 'Uncle Dickie' and 'Auntie Nancy' then?"

"Technically, yes, but I personally feel that the honorific should be earned. Dickie and Nancy have never given a flying fuck about me, so why should I bother?"

Rachel raised her eyebrows. "Well, thanks for the crash course on the T'siens. Now, how about the third branch?"

"Ah yes, the Shangs."

"I don't think I've met any of them yet."

"Well, none of them are here, of course. We're not supposed to *ever* talk about them, but the imperial Shangs flee to their grand country estates in England every April and stay until September, to avoid the hottest months. But not to worry, I think my cousin Cassandra Shang will be back for the wedding next week, so you will get a chance to bask in her incandescence."

Rachel grinned at his florid remark—this Oliver was such a trip. "And how are they related exactly?"

"Here's where it gets interesting. Pay attention. So my grandmother's eldest daughter, Aunt Mabel T'sien, was married off to Nick's grandmother's younger brother Alfred Shang."

"Married off? Does that mean it was an arranged marriage?"

"Yes, very much so, plotted by my grandfather T'sien Tsai Tay and Nick's great-grandfather Shang Loong Ma. Good thing they actually liked each other. But it was quite a masterstroke, because it strategically bound together the T'siens, the Shangs, and the Youngs."

"What for?" Rachel asked.

"Oh come on, Rachel, don't play the naïf with me. For the *money*, of course. It joined together three family fortunes and kept everything neatly locked up."

"Who's getting locked up? Are they finally locking you up, Ollie?" Nick said, as he approached the table with Astrid.

"They haven't been able to pin anything on me yet, Nicholas," Oliver retorted. He turned to Astrid and his eyes widened. "Holy Mary Mother of Tilda Swinton, look at those earrings! Wherever did you get them?"

"Stephen Chia's . . . they're VBH," Astrid said, knowing he would want to know who the designer was.

"Of course they are. Only Bruce could have dreamed up something like that. They must have cost *at least* half a million dollars. I wouldn't have thought they were quite your style, but they do look fabulous on you. Hmm . . . you still can surprise me after all these years."

"You know I try, Ollie, I try."

Rachel stared with renewed wonder at the earrings. Did Oliver really say half a million dollars? "How's Cassian doing?" she asked.

"It was a bit of a struggle at first, but now he'll sleep till dawn," Astrid replied.

"And where is that errant husband of yours, Astrid? Mr. Bedroom Eyes?" Oliver asked.

"Michael's working late tonight."

"What a pity. That company of his really keeps him toiling away, don't they? Seems like ages since I've seen Michael—I'm beginning to take it quite personally. Though the other day I could have *sworn* I saw him walking up Wyndham Street in Hong Kong with a little boy. At first I thought it was Michael and Cassian, but then the little boy turned around and he wasn't nearly as cute as Cassian, so I knew I had to be hallucinating."

"Obviously," Astrid said as calmly as she could, feeling like she had just been punched in the gut. "Were you in Hong Kong before this, Ollie?" she asked, her brain furiously trying to ascertain whether Oliver had been in Hong Kong at the same time as Michael's last "business trip."

"I was there last week. I've been shuttling between Hong Kong, Shanghai, and Beijing for the past month for work."

Michael was supposedly in Shenzhen then. He could have easily taken a train to Hong Kong, Astrid thought.

"Oliver is the Asian art and antiquities expert for Christie's in London," Nick explained to Rachel.

"Yes, except that it's no longer very efficient for me to be based in London. The Asian art market is heating up like you wouldn't believe."

"I hear that every new Chinese billionaire is trying to get their hands on a Warhol these days," Nick remarked.

"Well, yes there are certainly quite a few wannabe Saatchis around, but I'm dealing more with the ones trying to buy back the great antiquities from European and American collectors. Or, as they like to say, stuff stolen by the foreign devils," Oliver said.

"It wasn't truly *stolen*, was it?" Nick asked.

"Stolen, smuggled, sold off by philistines, isn't it all the same? Whether the Chinese want to admit it or not, the true connoisseurship of Asian art was outside of China for much of the last century, so that's where a lot of the museum-quality pieces ended up—in Europe and America. The demand was there. The moneyed Chinese didn't really appreciate what they had. With the exception of a few families, no one bothered to collect Chinese art and antiquities, not with any real discernment, anyway. They wanted to be modern and sophisticated, which meant emulating the Europeans. Why, even in this house there's probably more French art deco than there are Chinese pieces. Thank God there are some fabulous signed Ruhlmann pieces, but if you think about it, it's a pity that your great-grandfather went mad for art deco when he could have been snapping up all the imperial treasures coming out of China."

"You mean the antiques that were in the Forbidden City?" Rachel asked.

"Absolutely! Did you know that in 1913, the imperial family of China actually tried to *sell* their entire collection to the banker J. P. Morgan?" Oliver said.

"Come on!" Rachel was incredulous.

"It's true. The family was so hard up, they were willing to let all of it go for four million dollars. All the priceless treasures, collected over a span of five centuries. It's quite a sensational story—Morgan received the offer by telegram, but he died a few days later. Divine intervention was the only thing that prevented the most irreplaceable treasures of China from ending up in the Big Apple."

"Imagine if that had actually happened," Nick remarked, shaking his head.

"Yes indeed. It would be a loss greater than the Elgin Marbles going to the British Museum. But thankfully the tide has turned. The Mainland Chinese are finally interested in buying back their own heritage, and they only want the best," Oliver said. "Which reminds me, Astrid—are you still looking for more *Huanghuali*? Because I know of an important Han dynasty puzzle table coming up for auction next week in Hong Kong." Oliver turned to Astrid, noticing that she had a faraway look on her face. "Earth to Astrid?"

"Oh . . . sorry, I got distracted for a moment," Astrid said, suddenly flustered. "You were saying something about Hong Kong?"

3

Peik Lin

•

SINGAPORE

Wye Mun and Neena Goh were stretched out on teal-colored leather recliners in their screening room at Villa d'Oro, munching on salted watermelon seeds and watching a Korean soap opera, when Peik Lin burst into the room.

"Mute the TV! Mute the TV!" she demanded.

"What's wrong, what's wrong?" Neena asked in alarm.

"You're not going to believe where I just came from!"

"Where?" Wye Mun asked, a little annoyed that his daughter had interrupted during a pivotal moment of his favorite show.

"I just came from Nicholas Young's grandma's house."

"So?"

"You should have seen the size of the place."

"*Dua geng choo, ah?*"* Wye Mun said.

"*Dua* doesn't even begin to describe it. The house was huge, but you should have seen the land. Do you know that there is an *enormous* piece of private land right next door to the Botanic Gardens?"

"Next to Botanic Gardens?"

"Yes. Off Gallop Road. It's on a street I've never even heard of called Tyersall Avenue."

* Hokkien for "big house."

"Near those old wooden houses?" Neena asked.

"Yes, but this wasn't one of the colonial houses. The architecture was very unusual, sort of Orientalist, and the gardens were unbelievable—probably around fifty acres or more."

"Bullshit, *lah!*" Wye Mun said.

"Papa, I'm telling you—the property was immense. It was like the *Istana*. The driveway itself went on for miles."

"Cannot be! Two or three acres I might believe, but fifty? No such thing, *lah.*"

"It was fifty acres *at least*, probably more. I thought I was dreaming. I thought I was in another country."

"*Lu leem ziew, ah?*"* Neena looked at her daughter in concern. Peik Lin ignored her.

"Show me," Wye Mun said, his interest piqued. "Let's see it on Google Earth." They walked over to the computer desk in the corner, pulled up the program, and Peik Lin began searching for the place. As they zoomed in on the topographical screen, she immediately noticed something amiss in the satellite image.

"Look, Papa—this whole patch is empty! You think it's part of the Botanic Gardens, but it's not. This is where the house is. But why are there no images? It doesn't appear on Google Earth at all! And my GPS couldn't find the address either."

Wye Mun stared at the screen. The place his daughter claimed to have seen was literally a black hole on the map. It did not officially exist. How very strange.

"Who is this fellow's family?" he asked.

"I don't know. But there were a lot of VIP cars in the driveway. I saw quite a few diplomatic license plates. Old Rolls-Royces, vintage Daimlers, that type of car. These people must be loaded beyond belief. Who do you think they are?"

"I can't think of anyone specifically who lives in this area." Wye Mun ran the cursor over the perimeter of the blacked-out area. His family had been in the property development and construction business in Singapore for more than forty years, but he had never come across anything like this. "Wah, this is prime, prime land—right in the middle of the island. The value would be incalculable. Cannot be one property, *lah!*"

* Hokkien for "Have you been drinking?"

"Yes it is, Papa. I saw it with my own eyes. And supposedly Nick's grandmother grew up there. It's *her* house."

"Make Rachel find out the grandma's name. And the grandpa. We need to know who these people are. How can one person own this much private land in one of the most crowded cities in the world?"

"Wah, it looks like Rachel Chu has hit jackpot. I hope she marries this guy!" Neena chimed in from her recliner.

"Aiyah, who cares about Rachel Chu? Peik Lin, *you* go after him!" Wye Mun declared.

Peik Lin grinned at her father, and began texting Rachel.

Wye Mun patted his wife on the shoulder. "Come, call the driver. Let's take a drive down Tyersall Road. I want to see this place for myself."

They decided to take the Audi SUV in an effort to be as inconspicuous as possible. "See, I think this is where the property actually begins," Peik Lin noted as they turned onto the curving, densely wooded road. "I think all this on the left side is the southern boundary of the land." When they reached the gray iron gates, Wye Mun made the driver stop the car for a minute. The place looked completely deserted. "See, you wouldn't think there's anything here. It looks like some old section of the Botanic Gardens. There's another guard house farther down this road, a high-tech one manned by Gurkha guards," Peik Lin explained. Wye Mun stared down the unlit, overgrown road, completely fascinated. He was one of Singapore's leading property developers, and he knew every square inch of land on the island. Or at least he thought he did.

4

Rachel and Nick

•

"The *tan huas* are coming into bloom!" Ling Cheh announced excitedly to everyone on the terrace. As the guests began to head back in through the conservatory, Nick pulled Rachel aside. "Here, let's take a shortcut," he said. Rachel followed him through a side door, and they wandered down a long hallway, past many darkened rooms that she longed to peek into. When Nick led her through an arch at the end of the passage, Rachel's jaw dropped in disbelief.

They were no longer in Singapore. It was as if they had stumbled onto a secret cloister deep within a Moorish palace. The vast courtyard was enclosed on all sides but completely open to the sky. Elaborately carved columns lined the arcades around its perimeter, and an Andalusian fountain protruded from the stone wall, spouting a stream of water from a lotus blossom sculpted out of rose quartz. Overhead, hundreds of copper lanterns had been meticulously strung across the courtyard from the second-floor walkway, each flickering with candlelight.

"I wanted to show you this place while it was still empty," Nick said in a hushed voice, pulling Rachel into an embrace.

"Pinch me, please. Is any of this real?" Rachel whispered as she looked into Nick's eyes.

"This place is very real. *You're* the dream," Nick answered as he kissed her deeply.

A few guests began to trickle in, disrupting the spell they had momentarily been under. "Come, it's dessert time!" Nick said, rubbing his hands together in anticipation.

Along one of the arcades stretched long banquet tables that displayed a wondrous selection of desserts. There were elaborate cakes, soufflés, and sweet puddings, there was *goreng pisang** drizzled with Lyle's Golden Syrup, *nyonya kuehs* in every color of the rainbow, and tall polished samovars filled with different steaming-hot elixirs. Servers wearing white toques stood behind each table, ready to dish out the delicacies.

"Tell me this isn't how your family eats every day," Rachel said in amazement.

"Well, tonight was leftovers night," Nick deadpanned.

Rachel elbowed him in the ribs playfully.

"Ow! And I was about to offer you a slice of the best chocolate chiffon cake in the world."

"I just stuffed my face with eighteen different types of noodles! I couldn't possibly eat dessert," Rachel groaned, pressing her palm against her stomach momentarily. She walked to the center of the courtyard, where chairs were arranged around a reflecting pool. In the middle of the pool were huge terra-cotta urns that held the painstakingly cultivated *tan huas*. Rachel had never seen a species of flora quite so exotic. The tangled forest of plants grew together into a tall profusion of large floppy leaves the color of dark jade. Long stems sprouted from the edges of the leaves, curving until they formed huge bulbs. The pale reddish petals curled tightly like delicate fingers grasping a silken white peach. Oliver stood by the flowers, scrutinizing one of the bulbs closely.

"How can you tell they are about to bloom?" Rachel asked him.

"See how swollen they've become, and how the whiteness of the bulbs are peeking through these red tentacles? Within the hour, you will see them open fully. You know, it's considered to be very auspicious to witness *tan huas* blooming in the night."

"Really?"

---

* Banana fritters deep-fried in batter, a Malay delicacy. Some of the best *goreng pisang* used to be found in the school canteen of the Anglo-Chinese School and were often used by teachers (especially Mrs. Lau, my Chinese teacher) as a reward for good grades. Because of this, a whole generation of Singaporean boys from a certain social milieu have come to regard the snack as one of their ultimate comfort foods.

"Yes, indeed. They bloom so rarely and so unpredictably, and it all happens so fast. It's a once-in-a-lifetime event for most people, so I'd say you're very lucky to be here tonight."

As Rachel strolled around the reflecting pool, she noticed Nick under an arcade chatting intently with the striking lady who had been sitting next to Nick's grandmother. "Who is that woman talking to Nick? You were with her earlier," Rachel asked.

"Oh, that's Jacqueline Ling. An old family friend."

"She looks like a movie star," Rachel commented.

"Yes, doesn't she? I've always thought that Jacqueline looks like a Chinese Catherine Deneuve, only more beautiful."

"She *does* look like Catherine Deneuve!"

"And aging better too."

"Well, she's not *that* old. What is she, in her early forties?"

"Try adding twenty years to that."

"You're kidding!" Rachel said, staring in awe at Jacqueline's ballerina-like figure, shown to great advantage by the pale yellow halter top and palazzo pants that she wore with a pair of silver stilettos.

"I've always thought it a bit of a pity that she hasn't done more with herself than disarm men with her looks," Oliver observed.

"Is that what she's done?"

"Widowed once, almost married a British marquess, and since then she's been the companion of a Norwegian tycoon. There's a story I heard as a child: Jacqueline's beauty was so legendary that when she visited Hong Kong for the first time in the sixties, her arrival attracted a throng of spectators, as if she were Elizabeth Taylor. All the men were clamoring to propose to her, and fights broke out at the terminal. It made the newspapers, apparently."

"All because of her beauty."

"Yes, and her bloodline. She's the granddaughter of Ling Yin Chao."

"Who's that?"

"He was one of Asia's most revered philanthropists. Built schools all over China. Not that Jacqueline is following in his footsteps, unless you consider her donations in aid of Manolo Blahnik."

Rachel laughed, as both of them noticed that Jacqueline had one hand on Nick's upper arm, stroking it gently.

"Don't worry—she flirts with everyone," Oliver quipped. "Do you want another piece of juicy gossip?"

"Please."

"I'm told Nick's grandmother very much wanted Jacqueline for Nick's father. But she didn't succeed."

"He wasn't swayed by her looks?"

"Well, he already had another beauty on his hands—Nick's mother. You haven't met Auntie Elle yet, have you?"

"No, she went away for the weekend."

"Hmm, how *interesting*. She never goes away when Nicholas is in town," Oliver said, turning around to make sure no one was within earshot before leaning closer in. "I'd tread extra carefully around Eleanor Young if I were you. She maintains a rival court," he said mysteriously before walking off toward the cocktails table.

———

Nick stood at one end of the desserts, wondering what to have first: the *goreng pisang* with ice cream, the blancmange with mango sauce, or the chocolate chiffon cake.

"Oh, your cook's chocolate chiffon! Now *this* is the reason I came tonight!" Jacqueline ran her fingers through her shoulder-length curls and then brushed her hand softly against his arm. "So tell me, why haven't you been calling Amanda? You've only seen her a handful of times since she moved to New York."

"We tried getting together a couple of times this spring, but she's always overbooked. Isn't she dating some high-flying hedge-fund guy?"

"It's not serious; that man is twice her age."

"Well, I see her pictures in the newspapers all the time."

"That's just the problem. That has to stop. It's so unseemly. I want my daughter to mix with quality people, not the so-called Asian jet set in New York. All those pretenders are riding Amanda's coattails—she's just too naïve to see that."

"Oh, I don't think Mandy's that naïve."

"She needs proper company, Nicky. *Gar gee nang.** I want you to look out for her. Will you promise to do that for me?"

"Of course. I spoke to her last month and she told me that she was too busy to come back for Colin's wedding."

———

* Hokkien for "same kind" or "our own people," usually used to refer to family or clan associations.

"Yes, it's too bad, isn't it?"

"I'll call her when I'm back in New York. But I do think I'm far too boring for Amanda these days."

"No, no, she would benefit from spending more time with you—you were so close once upon a time. Now tell me about this charming girl you've brought home to meet your grandmother. I see she's already won over Oliver. You better tell her to be careful with him—he's such a vicious gossip, that one."

———

Astrid and Rachel sat by the lotus fountain, watching a lady dressed in flowing apricot silk robes play a *guqin*, the traditional Chinese zither. Rachel was entranced by the mesmerizing speed of the lady's long red fingernails plucking gracefully at the strings, while Astrid desperately tried to stop obsessing over what Oliver had said earlier. Could he have really seen Michael walking with some little boy in Hong Kong? Nick sank into the chair next to her, dexterously balancing two steaming cups of tea with one hand and holding a plate of half-eaten chocolate chiffon cake with the other. He handed the cup with smoked lychee tea to Astrid, knowing it was her favorite, and offered some cake to Rachel. "You've got to try this—it's one of our cook Ah Ching's greatest hits."

"*Alamak*, Nicky, get her a proper piece of her own," Astrid scolded, temporarily snapping out of her funk.

"It's okay, Astrid. I'll just eat most of his, like always," Rachel explained with a laugh. She tasted the cake, her eyes widening instantly. It was the perfect combination of chocolate and cream, with an airy melt-in-your-mouth lightness. "Hmmm. I like that it isn't too sweet."

"That's why I can never eat other chocolate cakes. They're always too sweet, too dense, or have too much frosting," Nick said.

Rachel reached over for another bite. "Just get the recipe and I'll try making it at home."

Astrid arched her eyebrows. "You can try, Rachel, but trust me, my cook has tried, and it never comes out quite this good. I suspect Ah Ching's withholding some secret ingredient."

As they sat in the courtyard, the tightly rolled red petals of the *tan huas* unfurled like a slow-motion movie to reveal a profusion of feathery white petals that kept expanding into an explosive sunburst pattern. "I can't believe how big these flowers are getting!" Rachel observed excitedly.

"It always reminds me of a swan ruffling its wings, about to take flight," Astrid remarked.

"Or maybe about to go into attack mode," Nick added. "Swans can get really aggressive."

"My swans were never aggressive," Great-aunt Rosemary said as she walked up, overhearing Nick's comment. "Don't you remember feeding the swans in my pond when you were a little boy?"

"I remember being rather afraid of them actually," Nick replied. "I would break off little bits of bread, throw them into the water, and then run for cover."

"Nicky was a little wimp," Astrid teased.

"Was he?" Rachel asked in surprise.

"Well, he was so tiny. For the longest time everyone was afraid that he would never grow—I was so much taller than him. And then suddenly he shot up," Astrid said.

"Hey, Astrid, stop discussing my secret shame," Nick said with a mock frown.

"Nicky, you have nothing to be embarrassed about. After all, you've grown up to be quite the strapping specimen, as I'm sure Rachel would agree," Great-aunt Rosemary said saucily. The women all laughed.

As the flowers continued to transform before her eyes, Rachel sat sipping lychee tea from a red porcelain cup, entranced by everything around her. She watched the sultan taking pictures of his two wives in front of the blossoms, their jewel-embroidered *kebayas* reflecting shards of light every time the camera flash went off. She observed the cluster of men sitting in a circle with Astrid's father, who was engrossed in a heated political debate, and she looked at Nick, now crouched beside his grandmother. She was touched to see how caring Nick seemed to be with his grandmother, holding the old lady's hands as he whispered into her ear.

"Is your friend having a nice time tonight?" Su Yi asked her grandson in Cantonese.

"Yes, Ah Ma. She's having a lovely time. Thank you for inviting her."

"She seems to be quite the talk of the town. Everyone is either trying delicately to ask me about her or trying delicately to tell me things about her."

"Really? What have they been saying?"

"Some are wondering what her intentions are. Your cousin Cassandra even called me from England, all flustered up."

Nick was surprised. "How does Cassandra even know about Rachel?"

"Aiyah, only the ghosts know where she gets her information! But she is very concerned for you. She thinks you are going to get trapped."

"Trapped? I'm just on holiday with Rachel, Ah Ma. There is nothing to be concerned about," Nick said defensively, annoyed that Cassandra had been gossiping about him.

"That's *exactly* what I told her. I told her that you are a good boy, and that you would never do anything without my blessing. Cassandra must be bored out of her mind in the English countryside. She's letting her imagination run as wild as her silly horses."

"Would you like me to bring Rachel over, Ah Ma, so that you can get to know her better?" Nick ventured.

"You know I won't be able to stand all the craning necks if that happens. Why don't you both just come to stay next week? It's so silly to be staying at a hotel when your bedroom is waiting right here."

Nick was thrilled to hear these words from his grandmother. He had her seal of approval now. "That would be wonderful, Ah Ma."

———

In a corner of the darkened billiard room, Jacqueline was in the midst of a heated phone conversation with her daughter, Amanda, in New York. "Stop making excuses! I don't give a damn what you told the press. Do what you have to do, but just make sure you're back next week," she fumed.

Jacqueline ended her call, looking out the window at the moonlit terrace. "I know you're there, Oliver," she said sharply, not turning around. Oliver emerged from the shadowy doorway and approached slowly.

"I can smell you from a mile away. You need to lay off the Blenheim Bouquet—you're not the Prince of Wales."

Oliver arched his eyebrows. "Aren't we getting testy! Anyway, it's quite clear to me that Nicholas is completely smitten. Don't you think it's a little too late for Amanda?"

"Not at all," Jacqueline replied, carefully rearranging her hair. "As you yourself have often said, *timing is everything.*"

"I was talking about investing in art."

"My daughter is an exquisite piece of art, is she not? She belongs only in the finest collection."

"A collection you failed to become part of."

"Fuck you, Oliver."

"*Chez toi ou chez moi?*" Oliver naughtily arched an eyebrow as he sauntered out of the room.

In the Andalusian courtyard, Rachel allowed her eyes to close for a moment. The strums of the Chinese zither created a perfect melody with the trickling waters, and the flowers in turn seemed to be choreographing their bloom to the mellifluous sounds. Every time a breeze blew, the copper lanterns strung against the evening sky swayed like hundreds of glowing orbs adrift in a dark ocean. Rachel felt like she was floating along with them in some sybaritic dream, and she wondered if life with Nicholas would always be like this. Soon, the *tan huas* began to wilt just as swiftly and mysteriously as they had bloomed, filling the night air with an intoxicating scent as they shriveled into spent, lifeless petals.

5

Astrid and Michael

SINGAPORE

Whenever her grandmother's parties ran late, Astrid would normally opt to spend the night at Tyersall Park. She preferred not to wake Cassian if he was sleeping soundly, and she would head for the bedroom (just opposite from Nick's) that had been set aside for her frequent visits since she was a little girl. Her adoring grandmother had created an enchanted emporium for her, commissioning whimsical hand-carved furniture from Italy and walls painted with scenes from her favorite fairy tale, "The Twelve Dancing Princesses." Astrid still loved the occasional night spent in this childhood bedroom, cosseted by the most fantastical dolls, stuffed animals, and tea sets that money could buy.

Tonight, however, Astrid was determined to get home. Even though it was well past midnight, she swept Cassian into her arms, buckled him into his child seat, and headed for her apartment. She was desperate to know if Michael was back "from work" yet. She was kidding herself in thinking she could just look the other way while Michael carried on. She was not like those wives. She was not going to be a victim, like Eddie's wife, Fiona. All these weeks of speculation and uncertainty had become a crushing weight on her, and she had to resolve this issue once and for all. She needed to see her husband with her own eyes. She needed to smell him. She needed to know whether there truly was another woman. Although, if she was being brutally honest with herself, she had known the truth ever since those four simple words flashed across his iPhone screen. This was the price she had to pay for falling for Michael. He was a man whom all women found irresistible.

SINGAPORE, 2004

The first time Astrid laid eyes on Michael, he was in a camouflage-print speedo. The sight of anyone over the age of ten in one of these banana hammocks was usually repellant to Astrid's aesthetic sensibilities, but when Michael strutted down the runway in his Custo Barcelona speedo, his arm around an Amazonian girl clad in a sheer black Rosa Cha bathing suit and emerald necklace, Astrid was transfixed.

She had been dragged to Churchill Club for a charity fashion show organized by one of her Leong cousins and had sat bored stiff throughout the proceedings. For someone used to a front-row seat at Jean Paul Gaultier's elaborate flights of stagecraft, this hastily constructed catwalk lit with yellow gels, fake palm fronds, and flashing strobe lights seemed like underfunded community theater.

But then Michael appeared, and suddenly everything went into slow motion. He was taller and bigger than most Asian men, with a gorgeous nut-brown tan that wasn't the sort you could spray on at a salon. His severe military buzz cut served to accentuate a hawklike nose that seemed so incongruous to the rest of his face, it took on an overtly sexual quality. Then there were those piercing, deep-set eyes and the washboard abs rippling along his lean torso. He was only on the runway for less than thirty seconds, but she immediately recognized him a few weeks later at Andy Ong's birthday party even though he was fully clothed in a V-neck T-shirt and faded gray jeans.

This time it was Michael who noticed her first. He was leaning against a ledge at the bottom of the garden at the Ong bungalow with Andy and some friends when Astrid appeared on the terrace in a long white linen dress with delicate lace cutouts. Here's a girl who does *not* belong at this party, he thought to himself. The girl soon spotted the birthday boy, and made a beeline toward them, giving Andy a big hug. The guys around him stared openmouthed.

"Many happy returns!" she exclaimed, handing over a small present exquisitely wrapped in purple silk fabric.

"Aiyah, Astrid, *um sai lah*!"* Andy said.

"It's just a little something I thought you'd like from Paris, that's all."

"So did you get that city totally out of your system? Back for good now?"

"I'm not sure yet," Astrid said carefully.

The guys were all jockeying for position, so as reluctant as he was, Andy felt that it would be rude not to introduce them. "Astrid, allow me to introduce Lee Shen Wei, Michael Teo, and Terence Tan. All army buddies."

Astrid smiled sweetly at everyone before fixing her gaze on Michael. "If I'm not mistaken, I've seen *you* in a speedo," she said.

The guys were equal parts stunned and baffled by her statement. Michael just shook his head and laughed.

"Er . . . what is she talking about?" Shen Wei asked.

Astrid peered at Michael's sculpted torso, which was clearly evident despite his loose T-shirt. "Yes, it *was* you, wasn't it? At Churchill Club's fashion show to benefit juvenile shopaholics?"

"Michael, *you modeled in a fashion show*?" Shen Wei said in disbelief.

"In a speedo?" Terence added.

"It was for charity. I got dragged into it!" Michael sputtered, his face turning beet red.

"So you don't model professionally?" Astrid asked.

The guys all started laughing. "He does! He does! He's Michael Zoolander," Andy cracked.

"No, I'm serious," Astrid insisted. "If you ever want to model professionally, I know a few agencies in Paris that would probably love to represent you."

Michael just looked at her, not knowing how to respond. There was a palpable tension in the air, and none of the guys knew what to say.

"Listen, I'm famished, and I think I have to have some of that delicious-looking *mee rebus*† back at the house," Astrid said, giving Andy a quick peck on the cheek before striding back toward the house.

---

* Cantonese for "You really didn't have to."

† Malay egg noodles in a spicy-sweet curry gravy.

"Okay, *laeng tsai*,* what are you waiting for? She was obviously into you," Shen Wei said to Michael.

"Don't want to get your hopes up, Teo, but she's *untouchable*," Andy warned.

"What do you mean *untouchable*?" Shen Wei asked.

"Astrid doesn't date in our stratosphere. You know who she almost married? Charlie Wu, the tech billionaire Wu Hao Lian's son. They were engaged, but then she broke it off at the last minute because her family felt that even *he* wasn't good enough," Andy said.

"Well, Teo here is going to prove you wrong. Mike, that was an open invitation if I've ever seen one. Don't be so *kiasu*,† man!" Shen Wei exclaimed.

Michael did not know what to make of the girl sitting across the table from him. First of all, this date should not even be happening. Astrid wasn't his type. This was the kind of girl he would see shopping at one of those pricey boutiques on Orchard Road or sitting in the lobby café of some fancy hotel having a double decaf macchiato with her banker boyfriend. He wasn't even sure why he had asked her out. It wasn't his style to go after girls in such an obvious way. All his life, he had never needed to chase after women. They had always given themselves freely to him, starting with his older brother's girlfriend when he was fourteen. Technically, Astrid had made the first move, so he didn't mind going after her. Andy's talk about her being "out of his league" really irked him, and he thought it would be fun to bed her, just to shove it in Andy's face.

Michael never expected she would say yes to the date, but here they were, barely a week later, sitting at a restaurant in Dempsey Hill with cobalt-blue glass votives on every table (the trendy sort of place filled with *ang mors* that he hated) with nothing much to say to each other. They had nothing in common, except for the fact that they both knew Andy. She didn't have a job, and since all his work was classified, they couldn't really talk about that. She had been living in Paris for the past few years, so she was out of touch with Singapore.

* Cantonese for "pretty boy."

† Hokkien for "afraid to lose."

Hell, she didn't even seem like a true Singaporean—with her Englishy accent and her mannerisms.

Yet he couldn't help but feel incredibly drawn to her. She was the complete opposite of the type of girls he normally dated. Even though he knew she came from a rich family, she wasn't wearing brand-name clothes or any jewelry. She didn't even appear to be wearing makeup, and still she looked smoking hot. This girl wasn't as *seow chieh*[*] as he had been led to believe, and she even challenged him to a game of pool after dinner.

She turned out to be pretty lethal at billiards, and it made her even sexier. But this was obviously not the kind of girl he could have a casual fling with. He felt almost embarrassed about it, but all he wanted to do was keep staring at her face. He couldn't get enough of it. He was sure he lost the game partly because he was just too distracted by her. At the end of the date, he walked her out to her car (surprisingly, just an Acura) and held the door open as she got in, convinced he would never see her again.

Astrid lay in bed later that night, trying to read Bernard-Henri Lévy's latest tome but having no luck focusing. She couldn't stop thinking about her disastrous date with Michael. The poor guy really didn't have much in the way of conversation, and he was hopelessly unsophisticated. Figures. Guys who looked like that obviously did not have to work hard to impress a woman. There was *something* to him, though, something that imbued him with a beauty that seemed almost feral. He was simply the most perfect specimen of masculinity she had ever seen, and it unleashed a physiological response in her that she did not realize she possessed.

She turned off her bedside lamp and lay in the dark under the mosquito netting of her heirloom Peranakan bed, wishing Michael could read her mind at this very moment. She wanted him to dress up in night camouflage and scale the walls of her father's house, evading the guards in the sentry house and the German shepherds on patrol. She wanted him to climb the guava tree by her window and enter her bedroom without a sound. She wanted him to stand at the foot of her bed for a while, nothing but a leering black shadow. Then she wanted him to rip off her clothes, cover her mouth with his earthy hand, and ravish her nonstop till dawn.

[*] Mandarin for "prissy" or "high maintenance."

She was twenty-seven years old, and for the first time in her life, Astrid realized what it *really* felt like to crave a man sexually. She reached for her cell phone and, before she could stop herself, dialed Michael's number. He picked up after two rings, and Astrid could hear that he was in some sort of noisy bar. She hung up immediately. Fifteen seconds later, her phone rang. She let it ring about five times before answering.

"Why did you call me and hang up?" Michael said in a calm, low voice.

"I didn't call you. My phone must have rung your number accidentally while it was in my purse," Astrid said nonchalantly.

"Uh-huh."

There was a long pause, before Michael casually added, "I'm at Harry's Bar now, but I'm going to drive over to the Ladyhill Hotel and check into a room. The Ladyhill is quite near you, isn't it?"

Astrid was taken aback by his audacity. Who the hell did he think he was? She felt her face go hot, and she wanted to hang up on him again. Instead, she found herself turning on her bedside lamp. "Text me the room number," she said simply.

SINGAPORE, 2010

Astrid drove along the meandering curves of Cluny Road, her head swimming in thoughts. At the start of the evening at Tyersall Park, she had entertained the fantasy that her husband was at some one-star hotel engaged in a torrid affair with the Hong Kong sexting tramp. Even while she was on conversational autopilot with her family, she envisioned herself bursting in on Michael and the tramp in their sordid little room and flinging every available object at them. The lamp. The water pitcher. The cheap plastic coffeemaker.

After Oliver's comment, however, a darker fantasy began to consume her. She was now convinced that Oliver had not made a mistake, and that it was indeed her husband he had spotted in Hong Kong. Michael was too distinctive to be mistaken for anyone else, and Oliver, who was equal parts schemer and diplomat, was obviously sending her a coded message. But who was the little boy? Could Michael have fathered another child? As Astrid turned right onto Dalvey Road, she almost didn't notice the truck parked just a few yards ahead, where a nighttime construction crew stood repairing a tall streetlamp. One of the workers suddenly flung open the truck door, and before Astrid could even gasp, she swerved hard to the right. The windshield shattered, and the last thing she saw before she lost consciousness was the complex root system of an ancient banyan tree.

6

Nick and Rachel

•

When Rachel awoke the morning after the *tan hua* party, Nick was talking softly on the phone in the sitting room of their suite. As her vision slowly came into focus, she lay there silently, looking at Nick and trying to take in everything that had happened in the past twenty-four hours. Last night had been magical, and yet she couldn't help but feel a burgeoning sense of unease. It was as if she had stumbled into a secret chamber and discovered that her boyfriend had been living a double life. The ordinary life they shared as two young college professors in New York bore no resemblance to the life of imperial splendor that Nick seemed to lead here, and Rachel didn't know how to reconcile the two.

Rachel was by no means an ingenue in the realms of wealth. After their early struggles, Kerry Chu had landed on her feet and gotten her real estate license right when Silicon Valley was entering the Internet boom. Rachel's Dickensian childhood was replaced by teenage years growing up in the affluent Bay Area. She went to school at two of the nation's top universities—Stanford and Northwestern—where she encountered the likes of Peik Lin and other trust-fund types. Now she lived in America's most expensive city, where she mingled with the academic elite. None of this, though, prepared Rachel for her first seventy-two hours in Asia. The exhibitions of wealth here were so extreme, it was unlike anything she had ever witnessed, and not for a moment would she have fathomed that her boyfriend could be part of this world.

Nick's lifestyle in New York could be described as modest, if not downright frugal. He rented a cozy alcove studio on Morton Street that didn't seem to contain anything of value aside from his laptop, bike, and stacks of books. He dressed distinctively but casually, and Rachel (having no reference for British bespoke menswear) never realized just how much those rumpled blazers with the Huntsman or Anderson & Sheppard labels cost. Otherwise, the only splurges she had known Nick to make were on overpriced produce at the Union Square Greenmarket and good seats to a concert if some great band came to town.

But now it was all beginning to make sense. There had always been a certain quality to Nick, a quality Rachel was unable to articulate even to herself, but it set him apart from anyone she had ever known. The way he interacted with people. The way he leaned against a wall. He was always comfortable fading into the background, but in that way, he stood out. She had chalked it up to his looks and his for-midable intellect. Someone as blessed as Nick had nothing to prove. But now she knew there was more to it. This was a boy who had grown up in a place like Tyersall Park. Everything else in the world paled by comparison. Rachel longed to know more about his child-hood, about his intimidating grandmother, about the people she had met last night, but she didn't want to start the morning peppering him with a million questions, not when she had the whole summer to discover this new world.

"Hey, Sleeping Beauty," Nick said, finishing his call and noticing that Rachel was awake. He loved the way she looked when she was just waking up, with her long hair so alluringly disheveled, and the sleepy, blissful smile she always gave when she first opened her eyes.

"What time is it?" Rachel asked, stretching her arms against the padded headboard.

"It's about nine thirty," he said, striding over and slipping under the sheets, wrapping his arms around her from behind, and pulling her body against his. "Spooning time!" he declared playfully, kissing the nape of her neck several times. Rachel turned around to face him and began to trace a line from his forehead to his chin.

"Did anyone ever tell you . . ." she began.

". . . that I have the most perfect profile?" Nick said, finishing her question with a laugh. "I only hear that every single day from my beautiful girlfriend, who is clearly deranged. Did you sleep well?"

"Like a log. Last night really took it out of me."

"I'm so proud of you. I know it must have been exhausting having to meet so many people, but you really charmed the socks off everyone."

"Arggh. That's what you say. I don't think that aunt of yours in the Chanel suit felt the same way. Or your uncle Harry—I should have spent a full year studying up on Singapore history, and politics, and art—"

"Come on, no one was expecting you to be a scholar of Southeast Asian affairs. Everyone just enjoyed meeting you."

"Even your grandmother?"

"Definitely! In fact, she's invited us to come stay next week."

"Really?" Rachel said. "We're going to stay at Tyersall Park?"

"Of course! She liked you, and she wants to get to know you better."

Rachel shook her head. "I can't believe I made *any* sort of impression on her."

Nick took a stray lock of hair hanging down her forehead and gently tucked it behind her ear. "First of all, you have to realize that my grandmother is exceedingly shy, and sometimes that comes across as being standoffish, but she is an astute observer of people. Second, you don't *need* to make any sort of impression on her. Just being yourself is quite enough."

Based on what she'd gleaned from everyone else, she wasn't so sure about that, but she decided not to worry about it for the moment. They lay entwined in bed, listening to the sounds of splashing water and children shrieking as they did cannonballs into the pool. Nick suddenly sat up. "You know what we haven't done yet? We haven't ordered from room service. You know that's one of the things I love most about staying in a hotel! Come on, let's see how good their breakfast is."

"You read my mind! Hey, does Colin's family really own this hotel?" Rachel asked, picking up the leather-bound menu by the side of the bed.

"Yes, they do. Did Colin tell you?"

"No, Peik Lin did. I mentioned yesterday that we were going to Colin's wedding, and her whole family almost had a fit."

"Why?" Nick asked, momentarily perplexed.

"They were just very excited, that's all. You didn't tell me that Colin's wedding was going to be *such* a big deal."

"I didn't think it was going to be."

"It's apparently front-page news in every newspaper and magazine in Asia."

"You'd think the newspapers would have better things to write about, with everything that's happening in the world."

"Come on, nothing sells like a big fancy wedding."

Nick sighed, rolling onto his back and staring at the wood-beamed ceiling. "Colin is so stressed. I'm really worried about him. A big wedding is the last thing he wanted, but I guess it was unavoidable. Araminta and her mum just took over, and from what I hear, it's going to be quite a production."

"Well, thankfully I can just sit in the audience," Rachel smirked.

"You can, but I'll be up there in the middle of the three-ring circus. That reminds me, Bernard Tai is organizing the bachelor party, and it seems he's planned quite the extravaganza. We're all meeting at the airport and going to some secret destination. Would you mind terribly if I abandoned you for a couple of days?" Nick asked, stroking her arm lightly.

"Don't worry about me—you do your duty. I'll do some exploring on my own, and Astrid and Peik Lin both offered to show me around this weekend."

"Well, here's another option—Araminta called this morning, and she really *does* want you to come to her bachelorette party this afternoon."

Rachel pursed her lips for a moment. "Don't you think she was only being polite? I mean, we just met. Wouldn't it be kind of weird if I show up to a party of her close friends?"

"Don't look at it like that. Colin's my best friend, and Araminta's a big social butterfly. I think it's going to be a large group of girls, so it will be fun for you. Why don't you call her and talk it over?"

"Okay, but let's order some of those Belgian waffles with maple butter first."

7

Eleanor
·

SHENZHEN

Lorena Lim was talking on her cell phone in Mandarin when Eleanor entered the breakfast room. She sat down across from Lorena, taking in the hazy morning view from this glass aerie. Every time she visited, the city seemed to have doubled in size.[*] But like a gangly teenager in the middle of a growth spurt, many of the hastily erected buildings—barely a decade old—were already being torn down to make way for shinier towers, like this place Lorena had recently bought. It was shiny all right, but sorely lacking in the taste department. Every surface in this breakfast room, for instance, was covered in a particularly putrid shade of orange marble. Why did all these Mainland developers think that more marble was a good thing? As Eleanor tried to imagine the countertops in a neutral Silestone, a maid placed a bowl of steaming fish porridge in front of her. "No, no porridge for me. Can I have some toast with marmalade?"

[*] What was formerly a sleepy fishing village on the Guangdong coast is now a metropolis crammed with tragically gaudy skyscrapers, gargantuan shopping malls, and rampant pollution—in other words, Asia's version of Tijuana. Shenzhen has become a favorite cheap getaway for its richer neighbors. Tourists from Singapore and Hong Kong, in particular, enjoy the thrill of feasting on gourmet delicacies like abalone and shark-fin soup, shopping until midnight at bargain-basement emporiums filled with fake designer goods, or indulging in hedonistic spa treatments—all at a fraction of what they would have to pay back home.

The maid did not appear to understand Eleanor's attempt at Mandarin.

Lorena finished her call, flipped off her phone, and said, "Aiyah, Eleanor, you're in China. At least try some of this delicious porridge."

"Sorry, I can't eat fish first thing in the morning—I'm used to my morning toast," Eleanor insisted.

"Look at you! You complain your son is too Westernized, and yet you can't even enjoy a typical Chinese breakfast."

"I've been married to a Young for too many years," Eleanor said simply.

Lorena shook her head. "I just spoke to my *lobang*.* We are going to meet him in the lobby of the Ritz-Carlton tonight at eight, and he is going to escort us to the person with the inside information about Rachel Chu."

Carol Tai swept into the breakfast room in a luxuriant lilac peignoir. "Who are these people you are taking Eleanor to meet? Are you sure it's safe?"

"Aiyah, don't worry. It will be just fine."

"So what should we do until then? I think Daisy and Nadine want to go to that enormous mall by the train station," Eleanor said.

"You're talking about Luohu. I have an even better place to take all of you first. But it must remain top secret, okay?" Carol whispered conspiratorially.

After the ladies had breakfasted and beautified themselves for the day, Carol took the group to one of the many anonymous office buildings in downtown Shenzhen. A lanky youth standing at the curb of the building, who seemed to be texting away furiously on his cell phone, looked up when he saw the two late-model Mercedes sedans pull up and a bevy of women emerge.

"Are you Jerry?" Carol asked in Mandarin. She squinted at the boy in the scorching noonday sun, noticing that he was playing a computer game on his cell phone.

The young man scrutinized the group of ladies for a minute, making sure they weren't undercover police. Yes, these were obviously a bunch of rich wives and, judging from the way they looked, they were from Singapore. These Singaporeans dressed in their own distinct hodgepodge of styles and wore less jewelry since they were

* Malay slang for "contact."

always so scared of being robbed. Hong Kong women tended to dress alike and sport huge rocks, while the Japanese ladies with their sun visors and fanny packs looked like they were on the way to the golf course. He gave them a big toothy grin and said, "Yes, I'm Jerry! Welcome, ladies, welcome. Follow me, please."

He led them through the smoked-glass doors of the building, down a long corridor, and through a back door. They were suddenly outdoors again on a side street, across from which stood a smaller office tower that looked like it was either still under construction or about to be condemned. The lobby inside was pitch-black, its only source of light coming from the door that Jerry had just propped open. "Be careful, please," he warned, as he led them through the dark space littered with boxes of granite tiles, plywood, and construction equipment.

"Are you sure this is safe, Carol? I wouldn't have worn my new Roger Vivier heels if I knew we were coming to a place like this," Nadine complained nervously. At any moment she felt like she was going to trip over something.

"Trust me, Nadine, nothing is going to happen. You will be thanking me in a minute," Carol replied calmly.

A doorway finally led to a dimly lit elevator vestibule, and Jerry jabbed repeatedly at the decayed elevator call button. Finally the service elevator arrived. The ladies all crammed in, cowering together to avoid accidentally brushing against the dusty walls. On the seventeenth floor, the elevator opened to reveal a bright, fluorescent-lit vestibule. There were two steel double doors on either end of the space, and Eleanor couldn't help but notice two sets of closed-circuit cameras installed on the ceiling. A very skinny girl in her early twenties emerged from one of the doors. "Hello, hello," she said in English, nodding at the ladies. She inspected them briefly, and then said in a surprisingly stern, staccato tone, "Please turn off phone, no camera allowed." She moved toward an intercom, which she spoke into in a rapid-fire dialect that none of them could discern, and a set of secure locks clicked open loudly.

The ladies walked through the door and abruptly found themselves in a sumptuously designed boutique. The floor was polished pink marble, the walls upholstered in pale pink moiré fabric, and from where they stood, they could peer down the corridor into some of the adjacent showrooms. Each room was devoted to a different luxury brand, with floor-to-ceiling display cabinets crammed full of the most current handbags and accessories. The designer treasures seemed to glow under the carefully positioned halogen spotlights, and well-attired shoppers filled each showroom, eagerly perusing the merchandise.

"This place is known for the very best fakes," Carol declared.

"Holy Jesus!" Nadine shrieked excitedly, while Carol glared at her for using the Lord's name in vain.

"Italy this side, French the other side. What you want?" the skinny girl asked.

"Do you have any handbags by Goyard?" Lorena asked.

"Hiyah! Yes, yes, everybody want Goya right now. We have best Goya," she said, leading Lorena into one of the showrooms. Behind the counter were rows and rows of the latest must-have Goyard tote bag in every color imaginable, and a Swiss couple stood in the middle of the room testing the wheels on one of the Goyard carry-on suitcases.

Daisy whispered into Eleanor's ear, "See, the only people shopping here are tourists like us. These days, the Mainlanders only want the real thing."

"Well, for once I agree with the Mainlanders. I've never understood why anyone would want a fake designer handbag. What is the point of pretending to carry one if you can't afford it?" Eleanor sniffed.

"Aiyah, Eleanor, if you or I carried one of these, who would ever think it was fake?" Carol said. "Everyone knows we can afford the real thing."

"Well, these are *absolutely identical* to the real thing. Not even the people who work at Goyard would be able to tell," Lorena said, shaking her head in disbelief. "Just look at the stitching, the embossing, the label."

"They look so real because they practically *are* real, Lorena," Carol explained. "These are what they call 'real fakes.' The factories in China are commissioned by all the luxury brands to manufacture the leather. Say the company places an order for ten thousand units, but they actually make twelve thousand units. Then they can sell the remaining two thousand off the books on the black market as 'fakes,' even though they are made with the exact same material as the real ones."

"Hey ladies, *guei doh say, ah!** These aren't bargains at all," Daisy warned, scrutinizing one of the price tags.

"It's still a bargain. This bag is forty-five hundred in Singapore. Here it's six hundred, and it looks exactly the same," Lorena said, feeling the distinctive texture of the bag.

"My God, I want one in every color!" Nadine squealed. "I saw this handbag on *British Tatler*'s 'It List' last month!"

"I'm sure Francesca would want a few of these bags too," Lorena said.

"No, no, I dare not buy anything for that fussy daughter of mine—Francesca will only carry originals, and they have to be from *next* season," Nadine replied.

Eleanor wandered into the next room, which was filled with racks and racks of clothing. She scrutinized a fake Chanel suit, shaking her head in disapproval at the gold buttons with interlocking *C*s running up the sleeves of the jacket. She had always felt that wearing a stiffly tailored designer dress of this sort, as women of her age and social milieu might be inclined to do, only served to reinforce one's age. Eleanor's style was a deliberate one—she preferred the more youthful, trendy clothes that she found in the boutiques of Hong Kong, Paris, or wherever she happened to be traveling, as this achieved three goals: she always wore something distinctive that no one else in Singapore had, she spent far less money on clothes than the rest of her friends, and she looked at least a decade younger than her real age. She tucked the sleeve of the Chanel suit back into its rack properly and walked into what appeared to be a room devoted to Hermès, finding herself face-to-face with none other than Jacqueline Ling. *Speak of age-defying, this one had made some pact with the devil.*

"What are you doing here?" Eleanor asked in surprise. Jacqueline was one of her least favorite people, but even she would never have imagined that Jacqueline might carry a designer fake.

"I just flew in this morning and a friend insisted that I come here and pick up one of these ostrich-leather purses for her," Jacqueline said, a little flustered to be seen by Eleanor at a place like this. "How long have you been here? No wonder I didn't see you at Tyersall Park last night."

"I'm here for a spa weekend with some girlfriends. So, you were

---

* Cantonese for "so expensive I could die."

at my mother-in-law's for Friday-night dinner?" Eleanor asked, not entirely surprised. Jacqueline was always sucking up to Nicky's grandmother whenever she visited Singapore.

"Yes, Su Yi decided to have a little party at the last minute because her *tan huas* were in bloom. She had quite a few people over. I saw your Nicky . . . and I met *the girl.*"

"Well, what was she like?" Eleanor asked impatiently.

"Oh, you haven't met her yet?" Jacqueline thought that Eleanor would surely want to assess the interloper as early as possible. "You know, she's typical ABC. Overconfident and overfamiliar. I would never have thought that Nicky would go for someone like that."

"They are just dating, *lah*," Eleanor said a little defensively.

"I wouldn't be so sure of that if I were you. This girl is already best friends with Astrid and Oliver, and you should have seen the way she was staring openmouthed at everything around the house," Jacqueline said, even though she had witnessed nothing of the sort.

Eleanor was taken aback by Jacqueline's comment, but it soon dawned on her that on this score at least, their interests were uniquely aligned. "How is your Mandy doing these days? I hear she's dating some Jewish banker twice her age."

"Oh, you know that's *really* just idle gossip," Jacqueline replied quickly. "The press over there is so fascinated by her, and they try to link her with all the eligible men in New York. Anyway, you can ask Amanda yourself—she'll be back for the Khoo wedding."

Eleanor looked surprised. Araminta Lee and Amanda Ling were archrivals, and two months ago, Amanda had caused something of a mini-scandal when she told the *Straits Times* that "she didn't understand what all the fuss was over the Khoo wedding—she was far too busy to come rushing back to Singapore for every social climber's wedding."*

At that moment, Carol and Nadine entered the Hermès room. Nadine recognized Jacqueline immediately, having seen her from afar many years ago at a gala movie premiere. Here was her chance to get an introduction. "Look at you, Elle, always running into people you know everywhere you go," she said cheerily.

Carol, who was much more interested in the fake Hermès Kelly bags, smiled at them from across the room but carried on shopping,

---

* Yes, the Khoos and the Lings are related by marriage as well.

while Nadine made a beeline for the ladies. Jacqueline glanced at the woman coming toward her, taken aback by the sheer volume of makeup she was wearing. *Oh my God, this was that awful Shaw woman whose pictures were always in the society pages, preening away with her equally vulgar daughter. And Carol Tai was the wife of that scoundrel billionaire. Of course Eleanor would be hanging around with* this *crowd.*

"Jacqueline, so nice to meet you," Nadine said effusively, extending her hand.

"Well, I must be off," Jacqueline said to Eleanor, not making eye contact with Nadine and stepping toward the exit nimbly before the woman could claim a proper introduction.

When Jacqueline had left the room, Nadine began to gush. "You never told me you knew Jacqueline Ling! Wow, she still looks stunning! How old must she be by now? Do you think she had a facelift?"

"*Alamak*, don't ask me such things, Nadine! How would I know?" Eleanor said, feeling irritated.

"You seemed to know her quite well."

"I've known Jacqueline for years. I even made a trip to Hong Kong with her a long time ago, where she couldn't stop making a spectacle of herself, and all these idiotic men kept following us everywhere, proclaiming their love for her. It was a nightmare."

Nadine wanted to keep talking about Jacqueline, but Eleanor's mind was already elsewhere. So Amanda had changed her mind and was coming home for Colin's wedding after all. How very interesting. As much as she detested Jacqueline, she had to admit that Amanda would be a superb match for Nicky. The stars were beginning to align, and she could hardly wait for whatever lay in store with Lorena's secret informer tonight.

8

Rachel

•

SINGAPORE

The first hint that Araminta's bachelorette party was going to be no ordinary affair occurred when Rachel's taxi dropped her off at the JetQuay CIP Terminal, which served the private-jet crowd. The second hint came when Rachel walked into the sleek lounge and came face-to-face with twenty girls who looked as if they had spent the last four hours in hair and makeup. Rachel thought that her outfit—a seafoam blue tunic top paired with a white denim skirt—was rather cute, but now it seemed a little shabby compared to the girls in their fresh-off-the-catwalk ensembles. Araminta was nowhere to be seen, so Rachel just stood around smiling at everyone as snippets of conversation drifted her way.

"I searched the world for that handbag, and even L'Eclaireur in Paris couldn't get it for me . . ."

"It's a three-bedroom in that old complex on Thompson Road. I have a gut feeling it's going to go en bloc and I'll triple my money . . ."

"OMG, I found the best new place for chili crab, you won't believe where . . ."

"I like the Lanesborough's suites more than Claridge's, but really, the Calthorpe is where you want to be . . ."

"Nonsense, lah! No Signboard Seafood still has the best chili crab . . ."

"This isn't cashmere, you know. It's baby vicuña . . ."

"Did you hear Swee Lin sold her Four Seasons flat for seven-point-five mil? A young Mainland Chinese couple, paid in cash . . ."

Yep, this was definitely not her crowd. Suddenly an overly tan girl with fake blond hair extensions came into the lounge, shouting, "Araminta just pulled up!" The room got quiet as everyone craned their necks toward the sliding glass door. Rachel hardly recognized the girl who entered. In place of the schoolgirl in pajama pants of a few nights ago was a woman in a matte-gold jumpsuit with gold stiletto boots, her wavy dark brown hair piled into a loose beehive. With a light dusting of expertly applied makeup, her girlish features were transformed into that of a supermodel. "Rachel, I'm so glad you made it!" Araminta said excitedly, giving her a big hug. "Come with me," she said, taking Rachel by the hand and leading her to the center of the room.

"Hello, everyone! First things first—I want to introduce all of you to my fabulous new friend Rachel Chu. She's visiting from New York, as the guest of Colin's best man, Nicholas Young. Please give her a very warm welcome." All eyes were on Rachel, who flushed a little and could do nothing but smile politely at the assembled crowd that was now dissecting every inch of her. Araminta continued. "You are all my dearest friends, so I wanted to give you a special treat." She paused for effect. "Today we're heading to my mum's private island resort in eastern Indonesia!" There were gasps of astonishment from the crowd. "We're going to dance on the beach tonight, feast on delish low-calorie cuisine, and pamper ourselves silly with spa treatments all weekend! Come on, girls, let's get this party started!"

Before Rachel could fully process what Araminta had said, they were ushered on board a customized Boeing 737-700, where she found herself in a dramatically chic space with streamlined white saddle-stitched leather sofas and glistening shagreen console tables.

"Araminta, this is just too much! Is this your dad's new plane?" one of the girls asked incredulously.

"Actually it's my mum's. Bought from some oligarch in Moscow who needed to lower his profile and go into hiding, from what I hear."

"Well, let's hope no one blows this plane up by mistake, then," the girl joked.

"No, no, we had it repainted. It used to be cobalt blue, and of course my mom had to do her Zen makeover thing. She had it repainted three times before she was satisfied with the right shade of glacier white."

Rachel wandered into the next cabin and encountered two girls chattering animatedly.

"Told you it was her!"

"She's not at all what I was expecting. I mean, her family is supposed to be one of the richest in Taiwan, and she shows up looking like some—"

Upon noticing Rachel, the girls abruptly went silent and smiled sheepishly at her before fleeing down the corridor. Rachel hadn't paid any attention to their exchange—she was far too distracted by the dove-gray leather banquettes and handsome polished-nickel reading lamps extending down from the ceiling. One wall was lined with a bank of flat-screen televisions, while the other consisted of silver ladder racks hung with the latest fashion magazines.

Araminta entered the cabin, leading some girls on a tour. "Here is the library-slash-media room. Don't you love how cozy it is? Now let me show you my favorite space on the plane, the yoga studio!" Rachel followed the group into the next room, in utter disbelief that there were people rich enough to install a state-of-the-art Ayurvedic yoga studio with inlaid pebble walls and heated pine floors in their private jet.

A group of girls came in squealing with laughter. "*Alamak*, Francesca has already cornered that hunky Italian steward and commandeered the master bedroom!" the overly bronzed girl exclaimed in her singsongy accent.

Araminta frowned in displeasure. "Wandi, tell her the bedroom is off-limits, and so is Gianluca."

"Maybe we should all get inducted into the mile-high club with these Italian stallions," one of the giggly girls said.

"Who needs to be inducted? I've been a member since I was thirteen," Wandi boasted, tossing back her blond-streaked hair.

Rachel, at a loss for words, decided to buckle herself into the nearest armchair and prepare for takeoff. The demure-looking girl sitting beside her smiled. "You'll get used to Wandi. She's a Meggaharto, you know. I don't think you need me to tell you how that family is. By the way, I'm Parker Yeo. I know your cousin Vivian!" she said.

"I'm sorry, but I don't have a cousin named Vivian," Rachel replied in amusement.

"Aren't you Rachel Chu?"

"Yes."

"Isn't your cousin Vivian Chu? Doesn't your family own Taipei Plastics?"

"Afraid not," Rachel said, trying not to roll her eyes. "My family is originally from China."

"Oh sorry, my mistake. So what does your family do?"

"Um, my mother is a real estate agent in the Palo Alto area. Who are these Taipei Plastics people everyone keeps talking about?"

Parker simply smirked. "I'll tell you, but excuse me for just one moment." She unbuckled her seat belt and made a beeline for the back cabin. It was the last time Rachel would see her during the entire flight.

"Girls, I have the scoop of all scoops!" Parker burst in on the girls crowded into the master cabin. "I was just sitting next to that Rachel Chu girl, and guess what? She isn't related to the Taipei Chus! She hasn't even *heard* of them!"

Francesca Shaw, lounging in the middle of the bed, gave Parker a withering look. "Is that all? I could have told you that months ago. My mother is best friends with Nicky Young's mother, and I know enough about Rachel Chu to sink a ship."

"Come on, *lah*—give us all the dirt!" Wandi pleaded, bouncing up and down on the bed in anticipation.

After a dramatic landing on a perilously short runway, Rachel found herself on a sleek white catamaran, the salty ocean breeze whipping through her hair as they sped toward one of the more remote islands. The water was an almost blinding shade of turquoise, interrupted by tiny islands dropped onto the calm surface here and there like dollops of fresh cream. Soon the catamaran made a sharp turn toward one of the bigger islands, and as they approached, a striking series of wooden buildings with undulating thatched canopies came into view.

This was the paradise dreamed up by Araminta's hotelier mother, Annabel Lee, who spared no expense in creating the ultimate retreat according to her exacting vision of what chic, modern luxury should be. The island, actually just a quarter-mile-long spit of coral, consisted of thirty villas built on stilts that extended out over the shallow coral reefs. As the boat pulled up to the jetty, a line of waiters in saffron-colored uniforms stood stiffly at attention holding Lucite trays of mojitos.

Araminta was helped out of the boat first, and when all the girls were assembled on the dock with cocktails in hand, she announced, "Welcome to Samsara! In Sanskrit, the word means 'to flow on'—to pass through states of existence. My mum wanted to create a special place where you could experience rebirth, where you could pass through different levels of bliss. So this island is ours, and I hope you will find your bliss with me this weekend. But first, I've arranged a shopping spree at the resort's boutique! Girls, as a gift from my mum, each of you can pick out five new outfits. And to make this just a little more fun, and also because I don't want to miss cocktails at sunset, we're going to make this a challenge. I'm giving you only twenty minutes to shop. Grab whatever you can, because in twenty minutes, the boutique closes!" The girls shrieked in excitement and began a mad dash down the jetty.

With its soothing mother-of-pearl varnished walls, Javanese teak floors, and windows overlooking a lagoon, the Samsara Collection was normally a haven of civilized tranquillity. Today it was like Pamplona during the running of the bulls as the girls charged in and ransacked the place in search of outfits that would outdo one another. A fashionista tug-of-war broke out as they began clawing over the most coveted pieces.

"Lauren, let go of this Collette Dinnigan skirt before you tear it to pieces!"

"Wandi, you bitch, I saw that Tomas Maier top first and you'll never fit into it with your new boobs!"

"Parker, put down those Pierre Hardy flats or I'll poke your eyes out with these Nicholas Kirkwood stilettos!"

Araminta perched on a counter savoring the scene, adding more tension to her little game by calling out the remaining time at one-minute intervals. Rachel tried to steer clear of the rampage, taking refuge at a rack overlooked by the rest of the girls, probably because there weren't any quickly recognizable labels on any of the garments. Francesca stood at a nearby rack picking through the clothes as if she was surveying medical photos of genital deformities. "This is impossible. Who are all these no-name designers?" she called out to Araminta.

"What do you mean 'no-name'? Alexis Mabille, Thakoon, Isabel Marant—my mum personally selects the hottest designers for this boutique," Araminta said defensively.

Francesca tossed back her long, wavy black locks and sniffed. "You know I *only* wear six designers: Chanel, Dior, Valentino, Etro, my dear friend Stella McCartney, and Brunello Cucinelli for country weekends. I wish you'd told me we were coming here, Araminta. I could have brought my latest Chanel resort wear—I bought this season's entire collection at Carol Tai's Christian Helpers fashion benefit."

"Well, I guess you'll just have to slum it for two nights without your Chanel," Araminta retorted. She gave Rachel a conspiratorial wink and whispered, "When I first met Francesca in Sunday school, she had a plumpish round face and was wearing hand-me-downs. Her grandpa was a famous miser, and the whole family lived crammed together in an old shop house on Emerald Hill."

"That's hard to picture," Rachel said, glancing over at Francesca's perfectly executed makeup and ruffled emerald-green wrap dress.

"Well, her grandpa had a massive stroke and went into a coma, and her parents finally got control of all the money. Almost overnight, Francesca got herself new cheekbones and a wardrobe from Paris—you won't believe how fast she and her mother transformed themselves. Speaking of fast, the minutes are running out, Rachel—you should be shopping!"

Even though Araminta had invited everyone to pick out five pieces, Rachel didn't feel comfortable taking advantage of her generosity. She picked out a cute white linen blouse with tiny ruffles along the sleeves and came across a couple of summery cocktail dresses made out of the lightest silk batiste, which reminded her of the simple shift dresses Jacqueline Kennedy wore in the sixties.

As Rachel was trying on the white blouse in the dressing room, she overheard two girls in the next dressing room chatting away.

"*Did you see what she was wearing? Where did she get that cheap-looking tunic top—Mango?*"

"*How can you expect her to have any style? Think she gets it from reading American* Vogue? *Hahaha.*"

"*Actually, Francesca says that she's not even ABC—she was born in Mainland China!*"

"*I knew it! She's got that same desperate look that all my servants have.*"

"Well here's a chance for her to get some decent clothes at last!"

"Just you watch, with all that Young money she's going to upgrade pretty damn quick!"

"We'll see—all the money in the world can't buy you taste if you weren't born with it."

Rachel realized with a start that the girls were talking about her. Shaken, she rushed out of the dressing room, almost colliding into Araminta.

"Are you okay?" Araminta asked.

Rachel quickly recovered. "Yes, yes, just trying not to get caught up in the panic, that's all."

"It's the panic that makes it so much fun! Let's see what you found," Araminta said excitedly. "Ooh, you have a great eye! These are done by a Javanese designer who hand-paints all of the dresses."

"They're so lovely. Let me pay for these—I can't possibly accept your mom's generosity. I mean, she doesn't even know me," Rachel said.

"Nonsense! They are yours. And my mum is *so* looking forward to meeting you."

"Well, I have to hand it to her—she's created quite a shop. Everything is so unique, it reminds me of the way Nick's cousin dresses."

"Ah, Astrid Leong! '*The Goddess*,' as we used to call her."

"Really?" Rachel laughed.

"Yes. All of us absolutely worshipped her when we were schoolgirls—she always looked so fabulous, so effortlessly chic."

"She *did* look amazing last night," Rachel mused.

"Oh, you saw her last night? Tell me exactly what she was wearing," Araminta asked eagerly.

"She had on this white sleeveless top with the most delicately embroidered lace panels I've ever seen, and a pair of skinny Audrey Hepburn-esque gray silk pants."

"Designed by . . . ?" Araminta prodded.

"I have no idea. But oh, what really stood out were these show-stopping earrings she had on—they sort of looked like Navajo dream catchers, except that they were made entirely of precious gems."

"How fabulous! I wish I knew who designed *those*," Araminta said intently.

Rachel smiled, as a cute pair of sandals at the bottom of a Balinese cupboard suddenly caught her eye. Perfect for the beach, she thought, walking over to take a better look. They were slightly too big, so Rachel returned to her section, only to discover that two of her outfits—the white blouse and one of the hand-painted silk dresses—had vanished. "Hey, what happened to my—" she began to ask.

"Time's up, girls! The boutique is now closed!" Araminta declared.

Relieved that the shopping spree was finally over, Rachel went in search of her room. Her card read "Villa No. 14," so she followed the signs down the central jetty that wound into the middle of the coral reef. The villa was an ornate wood-crafted bungalow with pale coral walls and airy white furnishings. At the back, a set of wooden screen doors opened onto a deck with steps leading straight into the sea.

Rachel sat on the edge of the steps and dipped her toes into the water. It was perfectly cool and so shallow she could sink her feet into the pillowy white sand. She could hardly believe where she was. How much must this bungalow cost per night? She always wondered if she would be lucky enough to visit a resort like this once in her life—for her honeymoon, perhaps—but never did she expect to find herself here for a bachelorette party. She suddenly missed Nick, and wished he could be here to share this private paradise with her. It was because of him that she had suddenly been thrust into this jet-set lifestyle, and she wondered where he could be at this very moment. If the girls went to an island resort in the Indian Ocean, where in the world did the boys go?

9

Nick
•

MACAU

"Please tell me we're not riding in one of *those*," Mehmet Sabançi grimaced to Nick as they disembarked from the plane and saw the fleet of matching white stretch Rolls-Royce Phantoms awaiting them.

"Oh, this is typical Bernard," Nick smiled, wondering what Mehmet, a classics scholar who hailed from one of Istanbul's most patrician families, made of the sight of Bernard Tai emerging from a limo in a mint-green chalk-striped blazer, orange paisley ascot, and yellow suede loafers. The only son of *Dato'* Tai Toh Lui, Bernard was famed for his "brave sartorial statements" (as *Singapore Tattle* so diplomatically put it) and for being Asia's biggest bon vivant, perpetually hosting wild parties at whatever louche jet-set resort was in fashion that year—always with the hippest DJs, the chillest drinks, the hottest babes, and, many whispered, the best drugs. "Niggas in Macauuuuw!" Bernard exulted, raising his arms rapper style.

"B. Tai! I can't believe you made us fly in this old sardine can! Your G5 had a time-to-climb I could grow a beard in! We should have taken my family's Falcon 7X," Evan Fung (of the Fung Electronics Fungs) complained.

"My dad's waiting for the G650 to launch into service, and then you can kiss my ass, Fungus!" Bernard retorted.

Roderick Liang (of the Liang Finance Group Liangs) chimed

in, "I'm a Bombardier man myself. Our Global 6000 has such a big cabin, you can do backflips down the aisle."

"Can you *ah guahs** stop comparing the size of your planes and let's hit the casinos, please?" Johnny Pang (his mother is an Aw, of *those* Aws) cut in.

"Well guys, hold on to your balls, because I have a very special treat arranged for all of us!" Bernard declared.

Nick climbed wearily into one of the tanklike cars, hoping that Colin's bachelor weekend would proceed without incident. Colin had been on edge all week, and heading to the gambling capital of the world with a group of testosterone-and-whiskey-fueled guys was a recipe for disaster.

"This wasn't the Oxford reunion I was expecting," Mehmet said to Nick in a low voice.

"Well, aside from his cousin Lionel and the two of us, I don't think Colin knows anyone here either," Nick remarked wryly, glancing at some of the other passengers. The lineup of Beijing princelings and Taiwanese trust-fund brats was definitely more Bernard's crowd.

As the convoy of Rolls-Royces sped along the coastal highway that skirted the island, gigantic billboards flashing the names of casinos could be seen from miles away. Soon the gaming resorts came into view like small mountains—behemoth blocks of glass and concrete that pulsated with lurid colors in the midafternoon haze. "It's just like Vegas, except with an ocean view," Mehmet remarked in awe.

"Vegas is the kiddie pool. This is where the real high rollers come to play," Evan remarked.[†]

As the Rolls squeezed through the narrow lanes of Felicidade in Macau's old town, Nick admired the colorful rows of nineteenth-century Portuguese shop houses, thinking that this could be a nice place to bring Rachel after Colin's wedding. The limos finally pulled up in front of a row of dingy shops on rua de Alfandega. Bernard led the group into what appeared to be an old Chinese apothecary with scratched glass cabinets selling ginseng root, edible bird nests,

---

* The Singlish equivalent of "faggot" or "fairy" (Hokkien).

† With 1.5 billion eager gamblers on the Mainland, the annual gambling revenue of Macau exceeds $20 billion—that's three times more than what Las Vegas takes in every year. (Celine Dion, where are you?)

dried shark fins, fake rhino tusks, and all manner of herbal curiosities. A few elderly ladies sat clustered in front of a small television set, watching a Cantonese soap opera, while a rail-thin Chinese man in a faded Hawaiian shirt leaned against the back counter eyeing the group with a bored look.

Bernard looked at the man and asked brashly, "I'm here to buy ginseng royal jelly."

"What type you want?" the fellow said disinterestedly.

"Prince of Peace."

"What size jar?"

"Sixty-nine ounces."

"Let me see if we have some. Follow me," the man said, his voice suddenly shifting into a rather unexpected Aussie accent. The group followed him toward the back of the shop and through a dim storeroom lined from floor to ceiling with neatly stacked rows of cardboard cartons. Every carton was stamped "China Ginseng for Export Only." The man pushed lightly against a stack of wide boxes in the corner, and the whole section seemed to collapse backward effortlessly, revealing a long passageway glowing with cobalt-blue LED lights. "Straight through here," he said. As the guys wandered down the passageway, the muffled roar became louder and louder, and at the end of the hall, smoked-glass doors parted automatically to reveal an astonishing sight.

The space, which resembled a sort of indoor gymnasium with bleachers on both sides of a sunken pit, was packed standing room only with a boisterous cheering crowd. Though they could not see past the audience, they could hear the blood-curdling growls of dogs tearing into each other's flesh.

"Welcome to the greatest dogfighting arena in the world!" Bernard proudly announced. "They only use Presa Canario mastiffs here—they are a hundred times more vicious than pit bulls. This is going to be damn *shiok*,* man!"

"Where do we place the bets?" Johnny asked excitedly.

"Er . . . isn't this illegal?" Lionel asked, peering nervously at the main fighting cage. Nick could tell Lionel wanted to look away but found himself curiously drawn to the scene of two huge dogs, all

* Malay slang term used to denote an experience that is amazing or something (usually food) that's out of this world.

muscle and sinew and fangs, rolling viciously in a pit smeared with their own blood.

"Of course it's illegal!" Bernard answered.

"I don't know about this, Bernard. Colin and I cannot risk being caught at some illegal dogfight right before the wedding," Lionel continued.

"You are *such* a typical Singaporean! So damn scared of everything! Don't be so fucking *boring*," Bernard said contemptuously.

"That's not the point, Bernard. This is just plain cruel," Nick interjected.

"*Alamak*, are you a member of Greenpeace? You're witnessing a great sporting tradition! These dogs have been bred for centuries in the Canary Islands to do nothing but fight," Bernard huffed, squinting his eyes.

The chanting of the crowd became deafening as the match reached its grisly climax. Both dogs had clamped tightly onto each other's throats, locked in a Sisyphean chokehold, and Nick could see that the skin around the brown dog's throat was half torn off, flapping against the snout of the other dog. "Well I've seen enough," he grimaced, turning his back on the fight.

"Come on, *lah*. This is a BACHELOR PARTY! Don't shit on my fun, Nickyboy," Bernard shouted over the chanting. One of the dogs gave a piercing shriek as the other mastiff snapped into the soft of its belly.

"There's nothing fun about this," Mehmet said firmly, nauseated by the sight of the fresh warm blood squirting everywhere.

"Ay, *bhai singh*,* isn't goat-fucking a tradition in your country? Don't you all think goat pussy is the closest thing to real vag?" Bernard countered.

Nick's jaw tightened, but Mehmet just laughed. "You sound like you're speaking from experience."

Bernard flared his nostrils, trying to figure out whether he should feel insulted.

"Bernard, why don't you stay? Those who don't want to be here can head to the hotel first, and we can all meet up later," Colin suggested, trying to play the diplomat.

---

* Racial slur for a Sikh person, used in this instance to refer to anyone of Middle Eastern origins.

"Suits me fine."

"Okay, then, I'll take the group to the hotel and we'll meet up at—"

"*Wah lan!** I organized this specially for you, and *you're* not staying?" Bernard sounded frustrated.

"Er . . . to be honest, I don't care for this either," Colin said, trying to look apologetic.

Bernard paused for a moment, supremely conflicted. He wanted to enjoy the dogfights, but at the same time he wanted everyone to witness the profuse ass-kissing he would receive from hotel management the minute they pulled up to the resort.

"'Kay *lah*, it's your party," Bernard muttered sulkily.

The sumptuous lobby of the Wynn Macau boasted a huge gilt mural on the ceiling that featured animals of the Chinese zodiac, and at least half the assembled group were relieved to be someplace where the animals were covered in twenty-two-carat gold instead of blood. At the reception desk, Bernard was having one of the classic fits he was renowned for the world over.

"What the fuck! I'm a VVIP here, and I booked the most expensive suite in this entire hotel *almost a week ago.* How can it not be ready?" Bernard raged to the manager.

"I do apologize, Mr. Tai. Checkout time for the Presidential Penthouse is four o'clock, so the previous guests have not yet vacated the room. But as soon as they do, we'll have the suite serviced and turned around for you in no time at all," the manager said.

"Who are these bastards? I'll bet they're Hongkies! Those *ya ya*† Hongkies always think they own the world!"

The manager never broke his smile throughout Bernard's tirade. He didn't want to do anything to jeopardize the business of *Dato'* Tai Toh Lui's son—the boy was such a bloody brilliant loser at the baccarat tables. "Some of the grand salon suites reserved for your party are ready. Please allow me to escort you there with a few bottles of your favorite Cristal."

---

* Hokkien for "oh penis." This extremely popular and versatile term can be used—depending on the tone—to convey anything from "oh wow" to "oh fuck."

† Singlish slang of Javanese origin meaning "arrogant," "show-off."

"I'm not going to dirty my Tod's setting foot in one of those rat holes! I want my duplex or nothing," Bernard said petulantly.

"Bernard, why don't we visit the casino first?" Colin calmly suggested. "It's what we would have done anyway."

"I'll go to the casino, but you guys need to give us the best private VVIP gambling salon right now," Bernard demanded of the manager.

"Of course, of course. We *always* have our most exclusive gaming salon available to you, Mr. Tai," the manager said deftly.

Just then, Alistair Cheng wandered into the lobby, looking slightly disheveled.

"Alistair, so glad you found us!" Colin greeted him heartily.

"Told you it wouldn't be a problem. Hong Kong's just thirty minutes away by hydrofoil, and I know Macau like the back of my hand—I used to skip school and come here all the time with my classmates," Alistair said. He caught sight of Nick and went over to give him a hug.

"Aiyoh, how sweet. Is this your boyfriend, Nickyboy?" Bernard said mockingly.

"Alistair's my cousin," Nick replied.

"So you guys played with each other's cocks while growing up," Bernard taunted, laughing at his own joke.

Nick ignored him, wondering how it was possible that Bernard hadn't changed one bit since they were in primary school. He turned back to his cousin and said, "Hey, I thought you were coming to visit me in New York this spring. What happened?"

"A girl happened, Nick."

"Really? Who's the lucky girl?"

"Her name's Kitty. She's an amazingly talented actress from Taiwan. You'll meet her next week—I'm bringing her to Colin's wedding."

"Wow, I can't wait to meet the girl who finally stole the heartbreaker's heart," Nick teased. Alistair was just twenty-six, but his baby-face good looks and laid-back persona had already made him renowned for leaving a trail of broken hearts all over the Pacific Rim. (Aside from ex-girlfriends in Hong Kong, Singapore, Thailand, Taipei, Shanghai, and one summer fling in Vancouver, a diplomat's daughter at his college in Sydney famously became so obsessed that she attempted to overdose on Benadryl just to get his attention.)

"Hey, I heard you brought *your* girlfriend to Singapore too," Alistair said.

"Word travels fast, doesn't it?"

"My mum heard it from Radio One Asia."

"You know, I'm beginning to suspect that Cassandra has me under surveillance," Nick said wryly.

The group entered the sprawling casino where the gaming tables seemed to glow with a peachy, golden light. Colin crossed the opulent sea anemone–patterned carpet and approached the Texas hold 'em table. "Colin, the VIP salons are this way," Bernard said, trying to steer Colin toward the sumptuous salons reserved for high rollers.

"But it's more fun to play five-dollar poker," Colin argued.

"No, no, we're moguls, man! I created that whole scene with the manager just so we could score the best VIP room. Why would you want to mix with all these smelly Mainlanders out here?" Bernard said.

"Let me just play a couple of rounds here and then we'll go to the VIP room, okay?" Colin pleaded.

"I'll join you, Colin," Alistair said, sliding into a seat.

Bernard smiled tightly, looking like a rabid Boston terrier. "Well I'm going to our VIP room. I can't play at these kiddie tables—I only get hard when I'm betting at least thirty thousand per hand," he said with a sniff. "Who's with me?" Most of Bernard's entourage peeled off with him, with the exception of Nick, Mehmet, and Lionel. Colin's face clouded over.

Nick took the other seat beside Colin. "I have to warn you guys, two years in New York has made me quite a cardsharp. Prepare to be schooled by the master . . . Colin, remind me what game this is?" he said, trying to lighten the mood. As the dealer began to expertly flick the cards across the table, Nick quietly fumed. Bernard had always been a troublemaker. Why should things be any different this weekend?

SINGAPORE, 1986

It all happened so fast, the next thing Nick remembered was the feeling of cold damp mud against his neck and a strange face looking down on him. Dark skin, freckles, a shock of brownish-black hair.

"Are you okay?" the dark boy asked.

"I think so," Nick said, his vision coming back into focus. His entire back was soaked in muddy water from being pushed into the ditch. He got up slowly and looked around to see Bernard leering at him, red-faced, arms crossed like an angry old man.

"I'm going to tell your mum that you hit me!" Bernard shouted at the boy.

"And I'm going to tell your mum that you're a bully. Plus, I didn't hit you—I just pushed you away," the boy replied.

"It was none of your bloody business! I'm trying to teach this little dick here a lesson!" Bernard seethed.

"I saw the way you shoved him into the ditch. You could have really hurt him. Why don't you pick on someone your own size?" the boy replied calmly, not the least intimidated by Bernard.

At that point, a metallic-gold Mercedes limousine pulled up to the driveway outside the school. Bernard glanced at the car briefly, and then turned back to Nick. "This isn't over. Get ready for part two tomorrow—I'm really going to *hun tum** you!" He got into the backseat of the car, slammed the door, and was driven away.

The boy who had come to Nick's rescue looked at him and said, "You okay? Your elbow's bleeding."

Nick looked down and noticed the bloody scrape on his right elbow. He wasn't sure what to do about it. At any moment, one of his parents could arrive to pick him up, and if it happened to be his mother, he knew she would get all *gan cheong*† if she saw him bleeding like this. The boy took a white, perfectly folded handkerchief out of his pocket and handed it to Nick. "Here, use this," he said.

Nick took the handkerchief from his rescuer and held it to his elbow. He had seen this boy around. Colin Khoo. He had transferred in this semester, and he was hard to miss, with his deep-caramel skin and wavy hair with the strange light brown streak in the front. They weren't in the same class, but Nick had noticed during PE that the boy had swim practice alone with Coach Lee.

"What did you do to piss off Bernard so much?" Colin asked.

Nick had never heard someone use the term "piss off" before, but he knew what it meant. "I caught him trying to cheat off my

---

* Malay slang meaning to pummel, beat up, or basically kick someone's ass.

† Cantonese for "panicky," "anxious."

maths test, so I told Miss Ng. He got in trouble and was sent to Vice Principal Chia's office, so now he wants to pick a fight."

"Bernard tries to pick a fight with everyone," Colin said.

"Are you good friends with him?" Nick asked carefully.

"Not really. His father does business with my family, so I'm told I have to be nice to him," Colin said. "But to tell you the truth, I can't really stand him."

Nick smiled. "Whew! For a second I thought Bernard actually had one friend!"

Colin laughed.

"Is it true you're from America?" Nick asked.

"I was born here, but I moved to Los Angeles when I was two."

"What's LA like? Did you live in Hollywood?" Nick asked. He had never met anyone his age who had lived in America.

"Not Hollywood. But we weren't very far—we lived in Bel Air."

"I'd like to visit Universal Studios. Did you ever see famous movie stars?"

"All the time. It's no big deal when you live there." Colin looked at Nick, as if assessing him for a moment, before continuing. "I'm going to tell you something, but first you have to swear not to tell anyone."

"Okay. Sure," Nick replied earnestly.

"Say, 'I swear.'"

"I swear."

"Have you heard of Sylvester Stallone?"

"Of course!"

"He was my neighbor," Colin said, almost in a whisper.

"Come on, that's bullshit," Nick said.

"I'm not bullshitting you. It's the truth. I have a signed photo from Stallone in my bedroom," Colin said.

Nick jumped up onto the metal guardrail in front of the ditch, balancing himself nimbly on the thin railing as he moved back and forth like a tightrope walker.

"Why are you here so late?" Colin inquired.

"I'm always here late. My parents are so busy, sometimes they forget to pick me up. Why are you here?"

"I had to take a special test in Mandarin. They don't think I'm good enough, even though I took classes every day in LA."

"I suck at Mandarin too. It's my least favorite subject."

"Join the club," Colin said, jumping up onto the railing with him. Just then, a large black vintage car pulled up. Ensconced in the backseat was the most curious woman Nick had ever seen. She was rotund with the most immense double chin, probably in her sixties, dressed entirely in black with a black hat and a black veil over her face, which was powdered an extreme shade of white. She looked like an apparition straight out of a silent film.

"Here's my ride," Colin said excitedly. "See you later." The uniformed chauffeur got out and opened the door for Colin. Nick noticed that the car door opened opposite from the way other cars normally did—outward from the end nearest to the driver's door. Colin climbed in beside the woman, who bent down to kiss him on the cheek. He looked out of the window at Nick, clearly embarrassed that Nick had witnessed this scene. The woman pointed at Nick, talking to Colin while the car idled. A moment later, Colin jumped out of the car again.

"My grandma wants to know if you need a ride home," Colin asked.

"No, no, my parents are on their way," Nick replied. Colin's grandmother rolled down the window and beckoned Nick to come closer. Nick approached hesitantly. The old lady looked pretty scary.

"It's almost seven o'clock. Who's coming to fetch you?" she asked in concern, noticing that it was already getting dark.

"Probably my dad," Nick said.

"Well, it's far too late for you to be waiting here all by yourself. What is your daddy's name?"

"Philip Young."

"Good gracious, Philip Young—James's boy! Is Sir James Young your grandfather?"

"Yes, he is."

"I know your family very well. I know all your aunties—Victoria, Felicity, Alix—and Harry Leong's your uncle. Why, we're practically family! I'm Winifred Khoo. Don't you live at Tyersall Park?"

"My parents and I moved to Tudor Close last year," Nick replied.

"That's very close to us. We live on Berrima Road. Come, let me call your parents just to make sure they are on their way," she said, reaching for the car phone on the console in front of her. "Do you know your telephone number, dearie?"

Colin's grandmother made fast work of it, and soon discovered from the maid that Mrs. Young had unexpectedly jetted off to Switzerland that afternoon, while Mr. Young was held up by a work emergency. "Please call Mr. Young at work and tell him that Winifred Khoo is going to be sending Master Nicholas home," she said. Before Nick knew what was happening, he found himself inside the Bentley Mark VI, sandwiched between Colin and the well-cushioned lady in the black veiled hat.

"Did you know your mother was going away today?" Winifred asked.

"No, but she does that a lot," Nick replied softly.

That Eleanor Young! So irresponsible! How on earth Shang Su Yi ever allowed her son to marry one of those Sung girls, I will never understand, Winifred thought. She turned to the boy and smiled at him. "*What* a coincidence! I'm so glad that you and Colin are friends."

"We just met," Colin interjected.

"Colin, don't be rude! Nicholas is a classmate of yours, and we've known his family for a long time. *Of course* you are friends." She looked at Nick, smiled her gum-baring smile, and continued. "Colin has made so few friends since moving back to Singapore, and he's rather lonely, so we must arrange for you to play together."

Colin and Nick sat there completely mortified, but in their own ways rather relieved. Colin was astonished by how friendly his normally disapproving grandmother was being toward Nick, especially since she had previously forbidden any guests at their house. He had recently tried to invite a boy from St. Andrew's over after a swim meet and had been disappointed when his grandmama told him, "Colin, we can't have just anyone over, you know. We must know who the family is first. This isn't like California—you have to be so very careful about what sort of people you associate with here."

As for Nick, he was just glad to be getting a ride home and excited that he might soon discover whether Colin really had an autographed photo of Rambo.

10

Eddie, Fiona, and the Children

HONG KONG

Eddie sat on the fleur-de-lis-patterned carpet of his dressing room, carefully unwrapping the tuxedo that had just arrived from Italy, which he had ordered especially for Colin's wedding. He took extra care to peel off the embossed sticker from the tissue-like wrapping paper that covered the large garment box, as he liked to save all the stickers and labels from his designer clothes in his Smythson leather scrapbook, and slowly eased the garment bag out of its box.

The first thing he did was try on the midnight-blue trousers. Fucky fuck, they were too tight! He tried fastening the button at the waist, but no matter how much he sucked his gut in, the damn thing wouldn't button. He took the trousers off in a huff and scrutinized the size label sewn into the lining. It read "90," which seemed correct, since his waistline was thirty-six inches. Could he have put on so much weight in just three months? No way. Those fucking Italians must have screwed up the measurements. So bloody typical. They made beautiful things, but there was always some problem or other, like the Lamborghini he once had. Thank God he got rid of that pile of cow dung and bought the Aston Martin. He would call Felix at Caraceni first thing tomorrow and tear him a new asshole. They needed to fix this before he left for Singapore next week.

He stood by the mirrored wall in nothing but his white dress shirt, black socks, and white briefs, and gingerly put on the double-breasted tuxedo jacket. Thank God, at least the jacket fit nicely. He buttoned the top button of the jacket and found to his dismay that the fabric pulled a little against his belly.

He walked over to the intercom system, pushed a button, and bellowed, "Fi! Fi! Come to my dressing room now!" A few moments later, Fiona entered the room, wearing just a black slip and her padded bedroom slippers. "Fi, is this jacket too tight?" he asked, buttoning the jacket again and moving his elbows around like a goose flapping its wings to test the sleeves.

"Stop moving your arms and I'll tell you," she said.

He put his arms down but kept shifting his weight from one foot to the other, impatiently awaiting her verdict.

"It's definitely too tight," she said. "Just look at the back. It's pulling at the center seam. You've put on weight, Eddie."

"Rubbish! I've hardly gained a pound in the last few months, and definitely not since they took my measurements for this suit back in March."

Fiona just stood there, not wanting to argue with him over the obvious.

"Are the children ready for inspection?" Eddie asked.

"I'm trying to get them dressed right now."

"Tell them they have five more minutes. Russell Wing is coming over at three to take some family pictures of us in the wedding clothes. *Orange Daily* might do a feature on our family attending the wedding."

"You didn't tell me Russell is coming over today!"

"I just remembered. I called him only yesterday. You can't expect me to remember everything when I have much more important matters on my mind, can you?"

"But you need to give me more time to prepare for a photo shoot. Don't you remember what happened the last time when they shot us for *Hong Kong Tattle*?"

"Well, I'm telling you now. So stop wasting time and go get ready."

Constantine, Augustine, and Kalliste stood obediently in a straight line in the middle of the sunken formal living room, all dressed up in their new outfits from Ralph Lauren Kids. Eddie sprawled on the plush velvet brocade sofa, inspecting each of his children, while Fiona, the Chinese maid, and one of the Filipino nannies hovered close by. "Augustine, I think you should wear your Gucci loafers with that outfit and not those Bally moccasins."

"Which ones?" Augustine asked, his little voice almost a whisper.

"What? Speak up!" Eddie said.

"Which ones do I wear?" Augustine said again, not much louder.

"Sir, which pair of Gucci loafers? He has two," Laarni, the Filipino nanny interjected.

"The burgundy ones with the red-and-green band, of course," Eddie said, giving his six-year-old son a withering look. "*Nay chee seen, ah?* You can't seriously think you can wear *black* shoes with khaki trousers, can you?" Eddie scolded. Augustine's face reddened, close to tears. "Okay, that covers the tea ceremony. Now, go and change into your wedding outfits. Hurry up, I'm going to give you five minutes." Fiona, the nanny, and the maid quickly ushered the children back to their bedrooms.

Ten minutes later, when Fiona came down the spiral stairs in a minimalist gray off-the-shoulder gown with one asymmetrical sleeve, Eddie could hardly believe his eyes. "*Yau moh gau chor?*[*] What on earth is *that*?"

"What do you mean?" Fiona asked.

"That dress! You look like you're in mourning!"

"It's Jil Sander. I love it. I showed you a picture and you approved."

"I don't remember seeing a picture of this dress. I never would have approved it. You look like some spinster widow."

"There's no such thing as a spinster widow, Eddie. Spinsters are unmarried," Fiona said drily.

"I don't care. How can you look like death warmed over when the rest of us look so good? See how nice and colorful your children look," he said, gesturing to the kids, who cowered in embarrassment.

"I will be wearing my diamond-and-jade necklace with it, and the jade art deco earrings."

"It will still look like you are going to a funeral. We're going to the wedding of the year, with kings and queens and some of the richest people in the world and all my relatives. I don't want people thinking that I can't afford to buy my wife a proper dress."

"In the first place, Eddie, I bought it with my own money, since

[*] Cantonese for "Did you make a mistake?"

you never pay for my clothes. And this is one of the most expensive dresses I've ever bought."

"Well, it doesn't look expensive enough."

"Eddie, you are always contradicting yourself," Fiona said. "First you tell me you want me to dress more expensively like your cousin Astrid, but then you criticize everything I buy."

"Well, I criticize you when you're wearing something that looks so cheap. It's a disgrace to me. It's a disgrace to your children."

Fiona shook her head in exasperation. "You don't have any idea what looks cheap, Eddie. Like that shiny tux you're wearing. *That* looks cheap. Especially when I can see the safety pins holding your pants on."

"Nonsense. This tux was six thousand euros. Everyone can see how expensive the fabric is and how well tailored it is, especially when they fix it properly. The pins are temporary. I'm going to button the jacket for the pictures and no one will see them."

The doorbell made an elaborate, symphonically excessive chime.

"That must be Russell Wing. Kalliste, take off your glasses. Fi, go and change your dress—now."

"Why don't you just go to my closet and pick out whatever you want me to wear?" Fiona said, not wanting to argue with him anymore.

At that moment, the celebrity photographer Russell Wing entered the living room.

"Look at you Chengs! Wah, *gum laeng, ah*!"* he said.

"Hello Russell," Eddie said, smiling broadly. "Thank you, thank you, we only look stylish for you!"

"Fiona, you look stunning in that dress! Isn't it Raf Simons for Jil Sander, from next season? How in the world did you get your hands on it? I just photographed Maggie Cheung in this dress last week for *Vogue China*."

Fiona said nothing.

"Oh, I always make sure my wife has the very best, Russell. Come, come, have some of your favorite cognac before we begin. *Um sai hak hei*,"† Eddie said cheerily. He turned to Fiona and said, "Darling, where are your diamonds? Go and put on your beautiful

* Cantonese for "how beautiful."

† Cantonese for "no need to be so polite."

art deco diamond-and-jade necklace and then Russell can start his photo shoot. We don't want to take up too much of his time, do we?"

As Russell was taking some of the final shots of the Cheng family posed in front of the huge bronze sculpture of a Lipizzan stallion in the front foyer, another worrying thought entered Eddie's head. As soon as Russell was out the door with his camera equipment and a gift bottle of Camus Cognac, Eddie called his sister Cecilia.

"Cecilia, what colors will you and Tony be wearing at Colin's wedding ball?"

"*Nay gong mut yeah?*"*

"The color of your dress, Cecilia. The one you're wearing to the ball."

"The color of my dress? How should I know? The wedding is a week away—I haven't begun to think about what I'm going to wear, Eddie."

"You didn't buy a new dress for the wedding?" Eddie was incredulous.

"No, why should I?"

"I can't believe it! What is Tony going to wear?"

"He will probably wear his dark blue suit. The one he always wears."

"He's not wearing a tux?"

"No. It's not like it's *his* wedding, Eddie."

"The invitation says *white tie*, Cecilia."

"It's *Singapore*, Eddie, and no one there takes those things seriously. Singaporean men have no style, and I guarantee you half the men won't even be in suits—they'll all be wearing those ghastly untucked batik shirts."

"I think you're mistaken, Cecilia. It's Colin Khoo and Araminta Lee's wedding—all of high society will be there and everyone will be dressed to impress."

"Well, you go right ahead, Eddie."

Fucky fuck, Eddie thought. His whole family was going to show up looking like peasants. So bloody typical. He wondered if he could convince Colin to change his seating so that he didn't have to be anywhere near his parents and siblings.

---

* Cantonese for "What are you saying?" or, better yet, "What the hell are you talking about?"

"Do you know what Mummy and Daddy are wearing?"

"Believe it or not, Eddie, I don't."

"Well—we still need to color coordinate as a family, Cecilia. There's going to be a lot of press there, and I want to make sure we don't clash. Just be sure you don't wear anything gray to the main event. Fiona is wearing a gray Jil Sander ball gown. And she's wearing a deep lavender Lanvin dress to the rehearsal dinner, and a champagne-colored Carolina Herrera to the church ceremony. Can you call Mummy and tell her?"

"Sure, Eddie."

"Do you need me to SMS you the color scheme again?"

"Sure. Whatever. I have to go now, Eddie. Jake is having another nosebleed."

"Oh, I almost forgot. What is Jake going to wear? My boys will all be wearing Ralph Lauren tuxedos with dark purple cummerbunds—"

"Eddie, I really have to go. Don't worry, Jake is not going to wear a tuxedo. I'll be lucky if I can get him to tuck in his shirt."

"Wait, wait, before you go, have you talked to Alistair yet? He's not still thinking of bringing that Kitty Pong, is he?"

"Too late. Alistair left yesterday."

"What? No one told me he was planning to go early."

"He was always planning to leave on Friday, Eddie. If you kept up with us more, you'd know that."

"But why did he go to Singapore so soon?"

"He didn't go to Singapore. He went to Macau for Colin's bachelor party."

"WHAAAT? Colin's bachelor party is this weekend? Who the hell invited Alistair to his bachelor party?"

"Do you really need me to answer that?"

"But Colin is better friends with ME!" Eddie screamed, the pressure building in his head. And then he felt a strange draft from behind. His pants had split open at the ass.

11

Rachel
•

SAMSARA ISLAND

The bachelorettes were enjoying a sunset dinner at a long table set under a pavilion of billowing orange silk on the pristine white sand, surrounded by glowing silver lanterns. With dusk transforming the gentle waves into an emerald froth, it could have been a photo shoot straight out of *Condé Nast Traveler*, except that the dinner conversation put a damper on that illusion. As the first course of baby Bibb lettuce with hearts of palm in a coconut-milk dressing was served, the cluster of girls to Rachel's left were busy skewering into the heart of another girl's boyfriend.

"So you say he just made senior vice president? But he's on the retail side, not the investment banking side, right? I spoke to my boyfriend Roderick, and he thinks that Simon probably makes between six to eight hundred thou base salary, if he's lucky. And he doesn't get millions in bonuses like the I-bankers," sniffed Lauren Lee.

"The other problem is his family. Simon's not even the eldest brother. He's the second youngest of five," Parker Yeo pontificated. "My parents know the Tings very well, and let me tell you, as respected as they are, they are not what you or I would consider rich—my mum says they have maybe two hundred million, max. You split that five ways and you'll be lucky if Simon gets forty mil at the end of the day. And that won't be for a loooong time—his parents are still quite young. Isn't his father going to run for parliament again?"

"We just want what's best for you, Isabel," Lauren said, patting her hand sympathetically.

"But . . . but I really think I love him—" Isabel stammered.

Francesca Shaw cut in. "Isabel, I'm going to tell it to you like it is, because everyone here is wasting your time being polite. You can't *afford* to fall in love with Simon. Let me break it down for you. Let's be generous and assume that Simon is making a measly eight hundred thousand a year. After taxes and CPF,* his take-home is only about half a million. Where are you going to live on *that* kind of money? Think about it—you have to factor a million dollars per bedroom, and you need at least three bedrooms, so you are talking three mil for an apartment in Bukit Timah. That's a hundred and fifty thousand a year in mortgage and property taxes. Then say you have two kids, and you want to send them to proper schools. At thirty thousand a year each for school fees that's sixty thousand, plus twenty thousand a year each on tutors. That's one hundred thousand a year on schooling alone. Servants and nannies—two Indonesian or Sri Lankan maids will cost you another thirty thousand, unless you want one of them to be a Swedish or French au pair, then you're talking eighty thousand a year spent on the help. Now, what are we going to do about your own upkeep? At the very least, you'll need ten new outfits per season, so you won't be ashamed to be seen in public. Thank God Singapore only has two seasons—hot and hotter—so let's just say, to be practical, you'll only spend four thousand per look. That's eighty thousand a year for wardrobe. I'll throw in another twenty thousand for one good handbag and a few pairs of new shoes every season. And then there is your basic maintenance—hair, facials, mani, pedi, brazilian wax, eyebrow wax, massage, chiro, acupuncture, Pilates,

---

* Central Provident Fund, a mandatory savings scheme that Singaporeans contribute to each month to fund their retirement, health care, and housing. It's a bit like the U.S. Social Security program, except that the CPF won't be going broke anytime soon. CPF account holders earn an average of five percent interest per year, and the government also periodically gifts its citizens with bonuses and special shares, making Singapore the only country in the world that gives dividends to all its citizens when the economy does well. (Now you know why that Facebook fellow became a Singaporean.)

yoga, core fusion, personal trainer. That's another forty thousand a year. We've already spent four hundred and seventy thousand of Simon's salary, which leaves just thirty thousand for everything else. How are you going to put food on the table and clothe your babies with that? How will you ever get away to an Aman resort twice a year? And we haven't even taken into account your membership dues at Churchill Club and Pulau Club! Don't you see? It's *impossible* for you to marry Simon. We wouldn't worry if you had your own money, but you know your situation. The clock is ticking on your pretty face. It's time to cut your losses and let Lauren introduce you to one of those eligible Beijing billionaires before it's too late."

Isabel was reduced to a puddle of tears.

Rachel couldn't believe what she had just heard—this crowd made Upper East Side girls look like Mennonites. She tried to shift her attention back to the food. The second course had just been served—a surprisingly tasty langoustine and calamansi lime geleé terrine. Unfortunately, the girls on her right seemed to be loudly fixating on some couple named Alistair and Kitty.

"Aiyah, I don't understand what he sees in her," Chloé Ho lamented. "With the fake accent and fake breasts and fake everything."

"I know *exactly* what he sees in her. He sees those fake breasts, and that's all he needs to see!" Parker cackled.

"Serena Oh told me that she ran into them at Lung King Heen last week, and Kitty was in Gucci, head to toe. Gucci purse, Gucci halter top, Gucci satin mini-shorts, and Gucci python boots," Chloé said. "She kept her Gucci sunglasses on all through dinner, and apparently even made out with him at the table with her sunglasses on."

"*Alamaaaaak*, how tacky can you get!" Wandi hissed, patting her diamond-and-aquamarine tiara.

Parker suddenly addressed Rachel from across the table. "Wait a minute, have *you* met them yet?"

"Who?" Rachel asked, since she was trying to tune the girls out rather than listen in on their salacious gossip.

"Alistair and Kitty!"

"Sorry, I wasn't really following . . . who are they?"

Francesca glanced at Rachel and said, "Parker, don't waste your time—it's obvious Rachel doesn't know anybody."

Rachel didn't understand why Francesca was being so icy toward her. She decided to ignore the comment and took a sip of her Pinot Gris.

"So Rachel, tell us how you met Nicholas Young," Lauren asked loudly.

"Well, it's not a very exciting story. We both teach at NYU, and we were set up by a colleague of mine," Rachel answered, noticing that all eyes at the table were fixed on her.

"Oh, who is the colleague? A Singaporean?" Lauren asked.

"No, she's Chinese American, Sylvia Wong-Swartz."

"How did she know Nicholas?" Parker asked.

"Um, they met on some committee."

"So she didn't know him very well?" Parker continued.

"No, I don't think so," Rachel replied, wondering what these girls were getting at. "Why the interest in Sylvia?"

"Oh, I love setting up my friends too, so I was just curious to know what motivated your friend to set the two of you up, that's all." Parker smiled.

"Well, Sylvia's a good friend, and she was always trying to set me up. She just thought Nick was cute and a total catch . . ." Rachel began, instantly regretting her choice of words.

"It sure sounds like she did her homework on *that*, didn't she?" Francesca said with a sharp laugh.

After dinner, while the girls took off for the disco marquee precariously erected on a jetty, Rachel headed alone to the beach bar, a picturesque gazebo overlooking a secluded cove. It was empty except for the tall, strapping bartender who grinned broadly when she entered. "Signorina, can I make you something special?" he asked in an almost comically seductive accent. *Hell, did Araminta's mother only hire dashing Italians?*

"I've actually been craving a beer. Do you have any beer?"

"Of course. Let's see, we have Corona, Duvel, Moretti, Red Stripe, and my personal favorite, Lion Stout."

"That's one I've never heard of."

"It's from Sri Lanka. It's creamy and bittersweet, with a rich tan head."

Rachel couldn't help giggling. It sounded like he was describing himself. "Well if it's your favorite, then I have to try it."

As he poured the beer into a tall frosted glass, a girl whom Rachel hadn't previously noticed strolled into the bar and slipped onto the stool next to her.

"Thank God there's someone else here who drinks beer! I am so sick of all those pissy low-cal cocktails," the girl said. She was Chinese, but spoke with an Australian accent.

"Cheers to that," Rachel replied, tipping her glass at the girl. The girl ordered a Corona, and grabbed the bottle from the bartender before he could pour it into a glass. He looked personally wounded as she tilted her head back and downed her beer in full-bodied gulps. "Rachel, isn't it?"

"That's right. But if you're looking for the Taiwanese Rachel Chu, you've got the wrong girl," Rachel shot back preemptively.

The girl smiled quizzically, a little baffled by Rachel's response. "I'm Astrid's cousin Sophie. She told me to look out for you."

"Oh, hi," Rachel said, disarmed by Sophie's friendly smile and deep dimples. Unlike the other girls sporting the latest resort fashions, she was dressed plainly in a sleeveless cotton shirt and a pair of khaki shorts. She had a no-nonsense pageboy haircut, and wore no makeup or jewelry except for a plastic Swatch on her wrist.

"Were you on the plane with us?" Rachel asked, trying to remember her.

"No, no, I flew in on my own and just arrived a little while ago,"

"You have your own plane too?"

"No, I'm afraid not." Sophie laughed. "I'm the lucky one who flew Garuda Airlines, economy class. I had some hospital rounds to do, so I couldn't get away until later this afternoon."

"You're a nurse?"

"Pediatric surgeon."

Once again, Rachel was reminded that one could never judge a book by its cover, especially in Asia. "So you're Astrid and Nick's cousin?"

"No, just Astrid's, on the Leong side. Her father is my mum's brother. But of course I know Nick—we all grew up together. And you grew up in the States, right? Where did you live?"

"I spent my teenage years in California, but I've lived in twelve different states. We moved around quite a bit when I was younger."

"Why did you move around so much?"

"My mom worked in Chinese restaurants."

"What did she do?"

"She usually started out as a hostess or a waitress, but she always managed to get promoted quickly."

"So she took you everywhere with her?" Sophie asked, genuinely fascinated.

"Yes—we lived the Gypsy life until my teenage years, when we settled down in California."

"Was it lonely for you?"

"Well, it was all I knew, so it seemed normal to me. I got to know the back rooms of suburban strip-mall restaurants very well, and I was pretty much a bookworm."

"And what about your father?"

"He died soon after I was born."

"Oh, I'm sorry," Sophie said quickly, regretting that she had asked.

"That's fine—I never knew him." Rachel smiled, trying to put her at ease. "And anyway, it wasn't all bad. My mom put herself through night school, got a college degree, and has been a successful real estate agent for many years now."

"That's amazing," Sophie said.

"Not really. We're actually one of the many clichéd 'Asian immigrant success stories' that politicians love to trot out every four years during their conventions."

Sophie chuckled. "I can see why Nick likes you—you both have the same dry wit."

Rachel smiled, looking away toward the disco marquee on the jetty.

"Am I keeping you from the dance party? I hear Araminta flew in some famous DJ from Ibiza," Sophie said.

"I'm enjoying this, actually. It's the first real conversation I've had all day."

Sophie glanced at the girls—most of whom were now writhing wildly with several of the Italian waiters to the pounding euro-trance-disco music—and shrugged. "Well, with this crowd, I can't say I'm surprised."

"Aren't these your friends?"

"A few, but most of these girls I don't know. I recognize them, of course."

"Who are they? Are some of them famous?"

"In their own minds, perhaps. These are the more *social* girls, the type that are always appearing in the magazines, attending all the charity galas. Far too glamorous a crowd for me. I'm sorry, but I work twelve-hour shifts and don't have the time to go to benefit parties in hotels. I have to benefit my patients first."

Rachel laughed.

"Speaking of which," Sophie added, "I've been up since five, so I'm going to turn in now."

"I think I will too," Rachel said.

They walked down the jetty toward their bungalows.

"I'm in the villa at the end of this walkway if you need anything," Sophie said.

"Good night," Rachel said. "It's been lovely talking with you."

"Likewise," Sophie said, flashing that deep-dimpled smile again.

Rachel entered her villa, gladly returning to some peace and quiet after a draining day. None of the lights were on in the suite, but the bright silvery moonlight glimmered through the open screen doors, casting serpentine ripples along the walls. The sea was so still that the sound of the water lapping slowly against the wood stilts had a hypnotic effect. It was the perfect setting for a night swim in the ocean, something she'd never done. Rachel padded toward the bedroom for her bikini. As she passed the vanity table, she noticed that the leather satchel she'd left hanging on the chair seemed to be leaking some sort of liquid. She walked toward the bag and saw that it was completely drenched, with brownish water dripping out of the corner into a large puddle on the bedroom floor. What the hell happened? She turned on the lamp by the table and opened the front flap of her bag. She screamed, jerking backward in horror and knocking over the table lamp.

Her bag was filled with a large fish that had been badly mutilated, blood seeping out from its gills. Violently scrawled on the vanity mirror above the chair in fish blood were the words "CATCH THIS, YOU GOLD-DIGGING CUNT!"

12

Eleanor
.

"Thirty thousand yuan? That's ridiculous!" Eleanor seethed at the man in the poly-blend gray jacket seated across from her in the lounge off the lobby of the Ritz-Carlton. The man looked around to make sure that Eleanor's outburst wasn't attracting too much attention.

"Trust me, it will be worth your money," the man said quietly in Mandarin.

"Mr. Wong, how can we be sure your information has any value when we don't even know what it is exactly?" Lorena asked.

"Listen, your brother explained to Mr. Tin what the situation was, and Mr. Tin and I go way back—I have worked for him for more than twenty years. We are the best at this sort of thing. Now, I'm not sure what exactly you're planning, and I don't want to know, but I can assure you that this information will be *extremely* beneficial to whoever possesses it," Mr. Wong said confidently. Lorena translated his response for Eleanor.

"Who does he think we are? There isn't any sort of information that's worth thirty thousand yuan to me. Does he think I'm made of money?" Eleanor was indignant.

"How about fifteen thousand?" Lorena asked.

"Okay, for you, twenty thousand," Mr. Wong countered.

"Fifteen thousand, and that's our last offer," Lorena insisted again.

"Okay, seventeen thousand five hundred, but that's *my* last offer," the man said, getting frustrated by all the bargaining. Mr. Tin had told him that these ladies were millionaires.

"No—ten thousand, or I leave," Eleanor suddenly declared in Mandarin. The man glared at her as if she had insulted all of his ancestors. He shook his head in dismay.

"Lorena, I'm done with this extortion," Eleanor huffed, getting up from her red velvet club chair. Lorena stood up as well, and both women began to walk out of the lounge into the soaring three-story atrium lobby, where there was a sudden traffic jam of men in tuxedos and women in black, white, and red ball gowns. "Must be some sort of big function going on," Eleanor noted, scrutinizing a woman ablaze with diamonds around her neck.

"Shenzhen is not Shanghai, that's for sure—all these women are dressed in fashions from three years ago," Lorena observed wryly as she tried to navigate her way through the crowd. "Eleanor, I think you've gone too far with your bargaining tactics this time. I think we've lost this guy."

"Lorena, trust me—keep walking and don't turn around!" Eleanor instructed.

Just as the ladies reached the front entrance of the hotel, Mr. Wong suddenly came running out of the lounge. "Okay, okay, ten thousand," he said breathlessly. Eleanor beamed in triumph as she followed the man back to the table.

Mr. Wong made a quick phone call on his cell, and then said to the ladies, "Okay, my informer will be here very soon. Until then, what would you ladies like to drink?"

Lorena was a little surprised to hear this—she had assumed that they would be taken to some other place to meet the informer. "Is it safe to meet right here?"

"Why not? This is one of the best hotels in Shenzhen!"

"I mean, it's so public."

"Don't worry, you'll see that it will be just fine," Mr. Wong said, grabbing a handful of macadamia nuts from the silver bowl on the table.

A few minutes later, a man entered the bar, walking with trepidation toward their table. Eleanor could tell just by looking at him that he was from some rural area and that it was the first time he had set foot in a hotel as fancy as this. He wore a striped polo shirt and ill-fitting dress pants, and carried a metallic-silver briefcase. It looked to Lorena like he had just picked up the suitcase an hour ago from one of those cheap luggage stalls at the train station, to make himself seem more professional. He looked nervously at the women as he approached the table. Mr. Wong had a short exchange with him in a dialect that neither woman could understand, and the man set his briefcase onto the granite-top table. He fiddled with the combination and clicked the locks on each side in unison before opening the briefcase lid ceremoniously.

The man took out three items from the suitcase and placed them on the table in front of the ladies. There was a small rectangular paper box, a manila envelope, and one photocopy of a newspaper clipping. Lorena opened the manila envelope and fished out a yellowed piece of paper, while Eleanor opened the box. She peered into it, and then looked at the piece of paper Lorena was holding. She only read very basic Mandarin, so she was mystified by it. "What does all this mean?"

"Just give me a minute to finish, Elle," Lorena said, scanning the last document up and down. "Oh my God, Elle," she exclaimed, suddenly staring at Mr. Wong and the informer. "Are you *sure* this is completely accurate? There will be big trouble for all of you if it isn't."

"I swear on the life of my firstborn son," the man replied haltingly.

"What is it? What is it?" Eleanor asked urgently, hardly able to contain herself. Lorena whispered into Eleanor's right ear. Her eyes grew large, and she looked up at Mr. Wong.

"Mr. Wong, I'll give you thirty thousand yuan in cash if you can take me right now," Eleanor commanded.

13

Rachel

.

Sophie was splashing some water on her face when she heard an urgent rapping. She went to the door and found Rachel standing there, her lips white and her whole body shaking.

"What's wrong? Are you cold?" Sophie asked.

"I . . . think . . . I think I'm in shock," Rachel stuttered.

"WHAT? What happened?"

"My room . . . I can't describe it. Go see for yourself," Rachel said numbly.

"Are you okay? Should I call for help?"

"No, no, I'll be fine. I'm just shaking involuntarily."

Sophie immediately slipped into doctor mode, grabbing hold of Rachel's wrist. "Your pulse *is* a bit elevated," she noted. She grabbed the cashmere throw on her chaise lounge and handed it to Rachel. "Sit down. Take long, slow breaths. Wrap this around yourself and wait right here," she instructed.

A few minutes later, Sophie returned to the villa, ablaze in anger. "I can't believe it! This is outrageous!"

Rachel nodded slowly, having calmed down a little by this point. "Can you call hotel security for me?"

"Of course!" Sophie headed for the phone and scanned the list on it, looking for the right button to press. She turned back to Rachel and gave her a thoughtful look. "Actually, I'm wondering whether it's the best idea to call security. What exactly could they do?"

"We can find out who did this! There are security cameras everywhere, and surely they must have footage of who went into my room," Rachel said.

"Well . . . what would that really achieve?" Sophie ventured. "Hear me out for a second . . . No one's committed any real crime. I mean, I feel bad for the fish, and it was certainly traumatizing for you, but if you think about it, this was just a nasty prank. We're on an island. We know it had to be one of these girls, or maybe even a group of them. Do you really care who did it? Are you going to confront someone and make a scene? They're just trying to mess with you—why give them more fuel? I'm sure they're on the beach right now just *waiting* for you to go hysterical and ruin Araminta's bachelorette party. They wanted to provoke you."

Rachel considered what Sophie had said for a moment. "You know, you're right. I'm sure these girls are just dying for some drama so they can talk about it back in Singapore." She got up from the sofa and paced around the room, not quite sure what to do next. "But there must be *something* we can do."

"Doing nothing can sometimes be the most effective form of action," Sophie remarked. "If you do nothing, you'll be sending a clear message: that you're stronger than they think you are. Not to mention a lot classier. Think about it."

Rachel mulled it over for a few minutes and decided that Sophie was right. "Did anyone ever tell you how brilliant you are, Sophie?" she said with a sigh.

Sophie smiled. "Here, I saw some verveine tea in the bathroom. Let me make some. It'll calm both our nerves."

With warm cups of tea nestled on their laps, Rachel and Sophie sat on a pair of lounge chairs on the deck. The moon hung like a giant gong in the sky, lighting the ocean so brightly that Rachel could see the tiny schools of fish shimmering as they darted around the wooden piers of the bungalow.

Sophie looked intently at Rachel. "You weren't prepared for any of this, were you? Astrid was so perceptive when she asked me to look out for you. She was a little worried about you tagging along with this particular crowd."

"Astrid is so sweet. I guess I just never expected to encounter this kind of viciousness, that's all. The way these girls are acting, it's as if Nick is the last man in all of Asia! Look, I get it now—his family's rich, he's considered a good catch. But isn't Singapore supposed to be filled with other rich families like his?"

Sophie sighed sympathetically. "First of all, Nick is so inordinately good-looking, most of these girls have had mad crushes on him since childhood. Then you have to understand something about his family. There's a certain mystique that surrounds them because they are so intensely private. Most people don't even realize they exist, but for the small circle of old families that do, they inspire a level of fascination that's hard to describe. Nick is the scion of this noble clan, and for some of these girls, that's all that matters. They may not know the first thing about him, but they are all vying to become Mrs. Nicholas Young."

Rachel took it all in quietly. It felt like Sophie was talking about some character of fiction, someone who bore no resemblance to the man she knew and had fallen in love with. It was as if she were Sleeping Beauty—only, she never asked to be awakened by a prince.

"You know, Nick has told me very little about his family. I still don't know much about them," Rachel mused.

"That's the way Nick was raised. I'm sure he was taught from a very young age never to talk about his family, where he lived, that sort of thing. He was brought up in such a cloistered environment. Can you imagine growing up in that house with no other kids around—no one but your parents, grandparents, and all those servants? I remember going over there as a child, and Nick always seemed so grateful whenever there were other kids to play with."

Rachel gazed at the moon. Suddenly the rabbit-like figure on the moon reminded her of Nick, a little boy stuck up there in that glittering palace all by himself. "Do you want to know the craziest part of all this?"

"Tell me."

"I just came for a summer vacation. Everyone here assumes that Nick and I are a done deal, that we're going to run off and tie the knot tomorrow or something. Nobody knows that marriage is something we've never even discussed."

"Really, you haven't?" Sophie asked in surprise. "But don't you ever think about it? Don't you want to marry Nick?"

"To be completely honest, Nick is the *first* guy I've dated who I could imagine being married to. But I was never raised to believe that marriage was supposed to be my life's goal. My mother wanted me to get the best education first. She never wanted me to end up having to wash dishes in a restaurant."

"That's not the case over here. No matter how advanced we've become, there's still tremendous pressure for girls to get married. Here, it doesn't matter how successful a woman is professionally. She isn't considered complete until she is married and has children. Why do you think Araminta is so eager to get married?"

"Do you think Araminta shouldn't be getting married, then?"

"Well, that's a difficult question for me to answer. I mean, she *is* about to become my sister-in-law."

Rachel looked at Sophie in surprise. "Wait a minute . . . Colin is *your brother?*"

"Yes." Sophie giggled. "I thought you knew that all along."

Rachel stared at her with renewed wonder. "I had no idea. I thought you were Astrid's cousin. So . . . the Khoos are related to the Leongs?"

"Yes, of course. My mother was born a Leong. She was Harry Leong's sister."

Rachel noticed that Sophie used the past tense in talking about her mother. "Is your mother no longer around?"

"She passed away when we were kids. She had a heart attack."

"Oh," Rachel said, realizing why she felt a connection with the girl she had met only hours earlier. "Don't take this the wrong way, but I understand now why you're so different from the other girls."

Sophie smiled. "Growing up with only one parent—especially in a place where everyone goes to such great lengths to present a picture-perfect family—really sets you apart. I was always the girl whose mother died too young. But you know, it had its advantages. It allowed me to get away from the frying pan. After my mum died, I was sent to school in Australia, and I stayed there all through uni. I suppose that's what makes me a little different."

"A *lot* different," Rachel corrected. She thought of another thing that made her like Sophie. Her candor and complete lack of pretension reminded her so much of Nick. Rachel peered up at the moon, and this time, the rabbit boy didn't look so alone anymore.

Astrid and Michael

SINGAPORE

The minute Harry Leong's Armani-suited security men entered her hospital room and did their usual sweep, Astrid knew that she had been found out. Minutes later, her parents rushed into the room in a huff. "Astrid, are you okay? How's Cassian? Where is he?" her mother asked anxiously.

"I'm fine, I'm fine. Michael is with Cassian in the children's ward, signing his release forms."

Astrid's father eyed the elderly Chinese woman a few feet away vigorously rubbing Tiger Balm onto her ankle. "Why did they bring you to a public hospital, and why on earth are you not in your own room? I'm going to tell them to move you immediately," Harry whispered irritatedly.

"It's okay, Daddy. I had a slight concussion, so they just put me in this ward for monitoring. Like I said, we're about to get released. How did you know I was here?" Astrid demanded, not bothering to hide her annoyance.

"Aiyoh, you've been in the hospital for two days without telling us, and all you care about is how we found out!" Felicity sighed.

"Don't get so *kan cheong*, Mum. Nothing happened."

"Nothing happened? Cassandra called up at seven this morning from England. She scared us half to death, making it sound like you were Princess Diana in that tunnel in Paris!" Felicity lamented.

"Just be glad she didn't call the *Straits Times*," Harry added.

Astrid rolled her eyes. Radio One Asia had struck again. How in the world did Cassandra know about her accident? She had specifically told the ambulance driver to take her to General Hospital—not one of the private hospitals like Mount Elizabeth or Gleneagles—so that she might avoid being recognized. Of course, that hadn't worked.

"This is it. You are no longer allowed to drive. You are going to get rid of that lousy Japanese car of yours and I am going to assign Youssef to you from now on. He can use one of the Vanden Plas," Harry declared.

"Stop treating me like a six-year-old, Daddy! It was such a minor accident. My concussion was from the air bag, that's all."

"The fact that your air bag deployed means that the accident was more serious than you think. If you don't value your life, do as you wish. But I'm not going to let you put my grandson's life in danger. What's the use of having all these drivers when no one uses them? Youssef will drive Cassian from now on," Harry insisted.

"Daddy, Cassian only got a few cuts."

"Aiyoh, a few cuts!" Felicity sighed, shaking her head in dismay just as Michael entered the room with Cassian. "Oh, Cassian, my poor darling," she exclaimed, rushing toward the child, who was happily clutching a red balloon.

"Where the hell were you on Friday night?" Harry barked at his son-in-law. "If you were doing your proper duty escorting her, this wouldn't have happened—"

"Daddy, stop it!" Astrid cut in.

"I was working late, sir," Michael said as calmly as possible.

"Working late, working late. You're always working late these days, aren't you?" Harry muttered contemptuously.

"Enough, Daddy, we're leaving now. Come on, Michael, I want to go home," Astrid insisted, getting out of the bed.

The minute they arrived home, Astrid put into motion the plan she had spent the past two days devising. She went into the kitchen and gave the cook and the maid the day off. Then she instructed Evangeline to take Cassian to play at the beach house in Tanah Merah. Michael was surprised by the sudden flurry of activity, but he assumed that Astrid just wanted some peace and quiet for the rest of the day. As soon as everyone was out of the flat and Astrid heard the elevator doors shut, she fixed her gaze on Michael. They were completely alone now, and she could suddenly hear her heartbeat fill her eardrums. She knew that if she didn't say the words she had carefully rehearsed in her head RIGHT NOW, she would lose her nerve.

"Michael, I want you to know what happened on Friday night," she began.

"You already told me, Astrid. It doesn't matter—I'm just glad that you and Cassian are okay," Michael said.

"No, no," Astrid said. "I want you to know the *real* reason I got into the car wreck."

"What are you talking about?" Michael asked, confused.

"I'm talking about how I became so distracted that I almost got our son killed," Astrid said, a note of anger hanging in her voice. "It *was* my fault. It was far too late, and too dark, especially those narrow lanes around the Botanic Gardens. I shouldn't have been driving, but I was. And all I could think about was where *you* were and what *you* were doing."

"What do you mean? I was home," Michael said matter-of-factly. "What were you so worried about?"

Astrid took a deep breath, and before she could stop herself, the words came tumbling out. "I know you think I'm some sort of delicate creature, but I'm a lot tougher than you think. I need you to be honest with me, completely honest. I saw a text message on your phone last month, Michael. *The dirty one.* I know you've been in Hong Kong when you were supposed to be in northern China—I found your dinner receipt from Petrus. And I know all about the charm bracelet you bought from Stephen Chia."

Michael sat down, the color draining from his face. Astrid watched him slump into the sofa, his body language speaking volumes. *He was guilty as hell.* She felt a surge of confidence that compelled her to ask the question she never imagined she would ever ask: "Have you been . . . are you having an affair?"

Michael sighed and shook his head almost imperceptibly. "I'm so sorry. I'm so sorry to have hurt you and Cassian. You're right—the car accident was my fault."

"Just tell me everything, Michael, and I . . . and I will try to understand," Astrid said softly, sitting down on the ottoman across from him, a calmness coming over her. "No more lies, Michael. Tell me, who is this woman you've been seeing?"

Michael could not bring himself to look up at his wife. He knew the time had finally come to say what he had been struggling to say for so long. "I'm so sorry, Astrid. I don't want to cause you any more pain. I'll go."

Astrid looked at him in surprise. "Michael, I'm asking you to tell me what happened. I want to know everything, so we can put this all behind us."

Michael got up from the sofa abruptly. "I don't know if that's possible."

"Why not?"

Michael turned away from Astrid and stared past the sliding glass doors of the balcony. He stared out at the trees lining Cavenagh Road, looking like giant bushy stalks of broccoli from up here. The trees marked the perimeter of the grounds that surrounded Istana, and beyond that, Fort Canning Park, River Valley Road, and then the Singapore River. He wished he had the power to fly off the balcony, to fly toward the river and away from this pain. "I . . . I've hurt you too much, and now I don't know if I can stop myself from hurting you even more," he finally said.

Astrid was silent for a moment, trying to decipher what he meant. "Is it because you're in love with this woman?" she asked, her eyes brimming with tears. "Or is it because you had another child with her?"

Michael smiled mysteriously. "What, does your father have me under surveillance or something?"

"Don't be ridiculous. A friend just happened to see you in Hong Kong, that's all. Who is the boy? And who is this woman you've been seeing?"

"Astrid, the boy and the woman are beside the point. You and I . . . it isn't working for us anymore. It hasn't really *ever* worked. We've just been pretending it has," Michael said emphatically, feeling that these were his first truly honest words to her in a very long time.

Astrid stared at him, stunned. "How can you say that?"

"Well, you want me to be honest, so I'm being honest. Your father was right—I haven't been doing my duty as a husband. I have been too consumed with my job, working my ass off trying to get this company off the ground. And you—you are consumed by your family obligations and traveling around the world fifty times a year. What kind of marriage do we have? We're not happy," Michael declared.

"I can't believe I'm hearing this. I've been happy. I was very happy until the day I discovered that damn text message," Astrid insisted, getting up and pacing around the room.

"Are you sure about that? Are you sure you've *truly* been happy? I think you're deceiving yourself, Astrid."

"I see what you're doing, Michael. You're just trying to find an easy way out of this. You're trying to blame me, to make this all about me, when *you're* the one who's guilty. Look, I'm not the one who broke our wedding vows. I'm not the one who cheated," Astrid seethed, her shock transforming into rage.

"Okay, I'm guilty. I admit it. I admit that I am a cheater. Happy now?"

"I'm not happy, and it will take me some time, but I'll learn to deal with it," Astrid said matter-of-factly.

"Well, I can't deal with it anymore!" Michael moaned. "So I'm going to pack."

"What's all this packing business? Who's asking you to leave? Do you think I want to kick you out of the house just because you cheated on me? Do you think I'm that simpleminded, that I think I'm the first woman whose husband ever had an affair? I'm not going *anywhere*, Michael. I'm standing right here, trying to work through this with you, for the sake of our marriage. For the sake of our son."

"Astrid, when have you ever really done anything for the sake of your son? I think Cassian will be much better off growing up with two parents who are happy, rather than with parents who are trapped in a bad marriage," Michael argued.

Astrid was perplexed. Who was this man standing in front of her? Where had he suddenly procured all this psychobabble? "It's because of that woman, isn't it? I see . . . you don't want to be part of this family anymore. You want to live with this . . . this whore, don't you?" she cried.

Michael took a deep breath before answering. "Yes. I don't want to live with you anymore. And I think that for both our sakes I should move out today." He knew that if he was ever going to leave, this was his chance. He began to walk toward the bedroom. Where was his large suitcase?

Astrid stood helplessly by the doorway to the bedroom, wondering what had just happened. This was not how it was supposed to go. She watched numbly as Michael began to grab his clothes and throw them haphazardly into his black Tumi suitcase. She had wanted to buy him a suite of Loewe luggage when they were in Barcelona last year, but he insisted on something cheaper and more practical. Now she had the distinct feeling of being trapped in a dream. None of this could really be happening. The fight they just had. The car accident. Michael's philandering. None of it. Her husband wasn't really leaving. There was no way he was leaving. This was just a nightmare. She hugged herself, pinching the flesh around her elbow repeatedly, willing herself to wake up.

15

Nick

•

MACAU

Nick ran his fingers along the leather-bound spines perfectly arranged on the neoclassical mahogany bookcase. *Lieutenant Hornblower. Islands in the Stream. Billy Budd.* All nautical-themed titles. He picked out a volume by Knut Hamsun that he had never heard of, *August*, and settled into one of the overstuffed club chairs, hoping he would be undisturbed for a while. Cracking open the stiff embossed cover, he could tell at once that its pages, like most of the others here, had probably never seen the light of day. Hardly surprising, considering that this sumptuous library was tucked away on the lower deck of a 388-foot yacht that boasted such distractions as a ballroom, a karaoke lounge for Bernard's dad, a chapel for his mother, a casino, a sushi bar complete with a full-time sushi chef from Hokkaido, two swimming pools, and an outdoor bowling alley on the uppermost deck that also converted into a runway for fashion shows.

Nick glanced at the door in dismay as footsteps could be heard coming down the spiral staircase just outside the library. If he'd been smarter, he would have locked the door behind him. Much to Nick's relief, it was Mehmet who peered in. "Nicholas Young—why am I not surprised to find you in the only intellectually inclined room on this entire vessel?" Mehmet remarked. "Mind if I join you? This looks to be the quietest place on the boat, and if I have to hear another Hôtel

Costes remix, I think I'm going to jump overboard and swim for the nearest buoy."

"You're most welcome here. How are the natives doing?"

"Incredibly restless, I would say. I left the pool deck just as the ice-cream-sundae contest began."

"They're making sundaes?" Nick cocked an eyebrow.

"Yes. On a dozen nude Macanese girls."

Nick shook his head wearily.

"I tried to rescue Colin, but he got trapped. Bernard anointed Colin the Whipped Cream King."

Mehmet slouched into a club chair and closed his eyes. "Colin should have listened to me and come to Istanbul for a relaxing get-away before the wedding. I told him to invite you too."

"Now *that* would have been nice." Nick smiled. "I would much rather be at your family's summer palace on the banks of the Bos-phorus than on this boat."

"You know, I'm surprised Colin had a bachelor party in the first place. It didn't strike me as his sort of thing."

"It's not, but I think Colin felt like he couldn't refuse Bernard, what with Bernard's father being the largest minority shareholder in the Khoo Organization," Nick explained.

"Bernard's doing a fine job, isn't he? He truly thinks Colin enjoys being part of the biggest drug and drinking binge I've witnessed since spring break in Cabo," Mehmet murmured.

Nick stared at him in surprise, never expecting to hear those words come out of Mehmet's mouth. Mehmet opened one eye and grinned. "Just kidding. I've never been to Cabo—I just always wanted to say that."

"You scared me for a second!" Nick laughed.

Just then, Colin stumbled into the library and plopped down on the nearest chair. "God help me! I don't think I'll ever be able to eat another maraschino cherry again!" He moaned, massaging his temples.

"Colin, did you actually eat off one of the girls?" Mehmet asked incredulously.

"Nooo! Araminta would kill me if she found out I ate a hot fudge sundae off some girl's pu . . . er, crotch. I only took one cherry, and then I told Bernard I really needed to go to the bathroom."

"Where did all these girls come from in the first place?" Mehmet asked.

"Bernard hired them from that brothel he forced all of us to go to last night," Colin mumbled through his pounding headache.

"You know, I think he was genuinely shocked when we turned down the girls he had procured for the night," Mehmet remarked.

"Poor bastard. We've completely ruined his bachelor weekend, haven't we? We didn't want to go to the dogfights, we didn't want to make sex videos with prostitutes, and we turned up our noses at his fancy Peruvian cocaine." Nick laughed.

Screams could be heard from the upper deck, followed by much panicked yelling. "I wonder what's happening now," Nick said. But none of them could muster up the effort to get out of the plush club chairs. The yacht began to slow, and several crewmen could be heard running along the lower decks.

Alistair strolled into the room, carefully balancing a white cup and saucer with what appeared to be a very frothy cappuccino.

"What's all the screaming on the deck?" Colin asked with a groan.

Alistair simply rolled his eyes and sat down in one of the chairs by the Regency drum table. "One of the girls slipped overboard during the oil-wrestling contest. Not to worry, her breasts make an excellent flotation device."

He began sipping his coffee, but then made a face. "The Aussie bartender lied to me. He told me he could make the perfect flat white, and this isn't even close. This is just a lousy latte!"

"What is a flat white?" Mehmet asked.

"It's a kind of cappuccino that they only do down in Oz. You use the steamed, frothy milk from the bottom of the jug, holding back the foam at the top so that you get this smooth, velvety texture."

"And that's good?" Mehmet continued, a little intrigued.

"Oh, it's the best. I had to have at least two a day back in my uni days in Sydney," Alistair said.

"God, now I'm craving one too!" Colin sighed. "This is a fucking nightmare. I just wish we could get off this boat and go have a decent cup of coffee somewhere. I know this is supposed to be one of the coolest new yachts in the world and I should be so grateful, but frankly, it feels like a floating prison to me." His face darkened, and Nick looked at him uneasily. Nick could sense that Colin was slipping fast into one of his deep funks. An idea began to take shape in his head. He whipped out his cell phone and began scrolling through his contacts, leaning over to Mehmet and whispering in his ear. Mehmet grinned and nodded eagerly.

"What are the two of you whispering about?" Alistair asked, leaning over curiously.

"I just had an idea. Colin, are you ready to bail out of this pathetically lame bachelor party?" Nick asked.

"I would like nothing more, but I don't think I can risk offending Bernard and, more important, his father. I mean, Bernard pulled out all the stops to entertain us in grand style this weekend."

"Actually, Bernard pulled out all the stops to entertain *himself*," Nick retorted. "Look how miserable you are. How much more of this do you want to endure, just so the Tais won't be offended? It's your last weekend as a single man, Colin. I think I have an exit strategy that won't offend anyone. If I can make it happen, will you play along?"

"Okay . . . why not?" Colin said a little trepidatiously.

"Hear, hear!" Alistair cheered.

———

"Quick, quick, we have a medical emergency. I need you to stop this boat, and I need our precise coordinates right now," Nick demanded as he rushed into the yacht's pilothouse.

"What's the matter?" the captain asked.

"My friend is suffering from acute pancreatitis. We have a doctor below, who thinks he might have begun bleeding internally. I'm on the line with the life-flight rescue chopper," Nick said, holding up his cell phone anxiously.

"Wait a minute, just wait a minute—I'm the captain of this ship. I'm the one who decides whether we call for medical evacuations. Who's the doctor below? Let me go see the patient," the captain gruffly demanded.

"Captain, with all due respect, we don't have a moment to waste. You can come look at him all you want, but right now, I just need the coordinates from you."

"But who are you speaking to? Macau Coast Guard? This is highly irregular protocol. Let me talk to them," the captain sputtered in confusion.

Nick put on his most condescendingly posh accent—honed from all his years at Balliol—and glowered at the captain. "Do you have any idea who my friend is? He's Colin Khoo, heir to one of the biggest fortunes on the planet."

"Don't get snooty with me, young chap!" the captain bellowed. "I don't care who your friend is, there are maritime emergency protocols I MUST FOLLOW, AND—"

"AND RIGHT NOW, my friend is below deck on your ship, quite possibly hemorrhaging to death, because you won't let me call for an emergency evacuation!" Nick interrupted, raising his voice to match the captain's. "Do you want to take the blame for this? Because you will, I can guarantee that. I'm Nicholas Young, and my family controls one of the world's largest shipping conglomerates. Please just give me the *fucking* coordinates now, or I promise you I'll personally see to it that you won't even be able to captain a piece of Styrofoam after today!"

Twenty minutes later, as Bernard sat in the diamond-shaped Jacuzzi on the uppermost deck while a half-Portuguese girl tried to swallow both of his testicles under the bubbly water jets, a white Sikorsky helicopter appeared out of the sky and began to descend onto the yacht's helipad. At first he thought he was hallucinating from all the booze. Then he saw Nick, Mehmet, and Alistair emerge onto the helipad, holding a stretcher on which lay Colin, tightly bundled up in one of the yacht's silk Etro blankets. "What the fuck is happening?" he said, getting out of the water, pulling on his Vilebrequin trunks and rushing up the steps toward the helipad.

He ran into Lionel in the corridor. "I was just coming to tell you—Colin is feeling horribly sick. He's been doubled over in pain for the past hour and throwing up uncontrollably. We think it's alcohol poisoning, from all of his boozing over the past two days. We're getting him off the boat and straight to the hospital."

They ran to the helicopter, and Bernard looked in at Colin, who was groaning softly, his face locked in a grimace. Alistair sat beside him, mopping his forehead with a damp towel.

"But, but, why the hell didn't anyone tell me sooner? I had no idea Colin was feeling this sick. *Kan ni na!* Now your family is going to blame me. And then it's going to get into all the gossip columns, all the papers," Bernard complained, suddenly becoming alarmed.

"Nothing's going to leak. No gossip, no newspapers," Lionel

said solemnly. "Colin doesn't want you to get any blame, which is why you have to listen to me now—we're going to take him to the hospital, and we won't tell anyone in the family what's happening. I've had alcohol poisoning before—Colin just needs to get detoxed and rehydrated. He'll be fine in a few days. You and the other guys need to keep pretending that nothing's wrong and keep partying, okay? Don't call the family, don't say a word to anyone, and we'll see you back in Singapore."

"Okay, okay," Bernard nodded rapidly, feeling relieved. Now he could get back to his blow job without feeling guilty.

As the helicopter lifted off from the yacht, Nick and Alistair began laughing uncontrollably at the figure of Bernard, his baggy swimming trunks whipping around his pale damp thighs, staring up at them in bewilderment.

"I don't think it even occurred to him that this isn't a medical helicopter but a chartered one." Mehmet chuckled.

"Where are we going?" Colin asked excitedly, throwing off the purple-and-gold paisley blanket.

"Mehmet and I have chartered a Cessna Citation X. It's all fueled up and waiting for us in Hong Kong. From there, it's a surprise," Nick said.

"The Citation X. Isn't that the plane that flies at six hundred miles per hour?" Alistair asked.

"It's even faster when we're just five people with no luggage." Nick grinned.

———

A mere six hours later, Nick, Colin, Alistair, Mehmet, and Lionel found themselves sitting on canvas chairs in the middle of the Australian desert, taking in the spectacular view of the glowing rock.

"I've always wanted to come to Ayers Rock. Or Uluru, or whatever they call it now," Colin said.

"It's so quiet," Mehmet said softly. "This is a very spiritual place, isn't it? I can really feel its energy, even from this distance."

"It's considered to be the most sacred site for the Aboriginal tribes," Nick answered. "My father brought me here years ago. Back in those days, we were still allowed to climb the rock. They stopped letting you do that a few years ago."

"Guys, I can't thank you enough. This was the perfect escape from a very misguided bachelor party. I'm sorry I put all of you through Bernard's bullshit. This is really all I ever hoped for—to be someplace amazing with my best friends."

A man in a white polo shirt and khaki shorts approached with a large tray from the luxury eco-resort nearby. "Well, Colin, Alistair—I thought that the only way to get you coffee snobs to stop bitching and moaning was to get you a decent flat white, one hundred percent made in Australia," Nick said, as the waiter put the tray down on the reddish earth.

Alistair brought the cup to his nose and inhaled the rich aroma deeply. "Nick, if you weren't my cousin, I'd kiss you right now," he joked.

Colin took a long sip of his coffee, its perfect velvety foam leaving a white frothy mustache on his upper lip. "This has got to be the best coffee I've ever tasted. Guys, I'll never forget this."

It was just past sunset, and the sky was shifting rapidly from shades of burnt orange into a deep violet blue. The men sat in awed silence, as the world's largest monolith glowed and shimmered a thousand indescribable shades of crimson.

16

Dr. Gu
.

SINGAPORE

Wye Mun sat at his desk, studying the piece of paper his daughter had just handed him. The ornate desk was a replica of the one Napoleon used at the Tuileries, with a satinwood veneer and ormolu legs of lions' heads and torsos that descended into elaborate claws. Wye Mun loved to sit in his burgundy velvet Empire chair and rub his socked feet against the bulbous golden claws, a habit his wife constantly scolded him for. Today, it was Peik Lin who substituted for her mother. "Dad, you're going to rub off all the gold if you don't stop doing that!"

Wye Mun ignored her and kept scratching his toes compulsively. He stared at the names Peik Lin had written down during her phone conversation a few days ago with Rachel: James Young, Rosemary T'sien, Oliver T'sien, Jacqueline Ling. Who were these people behind that mysterious old gate on Tyersall Road? Not recognizing any of these names bothered him more than he was willing to admit. Wye Mun couldn't help but remember what his father always said: "Never forget we are Hainanese, son. We are the descendants of servants and seamen. We always have to work harder to prove our worth."

Even from a young age, Wye Mun had been made aware that being the Chinese-educated son of a Hainanese immigrant put him at a disadvantage to the aristocratic Straits Chinese landowners or the Hokkiens that dominated the banking industry. His father had come to Singapore as a fourteen-year-old laborer and built a construction business out of sheer sweat and tenacity, and as their family business blossomed over the decades into a far-flung empire, Wye Mun thought that he had leveled the playing field. Singapore was a meritocracy, and whoever performed well was invited into the winner's circle. But those people—those people behind the gates were a sudden reminder that this was not entirely the case.

With his children all grown up now, it was time for the next generation to keep conquering new territory. His eldest son, Peik Wing, had done well by marrying the daughter of a junior MP, a Cantonese girl who was brought up a Christian, no less. P.T. was still fooling around and enjoying his playboy ways, so the focus now was on Peik Lin. Out of his three children, Peik Lin took after him the most. She was his smartest, most ambitious, and—dare he admit it—most attractive child. She was the one he felt confident would surpass all of them and make a truly brilliant match, linking the Gohs with one of Singapore's blue-blooded families. He could sense from the way his daughter spoke that she was onto something, and he was determined to help her dig deeper. "I think it's time we paid a visit to Dr. Gu," he said to his daughter.

Dr. Gu was a retired doctor in his late eighties, an eccentric who lived alone in a small, dilapidated house at the bottom of Dunearn Road. He was born in Xian to a family of scholars, but moved to Singapore in his youth for schooling. In the natural order of how Singapore society worked, Wye Mun and Dr. Gu might never have crossed paths had it not been for Dr. Gu's maddening stubbornness some thirty-odd years ago.

Goh Developments had been building a new complex of semi-detached houses along Dunearn Road, and Dr. Gu's little plot of land was the sole obstruction to the project getting under way. His neighbors had been bought out under extremely favorable terms, but Dr. Gu refused to budge. After all of his lawyers had failed in their negotiations, Wye Mun drove to the house himself, armed with his checkbook and determined to talk some sense into the old fart. Instead, the brilliant old curmudgeon convinced him to alter his entire scheme, and the revised development turned out to be even more of a success because of his recommendations. Wye Mun now found himself visiting his new friend to offer him a job. Dr. Gu refused, but Wye Mun would keep coming back, enthralled by Dr. Gu's encyclopedic knowledge of Singapore history, his acute analysis of the financial markets, and his wonderful Longjing tea.

Wye Mun and Peik Lin drove over to Dr. Gu's house, parking Wye Mun's shiny new Maserati Quattroporte just outside the rust-corroded metal gate.

"I can't believe he still lives here," Peik Lin said, as they walked down the cracked cement driveway. "Shouldn't he be in a retirement home by now?"

"I think he manages okay. He has a maid, and also two daughters, you know," Wye Mun said.

"He was smart not to sell out to you thirty years ago. This little piece of land is worth even more of a fortune now. It's the last undeveloped plot on Dunearn Road, we can probably even build a very sleek, narrow apartment tower here," Peik Lin commented.

"I tell you *lah*, he intends to die in this shack. Did I tell you what I heard from my stockbroker Mr. Oei many years ago? Dr. Gu is sitting on one million shares of HSBC."

"What?" Peik Lin turned to her father in amazed shock. "One million shares? That's more than fifty million in today's dollars!"

"He started buying HSBC shares in the forties. I heard this tidbit twenty years ago, and the stock has split how many times since then? I tell you, old Dr. Gu is worth hundreds of millions by now."

Peik Lin stared with renewed wonder as the man with a shock of unruly white hair came hobbling out onto his porch in a brown polyester short-sleeve shirt that looked like it had been tailored in pre-Castro Havana and a pair of dark green pajama bottoms. "Goh Wye Mun! Still wasting money on expensive cars, I see," he bellowed, his voice surprisingly robust for a man of his age.

"Greetings, Dr. Gu! Do you remember my daughter, Peik Lin?" Wye Mun said, patting the old man on the back.

"Aiyah, is this your daughter? I thought this pretty girl must surely be your latest mistress. I know how all you property tycoons are."

Peik Lin laughed. "Hello, Dr. Gu. My father wouldn't be standing here if I was his mistress. My mum would castrate him!"

"Oh, but I thought she did that a long time ago already." Everyone laughed, as Dr. Gu led them to a few wooden chairs arranged in his small front garden. Peik Lin noticed that the grass was meticulously mowed and edged. The fence that fronted Dunearn Road was covered in thick intertwining vines of morning glories, screening the bucolic little patch from the traffic along the busy thoroughfare. There isn't a single place like this left along this entire stretch, Peik Lin thought.

An elderly Chinese servant came out of the house with a large round wooden tray. On it was a ceramic teapot, an old copper kettle, three clay teacups, and three smaller snifter cups. Dr. Gu held the well-burnished kettle high above the teapot and began pouring. "I love watching Dr. Gu do his tea ritual," Wye Mun said to his daughter quietly. "See how he pours the water from high up. This is known as *xuan hu gao chong*—'rinsing from an elevated pot.'" Then, Dr. Gu began to pour the tea into each of the three cups, but instead of offering it to his guests, he flung the light caramel-colored tea dramatically from each cup onto the grass behind him, much to Peik Lin's surprise. He then refilled the teapot with a fresh batch of hot water.

"See, Peik Lin, that was the first rinse of the leaves, known as *hang yun liu shui*—'a row of clouds, running water.' This second pouring from a lower height is called *zai zhu qing xuan*—'direct again the pure spring,'" Wye Mun continued.

"Wye Mun, she could probably care less about these old proverbs," Dr. Gu said, before launching into a clinically precise explanation. "The first pouring was done from a height so that the force of water rinses the Longjing leaves. The hot water also helps to acclimate the temperature of the teapot and the cups. Then you do a second pouring, this time slowly and near the mouth of the pot, to gently coax the flavor out of the leaves. Now we let it steep for a while."

The sound of screeching truck brakes just beyond the fence interrupted the serenity of Dr. Gu's tea ritual. "Doesn't all this noise bother you?" Peik Lin asked.

"Not at all. It reminds me that I am still alive, and that my hearing is not deteriorating as quickly as I had planned," Dr. Gu replied. "Sometimes I wish I didn't have to hear all the nonsense that comes out of politicians' mouths!"

"Come on, *lah*, Dr. Gu, if it weren't for our politicians, do you think you would be able to enjoy this nice garden of yours? Think of how they've transformed this place from a backward island to one of the most prosperous countries in the world," Wye Mun argued, always on the defensive whenever anyone criticized the government.

"What rubbish! Prosperity is nothing but an illusion. Do you know what *my children* are doing with all this prosperity? My eldest daughter started a dolphin research institute. She is determined to rescue the white dolphins of the Yangtze River from extinction. Do you know how polluted that river is? This bloody mammal is already extinct! Scientists haven't been able to locate a single one of these creatures for years now, but she is determined to find them. And my other daughter? She buys old castles in Scotland. Not even the Scottish want those crumbling old pits, but my daughter does. She spends millions restoring them, and then no one comes to visit her. Her wastrel son, my only grandson and namesake, is thirty-six years old. Do you want to know what he does?"

"No . . . I mean, yes," Peik Lin said, trying not to giggle.

"He has a rock-and-roll band in London. Not even like those Beatles, who at least made money. This one has long oily hair, wears black eyeliner, and makes horrible noises with home appliances."

"Well, at least they are being *creative*," Peik Lin offered politely.

"Creatively wasting all my hard-earned money! I'm telling you, this so-called 'prosperity' is going to be the downfall of Asia. Each new generation becomes lazier than the next. They think they can make overnight fortunes just by flipping properties and getting hot tips in the stock market. Ha! Nothing lasts forever, and when this boom ends, these youngsters won't know what hit them."

"This is why I force my kids to work for a living—they are not going to get a single cent out of me until I am six feet underground," Wye Mun said, winking at his daughter.

Dr. Gu peeked into the teapot, finally satisfied with the brew. He poured the tea into the snifter cups. "Now this is called *long feng cheng xiang*, which means 'the dragon and phoenix foretells good fortune,'" he said, placing a teacup over the smaller snifter cup and inverting the cups deftly, releasing the tea into the drinking cup. He presented the first cup to Wye Mun, and the second cup to Peik Lin. She thanked him and took her first sip. The tea was bracingly bitter, and she tried not to make a face while swallowing it.

"So, Wye Mun, what really brings you here today? Surely you didn't come to hear an old man rant." Dr. Gu eyed Peik Lin. "Your father is very cunning, you know. He only comes calling when he needs to get something out of me."

"Dr. Gu, your roots go deep in Singapore. Tell me, have you ever heard of James Young?" Wye Mun asked, cutting to the chase.

Dr. Gu looked up from pouring his own tea with a start. "James Young! I haven't heard anyone utter that name in decades."

"Do you know him, then? I met his grandson recently. He's dating a good friend of mine," Peik Lin explained. She took another sip of the tea, finding herself appreciating its silky bitterness more and more with each sip.

"Who are the Youngs?" Wye Mun asked eagerly.

"Why are you suddenly so interested in these people?" Dr. Gu queried.

Wye Mun considered the question carefully before he answered. "We are trying to help my daughter's friend, since she is quite serious about the boy. I'm not familiar with the family."

"Of course you wouldn't know them, Wye Mun. Hardly anybody does these days. I have to admit that my own knowledge is very outdated."

"Well, what can you tell us?" Wye Mun pressed on.

Dr. Gu took a long sip of his tea and leaned into a more comfortable position. "The Youngs are descended, I believe, from a long line of royal court physicians, going all the way back to the Tang dynasty. James Young—Sir James Young, actually—was the first Western-educated neurologist in Singapore, trained at Oxford."

"He made his fortune as a doctor?" Wye Mun asked, rather surprised.

"Not at all! James was not the sort of person who cared about making a fortune. He was too busy saving lives in World War II, during the Japanese occupation," Dr. Gu said, staring at the crisscrossing patterns of ivy on his fence as they suddenly seemed to transform into diamond-like patterns, reminding him of a chain-link fence from a long time ago.

"So you knew him during the war?" Wye Mun asked, jarring Dr. Gu out of his recollection.

"Yes, yes, that's how I knew him," Dr. Gu said slowly. He hesitated for a few moments, before continuing. "James Young was in charge of an underground medical corps that I was briefly involved with. After the war, he set up his clinic in the old section of Chinatown, specifically to serve the poor and elderly. I heard that for years he charged his patients practically nothing."

"So how did he make his money?"

"There you go again, Wye Mun, always chasing after the money," Dr. Gu chided.

"Well, where did that huge house come from?" Wye Mun asked.

"Ah, I see the true nature of your interest now. You must be referring to the house off Tyersall Road."

"Yes. Have you been there?" Peik Lin asked.

"Goodness, no. I only heard about it. Like I said, I really did not know James very well; I would never have been invited."

"I dropped my friend off at the house last week, and I could hardly believe it when I saw the place."

"You must be joking! Is the house still there?" Dr. Gu said, looking quite shocked.

"Yes," Peik Lin replied.

"I would have thought that the place was long gone. I must say I'm quite impressed that the family never sold out in all these years."

"Yes, I'm quite shocked that there's a property this large on the island," Wye Mun cut in.

"Why should you be? The whole area behind the Botanic Gardens used to be full of great estates. The Sultan of Johore had a palace over there called Istana Woodneuk that burned to the ground many years ago. You say you were there last week?" Dr. Gu queried.

"Yes, but I did not go in."

"A pity. It would be a rare treat to see one of those houses. So few are left, thanks to all the brilliant developers," Dr. Gu said, glaring in mock anger at Wye Mun.

"So if James Young never made any money, how did—" Wye Mun began.

"You don't listen, Wye Mun! I said that James Young wasn't interested in making money, but I never said he didn't have any. The Youngs had money, generations of money. Besides, James married Shang Su Yi. And she, I can tell you for a fact, comes from a family so unfathomably rich, it would make your eyes water, Wye Mun."

"Who is she, then?" Wye Mun asked, his curiosity piqued to boiling point.

"All right, I will tell you and shut you up once and for all. She is the daughter of Shang Loong Ma. Never heard that name, either, right? He was an enormously wealthy banker in Peking, and before the Qing dynasty fell, he very smartly moved his money to Singapore, where he made an even greater fortune in shipping and commodities. The man had his tentacles in every major business in the region—he controlled all the shipping lines from the Dutch East Indies to Siam, and he was the mastermind behind uniting the early Hokkien banks in the thirties."

"So Nick's grandmother inherited all of that," Peik Lin surmised.

"She and her brother, Alfred."

"Alfred Shang. Hmm . . . another fellow I've never heard of," Wye Mun huffed.

"Well, that's not surprising. He moved to England many decades ago, but he is still—very quietly—one of the most influential figures in Asia. Wye Mun, you have to realize that before your generation of fat cats, there was an earlier generation of tycoons who made their fortunes and moved on to greener pastures. I thought most of the Youngs had long since dispersed from Singapore. The last time I heard any news, it was that one of the daughters had married into the Thai royal family."

"Sounds like a pretty well-connected bunch," Peik Lin said.

"Oh, yes indeed. The eldest daughter, for instance, is married to Harry Leong."

"Harry Leong, the fellow who is director of the Institute of ASEAN Affairs?"

"That's just a title, Wye Mun. Harry Leong is one of the king-makers in our government."

"No wonder I always see him in the prime minister's box at National Day celebrations. So this family is close to the center of power."

"Wye Mun, they *are* the center of power," Dr. Gu corrected, turning to Peik Lin. "You say your friend is dating the grandson? She's a fortunate girl, then, if she marries into this clan."

"I was beginning to think the same thing myself," Peik Lin said quietly.

Dr. Gu considered Peik Lin thoughtfully for a moment, and then he peered straight into her eyes, saying, "Remember, every treasure comes with a price." She caught his gaze for a moment, before looking away.

"Dr. Gu, it's always good to see you. Thank you for all your help," Wye Mun said, getting up. He was starting to get a backache from the rickety wooden chair.

"And thank you for the wonderful tea," Peik Lin said, helping Dr. Gu up from his seat.

"Will you ever accept my invitation and come over for dinner? I have a new cook who makes amazing *Ipoh hor fun*,* Dr. Gu."

"You're not the only one who has a good cook, Goh Wye Mun," Dr. Gu said wryly, walking them to their car.

As Wye Mun and Peik Lin merged into the early-evening traffic on Dunearn Road, Wye Mun said, "Why don't we invite Rachel and her boyfriend to dinner next week?"

Peik Lin nodded. "Let's take them somewhere classy, like Min Jiang."

Dr. Gu stood by his gate, watching as their car disappeared. The sun was setting just over the treetops, a few rays of light penetrating through the branches and glaring into his eyes.

He awoke with a start in the blinding sun to find his bleeding wrists bound tightly against the rusty chain-link fence. A group of officers walked by, and he noticed one uniformed man staring at him intently. Did he look familiar somehow? The man went up to the commanding officer and pointed directly at him. Curse to the gods. This was it. He looked at them, trying to muster up as much hate as he could in his expression. He wanted to die defiant, with pride. The man said calmly, in a British-accented English, "There's been a mistake. That one over there in the middle is just a poor idiot servant. I recognize him from my friend's farm, where he rears the pigs." One of the Japanese soldiers translated to the commanding officer, who sneered in disgust before barking out a few curt orders. He was cut loose, and brought to kneel in front of the soldiers. Through his bleary eyes, he suddenly recognized the man who had pointed him out. It was Dr. Young, who had taught one of his surgical classes when he was a medical trainee. "See, this is not a man of importance. He's not even worth your bullets. Let him go back to the farm where he can feed the dirty pigs," Dr. Young said, before walking off with the other soldiers. More arguing between the soldiers ensued, and before he knew what was happening, he found himself on a transport truck bound for the work farms in Geylang. Months later, he would run into Dr. Young at a meeting in the secret room hidden behind a shop house on Telok Ayer Street. He began thanking him profusely for saving his life, but Dr. Young brushed him off quickly. "Nonsense—you would have done the same for me. Besides, I couldn't let them kill yet another doctor. There are too few of us left," he said plainly.

* A delicacy from Ipoh, Malaysia—rice noodles served in a clear soup with prawns, shredded chicken, and fried shallots.

As Dr. Gu walked slowly back into his house, he felt a sudden pang of regret. He wished he hadn't said so much about the Youngs. Wye Mun, as usual, had steered him toward the stories about money, and he had missed the chance to tell them the real story, about a man whose greatness had nothing to do with wealth or power.

17

Rachel
•
SINGAPORE

"I've been trying to reach you for days! Where have you been? Did you get all the messages I left at the hotel?" Kerry asked her daughter in rapid-fire Mandarin.

"Mom, I'm sorry—I was away all weekend and only just got back," Rachel replied, raising her voice as she always did whenever she was talking to anyone long distance, even though she could hear her mother perfectly well.

"Where did you go?"

"I went to a remote island in the Indian Ocean for a bachelorette party."

"Huh? You went to India?" her mother asked, still confused.

"No, not India. It's an ISLAND in the INDIAN OCEAN, off the coast of Indonesia. It's an hour plane ride from Singapore."

"You took a plane trip just for two days? Hiyah, what a waste of money!"

"Well, I wasn't paying, and besides, I flew on a private plane."

"You flew on a private plane? Whose plane?"

"The bride's."

"Wah! So lucky, ah. Is the bride very rich?"

"Mom, these people . . ." Rachel began, before discreetly lowering her voice. "Both the bride and the groom come from very wealthy families."

"*Really?* What about Nick's family? Are they rich too?" Kerry asked.

How did she know this would be the next question out of her mom's mouth?

Rachel glanced toward the bathroom. Nick was still in the shower, but she decided to step out of the room anyway. She walked into the garden toward the quiet, shadier side of the pool. "Yes, Mom, Nick comes from a wealthy family," Rachel said, sitting down on one of the lounge chairs by the pool.

"You know, this is something I suspected all along. He's so well brought up. I can tell just by looking at how he behaves during dinner. Such lovely manners, and he always offers me the best part of the meat, like the fish cheek or the juiciest piece of duck."

"Well, it doesn't really matter, Mom, because it seems like *everyone* here is rich. I think I'm still in a bit of a culture shock, or maybe it's cash shock. The way these people spend money—the houses and the planes and the dozens of maids—you need to see it with your own eyes. It's as if the recession isn't happening here. Everything is ultra-modern and sparkling clean."

"That's all I hear from friends who visit Singapore. That it's clean, *too* clean." Kerry paused for a moment, her voice taking on a tone of concern. "Daughter, you need to watch out."

"What do you mean, Mom?"

"I know how those families can be, and you don't want to give them the impression that you are after Nick's money. From now on, you need to be extra-careful how you present yourself."

Too late for that, Rachel thought. "I'm just being myself, Mom. I'm not going to change how I behave." She wanted so much to tell her mother about the dreadful weekend, but she knew it would only worry her needlessly. She had done the same thing with Nick, sharing only the vaguest details. (Besides, they had spent most of the afternoon in a marathon lovemaking session, and she hadn't wanted to spoil their postcoital bliss with any horror stories.)

"Is Nick being good to you?" her mother asked.

"Of course, Mom. Nick is a sweetheart, as always. He's just rather distracted right now with his friend's wedding coming up. It's going to be the biggest wedding Asia has ever seen, Mom. All the newspapers have been covering it."

"Really? Should I get one of the Chinese newspapers when I go into San Francisco tomorrow?"

"Sure, you can try. The bride is Araminta Lee, and the groom is Colin Khoo. Look out for their names."

"What are Nick's parents like?"

"I don't know. I'm meeting them tonight."

"You have been there for almost *one week* and you still haven't met his parents?" Kerry remarked, warning lights flashing in her head.

"They were out of the country last week, Mom, and then we were away this weekend."

"So you are going to meet his parents today?"

"Yes, dinner at their house."

"But why aren't you staying with them?" Kerry asked, her concern growing. There were so many little signs that her Americanized daughter did not understand.

"Mom, stop overanalyzing this. Nick's friend owns the hotel, so we're staying here during the wedding period for the convenience. But we're moving to his grandmother's house next week."

Kerry didn't buy her daughter's explanation. In her mind, it still made no sense that the only son of a Chinese family would be staying in a hotel with his girlfriend instead of at his parents' house. Unless he was ashamed of Rachel. Or even worse, maybe the parents had forbidden him to bring her home.

"What are you bringing to his parents? Did you get the Estée Lauder gifts like I told you to?"

"No, I figured it would be too personal to give Nick's mom cosmetics without having even met her. There's a terrific florist in the hotel, and—"

"No, daughter, *never* bring flowers! Especially not those white ones you love. White flowers are only for funerals. You should bring them a big basket of mandarin oranges, and hand it to them with both hands. And make sure that you bow your head very deeply when you greet his mother and father for the first time. These are all gestures of respect."

"*I know*, Mom. You're acting like I'm five years old. Why are you suddenly getting so worried?"

"This is the first time you have been serious with a Chinese man. There is so much you don't know about the proper etiquette with these families."

"I didn't realize you could be so old-fashioned," Rachel teased. "Besides, Nick's family doesn't seem really Chinese at all. They seem more British if anything."

"It doesn't matter. You are Chinese, and you still need to behave like a properly brought-up Chinese girl," Kerry said.

"Don't worry, Mom. It's just dinner," Rachel said lightly, even though her anxiety was beginning to build.

18

The Youngs

•

SINGAPORE

With its prime position atop Cairnhill Road, *the Residences at One Cairnhill* was a striking marriage of architectural preservation and real estate wizardry. Originally the home of prominent banker Kar Chin Kee and built during the late-Victorian period, the house had long been a landmark. But as land values skyrocketed over the decades, all the other big houses gave way to the developers and high-rise towers sprang up around the graceful mansion like overgrown bamboo. By the time the great man died in 2006, the house was deemed far too historic to tear down, yet far too valuable to remain a single residence. So Kar Chin Kee's heirs decided to preserve the original structure, converting it into the base of a sleek thirty-story glass tower where Nick's parents now lived (when they were in Singapore, that is).

As the taxi climbed the hill toward the imposing Corinthian-columned portico, Nick explained its history to Rachel. "Uncle Chin Kee was a friend of my grandmother's, so we used to visit every Chinese New Year, and I would be made to recite some elaborate poem in Mandarin. Then the old man, who reeked of cigars, would give me a *hong bao** stuffed with five hundred dollars."

---

* Mandarin for the little red packets of money that are given out by married adults and the elderly during Chinese New Year to children and unmarried young people as an act of well-wishing. Originally a token coin or several dollars, the *hong bao* in

"That's insane!" Rachel exclaimed. "The biggest *hong bao* I ever got in my life was fifty dollars, and that was from this asshole dating my mom who was *really* trying to win me over. What did you do with all that money?"

"Are you kidding? My parents kept it, of course. They kept all my New Year money—I never saw a cent of it."

Rachel looked at him in horror. "That's just wrong! *Hong baos* are as sacred as Christmas presents."

"Don't get me started on what they did with my presents on Christmas morning!" Nick laughed. As they entered the elevator, Rachel inhaled deeply as she prepared to meet Nick's parents—these *hong bao* snatchers—for the first time.

"Hey, don't forget to breeeeathe," Nick said, massaging her shoulders gently. On the thirtieth floor, the elevator opened directly into the penthouse's foyer and they were greeted by an enormous pane of glass that framed a panoramic view of the Orchard Road shopping district. "Wow!" Rachel whispered, marveling at the deep purple dusk settling over the skyline.

A woman appeared from around the corner and said, "Aiyah, Nicky, why is your hair so long? You look like a ruffian! You better get it cut short before Colin's wedding."

"Hi, Mum," Nick said simply. Rachel was still reeling from the abruptness of this encounter when Nick continued, "Mum, I'd like you to meet Rachel Chu, *my girlfriend.*"

"Oh, *hello*," Eleanor said, as if she had no idea who the girl might be. *So this is the girl. She looks better than in that school yearbook picture obtained by the detective.*

"It's so nice to meet you, Mrs. Young," Rachel found herself saying, although her mind was still trying to accept the notion that this woman could actually *be* Nick's mother. Rachel had been expecting an imperious grande dame with a powdered white face and a tight perm dressed in some Hillary Clinton–esque pantsuit, but before her stood a striking woman in a trendy scoop-neck top, black leggings,

---

recent times has become a competitive sport, as wealthy Chinese strive to impress one another by giving ever larger sums. In the 1980s, $20 was considered customary and $50 was a big deal. These days, $100 has become the minimum in all the best houses. Since it is considered impolite to open a *hong bao* in the presence of the giver, this has led to the phenomenon of little children running off to the bathroom immediately after receiving one so they can peek at how much they've scored.

and ballet flats, looking far too young to have a thirty-two-year-old son. Rachel bowed her head and presented her gift of oranges.

"How lovely! Aiyah, you really shouldn't have!" Eleanor replied graciously. *Why in the world did she bring mandarin oranges—does she think it's Chinese New Year? And why is she bowing like some stupid Japanese geisha?* "Have you been enjoying Singapore so far?"

"Yes, very much," Rachel replied. "Nick's taken me to have the most fantastic hawker food."

"Where did you take her?" Eleanor looked at her son dubiously. "You're practically a tourist yourself—you don't know all the secret holes-in-the-wall like I do."

"We've been to Lau Pa Sat, Old Airport Road, Holland Village—" Nick began.

"Alamak! What is there to eat in Holland Village?" Eleanor exclaimed.

"Plenty! We had the best *rojak* for lunch," Nick said defensively.

"Nonsense! Everyone knows that the only place to go for *rojak* is that stall on the top floor of Lucky Plaza."

Rachel laughed, her nerves quickly dissipating. Nick's mother was so funny—why had she been so nervous?

"Well, this is it," Eleanor said to her son, gesturing at the space.

"I don't know what you were talking about, Mum, the place looks perfect."

"Alamak, you don't know how much of a headache this flat has caused me! We had to re-stain the floors six times to get the right finish." Nick and Rachel stared down at the beautiful gleaming white oak floors. "And then some of the custom furniture in the guest bedrooms had to be redone, and the automatic blackout curtains in my bedroom aren't dark enough. I've had to sleep in one of the guest bedrooms on the other side of the flat for more than a month now because the curtains are on back order from France."

The entry foyer opened into a great room with thirty-foot ceilings and a grid-like pattern of skylights that drenched the room with light. The space was made even more dramatic by a sunken oval pit in the center, with sleek Hermès-orange sofas perfectly contoured around both sides of the oval. From the ceiling, a spiral chandelier of sculptured gold and glass teardrops pirouetted down until it almost touched the oval driftwood coffee table. Rachel could hardly believe that Nick's parents lived in such a space—it looked more like the lobby of some impossibly hip hotel. A phone rang in another room, and a maid peered out of a doorway to announce, "It's Mrs. Foo and Mrs. Leong."

"Oh, Consuelo, please send them up," Eleanor said. *At last, the reinforcements are here.*

Nick looked at his mother in surprise. "You invited other people? I thought we were going to have a quiet family dinner."

Eleanor smiled. *We would have, if it were just our family.* "It's only the regular crowd, *lah.* The cook made *laksa,* and it's always better to have more people for that. Besides, everyone wants to see you, and they *can't wait* to meet Rachel!"

Nick smiled at Rachel in an attempt to cover up his dismay. He had wanted his parents to give their undivided attention to Rachel, but his mother was always springing last-minute surprises like this.

"Go wake your father, Nick—he's napping in his media room down that hall," Eleanor instructed.

Nick and Rachel walked toward the media room. The sounds of gunfire and explosions could be heard from within. As they approached the open door, Rachel could see Nick's father asleep on a Danish ergonomic recliner while *Battlestar Galactica* played on the flat-screen television built into the sandblasted oak wall. "Let's not disturb him," Rachel whispered, but Nick entered anyway.

"Wakey, wakey," he said softly.

Nick's father opened his eyes and looked up at Nick in surprise. "Oh, hello. Is it dinnertime?"

"Yes, Dad."

Nick's father got up from the chair and looked around, spotting Rachel standing shyly in the doorway.

"You must be Rachel Chu," he said, smoothing down the back of his hair.

"Yes," Rachel replied, coming into the room. Nick's father extended his hand. "Philip Young," he said with a smile, shaking her hand firmly. Rachel liked him instantly, and she could at last see where her boyfriend got his looks. Nick's large eyes and elegantly shaped mouth were exactly like his mother's, but the thin nose, prominent jawline, and thick jet-black hair were unmistakably his father's.

"When did you get in?" Nick asked his father.

"I caught the morning flight from Sydney. I wasn't planning to come until later in the week, but your mum insisted that I fly up today."

"Do you work in Sydney, Mr. Young?" Rachel asked.

"Work? No, I moved to Sydney *not* to work. It's far too beautiful a place for work. You get distracted by the weather and the sea, the long walks and the good fishing."

"Oh, I see," Rachel said. She noticed that his accent was a unique fusion of British, Chinese, and Australian.

Just then, there was a knock on the door, and Astrid peeked in. "I'm under strict orders to corral all of you," she announced.

"Astrid! I didn't know you were coming tonight," Nick said.

"Well, your mum wanted it to be a surprise. Surprise!" Astrid said, fluttering her fingers and giving him an ironic smile.

Everyone made their way back to the living room, where Nick and Rachel were surrounded by a flurry of dinner guests. Lorena Lim and Carol Tai shook Rachel's hand, while Daisy Foo embraced Nick. (It did not escape Rachel that Daisy was the first person who had hugged him all night.)

"Aiyah, Nicky, why have you been hiding your beautiful girl-friend for so long?" Daisy said, greeting Rachel with an effusive hug as well. Before Rachel could respond, she felt someone grabbing her arm. She looked down at the bing-cherry-size ruby ring and long red manicured claws before looking up in shock at a woman with teal-green eye shadow and rouge painted heavier than a drag queen's.

"Rachel, I'm Nadine," the woman said. "I've heard so much about you from my daughter."

"Really? Who's your daughter?" Rachel asked politely. Just then, she heard a high-pitched squeal right behind her. "Nicky! I've missed you!" a distinctive voice exclaimed. A chill came over Rachel. It was Francesca Shaw, greeting Nick with a tight bear hug and a kiss on the cheek. Before she could react, Francesca put on her biggest smile and swooped down on Rachel with another double-cheek kiss. "Rachel, lovely to see you so soon again!"

"Oh, were you at Araminta's bachelorette party?" Nick asked.

"Of course I was. We all had such a gloooorious time, didn't we, Rachel? Such a beautiful island, and wasn't the food marvelous? I heard you particularly enjoyed the *fish course*."

"Yes, it was quite an experience," Rachel replied slowly, stunned by Francesca's remarks. Was she admitting responsibility for the mutilated fish? She noticed that Francesca's lipstick had left a bright red imprint on Nick's cheek.

"I'm not sure if you remember my cousin Astrid," Nick said to Francesca.

"Of course!" Francesca rushed to greet her with a hug. Astrid stiffened up, taken aback by how familiar Francesca was being. Francesca scrutinized Astrid from head to toe. She was wearing a white drape-front silk georgette dress with navy blue trim. *The cut is so perfect, it must be couture. But who's the designer?*

"What a fantastic dress!" Francesca said.

"Thank you. You look lovely in red," Astrid responded.

"Valentino, of course," Francesca replied, pausing to wait for Astrid to reveal the designer of her outfit. But Astrid did not reciprocate. Without missing a beat, Francesca turned to Nick's mother and gushed, "What a fabulous place, Auntie Elle! I want to move in *right now*. It's all so Morris Lapidus, so Miami Modern! It makes me want to throw on a Pucci caftan and order a whiskey sour."

"Wah, Francesca, you hit it right on the head," Eleanor said in delight. "Everybody, we're going to do something different tonight— we're all going to *makan* in my little kitchen," she announced as she led her guests into a kitchen that to Rachel seemed anything but little. The cavernous space looked like a gourmand's idea of what heaven might be—a gleaming temple of white Calacatta marble, stainless-steel surfaces, and state-of-the-art appliances. A chef in white uniform stood by the commercial-grade Viking stove, busy monitoring bubbling copper pots, while three kitchen maids scurried around making final preparations. At the far end was an alcove with an art deco diner-style banquette.

As they took their seats, Carol glanced over at the chef deftly ladling crimson broth into large white clay soup bowls. "Wah, Eleanor—I feel like I'm dining at the chef's table of some chichi restaurant," she said.

"Isn't it fun?" Eleanor said merrily. She looked at Rachel and said, "I was never allowed to set foot in the kitchen at my mother-in-law's house. Now I get to eat in my *own* kitchen, and actually watch the food being cooked!" Rachel smiled in amusement—here was a woman who obviously had never cooked a meal in her life but seemed to relish the novelty of being inside a kitchen.

"Well, I love to cook. I can only dream of one day having a kitchen as beautiful as yours, Mrs. Young," Rachel said.

Eleanor smiled graciously. *I'm sure you can—with my son's money.*

"Rachel is an *amazing* cook. Without her, I'd probably be eating ramen noodles every night," Nick added.

"That would be just like you," Daisy commented. She looked at Rachel and said, "I used to call Nicky my 'Noodle Boy'—he was always so crazy over noodles as a kid. We would take him to the top restaurants in Singapore, and all he ever wanted was a plate of fried noodles with extra gravy."

As she said this, three maids entered the dining alcove and placed large steaming bowls of *laksa* noodle soup in front of each guest. Rachel marveled at the beautiful composition of butterfly shrimp, fried fish cake, pillowy tofu puffs, and hard-boiled egg halves beautifully arranged over the thick rice vermicelli and fiery soup. For a few minutes, the room lapsed into silence as everyone slurped down the distinctive noodles and savored the rich broth.

"I can taste the coconut milk in the soup, but what gives it the slightly tart, spicy kick? Is it Kaffir?" Rachel asked.

Show-off, Eleanor thought.

"Good guess. It's tamarind," Daisy answered. *This girl wasn't bullshitting—she* does *know how to cook.*

"Rachel, it's so impressive that you know your way around a spice rack," Francesca chirped, her fake-friendly tone barely masking her disdain.

"Apparently not as well as you know how to gut a fish," Rachel commented.

"You girls went fishing?" Philip looked up from his *laksa* in surprise.

"Oh, yes, we did. One of the girls even caught a bigger, endangered fish. We tried to convince her to put it back in the water, but she wouldn't, and it ended up biting her *very* hard. There was blood squirting all over the place," Francesca said, biting the head off her jumbo prawn and spitting it onto the side of the bowl.

"Serves her right, *lah*! Our oceans are getting so overfished, and we must respect all of God's creatures," Carol declared.

"Yes, I agree. You know, when you're just a *tourist*, you need to learn to respect the environment you're in," Francesca said, glaring at Rachel for a split second before shifting her gaze onto Astrid. "Now Astrid, when can I get you to join one of my committees?"

"What sort of committees?" Astrid asked more out of politeness than any real curiosity.

"Take your pick—I'm on the boards of the Singapore History Museum, the Museum of Contemporary Arts, the Heritage Society, the Pulau Club, the Cultural Arts Advisory Board at SBC, the steering committee of Singapore Fashion Week, the Singapore Zoo, the Lee Kong Chian Natural History Museum's Selection committee, the Wine Connoisseurs Society, Save the Shahtoosh, the junior committee of Christian Helpers, and, of course, the Shaw Foundation."

"Well, my three-year-old boy keeps me pretty busy—" Astrid began.

"Once he's in kindergarten and you have nothing to do, you really should consider joining one of my charities. I could fast-track you onto a committee. I think you'd be a natural."

"So Rachel, I hear you teach at NYU with Nick?" Lorena cut in. *This Francesca is getting on my nerves. We're here to interrogate RACHEL, not Astrid.*

"Yes, I do," Rachel replied.

"Which department?" Nadine asked, fully knowing the answer, since Eleanor had read the entire dossier on Rachel Chu to all the ladies while they were getting hour-long reflexology massages in Shenzhen.

"I'm in the Department of Economics, and I teach at the undergrad level."

"And how much do you get paid a year?" Nadine inquired.

Rachel was dumbstruck.

"Aiyah, Mummy, to Americans, it's very rude to ask how much somebody makes," Francesca said at last, clearly delighting in seeing Rachel squirm.

"Oh, is it? I was just curious to know how much a college teacher in America could possibly earn," Nadine said in her most innocent tone.

"Would you ever consider working in Asia?" Daisy asked.

Rachel paused. It seemed like a pretty loaded question, and she figured that the group would dissect whatever answer she gave. "Of course, if the right opportunity came along," she finally replied.

The ladies exchanged furtive looks, while Philip slurped on his soup.

After dinner, as the group adjourned to the living room for coffee and dessert, Astrid abruptly announced that she had to leave.

"Are you okay?" Nick asked. "You seem a little out of sorts tonight."

"I'm fine . . . I just got a text from Evangeline that Cassian is staging a coup and refusing to sleep, so I better dash off." In reality, Evangeline had informed her that Michael had stopped by and was reading Cassian a bedtime story. DO NOT LET HIM LEAVE, Astrid frantically texted back.

Nick and Rachel decided to seize this opportunity to make an exit as well, pleading fatigue from a long day of travel.

As soon as the elevator had closed on them, Eleanor announced, "Did you see the way that girl was staring at everything around the flat?"

"Darling, you've spent a year decorating. Of course people are going to stare—isn't that the whole point?" Philip interjected as he helped himself to a large slice of chocolate banana cake.

"Philip, that little economist brain of hers was busy calculating the value of everything. You could see her adding everything up with her big bulging eyes. And all that talk about cooking for Nick. What rot! As if that's going to impress me, knowing that she puts her rough peasant hands all over his food!"

"Well, you're in fine form tonight, darling," Philip said. "Frankly, I found her to be very pleasant, and her features quite nice." He was careful to emphasize the word *quite*, knowing that his wife would fly into even more of a jealous fit at the thought of another woman in her vicinity being unequivocally proclaimed a beauty.

"I have to agree with Philip. She was really quite pretty. Whether you care to admit it, Eleanor, your son at least has good taste," Daisy said, as she scrutinized the maid pouring her caffe latte.

"Really? You think she's as pretty as Astrid?" Eleanor asked.

"Astrid is a sultry, tempestuous beauty. This one is totally different. She has a simpler, more placid beauty," Daisy observed.

"But don't you think she's a little flat-chested?" Eleanor said.

Philip sighed. There was just no winning with his wife. "Well, good night everyone. It's time for my *CSI: Miami*," he said, getting up from the sofa and making a beeline for his media room. Francesca waited for him to round the corner before she spoke.

"Well, I for one think you are completely right about this girl, Auntie Elle. I spent the whole weekend with Rachel, and I saw her true colors. First of all, she picked out the most expensive dresses from the resort boutique when she found out that Araminta was paying. She was wearing one of them tonight."

"That plain lilac dress? *Alamak*, she has no taste!" Nadine exclaimed.

Francesca continued her assault. "Then, she spent all of yesterday taking different classes at the resort—yoga, Pilates, Nia, you name it. It was as if she was trying to avoid us and get her money's worth at the spa. And you should have heard her at dinner—she boldly announced that she went after Nicky because he is such a catch. Actually, I think her exact words were 'he's a TOTAL catch.'"

"Tsk, tsk, tsk, can you imagine!" Nadine said, shuddering openly.

"LeaLea, what are you going to do now that you've met her?" Carol asked.

"I think this girl needs to be sent packing. All you have to do is say the word, Auntie Elle, and as I told you, it would be my pleasure to help," Francesca said, giving Eleanor a meaningful look.

Eleanor took a few moments to answer, stirring her decaf cappuccino purposefully. She had been in a state of panic for weeks, but now that she had finally met this Rachel Chu, a preternatural calm had settled over her. She could see what needed to be done, and she knew she had to proceed covertly. She had witnessed firsthand the scars that blatant parental interference could inflict; why, even those assembled here were a reminder of that—Daisy's relationship with her sons was tenuous at best, while Lorena's eldest daughter no longer spoke to her after immigrating to Auckland with her Kiwi husband.

"Thank you, Francesca. You are always so helpful," Eleanor finally said. "For now, I don't think we need to do anything. We should all just sit back and watch, because things are about to get interesting."

"You're right, Elle—there's no need to rush into anything.

Besides, after Shenzhen, all the cards are in your hand," Lorena said gleefully as she scraped away the frosting from her cake.

"What happened in Shenzhen?" Francesca asked eagerly.

Eleanor ignored Francesca's question and smiled. "I might not even have to play the Shenzhen card. Let's not forget, all the Youngs and the Shangs are about to descend on Singapore for the Khoo wedding."

"Oh-ho! Who wants to bet she doesn't even last through the weekend?" Nadine cackled.

Part Three

*Let China sleep, for when she awakens
she will shake the world.*

NAPOLEON BONAPARTE

1

Tyersall Park

•

"Colin and I would speed down this slope on our bikes, hands in the air, seeing who could go the farthest without touching the handlebars," Nick said as they were driven up the long winding driveway to Tyersall Park. Arriving here with Nick was an entirely different experience for Rachel from her first time with Peik Lin. For starters, Nick's grandmother had sent a gorgeous vintage Daimler to pick them up, and this time Nick was pointing things out along the way.

"See that enormous rambutan tree? Colin and I tried to build a tree house in it. We spent three days working in secret, but then Ah Ma found out and was furious. She didn't want anything to ruin her precious rambutan fruit and forced us to dismantle it. Colin was so pissed off, he decided to pluck down as many of the rambutans as he could."

Rachel laughed. "You guys got into quite a bit of trouble, didn't you?"

"Yep—we were always getting into scrapes. I remember there was one *kampong** nearby we would sneak into to steal baby chickens."

---

* A traditional Malay village. Singapore was once scattered with many of these indigenous villages, where the native Malays lived as their ancestors had for centuries—in wooden huts with no electricity or plumbing. Today, thanks to the brilliant developers, there remains only one kampong on the entire island.

"Little rascals! Where was the adult supervision?"

"What adult supervision?"

The car pulled up to the porte cochere, and several servants emerged from a side door to remove their luggage from the trunk. The Indian butler came down the front steps to greet them.

"Good afternoon, Mr. Young, Miss Chu. Mrs. Young is expecting you for tea. She's in the star-fruit grove."

"Thanks, Sanjit, we'll head there now," Nick said. He guided Rachel past the red flagstone terrace and down a graceful allée, where white acanthus and colorful bursts of hibiscus mingled with lavish thickets of Egyptian papyrus.

"These gardens are even more glorious in the daytime," Rachel remarked, running her fingers along the row of papyrus stalks swaying gently in the breeze. Enormous dragonflies buzzed about, their wings sparkling in the sunlight.

"Remind me to show you the lily pond. We have these enormous lily pads there—*Victoria amazonica*, the largest in the world. You can practically sunbathe on them!"

As they approached the grove, a most curious sight awaited Rachel: Nick's ninety-something-year-old grandmother stood at the top of a wooden ladder that leaned precariously against the trunk of a tall star-fruit tree, painstakingly fussing over some plastic bags. Two gardeners stood at the foot of the rickety ladder, holding it steady, while a Gurkha and the two Thai lady's maids looked on placidly.

"Sweet Jesus, she's going to fall off that ladder and break her neck!" Rachel said in alarm.

"This is Ah Ma's thing. There's no stopping her," Nick said with a grin.

"But what exactly is she doing?"

"She inspects every single one of the young star fruits and wraps each of them in their own plastic bags. The humidity helps them to ripen and protects them from birds."

"Why doesn't she let one of the gardeners do it?"

"She loves doing it herself—she does this with her guavas too."

Rachel stared up at Nick's grandmother, immaculately dressed in a crisply pleated yellow gardening smock, and marveled at her dexterity. Su Yi looked down, noticing that she had a new audience, and said in Mandarin, "One minute—I just have two more to do."

When Nick's grandmother had safely descended the ladder

(much to Rachel's relief), the group proceeded down another pathway that led to a formal French walled garden where a profusion of African blue lilies were planted amid perfectly manicured boxwood hedges. In the middle of the garden stood a jewellike conservatory that appeared to have been transported straight out of the English countryside.

"This is where Ah Ma cultivates her prizewinning orchid hybrids," Nick informed Rachel.

"Wow," was all Rachel could say as she entered the greenhouse. Hundreds of orchid plants hung on different levels throughout the space, their subtle sweetness permeating the air. Rachel had never seen this many varieties—from intricate spider orchids and vividly colored vandas to the magnificent cattleyas and almost indecently suggestive slipper orchids. Tucked in the middle of all this was a round table that appeared to have been carved out of a single block of blue malachite. Its base consisted of four majestically fierce griffins facing in different directions, each poised to take flight.

As they made themselves comfortable on the cushioned wrought-iron chairs, a trio of servers appeared as if on cue, bearing an enormous five-tiered silver tray laden with delectable *nyonya kuehs*, finger sandwiches, gemlike *pâte de fruits*, and fluffy golden-brown scones. A tea cart was rolled toward them by one of the Thai lady's maids, and Rachel felt like she was hallucinating as she watched the maiden delicately pouring freshly steeped tea from a teapot intricately carved with multicolored dragons. She had never seen a more sumptuous tea service in her life.

"Here are my grandmother's famous scones—dig in," Nick said gleefully, licking his lips.

The scones were still warm as Rachel broke one apart and slathered it with a generous helping of clotted cream, just as she'd learned from Nick. She was about to put some of the strawberry jam onto the scone when Su Yi said in Mandarin, "You should try it with some of the lemon curd. My cook makes it fresh every day." Rachel didn't feel like she was in a position to defy her hostess, so she scooped on some lemon curd and took her first bite. It was pure heaven—the buttery lightness of the pastry combined with the decadent cream and the smooth hint of sweet lemon made for a perfect alchemy of flavors.

Rachel sighed audibly. "You were right, Nick, this *is* the best scone on the planet."

Nick grinned triumphantly.

"Mrs. Young, I am still discovering the history of Singapore. Was afternoon tea always a custom in your family?" Rachel asked.

"Well, I am not a native Singaporean. I spent my childhood in Peking, and we of course did not follow the British custom there. It was only when my family moved here that we picked it up, these colonial habits. It was something we first did for our British guests because they didn't much appreciate Chinese cooking. Then, when I married Nick's grandfather, who had spent many years abroad in England, he insisted on a proper afternoon tea with all the trimmings. And of course the children loved it. I suppose that's how I got used to it," Su Yi replied in her slow, deliberate way.

It was only then Rachel realized that Nick's grandmother had not touched any of the scones or finger sandwiches. Instead, she ate only a piece of *nyonya kueh* with her tea.

"Tell me, is it true that you are a professor of economics?" Su Yi asked.

"It is," Rachel replied.

"It is good that you had the opportunity to learn such things in America. My father was a businessman, but he never wanted me to learn about financial matters. He always said that within a hundred years, China would become the most powerful nation the world has ever seen. And that is something I always repeated to my children and grandchildren. Isn't that right, Nicky?"

"Yes, Ah Ma. That's why you made me learn my Mandarin," Nick confirmed. He could already see where this conversation was headed.

"Well I was right in doing that, wasn't I? I am fortunate enough to see my father's foresight come true in my lifetime. Rachel, did you watch the Beijing Olympics opening ceremony?"

"I did."

"Did you see how magnificent it was? No one in the world can doubt China's might after the Olympics."

"No, they really can't," Rachel replied.

"The future is in Asia. Nick's place is here, don't you think?"

Nick knew Rachel was headed straight into an ambush, and interrupted her before she could answer. "I have always said that I would return to Asia, Ah Ma. But right now I am still gaining valuable experience in New York."

"You said the same thing six years ago when you wanted to remain in England after your studies. And now you're in America. What's next, Australia, like your father? It was a mistake to send you abroad in the first place. You have become far too seduced by Western ways." Rachel couldn't help noting the irony in what Nick's grandmother was saying. She looked and sounded like a Chinese woman in the most traditional sense, and yet here they were in a walled garden straight out of the Loire Valley having English afternoon tea.

Nick didn't know how to respond. This was a debate he had been having with his grandmother for the past few years, and he knew he would never win. He started to pick apart the colored layers in a piece of *nyonya kueh*, thinking he should excuse himself for a moment. It would be good for Rachel to have some private time with his grandmother. He glanced at his watch and said, "Ah Ma, I think Auntie Alix and family will be arriving from Hong Kong any minute now. Why don't I go welcome them and bring them here?"

His grandmother nodded. Nick smiled at Rachel, giving her a look of assurance before stepping out of the conservatory.

Su Yi tilted her head to the left slightly, and one of the Thai lady's maids immediately sprang to her side, bending in one graceful motion onto her knees so that her ear was level with Su Yi's mouth.

"Tell the conservatory gardener that it needs to be five degrees warmer in here," Su Yi said in English. She turned her attention back to Rachel. "Tell me, where are your people from?" There was a forcefulness in her voice that Rachel had not previously noticed.

"My mother's family came from Guangdong. My father's family . . . I never knew," Rachel answered nervously.

"How come?"

"He died before I was born. And then I came to America as an infant with my mother."

"And did your mother remarry?"

"No, she never did." Rachel could feel the Thai lady's maids staring in silent judgment.

"So, do you support your mother?"

"No, quite the contrary. She put herself through college in America and is now a real estate agent. She's done well for herself and was even able to support me through my university studies," Rachel responded.

Su Yi was silent for a while, considering the girl before her. Rachel didn't dare to move at all. Finally, Su Yi spoke. "Did you know that I had quite a few brothers and sisters? My father had many concubines who bore him children, but only one supreme wife, my mother. She bore him six children, but out of all my siblings, only three were officially accepted. Myself, and two of my brothers."

"Why only the three of you?" Rachel ventured to ask.

"You see, my father believed he had a gift. He felt that he was able to ascertain a person's entire future based on their faces . . . the way they looked . . . and he chose to keep only the children he felt would go on to please him. He chose my husband for me this way as well, did you know that? He said, 'This man has a good face. He will never make any money, but he will never hurt you.' He was right on both counts." Nick's grandmother leaned in closer to Rachel and stared straight into her eyes. "I see your face," she said in a hushed tone.

Before Rachel could ask what she meant, Nick approached the conservatory door with a cluster of guests. The door burst open, and a man in a white linen shirt and bright orange linen pants bounded toward Nick's grandmother.

"Ah Ma, dearest Ah Ma! How I've missed you!" the man said dramatically in Cantonese, dropping to his knees and kissing her hands.

*"Aiyah, Eddie, cha si lang!"** Su Yi scolded, withdrawing her hands and smacking him across the head.

---

* Hokkien phrase that translates to "stop bothering me to death," used to scold people who are being noisy, annoying, or, as in Eddie's case, both.

2

11 Nassim Road

SINGAPORE

"God is in the details." Mies van der Rohe's iconic quote was the mantra Annabel Lee lived by. From the sculpted mango popsicles handed out to guests lounging by the pool to the precise placement of a camellia blossom on every eiderdown pillow, Annabel's unerring eye for detail was what made her chain of luxury hotels the favored choice for the most discriminating travelers. Tonight the object of scrutiny was her own reflection. She was wearing a high-collared champagne-colored dress woven from Irish linen, and trying to decide whether to layer it with a double strand of baroque pearls or an opera-length amber necklace. Were the Nakamura pearls too ostentatious? Would the amber beads be subtler?

Her husband, Peter, entered her boudoir wearing dark gray slacks and a pale blue shirt. "Are you sure you want me to wear this? I look like an accountant," he said, thinking his butler had surely made a mistake in laying out these clothes.

"You look perfect. I ordered the shirt specifically for tonight's occasion. It's Ede & Ravenscroft—they make all of the Duke of Edinburgh's shirts. Trust me, it's better to be underdressed with this crowd," Annabel said, giving him a careful once-over. Although there were grand events every single night of the week in the ramp-up to Araminta's wedding, the party that Harry Leong was throwing tonight in honor of his nephew Colin Khoo at the fabled Leong residence on Nassim Road was the one Annabel was secretly most eager to attend.

When Peter Lee (originally Lee Pei Tan of Harbin) made his first fortune in Chinese coal mining during the mid-nineties, he and his wife decided to move their family to Singapore, like many of the newly minted Mainlanders were doing. Peter wanted to maximize the benefits of being based in the region's preferred wealth management center, and Annabel (originally An-Liu Bao of Urümqi) wanted their young daughter to benefit from Singapore's more Westernized—and in her eyes, superior—education system. (The superior air quality didn't hurt, either.) Besides, she had tired of the Beijing elite, of all the interminable twelve-course banquets in rooms filled with bad replicas of Louis Quatorze furniture, and she longed to reinvent herself on a more sophisticated island where the ladies understood Armani and spoke perfect accentless English. She wanted Araminta to grow up speaking perfect accentless English.

But in Singapore, Annabel soon discovered that beyond the bold-faced names that eagerly invited her to all the glamorous galas, there hid a whole other level of society that was impervious to the flash of money, especially Mainland Chinese money. These people were snobbier and more impenetrable than anything she had ever encountered. "Who cares about those old mothball families? They're just jealous that we're richer, that we *really* know how to enjoy ourselves," her new friend Trina Tua (wife of the TLS Private Equity chairman Tua Lao Sai) said. Annabel knew this was something Trina said to console herself that she would never be invited to Mrs. Lee Yong Chien's legendary mah-jongg parties—where the women bet with serious jewelry—or get to peek behind the tall gates of the magnificent modernist house that architect Kee Yeap had designed for Rosemary T'sien on Dalvey Road.

Tonight she was finally going to be invited in. Even though she maintained homes in New York, London, Shanghai, and Bali, and even though *Architectural Digest* called her Edward Tuttle–designed house in Singapore "one of the most spectacular private residences in Asia," Annabel's heartbeat quickened as she passed through the austere wooden gates of 11 Nassim Road. She had long admired the house from afar—Black and Whites* like these were so exceedingly

* The exotic Black and White houses of Singapore are a singular architectural style

rare, and this one, which had been continuously occupied by the Leong family since the twenties, was perhaps the only one left on the island to retain all of its original features. Entering through the Arts and Crafts front doors, Annabel quickly soaked in every minute detail of the way these people lived. *Look at this whole row of Malay servants flanking the entrance hall in crisp white blazers. What are they offering on these Selangor pewter trays? Pimm's No. 1 with fizzy pineapple juice and fresh mint leaves. How quaint. I must copy that for the new Sri Lanka resort. Ah, here is Felicity Leong in tailored silk jacquard, wearing the most exquisite piece of lilac jade, and her daughter-in-law Cathleen, the constitutional law expert (this girl is always so plain, with not a drop of jewelry in sight—you would never guess she's married to the eldest Leong son). And here is Astrid Leong. What was it like for her to grow up in this house? No wonder she has such great taste—that robin's-egg blue dress she's wearing is on the cover of French* Vogue *this month. Who's this man whispering to Astrid at the foot of the stairs? Oh, it's her husband, Michael. What a stunning couple they make. And look at this drawing room, oh just look! The symmetry . . . the scale . . . the profusion of orange blossoms. Sublime. I need orange blossoms in all the hotel lobbies next week. Wait a second, is that Ru ware from the Northern Song dynasty? Yes it is. One, two, three, four, there are so many pieces. Unbelievable! This room alone must have thirty million dollars' worth of ceramics, strewn about as if they were cheap ashtrays. And these Peranakan-style opium chairs—look at the mother-of-pearl inlay—I've never seen a pair in such perfect condition. Here come the Chengs of Hong Kong. Look how adorable those children are, all dressed up like little Ralph Lauren models.*

Never had Annabel felt more content than right now, when at last she was breathing in this rarified air. The house was filling up with the sort of aristocratic families she had only heard about over the years, families that could trace their lineage back thirty generations or more. Like the Youngs, who had just arrived. *Oh look, Eleanor just waved at me. She's the only one who socializes outside the family. And here's her son, Nicholas—another looker. Colin's best friend. And the girl holding Nicholas's hand must be that Rachel Chu everyone is talking about, the one*

---

found nowhere else in the world. Combining Anglo-Indian features with the English Arts and Crafts movement, these white-painted bungalows with black trim detailing were ingeniously designed for tropical climes. Originally built to house well-to-do colonial families, they are now extremely coveted and available only to the crazy rich ($40 million for starters, and you might have to wait several decades for a whole family to die).

that's not one of the Taiwan Chus. One look and I could have told you that. This girl grew up drinking vitamin-D calcium-fortified American milk. But she still doesn't have a chance of catching Nicholas. And here comes Araminta with all the Khoos. Looking like she belongs.

Annabel knew at that moment she had made all the right decisions for her daughter—enrolling her at Far Eastern Kindergarten, choosing Methodist Girls' School over Singapore American School, forcing her to go to Youth Fellowship at First Methodist even though they were Buddhists, and whisking her away to Cheltenham Ladies' College in England for proper finishing. Her daughter had grown up as one of these people—people of breeding and taste. There wasn't a single diamond over fifteen carats in this crowd, not a single Louis Vuitton anything, no one looking over your shoulder for bigger fish. This was a family gathering, not a networking opportunity. These people were so completely at ease, so well mannered.

Outside on the east terrace, Astrid hid behind the dense row of Italian cypresses, waiting for Michael to arrive at her parents' house. As soon as she caught sight of him, she rushed to the front door to meet him so that it would appear they had arrived together. After the initial flurry of greetings, Michael was able to corner her by the staircase. "Is Cassian upstairs?" he mumbled under his breath.

"No, he isn't," Astrid said quickly before being swept into an embrace by her cousin Cecilia Cheng.

"Where is he? You've been hiding him from me all week," Michael pressed on.

"You'll see him soon enough," Astrid whispered as she beamed at her great-aunt Rosemary.

"This was your way of tricking me into coming tonight, wasn't it?" Michael said angrily.

Astrid took Michael by the hand and led him into the front parlor next to the staircase. "Michael, I promised you would see Cassian tonight—just be patient and let's get through dinner."

"That wasn't the deal. I'm leaving."

"Michael, you can't leave. We still have to coordinate plans for the wedding on Saturday. Auntie Alix is hosting a breakfast before the church ceremony and—"

"Astrid, I'm not going to the wedding."

"Oh come on, don't joke like this. *Everyone* is going."

"By 'everyone,' I suppose you are referring to everyone with a billion dollars or more?" Michael seethed.

Astrid rolled her eyes. "Come on, Michael, I know we've had a disagreement, and I know you're probably feeling ashamed, but as I said before, *I forgive you.* Let's not make a huge issue out of this. Come home."

"You don't get it, do you? I'm not coming home. I'm not going to the wedding."

"But what are people going to say if you don't show up at the wedding?" Astrid looked at him nervously.

"Astrid, I'm not the groom! I'm not even related to the groom. Who's going to give a shit whether I'm there or not?"

"You can't do this to me. Everyone will notice, and everyone will talk," Astrid pleaded, trying not to panic.

"Tell them I had to fly off at the last minute for work."

"Where are you going? Are you flying off to Hong Kong to see your mistress?" Astrid asked accusingly.

Michael paused a moment. He never wanted to resort to this, but he felt that he had been left with little choice. "If it makes you feel better to know—yes, I'm off to see my mistress. I'm leaving on Friday after work, just so I can get away from this carnival. I can't watch these people spend a gazillion dollars on a wedding when half the world is starving."

Astrid stared at him numbly, reeling from what he had said. At that moment, Cathleen, the wife of her brother Henry, walked into the room.

"Oh thank God you're here," Cathleen said to Michael. "The cooks are having a fit because some transformer blew and that damn high-tech commercial oven we put in last year won't work. Apparently it's gone into self-cleaning mode, and there are four Peking ducks roasting in there—"

Michael glared at his sister-in-law. "Cathleen, I have a master's degree from Caltech, specializing in encryption technology. I'm not your fucking handyman!" he fumed, before storming out of the room.

Cathleen stared after him in disbelief. "What's wrong with Michael? I've never seen him like this."

"Oh don't mind him, Cathleen," Astrid said, attempting a weak laugh. "Michael's upset because he just found out that he has to rush off to Hong Kong for some work emergency. Poor thing, he's afraid he might miss the wedding."

————

As the Daimler chauffeuring Eddie, Fiona, and their three children approached the gates of 11 Nassim Road, Eddie did one last run-through.

"Kalliste, what are you going to do when they start to serve the coffee and desserts?"

"I'm going to ask Great-aunt Felicity whether I can play the piano."

"And what are you going to play?"

"The Bach partita, and then the Mendelssohn. Can I also play my new Lady Gaga song?"

"Kalliste, I swear to God if you play any of that damn Lady Gaga I'm going to break every one of your fingers."

Fiona stared out the car window, ignoring her husband. This is how he was every time he was about to see his Singapore relatives.

"Augustine, what's the matter with you? Button your jacket," Eddie instructed.

The little boy obeyed, carefully buttoning the two gold buttons on his blazer.

"Augustine, how many times have I told you—do not ever, EVER button the last button, do you hear me?"

"Papa, you said never button the last button on my three-button jacket, but you never told me what to do when there's only two buttons," the boy whimpered, tearing up.

"Happy now?" Fiona said to her husband, taking the boy into her lap and gently smoothing out the hair on his forehead.

Eddie gave her an annoyed look. "Now everybody listen up . . . Constantine, what are we going to do when we get out of the car?"

"We are going to get into formation behind you and Mummy," his eldest son answered.

"And what is the order?"

"Augustine goes first, then Kalliste, then me," the boy droned in a bored voice.

"Perfect. Wait till everyone sees our splendid entrance!" Eddie said excitedly.

————

Eleanor entered the front hall behind her son and his girlfriend, eager to observe how the girl would be received. Nick had obviously been preparing her—Rachel was cleverly wearing a demure-looking navy blue dress and no jewelry except for tiny pearl earrings. Looking into the drawing room, Eleanor could see her husband's extended clan all clustered by the French doors leading out to the terrace. She remembered as if it were yesterday meeting them for the first time. It was at the old T'sien estate near Changi, before the place was turned into that frightful country club all the foreigners went to. The T'sien boys with their roving eyes were tripping over themselves to talk to her, but the Shangs barely deigned to look in her direction—those Shangs were only comfortable speaking to families they had known for at least two generations. But here Nick was boldly leading the girl straight into the frying pan, attempting to introduce Rachel to Victoria Young, the snottiest of Philip's sisters, and Cassandra Shang—the imperious gossip-monger otherwise known as Radio One Asia. *Alamak, this was going to be good.*

"Rachel, this is my aunt Victoria and my cousin Cassandra, just back from England."

Rachel smiled nervously at the ladies. Victoria, with her wiry chin-length bob and slightly rumpled peach cotton dress, had the look of an eccentric sculptress, while whippet-thin Cassandra—with her graying hair severely parted into a tight Frida Kahlo bun—wore an oversize khaki shirtdress and an African necklace festooned with little wooden giraffes. Victoria shook Rachel's hand coolly, while Cassandra kept her spindly arms crossed over her chest, her lips pursed in a tight smile as she assessed Rachel from head to toe. Rachel was about to inquire about their vacation when Victoria, looking over her shoulder, announced in that same clipped English accent that all of Nick's aunts had, "Ah, here come Alix and Malcolm. And there's Eddie and Fiona. Good grief, look at those children, all dressed up like that!"

"Alix was moaning on about how much money Eddie and Fiona spend on those kids. Seems they only wear *designer* clothes," Cassandra said, stretching out "deee-siiign-er" as if it were some sort of grotesque affliction.

"*Gum sai cheen!**" Where on earth does Eddie think he's taking

* Cantonese for "what a waste of money."

them? It's a hundred and five degrees outside and they are dressed for a shooting weekend at Balmoral," Victoria scoffed.

"They must be sweating like little pigs in those tweed jackets," Cassandra said, shaking her head.

Just then Rachel noticed a couple entering the room. A young man with the tousled hair of a Korean pop idol lumbered toward them with a girl dressed in a lemon-yellow and white-striped tube dress that clung to her body like sausage casing.

"Ah, here comes my cousin Alistair. And that must be Kitty, the girl he's madly in love with," Nick remarked. Even from across the room, Kitty's hair extensions, false eyelashes, and frosty-pink lipstick stood out dramatically, and as they approached, Rachel realized that the white stripes in the girl's dress were actually sheer, with her engorged nipples clearly showing through.

"Everyone, I'd like you all to meet my girlfriend Kitty Pong," Alistair proudly beamed.

The room went dead silent as everyone stood gaping at those chocolate-brown nipples. While Kitty basked in the attention, Fiona swiftly herded her children out of the room. Eddie glared at his kid brother, furious that his entrance had been upstaged. Alistair, thrilled by the sudden attention, blurted out, "And I want to announce that last night I took Kitty to the top of Mount Faber and asked her to marry me!"

"We're engaged!" Kitty squealed, waving around the large cloudy-pink diamond on her hand.

Felicity gasped audibly, looking at her sister, Alix, for some reaction. Alix gazed into the middle distance, not making eye contact with anyone. Her son nonchalantly continued. "Kitty, meet my cousin Nicky, my auntie Victoria, and my cousin Cassandra. And you must be Rachel."

Without missing a beat, Victoria and Cassandra turned to Rachel, cutting Alistair dead. "Now Rachel, I hear you are an economist? How fascinating! Will you explain to me why the American economy can't seem to dig out of its sorry state?" Victoria asked shrilly.

"It's that Tim Paulson fellow, isn't it?" Cassandra cut in. "Isn't he a puppet controlled by all the Jews?"

3

Patric's
•

"A lacy black thong? And you could really see it through the dress?" Peik Lin cried out, doubling over with laughter in the restaurant banquette she was sharing with Rachel.

"The thong, the nipples, all of it! You should have seen the look on all of their faces! She might as well have been naked," Rachel said.

Peik Lin wiped the tears of laughter from her eyes. "I can't believe all that's happened to you in the past week. Those girls. The dead fish. Nick's family. Leave it to you to walk right into the middle of all this."

"Oh Peik Lin, I wish you could see how Nick's family lives! Staying at Tyersall Park has been absolutely unreal. The bedroom we're in has all this exquisite French art deco furniture, and I feel like I've traveled back in time—the rituals, the decadence, the scale of everything . . . I mean, there must be at least twelve extra houseguests in town for the wedding, but there are so many maids around, I still have one dedicated just to me—this cute girl from Suzhou. I think she's a bit pissed off because I haven't let her do all her duties."

"What are her duties?" Peik Lin inquired.

"Well, the first night she offered to undress me and brush my hair, which I thought was a little creepy. So I said, 'No thanks.' Then she asked if she could 'draw me a bath'—I love that phrase, don't you?—but you know I prefer showers, even though the clawfoot tub looks amazing. So she offers to give me a shampoo and scalp massage! I'm like, no I don't need that. I just want her to leave the room so I can take my shower. Instead the girl rushes into the bathroom to adjust the old-fashioned shower taps until the water temperature is just perfect. I walked in and there were, like, twenty candles lit all around the room—for a friggin' shower!"

"*Alamak*, Rachel, why didn't you let her give you the works? All this royal pampering is totally wasted on you," Peik Lin chided.

"I'm not used to all this—it makes me uncomfortable that someone's entire job is to wait on me hand and foot. Another thing—their laundry service is *amazing*. Everything I wear is washed and pressed within a day of my wearing it. I noticed how fresh and wonderful all my clothes smelled, so I asked my maid what sort of detergent they used. She told me that everything is ironed with a special lavender water from Provence! Can you imagine? And every morning she wakes us up by bringing a 'calling tray' to the bedroom with tea for Nick, done just the way he likes it, coffee done just the way I like it, and a plate of these delicious cookies—'digestive biscuits,' Nick calls them. And this is *before* the huge buffet breakfast that's laid out, and always in a different part of the house. The first morning breakfast was served in the conservatory, the next morning it was on the second-floor veranda. So even going to breakfast is like a surprising treat every day."

Peik Lin shook her head in amazement, making a few mental notes. It was time to shake things up with the lazy maids at Villa d'Oro—they needed some new tasks. Lavender water in the irons, for starters. And tomorrow she wanted to have breakfast by the pool.

"I tell you, Peik Lin, between all the places Nick has taken me and all the lunches, teas, and dinners we've had to attend, I've never eaten like this in my entire life. You know, I never imagined that there could be so many big events surrounding one wedding. Nick warned me that tonight's party is on a boat."

"Yes, I read that it's going to be on *Dato'* Tai Toh Lui's new megayacht. So tell me about the outfits you're planning to wear this weekend," Peik Lin said excitedly.

"Um, *outfits*? I only brought one dress for the wedding."

"Rachel, you can't be serious! Aren't there going to be numerous events all weekend?"

"Well, there's the welcome party tonight on the yacht, the wedding tomorrow morning, which will be followed by a reception, and a wedding banquet in the evening. And then there's a tea ceremony on Sunday. I brought this cute cocktail-length black-and-white dress from Reiss, so I figure I can just wear it all day tomorrow and—"

"Rachel, you're going to need *at least* three outfits tomorrow. You can't be seen in the same dress from morning to night! And everyone is going to be decked out in jewels and ball gowns for the wedding banquet. It's going to be the grandest event of the decade—there'll be big-time celebrities and royalty there!"

"Well, there's no way I can compete with that," Rachel shrugged. "You know that fashion has never really been my thing. Besides, what can I do about it now?"

"Rachel Chu—I'm taking you shopping!"

"Peik Lin," Rachel protested, "I don't want to be running around some mall right now at the last minute."

"A mall?" Peik Lin gave her a look of disdain. "Who said anything about a *mall*?" She whipped out her cell phone and speed-dialed a number. "Patric, can you please slot me in? It's an emergency. We need to do an intervention."

———

Patric's atelier was a former shop house on Ann Siang Hill that had been transformed into an aggressively modern loft, and it was here that Rachel soon found herself standing on a glowing circular platform in nothing but her underwear, a three-way mirror behind her and an Ingo Maurer dome light hovering above, bathing her in warm, flattering light. Sigur Rós played in the background, and Patric (just Patric), wearing a white lab coat over a dramatically high-collared shirt and tie, scrutinized her intently, his arms crossed with one index finger on his pursed lips. "You're very long-waisted," he pronounced.

"Is that bad?" Rachel asked, realizing for the first time how contestants must feel during the swimsuit competition of a beauty pageant.

"Not at all! I know women who would *kill* for your torso. This means we can put you in some of the designers that normally wouldn't fit on very petite frames." Patric turned to his assistant, a young man in a gray jumpsuit with meticulously combed hair, and declared, "Chuaaaaan! Pull the plum Balenciaga, the naked peach Chloé, the Giambattista Valli that just came in from Paris, all the Marchesas, the vintage Givenchy, and that Jason Wu with the deconstructed ruffles on the bodice."

Soon half a dozen or so assistants, all dressed in tight black T-shirts and black denim, buzzed around the space with the urgency of bomb defusers, filling it up with rolling racks crammed with the most exquisite dresses Rachel had ever seen. "I suppose this is how all super-wealthy Singaporeans shop?" she asked.

"Patric's clients come from everywhere—all the Mainland Chinese, Mongolian, and Indonesian fashionistas who want the latest looks, and many of the privacy-obsessed Brunei princesses. Patric gets access to the dresses hours after they've walked the runways," Peik Lin informed her. Rachel gazed around in wonder as the assistants began hanging the dresses on a titanium rod that was suspended seven feet into the air, encircling the platform like a giant halo. "They're bringing in way too many dresses," she remarked.

"This is how Patric works. He needs to see different styles and colors around you first, then he edits. Don't worry, Patric has the most impeccable taste—he studied fashion at Central Saint Martins, you know. You can be sure that the dresses he picks out won't be seen on anyone else at the wedding."

"That's not my worry, Peik Lin. Look, no price tags anywhere—that's always a dangerous sign," Rachel whispered.

"Don't worry about price tags, Rachel. Your job is to try on the dresses."

"What do you mean? Peik Lin, I'm not letting you buy me a dress!"

"Shush! Let's not argue about this," Peik Lin said as she held up a translucent lace blouse to the light.

"Peik Lin, I mean it. None of your funny business here," Rachel warned as she thumbed through another rack. A dress that was hand-painted with watery blue-and-silver flowers caught her eye. "Now *this* is to die for. Why don't I try this one on?" she asked.

Patric reentered the room and noticed the dress Rachel was holding. "Wait, wait, wait. How did that Dries Van Noten get in here? Chuaaaan!" he yelled for his long-suffering aide-de-camp. "The Dries is reserved for Mandy Ling, who's on the way right now. Her mother will *kau peh kau bu*[*] if I let someone else have it." He turned back to Rachel and smiled apologetically. "I'm sorry, that Dries is already spoken for. Now, for starters let's see you in this oyster-pink number with the pretty bustle skirt."

Rachel soon found herself twirling around in one stunning dress after another and having more fun than she ever thought possible. Peik Lin would simply ooh and ahh over everything she put on, while reading aloud from the latest issue of *Singapore Tattle*:

> Expect private-jet gridlock at Changi Airport and road closures all over the CBD this weekend as Singapore witnesses its own royal wedding. **Araminta Lee** weds **Colin Khoo** at First Methodist Church on Saturday at high noon, with a private reception to follow at an undisclosed location. (Mother-of-the-bride **Annabel Lee** is said to have planned every last detail, blowing northward of forty million on the occasion.) Although the crème de la crème guest list has been more closely guarded than North Korea's nuclear weapons program, don't be surprised to see royalty, heads of state, and celebrities such as **Tony Leung, Gong Li, Takeshi Kaneshiro, Yue-Sai Kan, Rain, Fan BingBing,** and **Zhang Ziyi** in attendance. It's rumored that one of Asia's biggest pop divas will perform, and bookies are taking bets on who designed Araminta's bridal gown. Be on the lookout for Asia's most glittering to come out in full force, like the **Shaws,** the **Tais,** the **Mittals,** the **Meggahartos,** the Hong Kong AND Singapore **Ngs,** assorted **Ambanis,** the **David Tangs,** the L'Orient **Lims,** the **Taipei Plastics Chus,** and many others too fabulous to mention.

Meanwhile, Patric would dash in and out of the dressing room making definitive pronouncements:

"That slit is too high—you'll give all the choirboys erections wearing that one!"

"Gorgeous! You were genetically engineered to wear Alaïa!"

"NEVER, EVER wear green chiffon unless you want to look like bok choy that got gang-raped."

[*] Hokkien for "bitch me out" (or slang that translates to "cry to the father and cry to the mother").

"Now *that* looks stunning. That flared skirt would look even better if you were arriving on horseback."

Every outfit Patric selected seemed to fit Rachel more beautifully than the last. They found the perfect cocktail dress for the rehearsal dinner and an outfit that could work for the wedding. Just when Rachel finally decided that, *what the hell*, she would splurge on one great designer ball gown for the first time in her life, Peik Lin summoned for a whole rack of dresses to be wrapped up.

"Are you taking all those for yourself?" Rachel asked in astonishment.

"No, these are the ones that looked best, so I'm getting them for you," Peik Lin answered as she attempted to hand her American Express black card to one of Patric's assistants.

"Oh no you're not! Put that AMEX card down!" Rachel said sternly, grasping Peik Lin's wrist. "Come on, I only need one formal gown for the wedding ball. I can still wear my black-and-white dress to the wedding ceremony."

"First of all, Rachel Chu, you *cannot* wear a black-and-white dress to a wedding—those are mourning colors. Are you sure you're really Chinese? How could you not know that? Second, when was the last time I saw you? How often do I get to treat one of my best friends in the whole world? You can't deprive me of this pleasure."

Rachel laughed at the preposterous charm of her statement. "Peik Lin, I appreciate your generosity, but you just *can't* go around spending thousands of dollars on me. Now, I have money saved up for this trip, and I will gladly pay for my own—"

"Fantastic. Go buy some souvenirs when you're in Phuket."

———

In a dressing suite at the other end of Patric's atelier, two attendants were gingerly tightening the corseted bodice of a scarlet Alexander McQueen gown on Amanda Ling, still jet-lagged from having just stepped off a plane from New York.

"It needs to be tighter," her mother, Jacqueline, said, looking at the attendants, who each held one side of the gold silk cord hesitantly.

"But I can hardly breathe as it is!" Amanda protested.

"Take smaller breaths, then."

"This isn't 1862, Mummy. I don't think this is actually supposed to be worn like a *real* corset!"

"Of course it is. Perfection comes at a sacrifice, Mandy. Which naturally is a concept you seem to lack any understanding of."

Amanda rolled her eyes. "Don't get started again, Mummy. I knew *exactly* what I was doing. Things were going just fine in New York until you forced me to fly back for this insanity. I was so looking forward to blowing off Araminta's silly wedding."

"I don't know what planet you're living on, but things are not 'just fine.' Nicky is going to propose to this girl *any minute now*. What was the whole point of my sending you to New York? You had one simple mission to accomplish, and you failed miserably."

"You have no appreciation for what I've accomplished for myself. I'm part of New York society now," Amanda proudly declared.

"Who gives a damn about that? You think anyone here is impressed to see pictures of you in *Town & Country*?"

"He's not going to marry her, Mummy. You don't know Nicky like I do," Amanda insisted.

"Well, for your sake I hope you're right. I don't need to remind you—"

"Yes, yes, you've said it for years. You have nothing to leave me, I'm the girl, everything has to go to Teddy," Amanda lamented sarcastically.

"Tighter!" Jacqueline ordered the attendants.

First Methodist Church

SINGAPORE

"*Another* security checkpoint?" Alexandra Cheng complained, peering out the tinted window at the throngs of spectators lining Fort Canning Road.

"Alix, there are so many heads of state here, of course they have to secure the location. That's the Sultan of Brunei's convoy ahead of us, and isn't the vice premier of China supposed to be coming?" Malcolm Cheng said.

"It wouldn't surprise me if the Lees invited the entire Communist Party of China," Victoria Young snorted in derision.

Nick had departed at the crack of dawn to help Colin prepare for his big day, so Rachel caught a ride with his aunts and uncle in one of the fleets of cars leaving from Tyersall Park.

The burgundy Daimler finally arrived in front of First Methodist Church and the uniformed chauffeur opened the door, causing the crowd crammed behind barricades to roar in anticipation. As Rachel was helped out of the car, hundreds of press photographers hanging off metal bleachers began snapping away, the sound of their frenzied digital clicks like locusts descending on an open field.

Rachel heard a photographer yell to a newscaster standing on the ground, "Who's that girl? Is she someone? Is she someone?"

"No, it's just some rich socialite," the newscaster snapped back. "But look, here comes Eddie Cheng and Fiona Tung-Cheng!"

Eddie and his sons emerged from the car directly behind Rachel's. Both boys were dressed in outfits identical to their father's—dove-gray cutaway jackets and polka-dot lavender ties—and they flanked Eddie obediently while Fiona and Kalliste followed a few paces behind.

"Eddie Cheng! Look this way, Eddie! Boys, over here!" the photographers shouted. The newscaster thrust a microphone in front of Eddie's face. "Mr. Cheng, your family is always at the top of the best-dressed lists, and you certainly didn't disappoint us today! Tell me, who are you wearing?"

Eddie paused, proudly placing his arms around his boys' shoulders. "Constantine, Augustine, and I are in Gieves & Hawkes bespoke, and my wife and daughter are in Carolina Herrera," he grinned broadly. The boys squinted into the bright morning sun, trying to remember their father's instructions: look straight into the camera lens, suck your cheeks in, turn to the left, smile, turn to the right, smile, look at Papa adoringly, smile.

"Your grandsons look so cute all dressed up!" Rachel remarked to Malcolm.

Malcolm shook his head derisively. "Hiyah! Thirty years I have been a pioneering heart surgeon, but my son is the one who gets all the attention—for his bloody clothes!"

Rachel grinned. These big celebrity weddings all seemed to be about the "bloody clothes," didn't they? She was wearing an ice-blue dress with a fitted blazer trimmed with mother-of-pearl disks all along the lapel and sleeves. At first she felt rather overdressed when she saw what Nick's aunts were wearing back at Tyersall Park— Alexandra in a muddy-green floral dress that looked like eighties Laura Ashley, and Victoria in a geometric-patterned black-and-white knit dress (so much for Peik Lin's theory) that looked like something dug up from the bottom of an old camphor-wood chest. But here, among all the other chic wedding guests, she realized that she had nothing to worry about.

Rachel had never seen a crowd like this in the daytime—with the men sharply dressed in morning suits and the women styled to within an inch of their lives in the latest looks from Paris and Milan, many sporting elaborate hats or flamboyant fascinators. An even more exotic contingent of ladies arrived in iridescent saris, hand-painted kimonos, and intricately sewn *kebayas*. Rachel had secretly been dreading the wedding all week, but as she followed Nick's aunties up the slope toward the Gothic redbrick church, she found herself succumbing to the festive air. This was a once-in-a-lifetime event, the likes of which she would probably never witness again.

At the main doors stood a line of ushers dressed in pinstriped morning suits and top hats. "Welcome to First Methodist," an usher said cheerily. "Your names, please?"

"What for?" Victoria frowned.

"So I can tell you which rows you'll be sitting in," the young man said, holding up an iPad with a detailed seating chart glowing on its screen.

"What nonsense! This is *my* church, and I am going to sit in my regular pew," Victoria said.

"At least tell me if you're guests of the bride or groom?" the usher asked.

"*Groom*, of course!" Victoria huffed, brushing past him.

Entering the church for the first time, Rachel was surprised by how starkly modern the sanctuary looked. Silver-leaf latticework walls soared to the stonework ceilings, and rows of minimalist blond-wood chairs filled the space. There wasn't a single flower to be seen anywhere, but there was no need, because suspended from the ceiling were thousands of young Aspen trees, meticulously arranged to create a vaulted forest floating just above everyone's heads. Rachel found the effect stunning, but Nick's aunties were aghast.

"Why did they cover up the red brick and the stained glass? What happened to all the dark wooden pews?" Alexandra asked, disoriented by the complete transformation of the church she had been baptized in.

"Aiyah, Alix, don't you see? That Annabel Lee woman has transformed the church into one of her ghastly hotel lobbies!" Victoria shuddered.

The ushers inside the church rushed around in utter panic, since most of the eight hundred and eighty-eight[*] wedding guests were completely ignoring the seating chart. Annabel had been advised

---

[*] The number eight is considered by the Chinese to be an extremely lucky number, since in both Mandarin and Cantonese it sounds similar to the word for *prosperity* or *fortune*. Triple-eight means triple the luck.

on the seating protocol by no less an authority than *Singapore Tattle*'s editrix in chief, Betty Bao, but even Betty was unprepared for the ancient rivalries that existed among Asia's old-guard families. She would not have known, for instance, that the Hus should always be seated *in front* of the Ohs, or that the Kweks would not tolerate any Ngs within a fifty-foot radius.

Predictably, Dick and Nancy T'sien had commandeered two rows near the pulpit and were turning away anyone other than T'siens, Youngs, or Shangs (in rare exceptions, they were allowing in a few Leongs and Lynn Wyatt). Nancy, in a cinnabar-red dress and enormous matching feather-brimmed hat, gushed excitedly as Alexandra and Victoria approached. "Don't you love what they've done? It reminds me of the Seville Cathedral, where we attended the wedding of the Duchess of Alba's daughter to that handsome bullfighter."

"But we're *Methodists*, Nancy. This is a sacrilege! I feel like I'm in the middle of the Katyn forest, and someone is about to shoot me in the back of the head," Victoria seethed.

Rosemary T'sien walked up the central aisle escorted by her grandson Oliver T'sien and her granddaughter Cassandra Shang, nodding to people she knew along the way. Rachel could already tell by Cassandra's wrinkled nose that she did not approve of the decor. Radio One Asia slipped in between Victoria and Nancy and launched into the latest breaking news: "I just heard that Mrs. Lee Yong Chien is *furious*. She is going to talk to the bishop right after the service, and you know what *that* means—no more new library wing!"

Oliver, who was nattily dressed in a cream-colored seersucker suit, blue checked shirt, and yellow knit tie, slipped in next to Rachel. "I want to sit next to you—you're the best-dressed girl I've seen all day!" he declared, admiring the understated elegance of Rachel's outfit. As the church continued to fill up, Oliver's running commentary on the arriving VIP guests had Rachel alternately mesmerized and in stitches.

"Here comes the Malay contingent—assorted sultanas, princesses, and hangers-on. Hmm, it looks like *someone* got lipo. Lord have mercy, have you ever seen this many diamonds and bodyguards in all your life? Don't look now, I'm pretty sure that woman in the cloche hat is Faye Wong. She's an amazing singer and actress, famously elusive—the Greta Garbo of Hong Kong. Ah, look at Jacqueline Ling in that Azzedine Alaïa. On anyone else, that shade of pink would look slutty, but on her it looks drop-dead perfect. And see that really thin fellow with the comb-over being greeted so warmly by Peter and Annabel Lee? That's the man *everyone* here wants to talk to. He's the head of China Investment Corporation, which manages the Chinese Sovereign Wealth Fund. They have more than four hundred billion in reserves . . ."

On the bride's side of the aisle, Daisy Foo shook her head in awe. "The Lees got everyone, didn't they? The president and prime minister, all the Beijing top brass, Mrs. Lee Yong Chien, even Cassandra Shang flew back from London—and the Shangs never come to *anything*! Ten years ago the Lees were fresh off the boat from Mainland China, and look at them now—everyone who's anyone is here today."

"Speaking of *anyone*, look who just walked in . . . Alistair Cheng and Kitty Pong!" Nadine Shaw hissed.

"Well, she looks quite ladylike in that red-and-white polka-dot dress, doesn't she?" Carol Tai graciously offered.

"Yes, that ruffled skirt almost appears to cover her buttocks," Lorena Lim noted.

"*Alamak*, let's see what happens when she tries to sit with the Youngs. Wah, so *malu** for them! I bet she'll be thrown out of the row," Nadine said with glee. The ladies craned their necks to look, but much to their disappointment, Alistair and his new fiancée were greeted cordially by his relatives and ushered into the row.

"No such luck, Nadine. Those people are far too classy to make a public show out of it. But I bet you they are sharpening their knives in private. Meanwhile, that Rachel Chu looks like the Blessed Virgin compared to her. Poor Eleanor—her whole plan is backfiring!" Daisy sighed.

"Nothing is backfiring. Eleanor knows exactly what she's doing," Lorena said ominously.

At that moment, Eleanor Young walked up the aisle in a gunmetal-gray pantsuit that shimmered subtly, clearly delighting in the attention she was getting. She caught sight of Rachel and forced a smile. "Oh, hello there! Look Philip, it's Rachel Chu!" *In another designer dress. Every time I see this girl, she's wearing something more*

* Malay for "shameful," "embarrassing."

expensive than the last time. My God, she must be draining Nicky's money market account.

"Did you and Nicky stay up late last night? I bet you kids really went wild after we old fogies left the *dato*'s yacht, didn't you?" Philip asked with a wink.

"No, not at all. Nick needed to get to bed early, so we headed home soon after you left."

Eleanor smiled stiffly. *The cheek of this girl to call Tyersall Park "home"!*

Suddenly a hush fell over the crowd. Rachel thought at first that the ceremony was beginning, but when she glanced to the back of the church, all she saw was Astrid leading her grandmother up the aisle.

"My God, *Mummy's here!*" Alexandra gasped.

"What? You must be hallucinating," Victoria shot back, turning around in disbelief.

Oliver's mouth was agape, and every head on the groom's side of the church was trained on Astrid and her grandmother. Walking a few discreet paces behind them were the ubiquitous Thai lady's maids and several Gurkhas.

"What's the big deal?" Rachel whispered to Oliver.

"You don't know how monumental this is. Su Yi hasn't been seen at a public function like this in decades. She doesn't go out to other people's events—people come to *her.*"

A woman standing in the aisle suddenly dropped into a deep curtsy at the sight of Nick's grandmother.

"Who's that woman?" Rachel asked Oliver, mesmerized by the gesture.

"That's the wife of the president. She was born a Wong. The Wongs were saved by Su Yi's family during World War II, so they have always gone to great lengths to show their respect."

Rachel gazed at Nick's cousin and grandmother with renewed wonder, both so striking as they made their stately procession up the aisle. Astrid looked immaculately chic in a Majorelle-blue sleeveless halter-neck dress with gold cuff bracelets on both arms dramatically stacked all the way up to her elbows. Shang Su Yi was resplendent in a robe-like dress of pale violet that possessed the most distinctive gossamer sheen. "Nick's grandmother looks amazing. That dress . . ."

"Ah yes, that's one of her fabulous lotus-fabric dresses," Oliver said.

"As in lotus flowers?" Rachel asked, to clarify.

"Yes, from the stem of the lotus flower, actually. It's an extremely rare fabric that's handwoven in Myanmar, and normally available only for the most high-ranking monks. I'm told that it feels incredibly light and has an extraordinary ability to keep cool in the hottest climates."

As they approached, Su Yi was swarmed by her daughters.

"Mummy! Are you feeling okay?" Felicity asked in a worried tone.

"Why didn't you tell us you were coming?" Victoria snapped.

"Hiyah, we would have waited for you," Alexandra said excitedly.

Su Yi waved away all the fuss. "Astrid convinced me at the last minute. She reminded me that I wouldn't want to miss seeing Nicky as a best man."

As she uttered those words, two trumpeters appeared at the foot of the altar to herald the arrival of the groom. Colin entered the main sanctuary from a side alcove, accompanied by Nick, Lionel Khoo, and Mehmet Sabançi, all in dark gray morning suits and silvery blue ties. Rachel couldn't help but swell up with pride—Nick looked so dashing standing by the altar.

The lights in the sanctuary dimmed, and through a side door appeared a crowd of blond boys dressed in faun-like costumes of wispy white linen. Each rosy-cheeked boy clutched a glass jar filled with fireflies, and as more and more towheaded boys emerged to form two lines along both sides of the church sanctuary, Rachel realized there had to be at least a hundred of them. Illuminated by the flickering lights from their jars, the boys began to sing the classic English song "My True Love Hath My Heart."

"I don't believe it—it's the Vienna Boys' Choir! They flew in the fucking Vienna Boys' Choir!" Oliver exclaimed.

"Aiyah, what sweet little angels," Nancy gasped, overcome with emotion by the haunting alto voices. "It reminds me of the time King Hassan of Morocco invited us to his fort in the High Atlas Mountains—"

"Oh, do shut up!" Victoria said sharply, wiping tears from her eyes.

When the song ended, the orchestra, hidden in the transept, launched into the majestic strains of Michael Nyman's "Prospero's Magic" as sixteen bridesmaids in pearl-gray duchesse satin gowns entered the church, each holding an enormous curved branch of cherry blossom. Rachel recognized Francesca Shaw, Wandi Meggaharto, and a teary-eyed Sophie Khoo among them. The bridesmaids marched in choreographed precision, breaking off in pairs at different intervals so that they were spaced equally apart along the length of the aisle.

After the processional anthem, a young man in white tie stepped up to the altar with a violin in his hand. More murmurs of excitement filled the church as people realized that it was none other than Charlie Siem, the virtuoso violinist with matinee-idol looks. Siem began to play the first familiar chords of "Theme from *Out of Africa*," and sighs of delight could be heard from the audience. Oliver noted, "It's all about that chin, isn't it, clenched against the violin as if he's making savage love to it. That marvelous chin is what's making all the ladies cream their knickers."

The bridesmaids lifted their branches of cherry blossom high into the air, forming eight floral arches leading up to the altar, and the front doors of the church flung open dramatically. The bride appeared at the threshold, and there was a collective gasp from the crowd. For months magazine editors, gossip columnists, and fashion bloggers had speculated wildly over who might be designing Araminta's dress. Since she was both a celebrated model and one of Asia's budding fashion icons, expectations were high that she would wear a dress made by some avant-garde designer. But Araminta surprised everyone.

She walked down the aisle on her father's arm in a classically inspired wedding dress designed by Valentino, whom she lured out of retirement to make precisely the sort of gown that generations of European princesses had gotten married in, the sort of gown that would make her look every inch the proper young wife from a very traditional, old-money Asian family. Valentino's creation for Araminta featured a fitted high-necked lace bodice with long sleeves, a full skirt of overlapping lace and silk panels that unfurled like the petals of a peony as she moved, and a fifteen-foot train. (Giancarlo Giametti would later inform the press that the train, embroidered with ten thousand seed pearls and silver thread, took a team of twelve seamstresses nine months to sew and featured a pattern replicating the train Consuelo Vanderbilt wore when she fatefully wed the Duke of Marlborough in 1895.) Yet even in its baroque detail, the wedding gown did not overpower Araminta. Rather, it was the perfect extravagant foil against the stark minimalist wonderland her mother had so painstakingly created. Clutching a simple bouquet of stephanotis, with only a pair of antique pearl-drop earrings, the slightest hint of makeup, and her hair in a loose chignon adorned with nothing but a circlet of white narcissus, Araminta looked like a Pre-Raphaelite maiden floating through a sun-dappled forest.

From her seat in the front row, Annabel Lee, exultant in an Alexander McQueen dress of chiffon and gold lace, surveyed the faultlessly executed wedding procession and reveled in her family's social triumph.

Across the aisle, Astrid sat listening to the violin solo, relieved that her plan had worked. In the excitement over her grandmother's arrival, no one noticed that her husband was missing.

Sitting in his row, Eddie obsessed over which uncle could best introduce him to the chairman of the China Investment Corporation.

Standing by the altar, Colin gazed at the ravishing bride coming toward him, realizing that all the pain and fuss over the past few months had been worth it. "I can hardly believe it, but I don't think I've ever been happier," he whispered to his best man.

Nick, moved by Colin's reaction, searched the crowd for Rachel's face. Where was she? Oh, there she was, looking more gorgeous than she'd ever looked. Nick knew at that very moment that he wanted more than anything to see Rachel walk up that same aisle toward him in a white gown.

Rachel, who had been staring at the bridal procession, turned toward the altar and noticed Nick gazing intently at her. She gave him a little wink.

"I love you," Nick mouthed back to her.

Eleanor, witnessing this exchange, realized there was no more time to lose.

Araminta glided up the aisle, sneaking occasional peeks at her guests through her veil. She recognized friends, relatives, and many people she had only seen on television. Then she caught sight of Astrid. Imagine, Astrid Leong was at *her* wedding, and now they would be related through marriage. But wait a minute, that dress Astrid was wearing... wasn't that *the same* blue Gaultier she had worn to Carol Tai's Christian Helpers fashion benefit two months ago? As

Araminta reached the altar where her future husband awaited, with the Bishop of Singapore in front of her and the most important people in Asia behind her, one thought alone crossed her mind: Astrid Leong, *that damn bitch*, couldn't even be bothered to wear a new dress to her wedding.

5

Fort Canning Park

•

SINGAPORE

As the wedding guests began filtering into the park behind First Methodist Church for the reception, more gasps of astonishment could be heard.

"What now?" Victoria grumbled. "I'm so tired of all this 'oohing' and 'aiyahing'—I keep thinking somebody is going into cardiac arrest!" But as Victoria passed through the gates at Canning Rise, even she was momentarily silenced by the sight of the great lawn. In stark contrast to the church, the wedding reception looked like an atomic explosion of flowers. Thirty-foot-tall topiaries in gigantic pots and colossal spirals of pink roses encircled the field, where dozens of whimsical gazebos festooned in striped pastel taffeta had been built. In the center, an immense teapot spouted a waterfall of bubbly champagne into a cup the size of a small swimming pool, and a full string ensemble performed on what appeared to be a giant revolving Wedgwood plate. The scale of everything made the guests feel as if they had been transported to a tea party for giants.

"*Alamak*, someone pinch me!" *Puan Sri* Mavis Oon exclaimed as she caught sight of the food pavilions, where waiters in powdered white wigs and Tiffany-blue frock coats stood at tables piled mountain-high with sweets and savories.

Oliver escorted Rachel and Cassandra onto the great lawn. "I'm a bit confused—is this supposed to be the Mad Hatter's tea party or Marie Antoinette on a bad acid trip?"

"Looks like a combination of both," Rachel remarked.

"Now what do you suppose they're going to do with all these flowers once the reception ends?" Oliver wondered.

Cassandra stared up at the towering cascade of roses. "In this heat, they will all be rotten within three hours! I'm told the price of roses spiked to an all-time high this week at the Aalsmeer Flower Auction. Annabel bought up all the roses on the world market and had them flown in from Holland on a 747 freighter."

Rachel looked around at the guests parading the floral wonderland in their festive hats, their jewels glinting in the afternoon sun, and shook her head in disbelief.

"Ollie, how much did you say these Mainlanders spent?" Cassandra asked.

"Forty million, and for heaven's sake, Cassandra, the Lees have lived in Singapore for decades now. You need to stop calling them Mainlanders."

"Well, they still *behave* like Mainlanders, as this ridiculous reception proves. Forty million—I just don't see where all the money went."

"Well I've been keeping a tally, and I'm only up to five or six million so far. God help us, I think the motherlode is being spent on tonight's ball," Oliver surmised.

"I can't imagine how they're going to top this," Rachel said.

"Refreshments, anyone?" a voice behind her said. Rachel turned around to see Nick holding two glasses of champagne.

"Nick!" she cried excitedly.

"What did you all think of the wedding ceremony?" Nick asked, gallantly handing drinks to the ladies.

"Wedding? I could have sworn it was a coronation," Oliver retorted. "Anyway, who cares about the ceremony? The important question is: *What did everyone think of Araminta's dress?*"

"It was lovely. It looked deceptively simple, but the longer you stared at it, the more you noticed the details," Rachel offered.

"Ugh. It was awful. She looked like some kind of medieval bride," Cassandra sniggered.

"That was the point, Cassandra. I thought the dress was a triumph. Valentino at his best, channeling Botticelli's *Primavera* and Marie de' Medici's arrival in Marseilles."

"I have no idea what you just said, Ollie, but I agree." Nick laughed.

"You looked so serious up there at the altar," Rachel remarked.

"It was very serious business! Speaking of which, I'm going to steal Rachel away for a moment," Nick said to his cousins, grasping Rachel's hand.

"Hey—there are children around. No hanky-panky in the bushes!" Oliver warned.

"*Alamak*, Ollie, with Kitty Pong here, I don't think Nicky's the one we need to worry about," Cassandra said drily.

———

Kitty stood in the middle of the great lawn, staring in wonder at everything around her. Here at last was something worth getting excited about! Her trip to Singapore so far had been nothing but a series of disappointments. First of all, they were staying at that cool new hotel with the huge park on the roof, but all the suites were booked up and they were stuck in a lousy regular room. And then there was Alistair's family, who clearly weren't as rich as she had been led to believe. Alistair's auntie Felicity lived in an old wooden house with old Chinese furniture that wasn't even polished properly. They were nothing compared to the rich families she knew in China, who lived in huge newly built mansions decorated by the top designers from Paris France. Then there was Alistair's mother, who looked like one of those dowdy Family Planning Commission workers who used to come to her village in Qinghai to give advice about birth control. At last they were finally at this fairy-tale wedding reception, where she could be surrounded by the crème de la crème of society.

"Isn't that fellow in the bow tie the chief executive of Hong Kong?" Kitty whispered loudly to Alistair.

"Yes, I believe it is," Alistair answered.

"Do you know him?"

"I've met him once or twice—my parents know him."

"*Really?* Where are your parents, by the way? They disappeared so quickly after the wedding, I didn't even get a chance to say hi," Kitty said with a little pout.

"I'm not sure what you're talking about. My dad's right there piling his plate with langoustines, and my mum is over in that purple-striped gazebo with my grandmother."

"Oh, your Ah Ma is here?" Kitty said, peering at the gazebo. "There are so many old ladies in there—which one is she?"

Alistair pointed her out.

"Who is that woman talking to her right now? The one in the yellow head scarf, covered head to toe in *diamonds!*"

"Oh, that's one of my Ah Ma's old friends. I think she's some sort of Malay princess."

"Oooh, a *princess?* Take me to meet her now!" Kitty insisted, dragging Alistair away from the dessert tent.

In the gazebo, Alexandra noticed her son and *that strumpet* (she refused to call her his *fiancée*) walking intently toward her. *Hiyah, were they actually on their way here? Did Alistair not have the sense to keep Kitty away from his grandmother, especially when she was receiving Mrs. Lee Yong Chien and the Sultana of Borneo?*

"Astrid, it's getting a bit crowded. Will you please tell the sultana's bodyguards to make sure *no one else* is allowed in?" she whispered to her niece, her eyes darting frantically at Alistair and Kitty.

"Of course, Auntie Alix," Astrid said.

As Alistair and Kitty approached the gazebo, three guards in crisp military dress uniforms blocked the steps in front of it. "Sorry, no more people allowed in," a guard announced.

"Oh, but my family's in there. That's my mother and grandmother." Alistair pointed, peering over the guard's shoulder. He tried to catch his mother's eye, but she seemed to be engrossed in conversation with her cousin Cassandra.

"Yoohoo!" Kitty cried out. She took off her huge polka-dotted straw hat and began waving it excitedly, jumping up and down. "Yoohoo, Mrs. Cheng!"

Alistair's grandmother peered out and asked, "Who is that girl jumping about?"

Alexandra wished at that moment she had put an end to her son's ridiculous romance when she'd had the chance.

"It's nobody. Just someone trying to get a glimpse of Her Royal Highness," Astrid cut in, gesturing toward the sultana.

"Is that *Alistair* with the jumping girl?" Su Yi asked, squinting her eyes.

"Trust me, Mummy, just ignore them," Alexandra whispered nervously.

Cassandra decided that it would be far more amusing to throw a wrench into this little charade. "Aiyah, *Koo Por*,* that's Alistair's new girlfriend," she said mischievously, as Alexandra glared at her in exasperation.

"The Hong Kong starlet you were telling me about, Cassandra? Let her in—I want to meet her," Su Yi said. She turned to Mrs. Lee Yong Chien with a gleam in her eye. "My youngest grandson is dating some Hong Kong soap-opera actress."

"An *actress*?" Mrs. Lee made a face, as Alistair and Kitty were allowed into the gazebo.

"Ah Ma, I want you to meet my fiancée, Kitty Pong," Alistair boldly announced in Cantonese.

"Your fiancée? Nobody told me you got engaged," Su Yi said, shooting her daughter a look of surprise. Alexandra couldn't bear to make eye contact with her mother.

"So nice to meet you," Kitty said in a perfunctory tone, utterly disinterested in Alistair's elderly grandma. She turned to the sultana and dipped into a deep curtsey. "Your Honor, it is such a privilege to meet you!"

Cassandra turned away, trying to keep a straight face, while the other ladies glowered at Kitty.

"Wait a minute, are you the youngest sister in *Many Splendid Things*?" the sultana suddenly asked.

"Yes, she is," Alistair proudly answered for her.

"*Alamaaaaak*, I love your show!" the sultana exclaimed. "My God, you're so eeeeee-vil! Tell me, you didn't *really* die in that tsunami, did you?"

Kitty grinned. "I'm not telling you—you'll just have to wait for next season. Your Gracefulness, your jewels are magnificent. Is that diamond brooch real? It's bigger than a golf ball!"

The sultana nodded her head in amusement. "It's called the Star of Malaya."

"Ooooh, can I touch it, Your Highness?" Kitty asked. Mrs. Lee Yong Chien was about to protest, but the sultana eagerly leaned forward.

* Cantonese for "great-aunt."

"My God, feel the weight!" Kitty sighed, cupping the diamond in her palm. "How many carats?"

"One hundred and eighteen," the sultana declared.

"One day, you'll buy me something just like this, won't you?" Kitty said to Alistair unabashedly. The other ladies were aghast.

The sultana reached for her bejeweled handbag and pulled out an embroidered lace handkerchief. "Will you please autograph this?" she asked Kitty expectantly.

"Your Majesticness, it would be my pleasure!" Kitty beamed.

The sultana turned to Shang Su Yi, who had been surveying the whole exchange with bemused interest. "This is your grandson's fiancée? How delightful. Be sure you invite me to the wedding!" The sultana began to wiggle off one of the three humongous diamond rings on her left hand and handed it to Kitty, as the ladies looked on in horror. "Congratulations on your engagement—this is for you. *Taniah dan semoga kamu gembira selalu.*"*

The farther Nick and Rachel walked from the great lawn, the more the park began to change. The strains of the string ensemble gave way to birds with strangely hypnotic chirps as they entered a pathway shaded by the sprawling branches of two-hundred-year-old Angsana trees. "I love it over here—it's like we're on a whole other island," Rachel said, savoring the cool relief underneath the lush canopy.

"I love it here too. We're in the oldest part of the park, an area that's sacred to the Malays," Nick explained quietly. "You know, back when the island was called Singapura and was part of the ancient Majapahit empire, this is where they built a shrine to the last king."

"'The Last King of Singapura.' Sounds like a movie. Why don't you write the screenplay?" Rachel remarked.

"Ha! I think it'll draw an audience of about four," Nick replied.

They reached a clearing in the pathway, and a small colonial-era structure covered in moss came into view. "Whoa—is this the shrine?" Rachel asked, lowering her voice.

"No, this is the gatehouse. When the British came in the nineteenth century, they built a fort here," Nick explained as they

---

* Malay for "Congratulations and best wishes."

approached the structure and the pair of massive iron doors under the archway. The doors were wide open, flush against the inner wall of the tunnel-like gatehouse, and Nick slowly pulled on one of the heavy doors, revealing a dark narrow entrance cut into the thick stonework, and beyond it the steps leading to the roof of the gatehouse.

"Welcome to my hideout," Nick whispered, his voice echoing in the tight stairway.

"Is it safe to go up?" Rachel asked, assessing steps that looked like they hadn't been treaded on in decades.

"Of course. I used to come up here all the time," Nick said, bounding up the steps eagerly. "Come on!"

Rachel followed gingerly, taking care not to rub any part of her pristine dress against the dirt-caked stairway. The roof was covered in freshly fallen leaves, gnarled tree branches, and the remnants of an old cannon. "Pretty cool, isn't it? At one point, there were more than sixty cannons lining the battlements of the fort. Come take a look at this!" Nick said excitedly as he disappeared around the corner. Rachel could hear the schoolboy adventurer in his voice. Along the south wall, someone had scrawled long vertical lines of Chinese characters in what looked like a muddy-brown color. "Written with blood," Nick said in a hushed voice.

Rachel stared at the characters in amazement. "I can't make them out . . . it's so faded, and it's that old form of Chinese. What do you think happened?"

"We used to make up theories about it. The one I came up with was that some poor prisoner was chained here and left to die by Japanese soldiers."

"I'm getting sort of creeped out," Rachel said, shaking off a sudden chill.

"Well, you wanted to see the proverbial 'sacred cave.' This is as close to it as you're going to get. I used to bring my girlfriends up here to make out after Sunday school. This is where I had my first kiss," Nick announced brightly.

"Of course it is. I couldn't imagine a more eerily romantic hideout," Rachel said.

Nick pulled Rachel closer. She thought they were about to kiss, but Nick's expression seemed to shift into a more serious mode. He thought of the way she looked earlier that morning, with the light streaming in through the stained-glass windows and glinting on her hair.

"You know, when I saw you in the church today sitting with my family, do you know what I thought?"

Rachel could feel her heart suddenly begin to race. "Whh . . . what?"

Nick paused, gazing deeply into her eyes. "This feeling came over me, and I just knew tha—"

The sound of someone coming up the stairs suddenly interrupted them, and they broke away from their embrace. A ravishing girl with a short-cropped Jean Seberg hairstyle appeared at the top of the stairs, and behind her shuffled a portly Caucasian man. Rachel immediately recognized the hand-painted Dries Van Noten dress from Patric's atelier that the girl was wearing.

"Mandy!" Nick gasped in surprise.

"Nico!" the girl replied with a smile.

"What are you doing here?"

"What do you think I'm doing here, silly rabbit? I had to escape from that *taaaaacky* reception. Did you see that ghastly giant teapot? I half expected it to get up and start singing in Angela Lansbury's voice," she said, shifting her gaze onto Rachel.

Great. Another Singapore girl with a posh English accent, Rachel thought.

"Where are my manners?" Nick quickly recovered. "Rachel, this is Amanda Ling. You might remember meeting her mum, Jacqueline, the other night at Ah Ma's."

Rachel smiled and extended her hand.

"And this is Zvi Goldberg," Mandy reciprocated. Zvi nodded quickly, still trying to catch his breath. "Well, I came up here to show Zvi the place where I received my first kiss. And would you believe it, Zvi, the boy who kissed me is standing right before us," Mandy said, looking straight at Nick.

Rachel turned to Nick with a raised eyebrow. His cheeks were bright red.

"You gotta be kidding! You guys plan this reunion or something?" Zvi cracked.

"Swear to God we didn't. This is a complete coincidence," Mandy declared.

"Yes, I thought you were dead set against coming to the wedding," Nick said.

"Well, I changed my mind at the last minute. Especially since Zvi has this fabulous new plane that can zip around so quickly—our flight from New York only took fifteen hours!"

"Oh, you live in New York too?" Rachel inquired.

"Yes, I do. What, has Nico never mentioned me to you? Nico, I'm so hurt," Mandy said in mock outrage. She turned to Rachel with a placid smile. "I feel like I have an unfair advantage, since I've heard *loads* about you."

"You have?" Rachel couldn't hide her look of surprise. Why had Nick never once mentioned this friend of his, this beautiful girl who inexplicably kept calling him *Nico*? Rachel gave Nick a measured look, but he simply smiled back, oblivious to the nagging thoughts filling her mind.

"Well, I suppose we ought to get back to the reception," Mandy suggested. As the foursome made their way toward the stairs, Mandy halted abruptly. "Oh look, Nico. I can't believe it—it's still here!" She traced her fingers over a section of the wall right beside the staircase.

Rachel peered at the wall and saw the names *Nico* and *Mandi* carved into the rock, joined together by an infinity symbol.

6

Tyersall Park

.

Alexandra walked onto the veranda to find her sister, Victoria, and her daughter-in-law, Fiona, having afternoon tea with her mother. Victoria looked rather comical with a dramatic opera-length necklace of mine-cut cognac diamonds casually draped over her gingham shirt. Obviously, Mummy was doling out jewelry again, something she seemed to be doing with greater frequency these days.

"I've been labeling every piece in the vault and putting them in cases marked with all your names," Su Yi had informed Alexandra during her visit last year. "This way there is no fighting after I'm gone."

"There won't *be* any fighting, Mummy," Alexandra had insisted.

"You say that now. But look what happened to Madam Lim Boon Peck's family. Or the Hu sisters. Whole families torn apart over jewelry. And not even very good jewelry!" Su Yi had sighed.

As Alexandra approached the wrought-iron table where sweetly aromatic *kueh lapis** and pineapple tarts were arrayed on Longquan celadon dishes, Su Yi was taking out a diamond and cabochon sapphire choker. "This one my father brought back from Shanghai

---

* Also known as "thousand-layer cake," this decadently buttery cake with dozens of thin golden stripes is created by baking each layer of batter separately. Extremely laborious, but sinfully good.

in 1918," Su Yi said to Fiona in Cantonese. "My mother told me it belonged to a grand duchess who had escaped Russia on the Trans-Siberian Railway with all her jewels sewn into the lining of her coat. Here, try it on."

Fiona put the choker around her neck, and one of Su Yi's Thai lady's maids helped to fasten the delicate antique clasp. The other maid held up a hand mirror, and Fiona peered at her reflection. Even in the waning late-afternoon light, the sapphires glistened against her neck. "It's truly exquisite, Ah Ma."

"I've always liked it because these sapphires are so translucent—I've never quite seen a shade of blue like that," Su Yi said.

Fiona handed back the necklace, and Su Yi slipped it into a yellow silk pouch before handing it to Fiona. "Nah, you should wear it tonight to the wedding banquet."

"Oh, Ah Ma, I couldn't possibly—" Fiona began.

"Aiyah, *moh hak hei*,* it's yours now. Make sure it goes to Kalliste someday," Su Yi decreed. She turned to Alexandra and said, "Do you need something for tonight?"

Alexandra shook her head. "I brought my triple-strand pearls."

"You always wear those pearls," Victoria complained, casually twirling her new diamonds around her fingers as if they were toy beads.

"I like my pearls. Besides, I don't want to look like one of those Khoo women. Did you see how much jewelry they piled on this morning? Ridiculous."

"Those Khoos sure like to flaunt it, don't they," Victoria said with a laugh, popping one of the crumbly pineapple tarts into her mouth.

"Aiyah, who cares? Khoo Teck Fong's father came from a little village in Sarawak—I will always know him as the man who used to buy my mother's old silver," Su Yi said dismissively. "Now, speaking of jewelry, I want to talk about Alistair's girlfriend—*that starlet*."

Alexandra flinched, steeling herself for the onslaught. "Yes, Mummy, I'm sure you were as appalled as I was by that woman's behavior today."

"The audacity of her to accept that ring from the sultana! It was so undignified, not to mention—" Victoria began.

---

* Cantonese for "don't be formal."

Su Yi held out her hand to silence Victoria. "Why wasn't I told that Alistair was engaged to her?"

"It just happened a few days ago," Alexandra said bleakly.

"But who is she? Who are her people?"

"I don't know precisely," Alexandra said.

"How is it possible that you don't know the family, when your son wants to take her as his wife?" Su Yi said in astonishment. "Look at Fiona here—we have known her family for generations. Fiona, do *you* know this girl's family?"

Fiona grimaced, making no attempt to hide her disdain. "Ah Ma, I never set eyes on her until two days ago at Auntie Felicity's."

"Cassandra told me the girl showed up at Felicity's wearing a see-through dress. Is that true?" Su Yi asked.

"Yes," the three ladies droned in unison.

"Tien,* *ah,* what is this world coming to?" Su Yi shook her head, taking a slow sip from her teacup.

"Clearly the girl has not been brought up well," Victoria said.

"She's not been brought up at all. She's not Taiwanese, even though she claims to be, and she's certainly not from Hong Kong. I've heard that she is from some remote village in northern China," Fiona offered.

"Tsk, those northern Chinese are the worst!" Victoria huffed, nibbling on a slice of *kueh lapis.*

"Where she's from is irrelevant. My youngest grandson is not going to marry some actress, especially one of questionable lineage," Su Yi said simply. Turning to Alexandra, she said, "You will tell him to break off the engagement immediately."

"His father has agreed to talk to him when we return to Hong Kong."

"I don't think that will be soon enough, Alix. The girl needs to be sent packing before she does something more offensive. I can only imagine what she's going to wear to the ball tonight," Victoria said.

"Well, what about Rachel, that girlfriend of Nicky's?" Alexandra said, trying to deflect the focus from her son.

"What about her?" Su Yi asked, puzzled.

* Mandarin for "heavens!"

"Aren't you concerned about her as well? I mean, we know nothing of *her* family."

"Aiyah, she's just a pretty girl that Nicky's having fun with." Su Yi laughed, as if the idea of him marrying Rachel was too ridiculous to even consider.

"That's not the way it looks to me," Alexandra warned.

"Nonsense. Nicky has no intentions with this girl—he told me so himself. And besides, he would never do anything without my permission. Alistair simply needs to obey your wishes," Su Yi said with finality.

"Mummy, I'm not sure it's that simple. That boy can be so stubborn. I tried to get him to stop dating her months ago, but—" Alexandra began.

"Alix, why don't you just threaten to cut him off? Stop his allowance or something," Victoria suggested.

"*Allowance?* He doesn't get an allowance. Alistair isn't concerned about money—he supports himself with those odd jobs on films, so he has always done exactly as he pleases."

"You know, Alistair might not care about money, but I'll bet you that trollop does," Victoria expostulated. "Alix, you need to give her a good talking-to. Make her understand that it is impossible for her to marry Alistair, and that you will cut him off forever if she does."

"I don't know how I would even begin," Alexandra said. "Why don't you talk to her, Victoria? You're so good at this sort of thing."

"Me? Good grief, I don't intend to exchange *a single word* with that girl!" Victoria declared.

"*Tien, ah,* you are all hopeless!" Su Yi groaned. Turning to one of her lady's maids, she ordered, "Call Oliver T'sien. Tell him to come over right away."

———

On the way home from the wedding reception, Nick had assured Rachel that his relationship with Mandy was ancient history. "We dated on and off till I was eighteen and went off to Oxford. It was puppy love. Now we're just old friends who meet up every once in a while. You know, she lives in New York but we hardly ever meet—she's way too busy going to A-list parties with that Zvi fellow," Nick said.

Still, Rachel had sensed a distinctly territorial vibe coming from Mandy back at the fort, making her wonder if Mandy was truly over Nick. Now, as she was getting dressed for the most formal event she had ever been invited to, she wondered how she would compare to Mandy and all the other impossibly chic women in Nick's orbit. She stood in front of the mirror, assessing herself. Her hair had been swept up into a loose French twist and pinned with three violet orchid blossoms, and she was wearing a midnight blue off-the-shoulder gown that draped elegantly across her hips before flaring out just above the knees into luxuriant folds of silk organza scattered with tiny freshwater pearls. She scarcely recognized herself.

There was a jaunty rap on the door. "Are you decent?" Nick called out.

"Yes, come in!" Rachel replied.

Nick opened the bedroom door and stopped dead in his tracks. "Oh *wow*!" he said.

"You like it?" Rachel asked bashfully.

"You look stunning," Nick said, almost in a whisper.

"Do these flowers in my hair look silly?"

"Not at all." Nick circled around her, admiring how the thousands of pearls shimmered like faraway stars. "It makes you look glamorous and exotic at the same time."

"Thanks. You look pretty awesome yourself," Rachel declared, admiring how utterly debonair Nick looked in his dinner jacket, with its streamlined grosgrain lapels perfectly accentuating his crisp white bow tie.

"Ready for your carriage?" Nick asked, entwining his arm through hers in a courtly manner.

"I guess so," Rachel said, exhaling deeply. As they walked out of the bedroom, little Augustine Cheng came racing down the corridor.

"Whoa, Augustine, you're going to break your neck," Nick said, stopping him in his tracks. The little boy looked terrified.

"What's wrong, little man?" Nick asked.

"I need to hide." Augustine was panting.

"Why?"

"Papa's after me. I spilled Orange Fanta all over his new suit."

"Oh no!" Rachel said, trying not to giggle.

"He said he was going to kill me," the boy said, shaking, with tears in his eyes.

"Oh, he'll get over it. Come with us. I'll make sure your father doesn't kill you." Nick laughed, taking Augustine by the hand.

At the bottom of the stairs, Eddie was arguing in Cantonese with Ling Cheh, the head housekeeper, and Nasi, the head laundry maid, while Fiona stood next to him in her Weimaraner-gray evening gown looking exasperated.

"I'm telling you, this type of fabric needs to soak for a few hours if you want to get the stain out properly," the head laundry maid explained.

"A few hours? But we need to be at the wedding ball by seven thirty! This is an emergency, do you understand?" Eddie shouted, glaring at the Malay woman as if she didn't understand English.

"Eddie, there's no need to raise your voice. She understands," Fiona said.

"How many laundry maids does my grandmother keep? There must be at least ten of you! Don't tell me you people can't fix this right now," Eddie complained to Ling Cheh.

"Eddieboy, even if there were twenty of them, there's no way it will be ready for tonight," Ling Cheh insisted.

"But what am I going to wear? I had this tux specially made for me in Milan! Do you know how much it cost me?"

"I'm sure it was very, very expensive. And that's exactly why we need to be gentle and let the stain lift properly," Ling Cheh said, shaking her head. *Eddieboy had been a pompous little monster even when he was five.*

Eddie glanced up the staircase and noticed Augustine coming down with Nick and Rachel. "YOU LITTLE SHIT!" he screamed.

"Eddie, control yourself!" Fiona admonished.

"I'm going to teach him a lesson he'll never forget!" Incandescent with rage, Eddie began to storm up the stairs.

"Stop it, Eddie," Fiona said, grabbing hold of his arm.

"You're wrinkling my shirt, Fi!" Eddie scowled. "Like mother like son—"

"Eddie, you need to calm down. Just wear one of the other two tuxes you brought," Fiona said in a measured tone.

"Don't be stupid! I've already worn both of those the past two nights. I had everything perfectly planned until this little bastard came along! Stop hiding, you little bastard! Be a man and accept your punishment!" Eddie broke free from his wife and lunged toward the boy with his right arm outstretched.

Augustine whimpered, cowering behind Nick. "Eddie, you're not *really* going to hit your six-year-old son over a harmless accident, are you?" Nick said lightheartedly.

"Harmless? Fucky fuck, he's ruined everything! The monochromatic fashion statement I was planning for the whole family is RUINED because of him!"

"And you've just ruined the whole trip for me!" Fiona suddenly blurted out. "I'm so sick of all this. Why is it so damn important for us to look picture-perfect every time we walk out the door? Who exactly are you trying to impress? The photographers? The readers of *Hong Kong Tattle*? You really care so much about them that you'd rather hit your own son over an accident that *you caused in the first place* by screaming at him for wearing the wrong cummerbund?"

"But, but . . ." Eddie sputtered in protest.

Fiona turned to Nick, her serene expression returning. "Nick, can my children and I ride with you to the ball?"

"Er . . . if you'd like," Nick said cautiously, not wanting to further incite his cousin.

"Good. I have no desire to be seen with a tyrant." Fiona took Augustine by the hand and started up the stairs. She paused for a moment as she passed Rachel. "You look amazing in that dress. But you know what? It needs something." Fiona proceeded to take off the sapphire-and-diamond choker she had just been given by Su Yi and placed it around Rachel's neck. "Now the outfit looks complete. I insist that you borrow it for tonight."

"You're too kind, but what will you wear?" Rachel asked in astonishment.

"Oh, don't worry about me," Fiona said, giving her husband a dark stare. "I'm not going to be wearing a single piece of jewelry tonight. I was born a Tung, and I have *nothing* to prove to anyone."

7

Pasir Panjang Road

SINGAPORE

"Never, never let young people plan their own weddings, because this is what you end up with!" Mrs. Lee Yong Chien fumed to *Puan Sri* Mavis Oon. They were standing in the middle of an enormous warehouse in the Keppel Shipyard along with seven hundred other VIPs and VVIPs, utterly baffled by the Cuban band dressed in forties Tropicana splendor on the stage. People like Mrs. Lee were used to only one kind of Chinese wedding banquet—the kind that took place in the grand ballroom of a five-star hotel. There would be the gorging on salted peanuts during the interminable wait for the fourteen-course dinner to begin, the melting ice sculptures, the outlandish floral centerpieces, the society matron invariably offended by the faraway table she had been placed at, the entrance of the bride, the malfunctioning smoke machine, the entrance of the bride again and again in five different gowns throughout the night, the crying child choking on a fish ball, the three dozen speeches by politicians, token *ang mor* executives and assorted high-ranking officials of no relation to the wedding couple, the cutting of the twelve-tier cake, someone's mistress making a scene, the not so subtle counting of wedding cash envelopes by some cousin,* the ghastly Canto pop star flown in from

---

* The custom at Chinese weddings is for guests to contribute a cash gift meant to

Hong Kong to scream some pop song (a chance for the older crowd to take an extended toilet break), the distribution of tiny wedding fruitcakes with white icing in paper boxes to all the departing guests, and then *Yum seng!**—the whole affair would be over and everyone would make the mad dash to the hotel lobby to wait half an hour for their car and driver to make it through the traffic jam.

Tonight, however, there was none of that. There was just an industrial space with waiters bearing mojitos and a woman with short, slicked-back hair in a white tuxedo belting out "Besame Mucho." Glancing around, Rachel was amused by the looks of bafflement on the faces of the arriving guests decked out in their most ostentatious finery.

"These women really brought out the big guns tonight, didn't they?" Rachel whispered to Nick as she eyed a woman sporting a cape of metallic-gold feathers.

"Sure looks like it! Was that Queen Nefertiti who just walked by?" Nick joked.

"Shut your mouth, Nicholas—that's Patsy Wang. She's a Hong Kong socialite renowned for her avant-garde style. There are dozens of blogs out there devoted to her," Oliver commented.

"Who's the guy with her? The one in the diamond-studded jacket who looks like he's wearing eye shadow?" Rachel queried.

"That's her husband, Adam, and he *is* wearing eye shadow," Oliver answered.

"They're married? *Really?*" Rachel raised a doubting eyebrow.

"Yes, and they even have three children to prove it. You have to understand, many Hong Kong men revel in being fashionistas— they are dandies in the truest sense of the word. How flamboyantly dressed they might be is no indication of which team they play on."

"Fascinating," Rachel said.

"You can always tell Singapore men from Hong Kong men," Nick chimed in. "We're the ones dressed like we're still wearing our school uniforms, while they look more like—"

"David Bowie impersonators," Oliver finished.

---

help defray the cost of the lavish banquet, and it is usually the task of some unfortunate second cousin to collect and keep track of all these cash-stuffed envelopes.

* The traditional Singaporean toast, which literally means "finish drinking."

"Thanks, Ollie. I was going to go with Elton John." Nick chuckled.

As if on cue, the lights in the warehouse dimmed and the loading-dock doors behind the stage began to rise, revealing a line of sleek white ferries waiting harborside. Flaming torches lit the way to the pier, and a line of men dressed in Swedish sailor outfits stood ready to guide the guests onto the ferries. The crowd roared in approval.

"The other shoe drops," Oliver said gleefully.

"Where do you think we're going?" Rachel asked.

"You'll soon see," Nick said with a wink.

As the guests streamed onto the pier, Astrid made sure to board the ferry carrying a mix of international guests rather than the one filled with her nosy relatives. She had already been asked "Where's Michael?" too many times and was sick of parroting new variations of her excuse. As she leaned against the railing at the back of the ferry, peering at the frothy waves as the vessel pulled away from the embankment, she felt someone staring at her. She turned to see Charlie Wu, her old flame, on the upper deck. Charlie flushed bright red when he realized he'd been caught staring. He hesitated for a moment, and then decided to come downstairs.

"Long time no see," he said as nonchalantly as possible. In fact, it had been almost ten years since that fateful day when Astrid had thrown a Frosty in his face outside of the old Wendy's on Orchard Road.

"Yes," Astrid said with an apologetic smile. She assessed him for a moment, thinking that he looked better with a little age on him. Those rimless glasses suited him, his gangly frame had filled out, and the once problematic acne scarring now gave his face a finely weathered look. "How's life treating you? You moved to Hong Kong a few years ago, didn't you?"

"I can't complain. Too busy with work, but isn't that the case with everyone?" Charlie mused.

"Well, not everyone owns the largest digital technology company in Asia. Aren't they calling you the Asian Steve Jobs these days?"

"Yeah, unfortunately. Impossible shoes to fill." Charlie looked at her again, unsure of what to say. She looked more exquisite than ever in that chartreuse cheongsam. *Funny how you could be so intimate with someone for so many years, and yet feel so painfully awkward around them now.* "So I hear you got married to some hotshot army guy, and you have a son."

"Yes, Cassian . . . he's three," Astrid replied, adding preemptively, "and my husband works in the tech industry like you now. He had to run off to China at the last minute to handle some huge system meltdown. And you have a son and a daughter, don't you?"

"No, two daughters. Still no boy yet, much to my mother's dismay. But my brother Rob has three boys, which keeps her placated for the time being."

"And your wife? Is she here tonight?" Astrid asked.

"No, no, I'm the only one flying the flag for my family. You know, they only invited eight hundred and eighty-eight guests, so I hear that unless you were family, a head of state, or a member of royalty, your spouse didn't get invited."

"Is that so?" Astrid laughed. *I treated Charlie horribly. He didn't deserve to be chucked aside like that, but everyone was putting so much pressure on me about marrying Wu Hao Lian's son back in those days.* There was an awkward silence, but they were thankfully saved by the gasps of astonishment from the crowd. The ferry was fast approaching one of the outlying islands, and coming into view was what looked like a crystal palace glowing in the middle of the dense forest. Charlie and Astrid stared in awe as the full complexity of the structure became apparent.

The cathedral-like banquet hall consisted of immense trapezoidal canopies of glass that were seemingly integrated into the tropical rain forest. Trees grew out from some of the glass panels, while others were contained within its dramatically angled panes. Intersecting the main structure were cantilevered terraces of varying heights, with a profusion of tropical vines and flowers spilling out over each terrace. The whole place looked like a futuristic Hanging Gardens of Babylon, and standing at the harbor promenade flanked by a row of travertine columns were Colin and Araminta, both dressed in white, waving to the arriving guests.

Astrid took one look at them and deadpanned in a Latin accent, "Welcome to Fantasy Island!"

Charlie laughed. He had forgotten her wacky sense of humor.

"I guess this is how you spend forty million on a wedding," Astrid remarked drily.

"Oh, that thing costs way more than forty million," Charlie said.

Araminta, in a pleated white chiffon-silk gown with long straps of hammered gold and diamond links that crisscrossed her bodice, greeted her guests. Her hair was piled high into a mound of intricate braids and festooned with diamonds, baroque pearls, and moonstones. As the gown billowed around her in the ocean breeze, she could have been mistaken for an Etruscan goddess. Standing at her side, looking a little worn out from the day's festivities, was Colin in a white linen tuxedo.

Looking through the crowd, Araminta asked Colin, "Do you see your cousin Astrid anywhere?"

"I saw her brothers, but I haven't spotted her yet," Colin answered.

"Let me know the minute you spot her—I need to know what she's wearing tonight!"

"I spy Astrid disembarking from the third ferry," Colin reported.

"*Alamak*, she's wearing a *cheongsam*! Why didn't she wear one of her fabulous couture creations?" Araminta sighed.

"I think she looks lovely, and that cheongsam was probably handmade—"

"But I was *waiting* to see what designer she would turn up in! I go to all this trouble, and she doesn't even bother to make the effort. What's the whole fucking point of this wedding?" Araminta moaned.

When the last boatload of guests had disembarked, the illuminated crystalline façade of the banquet hall suddenly morphed into an intense shade of fuschia. Haunting New Age music boomed from the surrounding forest, and the trees were bathed in golden light. Slowly, almost imperceptibly, golden cords descended from the thick foliage. Wrapped cocoon-like in these cords were acrobats with bodies that had been painted gold. "Oh my goodness—I think it's Cirque du Soleil!" the guests began murmuring excitedly. As the acrobats started to unfurl and spin around the cords as effortlessly as lemurs, the crowd broke into rapturous applause.

Kitty jumped up and down like a hyperactive child.

"You seem to be having a good time," Oliver said, sidling up next to her and noticing that her breasts didn't seem to jiggle naturally inside that lacey turquoise gown. He also noticed that she had a thin sheen of body glitter on. *Bad combo*, he thought.

"I love Cirque du Soleil! I've gone to every single one of their performances in Hong Kong. Now, I must have these acrobats at my wedding too."

"My goodness, that will be costly," Oliver said in exaggerated awe.

"Oh, Alistair can handle it," Kitty replied breezily.

"You think so? I didn't realize Alistair was doing *that* well in the movie business."

"Hiyah, don't you think his parents will pay for the wedding?" Kitty said as she stared at the gold-painted acrobats while they began to form a human arch.

"Are you kidding me?" Oliver lowered his voice, continuing, "Do you have any idea how cheap his mother is?"

"She is?"

"Haven't you been to that flat of theirs on Robinson Road?"

"Er . . . no. I was never invited."

"That's probably because Alistair was too embarrassed to show it to you. It's a very basic three-bedroom flat. Alistair had to share a bedroom with his brother until he went to college. I went to visit in 1991, and there were these yellow floral bath mats in the toilet. And when I went again last month, the yellow floral bath mats were still there, except that they are grayish floral now."

"Really?" Kitty said in disbelief.

"Well, look at his mother. You think she wears those old eighties dresses on purpose? She wears them to save money."

"But I thought Alistair's father is a famous heart doctor?" Kitty was confused.

Oliver paused. Thank God she didn't seem to know about the Chengs' massive real estate holdings. "Do you have any idea how much malpractice insurance costs these days? Doctors don't make as much money as you think. Do you know how much it costs to send three children to study overseas? Eddie went to Cambridge, Cecilia went to UBC,* and Alistair—well, you know how long Alistair took to graduate from Sydney University. The Chengs spent most of their savings on their children's education."

"I had no idea."

"And you know how Malcolm is. He's a traditional Cantonese man—what remaining money he has will all go to his eldest son."

* University of British Columbia in Vancouver, commonly referred to by locals as "University of a Billion Chinese."

Kitty went quiet, and Oliver prayed he hadn't laid it on too thick.

"But of course, I know none of that is important to you," he added. "You're in love, and you don't really need Cirque du Soleil performing at your wedding, do you? I mean, you'll get to stare at that cute puppy-dog face of Alistair's every morning for the rest of your life. That's worth all the money in the world, isn't it?"

8

Pulau Samsara

OFF THE SOUTHERN COAST OF SINGAPORE

At nine o'clock sharp, the wedding-ball attendees were led into the vast banquet hall set amid the indigenous tropical rain forest. Along the south walls were archways that led to grotto-like alcoves, while the curved north wall consisted of a curtain of glass that overlooked a man-made lagoon and a dramatic waterfall tumbling over moss-covered boulders. All along the edge of the lagoon, a profusion of exotic flowers and plants seemed to glow in iridescent colors.

"Did they build all this just for the wedding banquet?" Carol Tai asked in astonishment.

"No, *lah*! Those Lees always have business on their mind—this building is the centerpiece of a new luxury eco-resort they are developing—Pulau Samsara, they're calling it," her husband revealed.

"What, are they going to try to sell us condos after the wedding cake is served?" Lorena Lim sniggered.

"They can give this resort some fancy new name, but I know for a fact the island used to be called *Pulau Hantu—'Ghost Island.'* It was one of the outlying islands where the Japanese soldiers took all the young able-bodied Chinese men and had them shot during World War II. This island is haunted with ghosts of the war dead," Daisy Foo whispered.

"*Alamak,* Daisy, if you truly have faith in the Lord, you won't believe in such things as ghosts!" Carol admonished.

"Well, what about the Holy Ghost, Carol? Isn't he a ghost too?" Daisy retorted.

———

Minutes after Rachel and Nick were seated, the dinner began with military precision as a battalion of waiters marched in with glowing LED-domed trays. The engraved menu card indicated that it was *Giant South Sea Scallop Consommé with Washington State Ginseng Vapors and Black Mushrooms,*[*] but Rachel wasn't quite sure what to do when the white-gloved waiter at her side lifted the shimmering dome off her plate. In front of her was a bowl, but encasing the surface of the bowl was what appeared to be a pinkish, membrane-like bubble that wobbled on its own accord.

"What are we supposed to do with this?" Rachel asked.

"Just pop it!" Nick encouraged.

Rachel looked at it, giggling. "I'm afraid! I feel like some alien creature is going to burst out of it."

"Here, stand back, I'll pop it for you," Mehmet, who was on her right, offered.

"No, no, I'll do it," Rachel said bravely. She gave it a jab with her fork, and the bubble immediately collapsed on itself, releasing a burst of pungent medicinal steam into the air. As the filmy pink membrane met the surface of the soup, it created a beautiful marbleized pattern across its surface. Rachel could now see an enormous poached scallop in the middle of the bowl and thinly julienned black mushrooms artfully positioned like sun rays around it.

"Hmm. I gather the bubble was the ginseng," Mehmet said. "It's always guesswork when you're eating molecular cuisine, even more so when it's Pacific Rim fusion molecular cuisine. What is the name of this culinary genius again?"

"I can't remember exactly, but supposedly he trained with Chan Yan-tak before going to do an apprenticeship at El Bulli," Nick replied. "It's really quite yummy, but I can see from my mum's expression that she's having a fit."

Four tables away, Eleanor was turning as red as the coral-beaded

---

[*] Among the ginseng connoisseurs of Asia, the ginseng from Washington State is more prized than anything from China. Go figure.

bolero jacket she wore over her intricately pleated Fortuny silk gown, but it had nothing to do with the soup. She had been in shock ever since she spotted Rachel on the promenade wearing the Grand Duchess Zoya sapphire necklace. Could her disapproving mother-in-law really have loaned the necklace to Rachel? Or, even more unthinkable, had she *given* Rachel the necklace? What sort of black magic was Rachel doing at Tyersall Park?

"Are you going to drink your soup or not?" Philip asked, interrupting her thoughts. "If you're not going to have it, hand over the bowl before it gets cold."

"I've lost my appetite tonight. Here, swap seats with me—I need to talk to your sister for a minute." Eleanor took her husband's seat and smiled prettily at Victoria, who was huddled in conversation with her cousin Dickie.

"Wah, Victoria, you should really wear jewelry more often—you look so pretty in these cognac diamonds."

Victoria wanted to roll her eyes. Eleanor had never once in three decades given her a compliment, but now, when she had this heap of vulgar stones on her chest, Eleanor was suddenly gushing. She was like all her other Sung sisters, so vain and materialistic. "Yes, isn't it fun? Mummy gave them to me. She was in a good mood today after the wedding and was doling out heaps of jewels to everyone."

"How nice for you," Eleanor said breezily. "And isn't that Mummy's sapphire necklace on Rachel Chu's neck?"

"Yes, doesn't it look *marvelous* on her? Mummy thought so too," Victoria said with a smile. She knew perfectly well that Fiona had been given the necklace and had loaned it to Rachel (after that delicious scene on the stairs with Eddie that Ling Cheh had breathlessly reenacted for her), but she chose not to share that detail with Eleanor. Far more amusing to see Eleanor get worked up over nothing.

"*Alamak,* aren't you the least bit concerned about Rachel?" Eleanor queried.

"Concerned about what?" Victoria asked, knowing full well what Eleanor meant.

"Well, her dubious family background, for starters."

"Oh, come on, Eleanor. You need to stop being so old-fashioned. Nobody cares about that kind of stuff anymore. Rachel is so well educated and down-to-earth. And she speaks perfect Mandarin." She took care to mention all the things Eleanor was not.

"I didn't know she spoke perfect Mandarin," Eleanor said, getting more worried by the minute.

"Yes, she's very accomplished. Why, I had the most fascinating conversation with her this morning about the importance of microlending in sub-Saharan Africa. You should feel lucky that Nicky has a girlfriend like her, and not someone like that spendthrift Araminta Lee. Can you imagine what the Khoos must be thinking right now, sitting here in the middle of this mosquito-infested jungle eating this absurd food? I'm so bloody sick of this Chinese fusion trend. I mean, it says on this menu card that this is *Caramelized Peking Duck y Chocolat Molé*, but it looks like peanut brittle. Where's the duck, I ask you? Where's the damn duck?"

"Will you excuse me a moment?" Eleanor said, getting up from the table abruptly.

Francesca was just about to take a pensive first bite into her *Hawaiian Suckling Pig Truffle Tacos* when Eleanor interrupted her. "Will you please come with me at once?"

Eleanor walked her into one of the cavern-like lounges surrounding the main banquet hall. She sank into a white mohair ottoman and inhaled deeply, as Francesca bent over her in concern, the ruffles on her flame-orange ball gown billowing around her like frothy waves. "Are you okay, Auntie Elle? You look like you're having a panic attack."

"I think I am. I need my Xanax. Can you get me some water? And please blow out all those candles. The smell is giving me a migraine."

Francesca quickly returned with a glass of water. Eleanor downed a few pills quickly and sighed. "It's worse than I thought. Far worse."

"What do you mean?"

"Did you see that sapphire necklace on *that girl*?"

"How could I miss it? Yesterday she was wearing Ann Taylor Loft and today she's in an Elie Saab gown *from next season* and those sapphires."

"It's my mother-in-law's. It used to belong to the Grand Duchess Zoya of St. Petersburg, and now it's been given to that girl. What's more, the whole family seems to have fallen in love with her, even my bitchy sister-in-law," Eleanor said, almost choking on the words.

Francesca looked grave. "Don't worry, Auntie Elle. I promised you I would see to it, and after tonight, Rachel Chu will wish she had never set foot on this island!"

———

After the sixth and final course had been served, the lights in the great hall dimmed, and a voice boomed out, "Ladies and gentlemen, please welcome our very special guest!" The live band struck up a tune, and the wall of glass behind the stage began to part. The water in the lagoon started to glow an iridescent aquamarine before draining away completely, and from the middle of the lagoon, the figure of a woman rose up as if by magic. As she walked slowly toward the banquet hall, someone screamed, "Oh my goodness, it's Tracy Kuan!" The usually grimfaced vice premier of China jumped out of his seat and began clapping like a man possessed, as everyone in the hall cheered and rose to a standing ovation.

"Who's that?" Rachel asked, amazed by the huge surge of excitement.

"It's Tracy Kuan—she's like the Barbra Streisand of Asia. Oh my God, I can die now!" Oliver practically swooned, getting all choked up.

"Tracy Kuan is still alive?" Cassandra Shang turned in astonishment to Jacqueline Ling. "The woman must be at least a hundred and three by now, and she doesn't look a day over forty! What on earth does she do to herself?"

"Whale vomit from New Zealand. Works miracles on your face," Jacqueline shot back in dead seriousness.

Tracy Kuan sang Dolly Parton's classic "I Will Always Love You," with alternating verses in English and Mandarin, as the lagoon outside began to shoot elaborate fountain jets of water into the sky, synchronized to the music. Colin led Araminta onto the dance floor, and the crowd oohed and aahed as they danced to the ballad. When the song was over, all of the surfaces along the stage suddenly transformed into giant LED panels, projecting rapid stop-motion video sequences as Tracy Kuan launched into her classic dance hit "People Like Us." The crowd roared in approval and rushed onto the dance floor.

Oliver grabbed Cecilia Cheng by the arm and said, "You are under orders from your grandmother to help me. I'm going to cut in on Alistair and Kitty, and you need to keep your baby brother distracted. All I need is one song alone with Kitty."

Kitty and Alistair were grinding against each other feverishly when Oliver and Cecilia cut in, Alistair giving up Kitty reluctantly. How was he supposed to dirty dance with his own sister? "You've got the best moves on the dance floor!" Oliver yelled into Kitty's ear, as Cecilia steered Alistair closer to the stage.

"I danced backup for Aaron Kwok. That's how I got my start in the industry," Kitty yelled back to Oliver as she continued to shimmy wildly.

"I know! I recognized you the minute I saw you the other day. You were wearing a short platinum blond wig in Aaron Kwok's music video," Oliver replied, expertly herding her toward a strategic point on the dance floor without her realizing it.

"Wow! You have a good memory," Kitty said, feeling flattered.

"I also remember you from your *other* video."

"Oh, which one?"

"The all-girl back-door-action one," Oliver said with a little wink.

Kitty didn't miss a beat. "Oh, I've heard about that video. That girl supposedly looks a lot like me," she shouted back at Oliver with a smirk.

"Yes, yes, she's your identical twin. Don't worry, Kitty, your secret is safe with me. I'm a survivor, just like you. And I know you didn't work your pretty ass off, quite literally I might add, to end up married to an upper-middle-class boy like my cousin."

"You're wrong about me. I love Alistair!" Kitty protested.

"Of course you do. I never said you didn't," Oliver replied, spinning her right next to Bernard Tai, who was dancing with Lauren Lee.

"Lauren Lee! My goodness, I haven't seen you since last year's Hong Kong art fair. Where have you been hiding yourself?" Oliver exclaimed as he switched partners with Bernard.

As Bernard began to ogle Kitty's skimpily swathed décolletage, Oliver whispered into Kitty's ear, "Bernard's father, *Dato'* Tai Toh Lui, has about four billion dollars. And he's the only son."

Kitty continued to dance as if she hadn't heard a single word.

Seeking respite from the ear-splitting music, Astrid headed outdoors and climbed onto one of the terraces overlooking a canopy of treetops. Charlie noticed her leaving the banquet hall, and it took every ounce of determination for him not to follow her. He was better off admiring her from afar, in the way that he always had. Even when they were living together in London, he loved nothing more than to watch her quietly as she drifted through a room in her inimitable way. Astrid had always stood apart from any woman he had ever known. Especially tonight, when the most stylish women in all of Asia were dressed to impress and drowning in diamonds, Astrid outdid all of them by appearing in a flawlessly elegant cheongsam and an exquisitely simple pair of chalcedony drop earrings. He knew from the tailoring and intricately embroidered peacock feathers that the cheongsam had to be vintage, likely one of her grandmother's. What the hell, he didn't care how she might feel—he needed to see her again up close.

"Let me guess . . . not a fan of Tracy Kuan?" Astrid asked when she saw Charlie walking up the steps onto the terrace.

"Not when I have no one to dance with."

Astrid smiled. "I'd happily dance with you, but you know the press would have a field day with that one."

"Heh, heh—we'd wipe this wedding off the front pages tomorrow, wouldn't we?" Charlie laughed.

"Tell me, Charlie, back in our day, were we anything like Colin and Araminta?" Astrid sighed, peering down at the fantastical harbor, its row of Grecian columns like leftover props from the set of *Cleopatra*.

"I'd like to think we weren't. I mean, kids these days . . . the spending is on a whole other level."

"'*Spending Ah Gong's* money,' as they say," Astrid quipped.

"Yes. But at least we had the sense to feel naughty doing it. And I think that back in those days when we lived in London, we were buying things we actually loved, not things to show off," Charlie mused.

"No one in Singapore gave a damn about Martin Margiela back then." Astrid laughed.

"It's a whole new world, Astrid." Charlie sighed.

"Well, I hope Colin and Araminta live happily ever after," Astrid said wistfully.

They were silent for a minute, taking in the calm of the rustling

* Hokkien for "grandpa."

trees mingling with the low bass thump coming from the great hall. Suddenly the relative quiet was broken, as Asia's bright young things flooded out onto the plaza in a raucous conga line led by the indefatigable Tracy Kuan doing her best rendition of the B-52s' "Love Shack."

"I can't lie to you, Astrid. My wife *was* invited tonight, but she's not here because we lead separate lives. We haven't lived together in more than two years," Charlie said over the din, slumping onto one of the Lucite benches.

"I'm sorry to hear that," Astrid said, jarred by his candor. "Well, if it makes you feel any better, my husband isn't really away on business. He's in Hong Kong with his mistress," she blurted out before she could stop herself.

Charlie stared at her, incredulous. "Mistress? How could anyone in his right mind be cheating on *you*?"

"That's what I've been asking myself all night. All week actually. I had been suspecting it for the past few months, but he finally came clean a week ago, before abruptly moving out."

"He moved to Hong Kong?"

"No, I don't think so. Actually, what am I talking about—I have no idea. I think his mistress lives there, and I think he went specifically this weekend just to spite me. It was the one weekend where his absence would surely be noticed."

"Fucker!"

"That's not all. I think he fathered a child with this woman," Astrid said sadly.

Charlie looked at her in horror. "You *think*? Or you know?"

"I don't really know, Charlie. There are so many things about this whole affair that don't make sense to me at all."

"Then why don't you go to Hong Kong yourself and find out?"

"How can I? There's no way I can run off to Hong Kong on my own to check up on him. You know how it is—no matter where I stay, someone is bound to recognize me, and there will be talk," Astrid said, rather resigned to her fate.

"Well, why don't we find out?"

"What do you mean 'we'?"

"I mean, I'm going to call my pilot right now to get the plane fueled up, and we can be in Hong Kong in three hours. Let me help you. You can stay with me, and no one will know you're in Hong Kong. It's unfortunate, but after my brother's kidnapping eight years ago, I have access to the best private investigators in the city. Let's get to the bottom of this," Charlie said eagerly.

"Oh Charlie, I can't just leave in the middle of all this."

"Why the hell not? I don't see you out there shaking your ass in that conga line."

Colin and Nick were standing by one of the alcoves, watching Peter Lee spin his daughter around the dance floor. "I can't quite believe I got married to that girl today, Nicky. This whole day has been a complete fucking blur." Colin sighed wearily.

"Yeah, it's been quite surreal," Nick admitted.

"Well, I'm glad you've been with me on this ride," Colin said. "I know I haven't been easy on you the last few days."

"Hey, what are friends for?" Nick said cheerily, putting his arm around Colin. He was not about to let Colin get maudlin on his wedding night.

"I'm going to do you the favor of *not* asking you when your turn's going to be, although I must say Rachel looks smashing tonight," Colin said, staring at her being whirled around by Mehmet.

"Doesn't she?" Nick grinned.

"I'd cut in on them if I were you. You know how lethal our Turkish friend can be, especially since he knows how to tango better than an Argentinean polo player," Colin warned.

"Oh, Mehmet already confessed to me that he thinks Rachel has the sexiest legs on the planet." Nick laughed. "You know how they say weddings are infectious. I think I really caught the bug today, watching you and Araminta during the ceremony."

"Does this mean what I think it does?" Colin asked, perking up.

"I think so, Colin. I think I'm finally ready to ask Rachel to marry me."

"Well hurry up, *lah*!" Colin exclaimed, clapping Nick on the back. "Araminta already told me she intends to get pregnant on our honeymoon, so you need to catch up. I'm counting on your kid to check my kid into rehab!"

It was almost midnight, and while the older guests were perched comfortably on terraces overlooking the promenade, sipping their

Rémy Martins or lapsang souchongs, Rachel was sitting with the few remaining girls in the banquet hall, catching up with Sophie Khoo. Lauren Lee and Mandy Ling were chatting several chairs away when Francesca sauntered up to the table.

"Wasn't that dinner a disappointment? That Edible Bird's Nest Semifreddo at the end—why would you ever puree bird's nest? Bird's nest is all about the texture, and that idiot chef transforms it into a half-frozen muck," Francesca complained. "We should all go for supper after the fireworks."

"Why don't we just go now?" Lauren suggested.

"No, we have to stay for the fireworks! Araminta told me in secret that Cai Guo-Qiang designed a pyrotechnics show even more spectacular than the one he did for the Beijing Olympics. But we'll take the first ferry the minute the show is over. Now, where should we go?"

"I don't know Singapore well at all anymore. If I was in Sydney right now, I'd be heading to BBQ King for a late-night snack," Sophie said.

"Oooh! BBQ King! I love that place! I think they have the best *siew ngarp* in the world!" Lauren declared.

"Aiyah, BBQ King is such a grease pit. Everyone knows that Four Seasons in London has the best roast duck in the world!" Mandy countered.

"I'm with Lauren, I think BBQ wins hands down," Francesca said.

"No, I find their roast duck too fatty. The duck at Four Seasons is *perfect*, because they raise the ducks on their own special organic farm. Nico would agree with me—we used to go there *all* the time," Mandy added with a flourish.

"Why do you call Nick 'Nico'?" Rachel turned to Mandy, the curiosity finally getting the better of her.

"Oh, when we were just teenagers, we spent one summer together on Capri. His auntie Catherine, the Thai one, took a villa there. We would follow the sun all day—start out sunbathing at the beach club by the Faraglioni rocks in the mornings, go swimming in Grotta Verde after lunch, and end up at Il Faro beach for sunset. We got so brown, and Nicky's hair got so long—he looked practically Italian! That's when the Italian kids we made friends with started calling him *Nico* and I was his *Mandi*. Oooh, it was such a *glorious* time."

"Sounds like it," Rachel said lightly, ignoring Mandy's blatant attempt to make her jealous by resuming her conversation with Sophie.

Francesca leaned into Mandy's ear. "Really, Mandy, I could have milked that story way better. Your mother is right—you have lost your edge living in New York."

"Go to hell, Francesca. I don't see you doing any better," Mandy said through gritted teeth as she got up from the table. She was fed up with the pressure coming at her from all sides, and wished she'd never agreed to come back. The girls looked up as Mandy stormed off.

Francesca shook her head slowly and gave Rachel a look. "Poor Mandy is so conflicted. She doesn't know what she wants anymore. I mean, that was such a pathetic attempt at inciting jealousy, wasn't it?"

For once, Rachel had to agree with Francesca. "It didn't work, and I don't understand why she keeps trying to make me jealous. I mean, why would I care about what Nick and her did when they were teenagers?"

Francesca burst out laughing. "Wait a minute, you thought she was trying to make *you* jealous?"

"Er . . . wasn't that what she was doing?"

"No, honey, she's not paying any attention to you. She was trying to make *me* jealous."

"You?" Rachel asked, puzzled.

Francesca smirked. "Of course. That's why she brought up the whole Capri story—I was there that summer too, you know. Mandy's never gotten over how into me Nick was when we had our three-some."

Rachel could feel her face get hot. Very hot. She wanted to bolt from the table but her legs seemed to have turned to glue.

Sophie and Lauren stared at Francesca, mouths agape.

Francesca looked straight into Rachel's face and kept on chattering lightly. "Oh, does Nick still do that trick with the underside of his tongue? Mandy was far too prissy to let him go down on her, but my God, on me he would stay down there *for hours.*"

Right then, Nick entered the banquet hall. "There you are! Why are you all sitting in here like statues? The fireworks are about to start!"

9

99 Conduit Road

HONG KONG

The elderly amah opened the door and broke out into a wide grin. "Hiyah, Astrid Leong! Can it be?" she cried in Cantonese.

"Yes, Ah Chee—Astrid will be our guest for a few days. Will you please make sure no one knows? And don't go telling any of the other maids who she is—I don't want them carrying tales to my mother's maids. This needs to remain *absolutely secret*, okay?" Charlie decreed.

"Yes, yes, of course, Charlieboy—now go and wash your hands," Ah Chee said dismissively, continuing to fuss over Astrid. "Hiyah, you are still so beautiful, I have dreamed about you often over the years! You must be so tired, so hungry—it's past three in the morning. Let me go and wake the cook up to make you something to eat. Some chicken congee maybe?"

"No need, Ah Chee. We came from a wedding banquet." Astrid smiled. She could hardly believe that Charlie's childhood nanny was still looking after him after all these years.

"Well, let me go make you some warm milk and honey. Or would you rather have Milo? Charlieboy always likes that when he's up late," Ah Chee said, rushing off to the kitchen.

"There's no stopping Ah Chee, is there?" Astrid laughed. "I'm so glad you still have her."

"She won't leave!" Charlie sputtered in exasperation. "I built her a house back in China—hell, I built all her relatives houses, got a satellite dish for the village, the whole nine yards, thinking she would want to return to China to retire. But I think she's much happier here bossing all the other maids around."

"It's very sweet of you to take care of her like that," Astrid said. They stepped into an expansive double-height living room that resembled the wing of a modern art museum, with its row of bronze sculptures placed like sentinels in front of the floor-to-ceiling windows. "Since when did you collect Brancusi?" she asked in surprise.

"Since you introduced me to him. Don't you remember that exhibition you dragged me to at the Pompidou?"

"Gosh, I'd almost forgotten," Astrid said, gazing at the minimalist curves of one of Brancusi's golden birds.

"My wife, Isabel, is mad for the French Provençal look, so she hates my Brancusis. They haven't had an airing until I moved in here. I've turned this apartment into a sort of refuge for my art. Isabel and the girls stay at our house on the Peak, and I'm here in the Mid-Levels. I like it because I can just walk out my door, take the escalator down to Central, and be at my office within ten minutes. Sorry it's a bit cramped—it's just a small duplex."

"It's gorgeous, Charlie, and much larger than my flat."

"You're kidding, right?"

"No, I'm not. I'm in a three-bedroom off Clemenceau Avenue. You know that eighties building across the street from the Istana?"

"What on earth are you doing living in that old teardown?"

"It's a long story. Basically, Michael didn't want to feel beholden to my dad. So I agreed to live in a place he could afford."

"I suppose that's admirable, although I just can't imagine how he could make you squeeze into a pigeonhole for the sake of his pride," Charlie huffed.

"Oh, I'm quite used to it. And the location is very convenient, just like here," Astrid said.

Charlie couldn't help but wonder what sort of life Astrid had made for herself since marrying this idiot. "Here, let me show you to your room," Charlie said. They climbed the sleek brushed-metal staircase and he showed her into a large, spartanly furnished bedroom with topstitched beige suede walls and masculine gray flannel bedding. The only decorative object was a photograph of two young girls in a silver frame by the bedside. "Is this your bedroom?" she asked.

"Yes. Don't worry, I'm going to sleep in my daughters' room," Charlie quickly added.

"Don't be silly! I'll take the girls' room—I can't make you give up your bedroom for me—" Astrid began.

"No, no, I insist. You'll be much more comfortable here. Try to get some sleep," Charlie said, closing the door gently before she could protest any more.

Astrid changed out of her clothes and lay down. She turned on her side and stared out the floor-to-ceiling windows that perfectly framed the Hong Kong skyline. The buildings were densely packed in this part of the city, staggered steeply on the mountainside in sheer defiance of the terrain. She remembered how, when she had first visited Hong Kong as a young girl, her aunt Alix had explained that the city's *feng shui* was particularly good, because wherever you lived, the dragon mountain was always behind you and the ocean was always in front of you. Even at this late hour, the city was a riot of lights, with many of the skyscrapers illuminated in a spectrum of colors. She tried to sleep, but she was still too wired from the past few hours—stealing away from the wedding just as the fireworks show was starting, rushing home to pack a few things, and now finding herself in the bedroom of Charlie Wu, the boy whose heart she had broken. The boy who, strangely enough, had awakened her to another way of life.

PARIS, 1995

Astrid leaped onto the king-size bed at the Hôtel George V, sinking into the plush feathertop mattress. "Ummmm . . . you need to lie down, Charlie. This is the most delicious bed I've ever slept on! Why don't we have beds like these at the Calthorpe? We really ought to— the lumpy mattresses we have probably haven't been changed since Elizabethan times."

"Astrid, we can enjoy the bed later, *lah*. We only have three hours left until the shops close! Come on, lazybones, didn't you sleep enough on the train?" Charlie cajoled. He couldn't wait to show Astrid the city he had come to know like the back of his hand. His mother and sisters had discovered the world of high fashion in the decade since his father had taken his tech company public, transforming the Wus almost overnight from mere centi-millionaires to billionaires. In the early days, before they were in the habit of chartering planes, Dad would buy up the entire first-class cabin of Singapore Airlines, and the whole family would sweep through the capitals of Europe—staying in the grandest hotels, eating at the restaurants with the most Michelin stars, and indulging in limitless shopping. Charlie had grown up knowing his Buccellati from his Boucheron, and he was eager to show this world to Astrid. He knew that—for all her pedigree—Astrid had been brought up practically in a nunnery. The Leongs did not eat in expensive restaurants—they ate food prepared by their cooks at home. They did not favor dressing up in designer clothes, preferring to have everything made by their family tailor. Charlie felt that Astrid had been far too stifled—all her life she had been treated like a hothouse flower, when in fact she was a wildflower that was never allowed to bloom fully. Now that they were eighteen and living together in London, they were finally free of family confines, and he would dress her like the princess she was, and she would be his forever.

Charlie led Astrid straight to the Marais, a neighborhood he had discovered on his own after tiring of tagging along with his family to the same shops within a three-block radius of the George V. As they strolled down rue Vieille du Temple, Astrid let out a sigh. "Aiyah, it's adorable here! So much cozier than those wide boulevards in the Eighth Arrondissement."

"There is one shop in particular that I stumbled on the last time I was here . . . it was so cool. I can just picture you wearing everything this designer makes, this tiny Tunisian guy. Let's see, which street was it on?" Charlie mumbled to himself. After a few more turns, they arrived at the boutique that Charlie wanted Astrid to see. The windows consisted of smoked glass, giving nothing away as to what treasures lay within.

"Why don't you go in first and I'll join you in a sec? I want to stop in at the pharmacy across the street to see if they have any camera batteries," Charlie suggested.

Astrid stepped through the door and found herself transported into a parallel universe. Portuguese fado music wailed through a space with black ceilings, obsidian walls, and poured-concrete floors stained a dark espresso. Minimalist industrial hooks protruded from the walls, and the clothes were artfully draped like pieces of sculpture and lit with halogen spotlights. A saleswoman with a wild, frizzy mane of red hair glanced briefly from behind an oval glass desk with elephant tusk legs before continuing to puff on her cigarette and page through an oversize magazine. After a few minutes, when it seemed like Astrid wasn't leaving, she asked haughtily, "Can I help you?"

"Oh, no, I'm just looking around. Thank you," Astrid replied in her schoolgirl French. She continued to circle the space and noticed a wide set of steps leading downstairs.

"Is there more downstairs?" she asked.

"Of course," the saleslady said in her raspy voice, getting up from her desk reluctantly and following Astrid down the stairs. Below was a space lined with glossy coral-red armoires where, once again, only one or two pieces were artfully displayed. Astrid saw a beautiful cocktail dress with a silvery chain-mail back and searched the garment for a tag indicating its size. "What size is this?" she asked the woman standing watch like a pensive hawk.

"It's couture. Do you understand? Everything made to order," the woman replied drolly, waving her cigarette hand around and flicking ash everywhere.

"So, how much would it cost for me to have this made in my size?" Astrid asked.

The saleswoman made a quick assessment of Astrid. Asians hardly ever set foot in here—they usually kept to the famous designer boutiques on the rue du Faubourg-Saint-Honoré or the avenue Montaigne, where they could inhale all the Chanel and Dior they wanted, God help them. Monsieur's collection was very avant-garde, and only appreciated by the chicest Parisiennes, New Yorkers, and a few Belgians. Clearly this schoolgirl in the rollneck fisherman's sweater, khakis, and espadrilles was out of her league. "Listen, *chérie*, everything here is *très, très cher*. And it takes five months for delivery. Do you really want to know how much it costs?" she said, taking a slow drag from her cigarette.

"Oh, I suppose not," Astrid said meekly. This lady obviously had no interest in helping her. She climbed the stairs and headed straight out the door, almost bumping into Charlie.

"So quick? Didn't you like the clothes?" Charlie queried.

"I do. But the lady in there doesn't seem to want to sell me anything, so let's not waste our time," Astrid said.

"Wait, wait a minute—what do you mean she doesn't want to sell you anything?" Charlie tried to clarify. "Was she being snooty?"

"Uh-huh," Astrid reported.

"We're going back in!" Charlie said indignantly.

"Charlie, let's just go to the next boutique on your list."

"Astrid, sometimes I can't believe you're Harry Leong's daughter! Your father bought the most exclusive hotel in London when the manager was rude to your mother, for chrissakes! You need to learn how to stand up for yourself!"

"I know perfectly well how to stand up for myself, but it's simply not worth making a fuss over nothing," Astrid argued.

"Well, it's not *nothing* to me. Nobody insults my girlfriend!" Charlie declared, flinging the door wide open with gusto. Astrid followed reluctantly, noticing that the redheaded saleslady was now joined by a man with platinum blond hair.

Charlie marched up and asked the man, in English, "Do you work here?"

"Oui," the man replied.

"This is my girlfriend. I want to buy a whole new wardrobe for her. Will you help me?"

The man crossed his arms lazily, slightly bemused by this scrawny teenager with a bad case of acne. "This is all haute couture, and the dresses start at twenty-five thousand francs. There is also an eight-month wait," he said.

"Not a problem," Charlie said boldly.

"Um, you pay cash? How are you going to guarantee payment?" the lady asked in thickly accented English.

Charlie sighed and whipped out his cell phone. He dialed a long series of numbers and waited for the other end to pick up. "Mr. Oei? It's Charlie Wu here. Sorry to disturb you at this time of night in Singapore, I'm in Paris at the moment. Tell me, Mr. Oei, does our bank have a relationship manager in Paris? Great. Will you call the fellow up and get him to make a call to this shop that I am at." Charlie looked up and asked them for the name, before continuing. "Tell him to inform these people that I am here with Astrid Leong. *Yes, Harry's daughter.* Yes, and will you be sure your fellow lets them know I can afford to buy anything I damn well please? Thank you."

Astrid watched her boyfriend in silence. She had never seen him behave in such an assertive manner. Part of her felt like cringing from the vulgarity of his swagger, and part of her found it to be remarkably attractive. A few long minutes passed, and finally the phone rang. The redhead picked it up quickly, her eyes widening as she listened to the tirade coming from the other end. *"Désolée, monsieur, très désolée,"* she kept saying into the phone. She hung up and began a terse exchange with her male colleague, not realizing that Astrid could understand almost every word they were saying. The man leaped off the table and gazed at Charlie and Astrid with a sudden vigor. "Please, mademoiselle, let me show you the full collection," he said with a big smile.

The woman, meanwhile, smiled at Charlie. "Monsieur, would you like some champagne? Or a cappuccino, maybe?"

"I wonder what my banker told them," Charlie whispered to Astrid as they were led downstairs into a cavernous dressing room.

"Oh, that wasn't the banker. It was the designer himself. He told them he was rushing over to personally supervise my fittings. Your banker must have called *him* directly," Astrid said.

"Okay, I want you to order ten dresses from this designer. We need to spend at least a few hundred thousand francs right now."

"Ten? I don't think I even *want* ten things from this place," Astrid said.

"Doesn't matter. You need to pick out ten things. Actually, make that twenty. As my father always says, the only way to get these *ang mor gau sai* to respect you is to smack them in the face with your *dua lan chiao** money until they get on their knees."

For the next seven days, Charlie led Astrid on a shopping spree to end all shopping sprees. He bought her a suite of luggage from Hermès, dozens of dresses from all the top designers that season, sixteen pairs of shoes and four pairs of boots, a diamond-encrusted Patek Philippe watch (that she never once wore), and a restored art nouveau lamp from Didier Aaron. In between the marathon shopping, there were lunches at Mariage Frères and Davé, dinners at Le Grand Véfour and Les Ambassadeurs, and dancing the night away in their new finery at Le Palace and Le Queen. That week in Paris, Astrid not only discovered her taste for haute couture; she discovered a new passion. She had lived the first eighteen years of her life sur-

---

* Hokkien for "big cock."

rounded by people who had money but claimed not to, people who preferred to hand things down rather than buy them new, people who simply didn't know how to enjoy their good fortune. Spending money the Charlie Wu way was absolutely exhilarating—honestly, it was better than sex.

10

Tyersall Park

•

Rachel was quiet all the way home from the wedding ball. She graciously returned the sapphire necklace to Fiona in the foyer and bounded up the stairs. In the bedroom, she grabbed her suitcase from the built-in cupboard and began shoving in her clothes as fast as she could. She noticed that the laundry maids had placed thin sheets of scented blotting paper between each folded piece of clothing, and she began tearing them out frustratedly—she didn't want to take a single thing from this place.

"What are you doing?" Nick said in bafflement as he entered the bedroom.

"What does it look like? I'm getting out of here!"

"What? Why?" Nick frowned.

"I've had enough of this shit! I refuse to be a sitting duck for all these crazy women in your life!"

"What on earth are you talking about, Rachel?" Nick stared at her in confusion. He had never seen her this angry before.

"I'm talking about Mandy and Francesca. And God only knows who else," Rachel cried, continuing to grab her things from the armoire.

"I don't know what you've heard, Rachel, but—"

"Oh, so you deny it? You deny that you had a threesome with them?"

Nick's eyes flared in shock. For a moment, he wasn't sure what to say. "I don't deny it, but—"

"You asshole!"

Nick threw his hands up in despair. "Rachel, I'm thirty-two, and as far as I know I've never mentioned joining the priesthood. I *do* have a sexual history, but I've never tried to conceal any of it from you."

"It's not that you concealed it. It's more that you never told me in the first place! You should have said something. You should have told me that Francesca and you had a past, so I didn't have to sit there tonight and get totally blindsided. I felt like a total fucking idiot."

Nick sat down on the edge of the chaise lounge, burying his face in his hands. Rachel had every right to be angry—it just never occurred to him to mention something that happened half a lifetime ago. "I'm so sorry—" he began.

"A threesome? With Mandy and *Francesca? Really?* Of all the women in the world," Rachel said contemptuously as she struggled with the zipper on her suitcase.

Nick sighed deeply. He wanted to explain that Francesca had been a very different girl back then, before her grandfather's stroke and all that money, but he realized that this was not the time to defend her. He approached Rachel slowly and put his arms around her. She tried to break away from him, but he locked his arms around her tightly.

"Look at me, Rachel. *Look at me,*" he said calmly. "Francesca and I just had a brief fling that summer in Capri. That's all it was. We were stupid sixteen-year-olds, all raging hormones. That was almost *two* decades ago. I was single for four years before I met you, and I think you know precisely how the last two years have gone—you are the center of my life, Rachel. *The absolute center.* What happened tonight? Who told you all these things?"

With that, Rachel broke down and it all came flooding out— everything that happened at Araminta's bachelorette weekend, all of Mandy's constant innuendoes, the stunt that Francesca had pulled at the wedding ball. Nick listened to Rachel's ordeal, feeling sick to his stomach the more he heard. Here he thought she had been having the time of her life. It pained him to see how shaken up she was, to see the tears spill down her pretty face.

"Rachel, I am *so* sorry. I can't even begin to tell you how sorry I am," Nick said earnestly.

Rachel stood facing the window, wiping the tears from her eyes. She was angry at herself for crying and confused by the tidal wave of emotion that had swept over her, but she just couldn't help it. The shock of the evening and the pent-up stress of the days leading up to it had brought her to this point, and now she was drained.

"I wish you had told me about the bachelorette weekend, Rachel. If I had known, I could have done more to protect you. I really had no clue those girls could be so . . . so vicious," Nick said, searching for the right word in his fury. "I'll make sure you never see them again. Just please, don't leave like this. Especially when we haven't even had a chance to enjoy our holiday together. Let me make it up to you, Rachel. Please."

Rachel kept silent. She stayed facing the window, suddenly noticing a strange set of shadows moving on the darkened expanse of lawn. A moment later, she realized it was just a uniformed Gurkha on his night patrol with a pair of Dobermans.

"I don't think you get it, Nick. I'm still mad at you. You didn't prepare me for any of this. I traveled halfway around the world with you, and you told me nothing before we left."

"What should I have told you?" Nick asked, genuinely perplexed.

"*All this*," Rachel cried, waving her hands around at the opulent bedroom they were standing in. "The fact that there's an army of Gurkhas with dogs protecting your grandmother while she sleeps, the fact that you grew up in friggin' Downton Abbey, the fact that your best friend was throwing the most expensive wedding in the history of civilization! You should have told me about your family, about your friends, about your life here, so I could at least know what I was getting myself into."

Nick sank onto the chaise lounge, sighing wearily. "Astrid did try to warn me to prepare you, but I was so sure that you'd feel right at home when you got here. I mean, I've seen how you are in different settings, the way you're able to charm the socks off everyone—your students, the chancellor, and all the university bigwigs, even that grouchy Japanese sandwich guy on Thirteenth Street! And I guess I just didn't know what to say. How could I have explained all this to you without your being here to see it yourself?"

"Well, I came and saw for myself, and now . . . now I feel like I don't know who my boyfriend is anymore," Rachel said forlornly.

Nick stared at Rachel openmouthed, stung by her remark. "Have

I really changed that much in the past couple of weeks? Because I feel like I'm the same person, and how I feel about you certainly hasn't changed. If anything, I love you more every day, and even more at this moment."

"Oh Nick." Rachel sighed, sitting down on the edge of the bed. "I don't know how to explain it. It's true, you *have* stayed exactly the same, but the world around you—this world around us—is so different from anything I'm used to. And I'm trying to figure out how I could possibly fit into this world."

"But don't you see how well you *do* fit in? You must realize that aside from a few inconsequential girls, *everyone* adores you. My best friends all think you're the bee's knees—you should have heard the way Colin and Mehmet were raving about you last night. And my parents like you, my whole family likes you."

Rachel shot him a look, and Nick could see that she wasn't buying it. He sat down next to her and noticed that her shoulders tightened almost imperceptibly. He longed to run a hand up and down her back soothingly, like he did almost every night in bed, but he knew better than to touch her now. What could he do to reassure her at this moment?

"Rachel, I never meant for you to get hurt. You know I'll do anything to make you happy," he said in a quiet voice.

"I know," Rachel said after a pause. As upset as she was, she couldn't stay mad at Nick for long. He had mishandled things, for sure, but she knew he wasn't to blame for Francesca's bitchiness. This was exactly what Francesca had been hoping to achieve—to make her doubt herself, to make her angry at Nick. Rachel sighed, leaning her head on his shoulder.

A sudden gleam came over Nick's eyes. "I have an idea—why don't we go away tomorrow? Let's skip the tea ceremony at the Khoos'. I don't think you really want to stand around and watch Araminta get piled with tons of jewelry from all her relatives anyway. Let's get out of Singapore and clear our heads. I know a special place we can go."

Rachel eyed him warily. "Is it going to involve more private jets and six-star resorts?"

Nick shook his head rapidly. "Don't worry, we're driving. I'm taking you to Malaysia. I'm taking you to a remote lodge in the Cameron Highlands, far away from all this."

11

Residences at One Cairnhill

.

SINGAPORE

Eleanor was just sitting down to her usual breakfast of toasted seven-grain bread, low-fat butter, and low-sugar marmalade when the phone rang. Whenever the phone rang this early in the morning, she knew it had to be one of her siblings in America. This was probably her brother in Seattle, begging for another loan. When Consuelo entered the breakfast room with the phone, Eleanor shook her head and mouthed silently, *"Tell him I'm still asleep."*

"No, no, ma'am, not Seattle brother. It's Mrs. Foo."

"Oh," Eleanor said, grabbing the phone as she took a bite of her toast. "Daisy, what are you doing up so early? Did you have indigestion too after that awful wedding banquet?"

"No, no, Elle, I have breaking news!" Daisy said excitedly.

"What, what?" Eleanor asked in anticipation. She said a quick prayer and hoped Daisy was going to report on the tragic breakup of Nicky and Rachel. Francesca had winked at her during the fireworks last night and whispered two words—*It's done*—and Eleanor noticed during the ferry ride home that Rachel looked like she had been hit in the face with a durian.

"Guess who just woke up from a coma?" Daisy announced.

"Oh. Who?" Eleanor asked, a little crestfallen.

"Just guess, *lah*!"

"I don't know . . . that von Bülow woman?"

"Aiyah, no *lah*! *Sir Ronald Shaw* woke up! Nadine's father-in-law!"

"*Alamak!*" Eleanor almost spat out her toast. "I thought he was a living vegetable."

"Well, somehow the vegetable woke up, and he's even talking! The cousin of my maid's daughter-in-law is the night nurse at Mount E, and apparently she got the shock of her life when Patient Shaw woke up at four this morning and started demanding his Kopi-O."*

"How long has he been in a coma?" Eleanor asked, looking up and noticing Nick stroll into the kitchen. *Oh my. Nick was over bright and early. Something must have happened!*

"Six years now. Nadine, Ronnie, Francesca, the whole family have rushed to his bedside, and the news crews are just arriving."

"Huh. Do you think we should go down too?" Eleanor asked.

"I think let's wait. Let's see. You know, I hear that sometimes these coma victims wake up right before they die."

"If he's asking for Kopi-O, something tells me he's not going to kick the bucket anytime soon," Eleanor surmised. She said goodbye to Daisy and focused her attention on Nick.

"Francesca's grandfather woke up from his coma this morning," Eleanor relayed, buttering another piece of toast.

"I didn't even realize he was still alive," Nick said disinterestedly.

"What are you doing here so early? Do you want some breakfast? Some *kaya* toast?"

"No, no, I already ate."

"Where's Rachel this morning?" Eleanor asked a little too eagerly. *Was the girl tossed out in the middle of the night like garbage?*

"Rachel's still asleep. I got up early to talk to you and Dad. Is he up yet?"

"*Alamak*, your father sleeps till ten, at the earliest."

"Well then, I'll tell you first. I'm going away with Rachel for a few days, and if all goes according to plan, I intend to propose to her while we're away," Nick declared.

Eleanor put down her toast and gave him a look of unconcealed horror. "Nicky, you can't be serious!"

"I'm totally serious," Nick said, taking a seat at the table. "I know you don't know her very well yet, but that's been my fault entirely—I haven't given you or Dad the chance to meet her until now. But I can

---

* A traditional black coffee served with sugar only.

assure you that you'll soon discover what an amazing human being she is. She is going to be a fantastic daughter-in-law to you, Mum."

"Why are you rushing into this?"

"I'm not rushing into anything. We've dated for nearly two years. We've practically been living together for the past year. I was planning to propose on our two-year anniversary this October, but some stuff happened, and I need to show Rachel how important she is to me, right now."

"What *stuff*?"

Nick sighed. "It's a long story, but Rachel's been treated badly by a few people since arriving—Francesca especially."

"What did Francesca do?" Eleanor asked innocently.

"It doesn't matter what she did. What matters is that I have to put things right."

Eleanor's mind raced in circles. *What the hell happened last night? That stupid Francesca!* Alamak, *her plan must have backfired.* "You don't have to marry her just to put things right, Nicky. Don't let this girl pressure you," Eleanor urged.

"I'm not being pressured. The truth is, I have been thinking about marrying Rachel almost since the day I met her. And now, more than ever, I know she is the one for me. She is so smart, Mum, and such a good person."

Eleanor was seething inside, but she tried to speak in a measured voice. "I'm sure Rachel is a nice girl, but she can *never* be your wife."

"And why is that?" Nick leaned back in his chair, amused by the absurdity of his mother's words.

"She is just not suitable for you, Nicky. She does not come from the right background."

"Nobody is ever going to come from 'the right background' in your eyes," Nick scoffed.

"I'm only telling you what *everyone* is already thinking, Nick. You haven't heard the horrible things I've heard. Do you know her family comes from Mainland China?"

"Stop it, Mum. I'm so fed up with this ridiculous snobbery you and your friends have toward the Mainland Chinese. We are all Chinese. Just because some people actually *work* for their money doesn't mean they are beneath you."

Eleanor shook her head and continued in a graver tone, "Nicky, you don't understand. She will never be accepted. And I'm not talking about your dad and me—I'm talking about your dear Ah Ma and the rest of the family. Take it from me—even though I have been married to your father for thirty-four years, I am *still* considered an outsider. I am a Sung—I came from a respectable family, a rich family, but in their eyes I was never good enough. Do you want to see Rachel suffer like that? Look at how they have frozen out that Kitty Pong girl!"

"How can you even compare Rachel to Kitty? Rachel isn't a soap-opera star who runs around in skimpy clothes—she's an economist with a PhD. And everyone in the family has been perfectly nice to her."

"It is one thing to be polite to your guest, but I can assure you that if they really thought she had any chance of being your wife, they would not be so nice."

"That's nonsense."

"No, Nicky, that is a *fact*," Eleanor snapped. "Ah Ma will never allow you to marry Rachel, no matter how accomplished she is. Come on, Nicky, you *know* this! It's been told to you a thousand times since you were a little boy. You are a *Young*."

Nick shook his head and laughed. "This is all so unbelievably archaic. We're living in the twenty-first century, and Singapore is one of the most progressive countries on the planet. I can assure you Ah Ma doesn't feel the way she did thirty years ago."

"*Alamak*, I've known your grandmother a lot longer than you have. You don't know how important bloodlines are to her."

Nick rolled his eyes. "To her, or to you? I haven't researched Rachel's genealogy, but if necessary I'm sure I can find some dead Ming emperor somewhere in her bloodline. Besides, she comes from a very respectable family. One of her cousins is even a famous film director."

"Nicky, there are things about Rachel's family that you don't realize."

"And how would you know this? Did Cassandra invent some story about Rachel's family or something?"

Eleanor kept silent on that score. She simply warned, "Save yourself and Rachel the heartache, Nicky. You have to give her up now, before things go any further."

"She's not something I can just *give up*, Mum. *I love her*, and I'm going to marry her. I don't need anyone's approval," Nick said forcefully, rising from the table.

"Stupid boy! Ah Ma will disinherit you!"

"Like I care."

"Nicky, listen to me. I haven't sacrificed my whole life for you just to see you waste everything on that girl," Eleanor said anxiously.

"*Sacrificed your whole life?* I'm not sure what you mean, when you're sitting here at the chef's table of your twenty-million-dollar apartment," Nick huffed.

"You have no idea! If you marry Rachel you will be ruining all our lives. Make her your mistress if you need to, but for heaven's sake, don't throw away your entire future by marrying her," Eleanor pleaded.

Nick snorted in disgust and stood up, kicking away the chair behind him as he stormed out of the breakfast alcove. Eleanor winced as the chrome chair legs cut across the Calacatta marble floor. She stared at the perfectly aligned rows of Astier de Villatte porcelain that lined the exposed stainless-steel shelves of her kitchen, reflecting on the heated exchange she had just endured. Every effort she had made to prevent her son from careening into this disastrous situation had failed, and now there was but one option left. Eleanor sat absolutely still for a few long moments, summoning the courage for the conversation she had been trying to avoid for so long.

"Consuelo!" she shouted. "Tell Ahmad to get the car ready. I need to go to Tyersall Park in fifteen minutes."

12

Wuthering Towers

•

HONG KONG

Astrid awoke to a shaft of sunlight on her face. What time was it? She looked at the clock on the side table and noticed it was after ten. She stretched into a yawn, crawled out of bed, and went to splash some water on her face. When she padded into the living room, she saw Charlie's elderly Chinese nanny sitting on one of the chrome-and-calfskin Le Corbusier lounge chairs frantically focused on a game on her iPad. Ah Chee pressed the screen furiously, muttering in Cantonese, "Cursed birds!" When she noticed Astrid passing by, she broke into a toothy grin. "Hiyah Astrid, did you sleep well? There's breakfast waiting for you," she said, her eyes never leaving the glowing screen.

A young maid rushed up to Astrid and said, "Ma'am, please, breakfast," gesturing toward the dining room. There she found a rather excessive spread laid out for her on the round glass table: pitchers of coffee, tea, and orange juice were accompanied by poached eggs and thick-cut bacon on a warming plate, scrambled eggs with Cumberland sausages, toasted English muffins, French toast, sliced mango with Greek yogurt, three types of breakfast cereals, silver-dollar pancakes with strawberries and Chantilly cream, fried crullers with fish congee. Another maid stood at attention behind Astrid, waiting to pounce forward and serve. Ah Chee came into the dining room and said, "We didn't know what you would want for breakfast, so the cook made a few options. Eat, eat. And then the car is waiting to take you to Charlieboy's office down the hill."

Astrid grabbed the bowl of yogurt and said, "This is all I need," much to Ah Chee's dismay. She went back to the bedroom and put on an ink-blue Rick Owens top over a pair of white jeans. After brushing her hair quickly, she decided to wear it in a low ponytail— something she never did—and rummaging through Charlie's bathroom drawers, she found a pair of Cutler and Gross horn sunglasses that fit her. This was as incognito as she was going to get. As she left the bedroom, one of the maids sprinted to the entrance foyer and summoned the elevator, while another held it open until Astrid was ready to enter. Astrid was mildly amused by how even an act as simple as exiting the flat was handled with such military urgency by these skittish girls. It was so different from the gracious, easygoing servants she had grown up with.

In the lobby, a chauffeur in a crisp black uniform with gold buttons bowed at Astrid. "Where's Mr. Wu's office?" Astrid asked.

"*Wu*thering Towers, on Chater Road." He gestured toward the forest-green Bentley parked outside, but Astrid said, "Thanks, but I think I'll walk," remembering the building well. It was the same place Charlie always had to go to pick up envelopes stuffed with cash from his father's secretary whenever they came to Hong Kong on weekend shopping binges. Before the chauffeur could protest, Astrid walked across the plaza to the Mid-Levels' escalator, strolling purposefully along the moving platform as it snaked its way down the hilly urban terrain.

At the base of the escalator on Queen Street, Astrid took a deep breath and plunged into the fast-moving river of pedestrians. There was something about Hong Kong's central district during the day, a special frenetic energy from the hustling and bustling crowd that always gave Astrid an intoxicating rush. Bankers in smart pinstripes walked shoulder to shoulder with dusty day laborers and teenagers in school uniforms, while chicly outfitted corporate women in don't-mess-with-me heels melded seamlessly with wizened old amahs and half-clothed street beggars.

Astrid turned left onto Pedder Street and entered the Landmark shopping mall. The first thing she saw was a long line of people. What was happening? Oh, it was just the usual queue of Mainland Chinese shoppers outside the Gucci store, anxiously awaiting their turn to go inside and get their fix. Astrid expertly negotiated her way through the network of pedestrian bridges and passageways that connected the Landmark to neighboring buildings—up the escalator to the mezzanine level of the Mandarin Oriental, through the shopping arcade at Alexandra House, down the short flight of steps by Cova Caffé, and here she was in the gleaming lobby of *Wu*thering Towers.

The reception counter appeared to have been sculpted from one massive block of malachite, and as Astrid approached, a man with an earpiece in a dark suit intercepted her and said discreetly, "Mrs. Teo, I'm with Mr. Wu. Please come with me." He waved her through the security checkpoint and into an express elevator that zipped straight up to the fifty-fifth floor. The elevator doors opened onto a serene, windowless room with alabaster-white walls inlaid with hairline circular patterns and a silvery blue sofa. The man ushered Astrid wordlessly past the three executive secretaries who sat at adjoining tables and through a pair of imposing etched-bronze doors.

Astrid found herself in Charlie's atrium-like office, which had a soaring pyramid-shaped glass ceiling and a bank of flat-screen televisions along one entire wall that silently flickered financial news channels from New York, London, Shanghai, and Dubai. A very tan Chinese man in a black suit and wire-frame glasses was seated on a nearby sofa.

"You almost gave my driver a panic attack," Charlie said, getting up from his desk.

Astrid smiled. "You need to cut your staff some slack, Charlie. They live in complete terror of you."

"Actually, they live in complete terror of *my wife*," Charlie responded with a grin. He gestured to the man seated on the black sofa. "This is Mr. Lui, who has already managed to find your husband by using the cell number you gave me last night."

Mr. Lui nodded at Astrid and began speaking in that distinctive, clipped, British-accented English that was so common in Hong Kong. "Every iPhone has a GPS locator, which makes it possible for us to track the owner very easily," Mr. Lui explained. "Your husband has been at an apartment in Mong Kok since last night."

Mr. Lui presented Astrid with his thin laptop computer, where a sequence of images awaited: Michael exiting the flat, Michael exiting the elevator, Michael clutching a bundle of plastic bags on the street.

The last picture, taken from a high angle, showed a woman opening the door of the flat to let Michael in. Astrid's stomach tightened into a knot. Here was the other woman. She scrutinized the picture for a long while, staring at the barefooted woman dressed in denim shorts and a skimpy tank top.

"Can we enlarge the picture?" Astrid asked. As Mr. Lui zoomed in on the blurry, pixilated face, Astrid suddenly sat back on the sofa. "There's something very familiar about that woman," she said, her pulse quickening.

"Who is she?" Charlie asked.

"I'm not sure, but I know I've seen her somewhere before," Astrid said, closing her eyes and pressing her fingers to her forehead. Then it hit her. Her throat seemed to close up, and she couldn't speak.

"Are you okay?" Charlie asked, seeing the look on Astrid's face.

"I'm okay, I think. I believe this girl was at my wedding. I think there's a picture of her in a group photo from one of my albums."

"Your *wedding*?" Charlie said in shock. Turning to Mr. Lui, he demanded, "What do you have on her?"

"Nothing on her yet. The flat's registered owner is Mr. Thomas Ng," the private investigator replied.

"Doesn't ring any bells," Astrid said numbly.

"We're still assembling a dossier," Mr. Lui said. An instant message flashed on his phone, and he reported, "The woman just left the flat with a young boy, approximately four years old."

Astrid's heart sank. "Have you been able to find out anything about the boy?"

"We have not. We did not know there was a boy inside the flat with them until this moment."

"So the woman has left with the boy and my husband is alone now?"

"Yes. We don't think anyone else is in the apartment."

"You don't think? Can you be sure there isn't someone else in there? Can't you use some sort of thermal sensor?" Charlie asked.

Mr. Lui gave a little snort. "Hiyah, this isn't the CIA. Of course, we can always escalate and bring in specialists if you wish, but for domestics such as these, we don't usually——"

"I want to see my husband," Astrid said matter-of-factly. "Can you take me to him now?"

"Ms. Teo, in these situations, we really don't advise—" the man delicately began.

"I don't care. I need to see him face-to-face," Astrid insisted.

A few minutes later, Astrid sat quietly in the back of the Mercedes with tinted windows while Mr. Lui rode in the front passenger seat, frantically barking orders in Cantonese to the team assembled around 64 Pak Tin Street. Charlie wanted to come along, but Astrid had insisted on going alone. "Don't worry, Charlie—nothing's going to happen. I'm just going to have a talk with Michael." Now her mind was reeling, and she was getting more and more antsy as the car inched through lunchtime traffic in Tsim Sha Tsui.

She just didn't know what to think anymore. Who exactly was this girl? It looked like the affair must have been going on since before their wedding, but then why had Michael married her? It clearly wasn't for money—her husband had always been so rabidly insistent about not wanting to benefit from her family's wealth. He had readily signed the hundred-and-fifty-page prenuptial agreement without so much as a blink, as well as the postnuptial her family's lawyers had insisted on after Cassian was born. Her money, and Cassian's money, was more secure than the Bank of China's. So what was it that motivated Michael to have a wife in Singapore, and a mistress in Hong Kong?

Astrid looked out her car window and noticed a Rolls-Royce Phantom next to her. Enthroned in the backseat was a couple, probably in their early thirties, dressed to the nines. The woman had short, smartly coiffed hair and was immaculately made up and dressed in a purple blouse with an enormous diamond-and-emerald floral brooch pinned to her right shoulder. The man at her side was sporting a florid Versace silk bomber jacket and Latin dictator–style dark sunglasses. Anywhere else in the world, this couple would have looked completely absurd—they were at least three decades too young to be chauffeured around so ostentatiously. But this was Hong Kong, and somehow it worked here. Astrid wondered where they came from, and where they were going. Probably off to lunch at the club. What secrets did they keep from each other? Did the husband have a mistress? Did the wife have a lover? Were there any children? Were they happy? The woman sat perfectly still, staring dead ahead, while the man slouched slightly away from her, reading the business section of the *South China Morning Post*. The traffic began to move again, and suddenly they were in Mong Kok, with its dense, hulking sixties apartment blocks crowding out the sunlight.

Before she knew it, Astrid was being led out of the car, flanked by four security men in dark suits. She looked around nervously as they escorted her to an old block of flats and into a small fluorescent-lit elevator with avocado-green walls. On the tenth floor, they emerged into an open-air hallway that skirted along an inner courtyard where lines of laundry hung from every available window. They walked past apartments with plastic slippers and shoes by the doorways, and soon they were in front of the metal-grille door of flat 10-07B.

The tallest man rang the doorbell once, and a moment later, Astrid could hear a few latches being undone. The door opened, and there he was. Her husband, standing right in front of her.

Michael glanced at the security detail surrounding Astrid and shook his head in disgust. "Let me guess, your father hired these goons to track me down."

13

Cameron Highlands

MALAYSIA

Nick borrowed his father's 1963 Jaguar E-Type roadster from the garage at Tyersall Park, and he and Rachel headed onto the Pan Island Expressway, bound for the bridge that linked Singapore to the Malay Peninsula. From Johor Bahru, they drove up the Utara-Selatan Highway, detouring to the seaside town of Malacca so that Nick could show Rachel the distinctive crimson-hued façade of Christ Church, built by the Dutch when the town was part of their colonial empire, and the charmingly ornate Peranakan row houses along Jalan Tun Tan Cheng Lock.

Afterward, they stayed on the old road that skirted along the Negeri Sembilan coast for a while. With the top down and the warm ocean breeze on her face, Rachel began to feel more relaxed than she had since arriving in Asia. The trauma of the past few days was dissipating, and at last it felt like they were truly on holiday together. She loved the wildness of these back roads, the rustic seaside hamlets that seemed untouched by time, the way Nick looked with day-old stubble and the wind whipping through his hair. A few miles north of Port Dickson, Nick turned down a dirt road thick with tropical vegetation, and as Rachel looked inland, she could glimpse miles and miles of uniformly planted trees.

"What are those perfect rows of trees?" Rachel asked.

"Rubber—we're surrounded by rubber plantations," Nick explained. They pulled up to a spot right by the beach, got out of the car, took off their sandals, and strolled onto the hot sand. A few Malay families were scattered about the beach having lunch, the ladies' colorful head scarves flapping in the wind as they bustled around canteens of food and children who were more interested in frolicking in the surf. It was a cloudy day, and the sea was a mottled tapestry of deep green with patches of azure where the clouds broke.

A Malay woman and her son came toward them, hauling a big blue-and-white Styrofoam cooler. Nick began talking animatedly with the woman, buying two bundles from her Igloo before bending down and asking the boy a question. The boy nodded eagerly and ran off, while Nick found a shady spot underneath the low-hanging branches of a mangrove tree.

He handed Rachel a still-warm banana-leaf packet tied with string. "Try Malaysia's most popular dish—*nasi lemak*," he said. Rachel undid the string and the glossy banana leaf unfolded to reveal a neatly composed mound of rice surrounded by sliced cucumbers, tiny fried anchovies, roasted peanuts, and a hard-boiled egg.

"Pass me a fork," Rachel said.

"There's no fork. You get to go native on this—use your fingers!" Nick grinned.

"You're kidding, right?"

"Nope, that's the traditional way. Malays believe the food actually tastes better when you eat with your hands. They only use the right hand to eat, of course. The left hand is used for purposes better left unmentioned."

"But I haven't washed my hands, Nick. I don't think I can eat like this," Rachel said, sounding a little alarmed.

"Come on, Miss OCD. Tough it out," Nick teased. He scooped some of the rice into his fingers and began eating the *nasi lemak* with gusto.

Rachel gingerly scooped some of the rice into her mouth, instantly breaking into a smile. "Mmmm . . . it's coconut rice!"

"Yes, but you haven't even gotten to the good part yet. Dig a little deeper!"

Rachel dug into her rice and discovered a curry sauce oozing out from the middle along with big chunks of chicken. "Oh my God," she said. "Does it taste this good because of all the different flavors or because we're sitting on this gorgeous beach eating it?"

"Oh, I think it's your hands. Your grotty hands are giving the food all the added flavor," Nick said.

"I'm about to slap you with my grotty curry hands!" Rachel scowled at him. Just as she was finishing her last bite, the little boy from earlier ran up with two clear-plastic drinking bags filled with rough chunks of ice and freshly squeezed sugarcane juice. Nick took the drinks from the boy and handed him a ten-dollar bill. *"Kamu anak yang baik,"** he said, patting the boy on the shoulder. The boy's eyes widened in delight. He tucked the money into the elastic band of his soccer shorts and scrambled off to tell his mother about his windfall.

"You never cease to amaze me, Nicholas Young. Why didn't I know you spoke Malay?" Rachel said.

"Only a few rudimentary words—enough to order food," Nick replied modestly.

"That conversation you had earlier didn't sound rudimentary to me," Rachel countered, sipping the icy sweet sugarcane through a thin pink straw tucked into the corner of the plastic bag.

"Trust me, I'm sure that lady was cringing at my grammar." Nick shrugged.

"You're doing it again, Nick," Rachel said.

"Doing what?"

"You're doing that annoying self-deprecating thing."

"I'm not sure I know what you mean."

Rachel sighed in exasperation. "You say you don't speak Malay when I hear you yapping away. You say, 'Oh, this old house,' when we're in a friggin' palace. You downplay *everything*, Nick!"

"I don't even realize when I'm doing it," Nick said.

"Why? I mean, you downplay things to the point that your parents don't even have a clue how well you're doing in New York."

"It's just the way I was brought up, I guess."

"Do you think it's because your family is so wealthy and you had to overcompensate by being super-modest?" Rachel suggested.

"I wouldn't put it quite like that. I was just trained to speak precisely and never to be boastful. Also, we're not *that* wealthy."

"Well then, what are you exactly? Are you guys worth hundreds of millions or billions?"

* "Good boy" in Malay.

Nick's face began to redden, but Rachel wouldn't let up.

"I know it makes you uncomfortable, Nick, but that's why I'm prodding you. You're telling me one thing, but then I hear other people speaking as if the entire economy of Asia revolves around your family, and you're, like, the heir to the throne. I'm an economist, for crying out loud, and if I'm going to be accused of being a gold digger, I'd like to know what I'm supposedly digging for," Rachel said bluntly.

Nick fidgeted with the remnant of his banana leaf nervously. Since he was old enough to remember, it had been ingrained into him that any talk of the family wealth was off-limits. But it was only fair that Rachel know what she was getting herself into, especially if he was (very shortly) going to ask her to accept the canary diamond ring hidden in the lower right pocket of his cargo shorts.

"I know this may sound silly, but the truth is I really don't know how rich my family is," Nick began tentatively. "Now, my parents live very well, mostly due to the legacy my mum received from her parents. And I have a private income that's not too shabby, mainly from stocks left to me by my grandfather. But we don't have the kind of money that Colin's or Astrid's family does, not even close."

"But how about your grandmother? I mean, Peik Lin says that Tyersall Park must be worth hundreds of millions just for the land alone," Rachel interjected.

"My grandmother has always lived in the manner that she has, so I can only presume that her holdings are substantial. Three times a year Mr. Tay, an elderly gentleman from the family bank, comes up to Tyersall Park in the same brown Peugeot he's driven ever since I was born and pays a visit to my grandmother. She meets with him alone, and it's the only time her lady's maids have to leave the room. So it's never crossed my mind to ask her how much she's worth."

"And your father never talked to you about it?"

"My father has never once brought up the subject of money—he probably knows even less than I do. You know, when there's always been money in your life, it's not something you spend much time thinking about."

Rachel tried to wrap her mind around that concept. "So why does everyone think you'll end up inheriting everything?"

Nick bristled. "This is Singapore, and the idle rich spend all their time gossiping about other people's money. Who's worth how much, who inherited how much, who sold their house for how much. But everything that's said about my family is pure speculation. The point is, I've never presumed that I will one day be the sole inheritor of some great fortune."

"But you must have known that you were different?" Rachel said.

"Well, I sensed that I was different because I lived in this big old house with all these rituals and traditions, but I never thought it had anything to do with money. When you're a kid, you're more concerned with how many pineapple tarts you're allowed to eat or where to catch the best tadpoles. I didn't grow up with a sense of entitlement like some of my cousins did. At least, I hope not."

"I wouldn't have been attracted to you if you went around acting like some pompous prick," Rachel said. As they walked back to the car, she slipped her arm around his waist. "Thank you for opening up. I know it wasn't easy for you to talk about these things."

"I want you to know everything about me, Rachel. I always have, which is why I invited you here in the first place. I'm sorry if it has felt like I wasn't forthcoming—I just didn't think any of this money talk was relevant. I mean, in New York, none of this really matters to our life, does it?"

Rachel paused for a while before answering. "It doesn't, especially now that I have a better understanding of your family. I just needed to be sure that you're the same person I fell in love with back in New York, that's all."

"Am I?"

"You're way cuter now that I know you're loaded."

Nick laughed and pulled Rachel tightly into his arms, giving her a long, lingering kiss.

"Ready for a complete change of scenery?" he asked, kissing her chin and then moving down to the tender spot on her throat.

"I think I'm ready to get a room. Any motels close by?" Rachel breathed, her fingers still entangled in his hair, not wanting him to stop.

"I don't think there are any motels you'd want to be in. Let's race to Cameron Highlands before it gets dark—it's only about three hours away. And then we can pick up where we left off on the most *ginormous* four-poster bed you've ever seen."

They made good time on the E1 highway, passing through the capital city of Kuala Lumpur toward Ipoh. When they reached the town of Tapah—the gateway to the Cameron Highlands—Nick turned onto the picturesque old road and they began the ascent up the mountain. The car climbed the steep hill, with Nick expertly negotiating the twists and turns, honking the horn at every blind curve.

Nick was anxious to get to the house before sunset. He had called ahead and given explicit instructions to Rajah, the majordomo. There were going to be votive candles in white paper bags lining the way down to the lookout point at the end of the lawn, and a stand with chilled champagne and fresh mangosteens right next to the carved wooden bench where they could sit and take in the scenic view. Then, just as the sun was sinking behind the hills and thousands of tropical birds descended into the treetops, he would get down on one knee and ask Rachel to be his forever. He wondered which was the correct knee to get down on? Right or left?

Rachel, meanwhile, found herself clutching at her seat-belt buckle tightly as she gazed out the window at sheer drops down into jungle-like ravines. "Uh, I'm in no hurry to die," she announced anxiously.

"I'm only going forty miles per hour. Don't worry, I can drive this road blindfolded—I used to come here almost every weekend during the summer holidays. Plus, don't you think it would be a glamorous way to die—careening down the side of a mountain in a classic Jag convertible?" Nick cracked, trying to diffuse the tension.

"If it's all right with you, I'd rather live a few days longer. *Annnnd*, I'd rather be in an old Ferrari, like James Dean," Rachel quipped.

"Actually, it was a Porsche."

"Smart-ass!"

The hairpin curves soon gave way to a breathtaking view of undulating green hills punctuated by bright swaths of color. In the distance, Rachel could make out flower orchards tucked along the hillsides and quaint little cottages.

"This is Bertam Valley," Nick said with a flourish. "We're about twelve hundred meters above sea level now. Back in the colonial days this was where British officers would come to escape the tropical heat."

Just past the town of Tanah Rata, they turned onto a narrow private road that snaked its way up a lushly planted hill. Behind another curve, a stately Tudor-style manor house on its own hillock suddenly reared into view. "I thought you promised you weren't going to take me to some luxury hotel," Rachel said in a half-chiding tone.

"This isn't a hotel, this is my grandmother's summer lodge."

"Why am I not surprised?" Rachel said, gazing at the beautiful structure. The lodge wasn't nearly as big as Tyersall Park, but it still looked formidably grand with its gabled roofs and black-and-white timbered woodwork. The whole place was aglow with lights blazing from the casement windows.

"Looks like we've been expected," Rachel said.

"Well, I called ahead for them to prepare for our arrival—there's a full staff all year round," Nick replied. The house was situated halfway up a gentle slope, with a long, paved stone path leading up to the front door. Its façade was partially covered in ivy and wisteria, and lining both sides of the slope were rosebushes that grew almost up to eye level.

Rachel sighed, thinking she had never seen such a romantic mountain haven in her life. "What enormous roses!"

"These are special Cameronian roses that only grow in this climate. Isn't the scent intoxicating?" Nick chatted on nervously. He knew he was only minutes away from one of the seminal moments of his life.

A young Malay butler wearing a crisp white dress shirt tucked into a gray-patterned sarong opened the door, bowing gallantly at them. Nick wondered where Rajah, the longtime butler, was. Rachel stepped into the front foyer and felt as if she had been transported once again into another era, to the colonial Malaya of a Somerset Maugham novel, perhaps. Anglo Raj wooden benches in the front hall were interspersed with wicker baskets brimming with freshly picked camellias, mica-shade lanterns hung from the mahogany-paneled walls, and a long, faded Tianjin silk carpet drew the eye straight back to the French doors and the glorious view of the highlands.

"Er, before I show you the rest of the house, let's, um, take in the sunset view," Nick said, feeling his throat go dry with anticipation. He led Rachel across the foyer and reached for the handle of the French doors leading out onto the terrace. Then suddenly he halted. He blinked a few times just to make sure he wasn't hallucinating. Standing at the edge of the expansive formal lawn having a smoke was Ahmad, his mother's chauffeur.

"Fuck me!" Nick swore under his breath.

"What? What's wrong?" Rachel asked.

"I think we've got company," Nick muttered darkly. He turned around, heading for the drawing room down the hall. Peering in, his suspicions were confirmed. Sure enough, perched on the floral chintz settee facing the door was his mother, who shot him a rather triumphant look as he entered the room. He was about to say something when his mother announced, a little too cheerily, "Oh look, Mummy, Nick and Rachel have arrived!"

Rachel spun around. Sitting in the armchair in front of the fireplace was Nick's grandmother, swaddled in an embroidered cashmere shawl, being poured a cup of tea by one of her Thai lady's maids.

"Ah Ma, what are you doing here?" Nick asked in astonishment.

"I received some very disturbing news, and so we rushed up here," Su Yi said in Mandarin, speaking slowly and deliberately.

Nick always found it disconcerting when his grandmother spoke to him in Mandarin—he associated that particular dialect with childhood scoldings. "What news? What has happened?" Nick asked, getting concerned.

"Well, I heard that you ran off to Malaysia, and that you mean to ask the girl to marry you," Su Yi said, not bothering to look at Rachel.

Rachel pursed her lips, shocked and thrilled at the same time.

"I was planning to surprise Rachel, but I guess *that's* ruined now," Nick huffed, staring at his mother.

"No matter, Nicky," his grandmother smiled. "I *do not* give you permission to marry her. Now let's stop all this nonsense and go home. I don't want to be stuck having dinner here, when the cook hasn't prepared properly for me. I'm sure she didn't get any fresh fish today."

Rachel's jaw dropped.

"Ah Ma, I'm sorry I don't have your blessing, but that doesn't change a thing. I intend to marry Rachel, if she'll have me," Nick said calmly, glancing at Rachel hopefully.

"Don't talk nonsense. This girl does not come from a proper family," Su Yi said.

Rachel felt her face go hot. "I've heard enough of this," she said in a quivering voice, turning to leave the room.

"No, Rachel, please don't go," Nick said, grabbing her by the arm. "I *need* you to hear this. Ah Ma, I don't know what stories you've been told, but I have met Rachel's family, and I like them very much. They have certainly shown me a great deal more courtesy, warmth, and *respect* than our family has shown to Rachel."

"Of course they should respect you—after all, you're a Young," Su Yi said.

"I can't believe you just said that!" Nick groaned.

Eleanor stood up and approached Rachel, looking her in the eye. "Rachel, I'm sure you're a nice girl. You must know I am doing you a favor. With your kind of background, you will be miserable in this family—"

"Stop insulting Rachel's family when you don't even know them!" Nick snapped. He put his arm on Rachel's shoulder and declared, "Let's get out of here!"

"You've met her family?" Eleanor called after him.

Nick turned back with a scowl. "Yes, I've met Rachel's mother many times, and I went to Thanksgiving at her uncle's in California, where I got to know many of her relatives."

"Even her father?" Eleanor asked, raising one eyebrow.

"Rachel's father died a long time ago, you already know that," Nick said impatiently.

"Well, that's a very convenient story, isn't it? But I assure you he's very much alive," Eleanor shot back.

"What?" Rachel said, confused.

"Rachel, you can stop pretending, *lah*. I know all about your father—"

"What?"

"Aiyoh, look at her act!" Eleanor twisted her face mockingly. "You know as well as I do that your father is still alive!"

Rachel looked at Eleanor as if she was talking to a deranged woman. "My father died in a horrible industrial accident when I was two months old. That's why my mother brought me to America."

Eleanor studied the girl for a moment, trying to discern whether she was giving the performance of a lifetime or speaking the truth. "Well, I'm sorry to be the one to break the news to you, Rachel. Your father did not die. He's in a prison outside Shenzhen. I met him myself a few weeks ago. The man was rotting away behind rusty bars, but he still had the nerve to demand an enormous dowry in exchange for you!"

Eleanor took out a faded manila envelope, the same envelope she had been given by the investigator in Shenzhen. She placed three pieces of paper on the coffee table. One was a copy of Rachel's original birth certificate. The next was a 1992 press clipping about the jailing of a man named Zhou Fang Min, after he had ordered illegal cost-cutting measures that led to a construction accident that killed seventy-four workers in Shenzhen (HUO PENG CONDO TRAGEDY UPDATE: MONSTER JAILED AT LAST! the headline screamed). The third was a notice of a reward from the Zhou family, for the safe return of a baby named Zhou An Mei, who had been kidnapped by her mother, Kerry Ching, in 1981.

Nick and Rachel took a few steps toward the table and stared at the papers in astonishment.

"What the hell did you do, Mum? You had Rachel's family *investigated*?" Nick kicked over the coffee table.

Nick's grandmother shook her head as she sipped her tea. "Imagine wanting to marry a girl from such a family! So disgraceful! Really, Nicky, what would Gong Gong say if he was alive? Madri, this tea needs a little more sugar."

Nick was livid. "Ah Ma, it's taken me about twenty years, but I finally understand why Dad moved to Sydney! He can't stand being around you!"

Su Yi put down her teacup, stunned by what her favorite grandson had just said.

Rachel grabbed at Nick's wrist urgently. He would never forget the look of devastation on her face. "I think . . . need air," she muttered, before collapsing into the wicker tea cart.

14

64 Pak Tin Street

•

The apartment was not the love nest Astrid had imagined—the living room was tiny, with a green vinyl sofa, three wooden dining-room chairs, and bright blue plastic buckets full of toys taking up one side of the room. Only the muffled sounds of a neighbor practicing "Ballade pour Adeline" on the electric keyboard filled the silence. Astrid stood in the middle of the cramped space, wondering how her life had come to this. How did it get to the point where her husband had resorted to fleeing to this sad romper room?

"I can't believe you got your dad's men to track me down," Michael muttered contemptuously, sitting down on the sofa and stretching his arms out along its back.

"My father had nothing to do with this. Can't you give me a little credit for having my own resources?" Astrid said.

"Great. You win," Michael said.

"So this is where you've been coming. Is this where your mistress lives?" Astrid finally ventured to ask.

"Yes," Michael said flatly.

Astrid was silent for a while. She picked up a little stuffed elephant from one of the buckets and gave it a squeeze. The elephant made a muffled electronic roar. "And these are your son's toys?"

Michael hesitated for a moment. "Yes," he finally answered.

"BASTARD!" Astrid screamed, throwing the elephant at him

with all her might. The elephant bounced off his chest, and Astrid sank to the floor, trembling as her body was racked with violent sobs. "I don't . . . care . . . who you fuck . . . but how could you do this . . . to *our son*?" She sputtered through her tears.

Michael leaned forward, burying his head in his hands. He couldn't stand seeing her like this. As badly as he wanted out of the marriage, he couldn't take hurting her anymore. Things had spiraled out of control, and it was time to come clean. He got up from the sofa and crouched down beside her.

"Listen to me, Astrid," he began, placing an arm on her shoulder. Astrid jerked backward and pushed his arm away.

"Listen to me. The boy isn't my son, Astrid."

Astrid looked up at him, not quite registering what he meant.

Michael looked Astrid directly in the eyes and said, "That's not my son, and there is no mistress."

Astrid's brow furrowed. "What do you mean? I know there was a woman here. I even recognize her."

"You recognize her because she's my *cousin*. Jasmine Ng—her mother is my auntie, and the little boy is her son."

"So . . . who have you been having an affair with?" Astrid asked, more confused than ever.

"Don't you get it? It's all been an act, Astrid. The text messages, the presents, everything! It's all fake."

"*Fake?*" Astrid whispered in shock.

"Yes, I faked everything. Well, except the dinner at Petrus. I took Jasmine as a treat—her husband has been working in Dubai and she's had a hard time managing on her own."

"I can't believe this . . ." Astrid said, her voice trailing off in astonishment.

"I'm sorry, Astrid. It was a stupid idea, but I didn't think I had any other choice."

"*Any other choice?* What do you mean?"

"I thought it would be far better for you to *want* to leave me than for me to divorce you. I would rather be labeled the cheating bastard with an illegitimate son, so that you could . . . your family could save face," Michael said rather dejectedly.

Astrid stared at him incredulously. For a few minutes, she sat completely still as her mind sifted through everything that had happened in the past few months. Then she spoke. "I thought I was going insane . . . I wanted to believe you were having an affair, but my heart kept telling me that you would never do such a thing to me. That just wasn't the man I married. I was so confused, so conflicted, and that's really what made it so painful. An affair or a mistress I could deal with, but something else didn't seem right, something kept gnawing away at me. It's finally beginning to make sense now."

"I never wanted this to happen," Michael said softly.

"Then why? What did I ever do to make you this miserable? What made you go to all the trouble to fake an entire affair?"

Michael sighed deeply. He got up off the floor and perched on one of the wooden chairs. "It's just never worked, Astrid. Our marriage. It hasn't worked from day one. We had a great time dating, but we should never have married. We were wrong for each other, but we both got so swept up in the moment—in, let's face it, the sex—that before I realized what was happening, we were standing in front of your pastor. I thought, what the hell, this is the most beautiful girl I've ever met. I'll never be this lucky again. But then reality hit . . . and things got to be too much. It just got worse, year after year, and I tried, I really tried, Astrid, but I can't face it anymore. You don't have a clue what it's like being married to Astrid Leong. Not you, Astrid, but everyone's idea of you. I could never live up to it."

"What do you mean? You *have* lived up to it—" Astrid began.

"Everyone in Singapore thinks I married you for your money, Astrid."

"You're wrong, Michael!"

"No, you just don't see it! But I can't face another dinner at Nassim Road or Tyersall Park with some minister of finance, some genius artist I don't get, or some tycoon who has a whole bloody museum named after him, feeling like I'm just a piece of meat. To them, I'm always 'Astrid's husband.' And those people—your family, your friends—they stare at me with such judgment. They're all thinking, *'Aiyah, she could have married a prince, a president—why did she marry this Ah Beng** from Toa Payoh?'"

"You're imagining things, Michael! Everyone in my family adores you!" Astrid protested.

"That's bullshit and you know it! Your father treats his fucking golf caddie better than me! I know my parents don't speak Queen's

---

* Derogatory Hokkien term for a lower-class young man who lacks education or taste.

English, I didn't grow up in a big mansion in Bukit Timah, and I didn't attend ACS—'American Cock Suckers,' as we used to call it—but I'm not some loser, Astrid."

"Of course you're not."

"Do you know how it feels to be treated like I'm the bloody tech-support guy all the time? Do you know how it feels when I have to visit your relatives every Chinese New Year in their incredible houses, and then you have to come with me to my family's tiny flats in Tampines or Yishun?"

"I've never minded, Michael. I like your family."

"But your parents don't. Think about it . . . in the five years we've been married, my mother and father haven't once—not even *once*—been invited to dinner at your parents' house!"

Astrid went pale. It was true. How could she not have realized it? How had her family been so thoughtless?

"Face it, Astrid, your parents will never respect my family the same way they respect your brothers' wives' families. We're not mighty Tans or Kahs or Kees—we're Teos. You can't really blame your parents. They were born that way—it's just not in their DNA to associate with anyone who isn't from their class, anyone who isn't born rich or royal."

"But you're on your way to doing just that, Michael. Look at how well your company is doing," Astrid said encouragingly.

"My company—ha! You want to know something, Astrid? Last December, when the company finally broke even and we did our first profit sharing, I got a bonus check for two hundred and thirty-eight thousand. For one minute, one whole minute, I was so happy. It was the most money I had ever made. But then it hit me . . . I realized that no matter how long I work, no matter how hard I sweat my ass off all day long, I will never make as much money in my whole life as you make in one month alone."

"That's not true, Michael, that's just not true!" Astrid cried.

"Don't patronize me!" Michael shouted angrily. "I know what your income is. I know how much those Paris dresses cost you! Do you know how it feels to realize that my pathetic two-hundred-thousand-dollar bonus can't even pay for one of your dresses? Or that I'll never be able to give you the type of house you grew up in?"

"I'm happy where we live, Michael. Have I ever complained?"

"I know about all your properties, Astrid, all of them."

"Who told you about them?" Astrid asked in shock.

"Your brothers did."

"My brothers?"

"Yes, your dear brothers. I never told you what happened when we got engaged. Your brothers called me one day and invited me to lunch, and they all showed up. Henry, Alex, and even Peter came down from K.L. They invited me to the snotty club on Shenton Way that they all belong to, took me into one of the private dining rooms, and sat me down. Then they showed me one of your financial reports. Just one. They said, *'We want you to have a glimpse of Astrid's financial picture, so you have an idea of what she netted last year.'* And then Henry said to me—and I'll never forget his words—*'Everything Astrid has is safeguarded by the best team of lawyers in the world. No one outside the Leong family will ever benefit from or come to control her money. Not if she divorces, not even if she dies. Just thought you should know, old chap.'"*

Astrid was horrified. "I can't believe it! Why didn't you tell me?"

"What good would that do?" Michael said bitterly. "Don't you see? From day one, your family didn't trust me."

"You don't ever have to spend a single minute with my family again, I promise. I am going to talk to my brothers. I am going to give them hell. And no one will ever ask you to recover their hard drives or reprogram their wine fridges again, I promise. Just please, don't leave me," she pleaded, the tears flooding down her cheeks.

"Astrid, you are talking nonsense. I would never want to deprive you of your family—your whole life revolves around them. What would you do if you weren't at Wednesday mah-jongg with your great-aunt Rosemary, Friday-night dinner at your Ah Ma's, or Pulau Club movie night with your dad?"

"I can give it up. I can give all of that up!" Astrid cried, burying her head in his lap and clinging to him tightly.

"I wouldn't want you to. You'll be happier without me in the long run. I'm just holding you back."

"But what about Cassian? How can you just abandon our son like this?"

"I'm not abandoning him. I will still spend as much time with him as you'll let me. Don't you see? If I was ever going to leave, this is the perfect time—before Cassian is old enough to be affected by it. I will never stop being a good father to him, but I can't stay married to you. I just don't want to live in your world anymore. There's no way

I can measure up to your family, and I don't want to keep resenting you for who you are. I made a terrible mistake, Astrid. Please, *please* just let me go," he said, his voice getting choked up.

Astrid looked up at Michael, realizing it was the first time she had ever seen him cry.

15

Villa d'Oro

SINGAPORE

Peik Lin knocked softly on the door. "Come in," Rachel said.

Peik Lin entered the bedroom gingerly, holding a gold tray with a covered earthenware bowl. "Our cook made some *pei daan zhook** for you."

"Please thank her for me," Rachel said disinterestedly.

"You can stay in here as long as you want, Rachel, but you need to eat," Peik Lin said, staring at Rachel's gaunt face and the dark circles under her eyes, puffy from all the crying.

"I know I look like hell, Peik Lin."

"Nothing a good facial won't fix. Why don't you let me whisk you away to a spa? I know a great place in Sentosa that has—"

"Thank you, but I just don't think I'm ready yet. Maybe tomorrow?"

"Okay, tomorrow," Peik Lin chirped. Rachel had been saying the same thing all week, but she had not left the bedroom once.

When Peik Lin left the room, Rachel took the tray and placed it against the wall next to the door. She hadn't had an appetite for days, not since the night she had fled from Cameron Highlands. After fainting in the drawing room in front of Nick's mother and grandmother, she had been quickly revived by the expert ministrations of

---

* Cantonese for "century-egg congee."

Shang Su Yi's Thai lady's maids. As she regained consciousness, she found a cold towel being dabbed on her forehead by one maid, while the other was performing reflexology on her foot.

"No, no, please stop," Rachel said, trying to get up.

"You mustn't get up so quickly," she heard Nick's mother say.

"The girl has such a weak constitution," she heard Nick's grandmother mutter from across the room. Nick's worried face appeared over her.

"Please Nick, get me out of here," she pleaded weakly. She had never wanted to leave someplace more desperately in her life. Nick scooped her into his arms and carried her toward the door.

"You can't leave now, Nicky! It's too dark to drive down the mountain, *lah*!" Eleanor called after them.

"You should have thought of that before you decided to play God with Rachel's life," Nick said through clenched teeth.

As they drove down the winding road away from the lodge, Rachel said, "You don't have to drive down the mountain tonight. Just drop me off at that town we passed through."

"We can go anywhere you want to, Rachel. Why don't we get off this mountain and spend the night in K.L.? We can get there by ten."

"No, Nick. I don't want to drive anymore. I need some time on my own. Just drop me off in town."

Nick was silent for a moment, thinking carefully before he responded.

"What are you going to do?"

"I want to check into a motel and go to sleep, that's all. I just want to be away from everyone."

"I'm not sure you should be alone right now."

"For God's sake, Nick, I'm not some basket case, I'm not going to slit my wrists or take a million Seconals. I just need some time to think," Rachel answered sharply.

"Let me be with you."

"I really need to be alone, Nick." Her eyes seemed glazed over.

Nick knew that she was in a deep state of shock—he was shocked himself, so he could scarcely imagine what she was going through. At the same time, he was racked with guilt, feeling responsible for the damage that had been done. It was his fault again. Intent on finding Rachel a tranquil haven, he had inadvertently led her right into a viper's nest. He even pulled her hand in to be bitten. His fucking mother! Maybe one night alone would do her no harm. "There's a little inn down in the lower valley called the Lakehouse. Why don't I drive you there and check you into a room?"

"That's fine," she responded numbly.

They drove in silence for the next half hour, Nick never taking his eyes off the treacherous curves, while Rachel stared at the rush of blackness out her window. They pulled up to the Lakehouse shortly after eight. It was a charming, thatched-roof house that looked like it had been transported straight out of the Cotswolds, but Rachel was too numb to notice any of it.

After Nick had checked her into a plushly decorated bedroom, lit the logs in the stone fireplace, and kissed her goodbye, promising to return first thing in the morning, Rachel left the room and headed straight to the reception desk. "Can you please stop payment on that credit card?" she said to the night clerk. "I won't be needing the room, but I will be needing a taxi."

Three days after arriving at Peik Lin's, Rachel crouched on the floor in the far corner of the bedroom and summoned the courage to call her mother in Cupertino.

"Aiyah, so many days I haven't heard from you. You must be having such a good time!" Kerry Chu said cheerily.

"Like hell I am."

"Why? What happened? Did you and Nick fight?" Kerry asked, worried by her daughter's strange tone.

"I just need to know one thing, Mom: Is my father still alive?"

There was a fraction of a pause on the other end of the line. "What are you talking about, daughter? Your father died when you were a baby. You know that."

Rachel dug her nails into the plush carpeting. "I'm going to ask you one more time: Is. My. Father. Alive?"

"I don't understand. What have you heard?"

"Yes or no, Mom. Don't waste my fucking time!" she spat out.

Kerry gasped at the force of Rachel's anger. It sounded like she was in the next room. "Daughter, you need to calm down."

"Who is Zhou Fang Min?" There. She had said it.

There was a long pause before her mother said nervously, "Daughter, you need to let me explain."

She could feel her heart pounding in her temples. "So it's true. He *is* alive."

"Yes, but—"

"So everything you've told me my entire life has been a lie! A BIG FUCKING LIE!" Rachel held the phone away from her face and screamed into it, her hands shaking with rage.

"No, Rachel—"

"I'm going to hang up now, Mom."

"No, no, don't hang up!" Kerry pleaded.

"You're a liar! A kidnapper! You've deprived me from knowing my father, my real family. How *could* you, Mom?"

"You don't know what a hateful man he was. You don't understand what I went through."

"That's not the point, Mom. You lied to me. About the most important thing in my life." Rachel shuddered as she broke down in sobs.

"No, no! You don't understand—"

"Maybe if you hadn't kidnapped me, he wouldn't have done all the horrible things he did. Maybe he wouldn't be in jail now." She looked down at her hand and realized she was pulling out tufts of the carpet.

"No, daughter. I had to save you from him, from his family."

"I don't know what to believe anymore, Mom. Who can I trust now? My name isn't even real. WHAT'S MY REAL NAME?"

"I changed your name to protect you!"

"I don't know who the fuck I am anymore."

"You're my daughter! My precious daughter!" Kerry cried, feeling utterly helpless standing in her kitchen in California while her daughter's heart was breaking somewhere in Singapore.

"I need to go now, Mom."

She hung up the phone and crawled onto the bed. She lay on her back, letting her head hang off the side. Maybe the rush of blood would stop the pounding, would end the pain.

The Goh family was just sitting down to some *poh piah* when Rachel entered the dining room.

"There she is!" Wye Mun called out jovially. "I told you Jane Ear would come down sooner or later."

Peik Lin made a face at her father, while her brother Peik Wing said, "*Jane Eyre* was the nanny, Papa, not the woman who—"

"*Ho lah, ho lah,** smart aleck, you get my point," Wye Mun said dismissively.

"Rachel, if you don't eat something you are going to deeesap-pear!" Neena chided. "Will you have one *poh piah*?"

Rachel glanced at the lazy Susan groaning with dozens of little plates of food that seemed completely random and wondered what they were having. "Sure, Auntie Neena. I'm absolutely starving!"

"That's what I like to hear," Neena said. "Come, come, let me make you one." She placed a thin wheat-flour crepe on a gold-rimmed plate and scooped a big serving of meat-and-vegetable filling onto the middle. Next she slathered some sweet hoisin sauce on one side of the crepe and reached for the little dishes, scattering plump prawns, crab meat, fried omelet, shallots, cilantro, minced garlic, chili sauce, and ground peanuts over the filling. She finished this off with another generous drizzle of sweet hoisin and deftly folded the crepe into what looked like an enormous bulging burrito.

"Nah—*ziak*!" Peik Lin's mother commanded.

Rachel began inhaling her *poh piah* ravenously, barely tasting the jicama and Chinese sausage in the filling. It had been a week since she had eaten much of anything.

"See? Look at her smile! There is nothing in the world that good food cannot fix," Wye Mun said, helping himself to another crepe.

Peik Lin got up from her seat and gave Rachel a big hug from behind. "It's good to have you back," she said, her eyes getting moist.

"Thank you. In fact, I really need to thank all of you, from the bottom of my heart, for letting me camp out here for so long," Rachel added.

"Aiyah, I'm just so happy you're eating again!" Neena grinned. "Now, time for mango ice-kleam sundaes!"

"Ice cream!" the Goh granddaughters screamed in delight.

"You've been through a lot, Rachel Chu. I'm glad we are able to help." Wye Mun nodded. "You are welcome to stay as long as you like."

"No, no, I've overstayed my welcome." Rachel smiled sheepishly,

* Hokkien slang for "it's all good."

wondering how she could have let herself hole up in their guest room for so many days.

"Have you thought about what you're going to do?" Peik Lin asked.

"Yeah. I'm going to head back to the States. But first," she paused, taking a deep breath, "I think I need to go to China. I've decided that, for better or for worse, I want to meet my father."

The whole table went silent for a moment. "What's the rush?" Peik Lin asked gently.

"I'm already on this side of the globe—why not meet him now?" Rachel said, trying to make it sound like it was no big deal.

"Are you going to go with Nick?" Wye Mun asked.

Rachel's face darkened. "No, he's the last person I want to go to China with."

"You *are* going to tell him, though?" Peik Lin inquired delicately.

"I might . . . . I haven't really decided yet. I just don't want a reenactment of *Apocalypse Now*. I'll be in the middle of meeting my father for the first time and next thing you know, one of Nick's relatives will land in the prison yard in a chopper. I'll be glad if I never have to see another private jet, yacht, or fancy car for the rest of my life," Rachel vehemently declared.

"Okay, Papa, cancel the NetJets membership," Peik Wing wisecracked.

Everyone at the table laughed.

"Nick's been calling every day, you know," Peik Lin said.

"I'm sure he has."

"It's been pretty pathetic," P.T. reported. "It was four times a day when you first got here, but he tapered off to once a day. He drove up here twice, hoping we might let him come in, but the guards told him he had to move along."

Rachel's heart sank. She could imagine how Nick was feeling, but at the same time, she didn't know how to face him. He had suddenly become a reminder of everything that had gone wrong in her life.

"You should see him," Wye Mun said gently.

"I disagree, Papa," Peik Wing's wife, Sheryl, piped in. "If I were Rachel, I would never want to see Nick or anyone in that evil family again. Who do those people think they are? Trying to ruin people's lives!"

"*Alamak*, why make the poor boy suffer? It's not his fault that his mother is a *chao chee bye*!" Neena exclaimed. The whole table exploded in laughter, except for Sheryl, who made a face as she covered her daughters' ears.

"Hiyah, Sheryl, they're too young to know what it means!" Neena assured her daughter-in-law.

"What does that mean?" Rachel asked.

"Rotten cunt," P.T. whispered with relish.

"No, no, *smelly* rotten cunt," Wye Mun corrected. Everyone roared again, Rachel included.

Recovering herself, Rachel sighed. "I guess I ought to see him."

———

Two hours later Rachel and Nick were seated at an umbrella-shaded table by the swimming pool of Villa d'Oro, the sound of trickling gilded fountains punctuating the silence. Rachel gazed at the water ripples reflecting off the gold-and-blue mosaic tiles. She couldn't bring herself to look at Nick. Strangely, what had been the most beautiful face in the world to her had become too painful to look at. She found herself suddenly mute, not quite knowing how to begin.

Nick swallowed nervously. "I don't even know how to begin to ask for your forgiveness."

"There's nothing to forgive. You weren't responsible for this."

"But I am. I've had a lot of time to think about it. I put you in one horrendous situation after another. I'm so sorry, Rachel. I've been recklessly ignorant about my own family—I had no idea how crazy my mum would get. And I always thought my grandmother wanted me to be happy."

Rachel stared at the sweaty glass of iced tea in front of her, not saying anything.

"I'm so relieved to see that you're okay. I've been so worried," Nick said.

"I've been well taken care of by the Gohs," Rachel said simply.

"Yes, I met Peik Lin's parents earlier. They're lovely. Neena Goh demanded that I come to dinner. Not tonight, of course, but . . ."

Rachel gave the barest hint of a smile. "The woman is a feeder, and you look like you've lost some weight." Actually, he looked terrible. She had never seen him like this—he looked like he had slept in his clothes, and his hair had lost its floppy sheen.

"I haven't been eating much."

"Your old cook at Tyersall Park hasn't been preparing all your favorite dishes?" Rachel said a little sarcastically. She knew her pent-up anger was misdirected at Nick, but in the moment she couldn't help herself. She realized he was as much a victim of circumstances as she was, but she wasn't able to look past her own pain just yet.

"Actually, I'm not staying at Tyersall Park," Nick said.

"Oh?"

"I haven't wanted to see anyone since that night in Cameron Highlands, Rachel."

"Are you back at the Kingsford Hotel?"

"Colin's let me crash at his house in Sentosa Cove while he's away on his honeymoon. He and Araminta have been very worried about you too, you know."

"How nice of them," she said flatly, staring out across the pool at the replica of *Venus de Milo*. An armless statue of a beautiful maiden fought over by collectors for centuries, even though its origins have never been verified. Maybe someone should chop off her arms too. Maybe she would feel better.

Nick reached out and placed his hand over Rachel's. "Let's go back to New York. Let's go home."

"I've been thinking . . . I need to go to China. I want to meet my father."

Nick paused. "Are you sure you're ready for that?"

"Is anyone ever ready to meet the father they never knew, who's in a prison?"

Nick sighed. "Well, when do we leave?"

"Actually, Peik Lin is coming with me."

"Oh," Nick said, a little taken aback. "Can I come? I'd like to be there for you."

"No, Nick, this is something I need to do on my own. It's already enough that Peik Lin insisted on coming. But her father has friends in China who are helping with the red tape, so I couldn't say no. I'll be in and out within a couple of days, and then I'll be ready to head back to New York."

"Well, just let me know when you want to change the return date on our plane tickets. I'm ready to go home anytime, Rachel."

Rachel inhaled deeply, bracing herself for what she was about to say. "Nick, I need to go back to New York . . . on my own."

"On your own?" Nick said in surprise.

"Yes. I don't need you to cut short your summer vacation and fly back with me."

"No, no, I'm as sick of this place as you are! I *want* to go home with you!" Nick insisted.

"That's the thing, Nick. I don't think I can deal with that right now."

Nick looked at her sadly. She was clearly still in a world of pain.

"And when I'm back in New York," she continued, her voice getting shaky, "I don't think we should see each other anymore."

"What? What do you mean?" Nick said in alarm.

"I mean exactly that. I'll get my things out of your apartment as soon as I get back, and then when you return—"

"Rachel, you're crazy!" Nick said, leaping out of his chair and crouching down beside her. "Why are you saying all this? I love you. I want to marry you."

"I love you too," Rachel cried. "But don't you see—it's never going to work."

"Of course it is. *Of course it is!* I don't give a damn what my family thinks—I want to be with you, Rachel."

Rachel shook her head slowly. "It's not just your family, Nick. It's your friends, your childhood friends—it's everyone on this island."

"That's not true, Rachel. My best friends think the world of you. Colin, Mehmet, Alistair, and there are so many friends of mine you haven't even had the chance to meet. But that's all beside the point. We live in New York now. Our friends are there, our life is there, and it's been great. It will continue to be great once we've left all this insanity behind."

"It's not that simple, Nick. You probably didn't notice it yourself, but you said 'we live in New York *now.*' But you won't always be living in New York. You'll be returning here someday, probably within the next few years. Don't kid yourself—your whole family is here, your legacy is here."

"Oh fuck all that! You know I couldn't care less about that bullshit."

"That's what you say now, but don't you see how things might change in time? Don't you think you might start to resent me in years to come?"

"I could never resent you, Rachel. You're the most important person in my life! You have no idea—I've barely slept, barely eaten—the past seven days have been absolute hell without you."

Rachel sighed, clamping her eyes shut for a moment. "I know you've been in pain. I don't want to hurt you, but I think it's really for the best."

"To break up? You're not making any sense, Rachel. I know how much you're hurting right now, but breaking up won't make it hurt any less. Let me help you, Rachel. Let me take care of you," Nick pleaded fervently, hair getting into his eyes.

"What if we have children? Our children will never be accepted by your family."

"Who cares? We'll have our own family, our own lives. None of this is significant."

"It's significant to me. I've been thinking about it endlessly, Nick. You know, at first I was so shocked to learn about my past. I was devastated by my mother's lies, to realize that even my name wasn't real. I felt like my whole identity had been robbed from me. But then I realized . . . none of it really matters. What is a name anyway? We Chinese are so obsessed with family names. I'm proud of my *own* name. I'm proud of the person I've become."

"I am too," Nick said.

"So you'll have to understand that, as much as I love you, Nick, I don't want to be your wife. I never want to be part of a family like yours. I can't marry into a clan that thinks it's too good to have me. And I don't want my children to ever be connected to such people. I want them to grow up in a loving, nurturing home, surrounded by grandparents and aunts and uncles and cousins who consider them equals. Because that's ultimately what I have, Nick. You've seen it yourself, when you came home with me last Thanksgiving. You see what it's like with my cousins. We're competitive, we tease each other mercilessly, but at the end of the day we support each other. That's what I want for my kids. I want them to love their family, but to feel a deeper sense of pride in who they are as individuals, Nick, not in how much money they have, what their last name is, or how many generations they go back to whatever dynasty. I'm sorry, but I've had enough. I've had enough of being around all these crazy rich Asians, all these people whose lives revolve around making money, spending money, flaunting money, comparing money, hiding money, controlling others with money, and ruining their lives over money. And if I marry you, there will be no escaping it, even if we live on the other side of the world."

Rachel's eyes were brimming with tears, and as much as Nick wanted to insist she was wrong, he knew nothing he could say now would convince her otherwise. In any part of the world, whether New York, Paris, or Shanghai, she was lost to him.

16

Sentosa Cove

•

SINGAPORE

It must have been a bird or something, Nick thought, waking up to a sound. There was a blue jay that liked to tap its beak against the sliding glass wall downstairs by the reflecting pool every morning. How long had he been sleeping? It was seven forty-five, so this meant he'd knocked off at least four and a half hours. Not bad, considering that he hadn't been able to sleep more than three hours a night since Rachel had broken up with him a week ago. The bed was bathed in a pool of light coming from the retractable glass roof, and now it was far too bright for him to go back to sleep. How did Colin manage to get any sleep in this place? There was something so impractical about living in a house that consisted mainly of reflecting pools and glass walls.

Nick turned over, facing the Venetian stucco wall with the large Hiroshi Sugimoto photograph. It was a black-and-white image from his cinema series, the interior of an old theater somewhere in Ohio. Sugimoto had left the camera shutter open for the duration of the film, so that the large screen became a glowing, rectangular portal of light. To Nick, it seemed like a portal to a parallel universe, and he wished he could just slip into all that whiteness and disappear. Maybe go back in time. To April, or May. He should have known better. He should never have invited Rachel to come here without first giving her a crash course in how to deal with his family. "Rich, Entitled, Delusional Chinese Families 101." Could he really be part of this family? The older he got, and the more years he spent abroad, the more he felt like a stranger in their midst. Now that he was in his thirties, the expectations kept growing, and the rules kept changing. He didn't know how to keep up with this place anymore. And yet he loved being back home. He loved the long rainy afternoons at his grandmother's house during monsoon season, hunting for *kueh tutu** in Chinatown, the long walks around MacRitchie Reservoir at dusk with his father . . .

There was the sound again. This time it didn't sound like the blue jay. He had fallen asleep without arming the security system, and now someone was definitely in the house. He threw on a pair of shorts and tiptoed out of the bedroom. The guest bedroom was accessed through a glass skywalk that stretched across the back section of the house, and looking down, he could see the flicker of a reflection as it moved across the polished Brazilian oak floors. Was the house being burglarized? Sentosa Cove was so isolated, and anyone reading the gossip rags knew Colin Khoo and Araminta Lee were away on their fabulous honeymoon yachting around the Dalmatian coast.

Nick hunted around for a weapon; the only thing he could find was a carved didgeridoo propped against the wall of the guest bathroom. (Would someone actually play the didgeridoo while sitting on the loo?) He crept down the floating titanium stairs and walked slowly toward the galley kitchen, raising the didgeridoo to strike just as Colin appeared from around the corner.

"Christ!" Nick swore in surprise, putting down his weapon.

Colin seemed unruffled by the sight of Nick in nothing more than a pair of soccer shorts, wielding a rainbow-colored didgeridoo. "I don't think that makes a good weapon, Nick," he said. "Should have gone for the antique samurai sword in my bedroom."

"I thought someone was breaking in!"

"There are no break-ins around here. This neighborhood is way too secure, and thieves can't be bothered to drive out here just to steal customized kitchen appliances."

"What are you doing back from your honeymoon so early?" Nick asked, scratching his head.

---

* This floral-shaped, steamed rice-flour cake filled with sweet shredded coconut is a traditional Singapore delicacy.

"Well, I heard disturbing rumors that my best friend was suicidal and wasting away in my house."

"Wasting away, but not suicidal." Nick groaned.

"Seriously, Nicky, you have a lot of people worried about you."

"Oh, like who? And don't say my mother."

"Sophie's been worried. Araminta. Even Mandy. She called me in Hvar. I think she feels really bad about how she acted."

"Well, the damage has been done," Nick said gruffly.

"Listen, why don't I make you a quick breakfast? You look like you haven't eaten in years."

"That'll be great."

"Watch, as the Iron Chef attempts to fry up some *hor bao daan*."*

Nick perched on a barstool at the island in the kitchen, wolfing down his breakfast. He held up a fork of eggs. "Almost as good as Ah Ching's."

"Pure luck. My *bao daan* usually end up as scrambled eggs."

"Well, it's the best thing I've eaten all week. Actually, it's the only thing I've eaten. I've just been parked on your sofa, bingeing on beer and episodes of *Mad Men*. By the way, you're out of Red Stripe."

"This is the first time you've ever really been depressed, isn't it? Finally the heartbreaker discovers how it feels to get his heart broken."

"I don't actually hold the trademark on that name. Alistair's the true heartbreaker."

"Wait a minute—you haven't heard? Kitty Pong dumped him!"

"Now that's a shocker," Nick remarked drily.

"No, you don't know the whole story! At the tea ceremony the day after the wedding, Araminta and I were in the middle of pouring tea for Mrs. Lee Yong Chien when we all heard this strange noise coming from somewhere. It sounded like a rattling crossed with some kind of farm animal giving birth. No one could figure out what it was. We thought maybe a bat was stuck somewhere in the house. So a few of us started looking around discreetly, and you know how my grandfather's colonial house on Belmont Road is—there are all these huge built-in closets everywhere. Well, little Rupert Khoo opens the door under the grand staircase and out tumble Kitty and Bernard Tai, right in front of all the guests!"

---

* Cantonese for "fried wrapped eggs," similar in style to sunny-side up or over-easy.

"NOOOOOOO!" Nick exclaimed.

"And that's not the worst of it. Bernard was bent over spread-eagle with his pants around his ankles, and Kitty still had two fingers up his bum when the door popped open!"

Nick broke out into hysterical fits, slapping the travertine counter repeatedly as tears ran down his cheeks.

"You should have seen the look on Mrs. Lee Yong Chien's face! I thought I was going to have to perform CPR!" Colin sniggered.

"Thanks for the laugh—I needed that." Nick sighed, trying to catch his breath. "I feel bad for Alistair."

"Oh, he'll get over it. I'm more worried about you. Seriously, what are you going to do about Rachel? We need to get you cleaned up and back on your white horse. I think Rachel could use your help now more than ever."

"I know that, but she's adamant about wanting me out of her life. She made it clear she never wanted to see me again, and those Gohs have done a damn good job of enforcing that!"

"She's still in shock, Nicky. With all that's happened to her, how could she possibly know what she wants?"

"I know her, Colin. When her mind is made up there's no going back. She's not a sentimentalist. She's very pragmatic, and she's so stubborn. She's decided that because of the way my family is, being together will never work. Can you blame her, after what they've done? Isn't it ironic? Everyone thinks she's some kind of gold digger, when she's the complete opposite. She broke up with me *because* of my money."

"I told you I liked her from the day we met—she's the real deal, isn't she?" Colin observed.

Nick gazed out the window at the view across the bay. In the morning haze, the Singapore skyline almost resembled Manhattan's. "I loved the life we had together in New York," he said wistfully. "I loved getting up early on Sunday mornings and going to Murray's to pick up bagel sandwiches with her. I loved spending hours wandering around the West Village, going to Washington Square Park to check out the dogs playing in the dog run. But I fucked it all up. I'm the reason her life has become a total mess."

"You're not the reason, Nicky."

"Colin—*I ruined her life.* Because of me, she no longer has a relationship with her mother, and they were like best friends. Because of me, she found out that her father is a convict, that everything she believed about herself has been a lie. None of this would have happened if I hadn't brought her here. As much as I want to believe there's a part of her that still loves me, we're trapped in an impossible situation." Nick sighed.

A sudden rapping noise, consistent as Morse code, echoed through the kitchen. "What's that?" Colin asked, looking around. "I sure hope it's not Kitty and Bernard again."

"No, that's the blue jay," Nick said, getting up from the barstool and heading toward the living room.

"What blue jay?"

"Don't you know? There's this blue jay that visits every morning without fail, and for about ten minutes it will keep flying into the glass wall and pecking at it."

"I guess I'm never up this early." Colin entered the living room and stared out the window, enthralled by the cobalt-blue bird darting through the air, its tiny black beak hitting against the glass pane for a moment before swooping away, only to return seconds later, like a tiny pendulum swinging against the glass.

"I keep wondering if he's just sharpening his beak, or whether he's really trying to come in," Nick said.

"Have you thought of opening the glass wall and seeing if he will fly in?" Colin suggested.

"Er . . . no," Nick said, looking at his friend as if it was the most brilliant thing he had ever heard. Colin picked up the house remote control and pressed a button. The glass panels began to open effortlessly.

The blue jay zipped into the living room at top speed, heading straight for the massive painting of brightly colored dots against the far wall, where it began pecking mercilessly at one of the bright yellow dots. "Oh my God, the Damien Hirst! It's been attracted to those bright dots all along!" Nick cried in amazement.

"Are you sure it's not the world's tiniest art critic?" Colin quipped. "Look at the way it's attacking the painting!"

Nick rushed up to the painting, waving his arms to shoo the bird off.

Colin sprawled onto his George Nakashima bench. "Well, Nicky, I hate to point out the obvious, but here's this tiny bird that's been trying to get through a huge bulletproof glass wall. A totally impossible situation. You tell me it's been here every day pecking away persistently for ten minutes. Well, today the glass wall came down."

"So you're saying I should free the bird? I should just let Rachel go?"

Colin gave Nick an exasperated look. "No, you idiot! If you love Rachel as much as you say you do, then you need to be that blue jay for her."

"Okay, so what would the blue jay do?" Nick asked.

"He would never give up trying. He would take an impossible situation and make *everything* possible."

17

Repulse Bay

•

HONG KONG

The Corsair speedboat collected Astrid from the jetty on the crescent-shaped beach and sped out into the deep emerald waters of Repulse Bay. Rounding the cove, Astrid caught her first glimpse of a majestic three-masted Chinese junk moored in Chung Hom Wan, with Charlie standing on its prow waving at her.

"How magnificent!" Astrid said as the speedboat pulled alongside the junk.

"I thought you could do with a little pick-me-up," Charlie said bashfully, as he helped her climb on deck. He had watched anxiously from the sidelines for the past couple of weeks as Astrid progressed through several stages of grief—going from shock to rage to despair while holed up at his duplex. When it seemed like she had come to a place of acceptance, he invited her for an afternoon sail, thinking that the fresh air would do her some good.

Astrid found her footing and smoothed out her navy capri pants. "Should I take off my shoes?"

"No, no. If you were wearing your usual stilettos, that would be one thing, but you're fine in those flats," Charlie assured her.

"Well, I wouldn't want to ruin any of this amazing woodwork." Astrid admired the gleaming golden teak surfaces around her. "How long have you had this junk?"

"Technically, it belongs to the company, since we're supposed to use it to impress clients, but I've been working on restoring it for the past three years. Weekend project, you know."

"How old is it?"

"She is from the eighteenth century—a pirate junk that smuggled opium in and out of all the tiny surrounding islands of southern Canton, which is precisely the course I've charted for today," Charlie said, as he gave the order to set sail. The massive tarpaulin sails were unfurled, turning from burnt sienna to a bright crimson in the sunlight as the vessel lurched into motion.

"There's a family legend that my great-great-grandfather dealt in opium, you know. In a very big way—that's how part of the family fortune was really made," Astrid said, turning her face into the breeze as the junk began to glide swiftly along.

"Really? Which side of the family?" Charlie raised an eyebrow.

"I shouldn't say. We're not allowed to talk about it, so I'm pretty sure it's true. My great-grandmother was apparently completely addicted and spent all her time horizontal in her private opium den."

"The daughter of the opium king became an addict? That's not a good business strategy."

"Karma, I guess. At some point, we all have to pay the price for our excesses, don't we?" Astrid said ruefully.

Charlie knew where Astrid was going with this. "Don't go beating yourself up again. I've said it a hundred times now—there was nothing you could have done to prevent Michael from doing what he wanted to do."

"Sure there was. I've been driving myself crazy thinking back on all the things I could have done differently. I could have refused when my lawyers insisted that he sign that prenup. I could have stopped going to Paris twice a year and filling up our spare bedroom with couture dresses. I could have given him less-expensive presents—that Vacheron for his thirtieth birthday was a huge mistake."

"You were only being yourself, and to anyone but Michael, it would have been perfectly okay. He should have known what he was getting himself into when he married you. Give yourself a little more credit, Astrid—you might have extravagant tastes, but that's never stopped you from being a good person."

"I don't know how you can say all this about me, when I treated you so horribly, Charlie."

"I never held a grudge against you, you know that. It was your parents I was mad at."

Astrid stared up at the blue sky. A lone seagull seemed to be flying in tandem with the ship, flapping its wings forcefully to keep up with it. "Well, now my parents will surely regret that I *didn't* marry you, once they find out that their precious daughter has been dumped by Michael Teo. Imagine, my parents were once so aghast at the prospect of you becoming their son-in-law. They stuck their noses up at your father's brand-new fortune, made from *computers*, and now your family is one of the most celebrated in Asia. Now the Leongs are going to have to face the shame of having a divorcée in the family."

"There's nothing shameful about it. Divorce is getting so common these days."

"But not in our kind of families, Charlie. You know that. Look at your own situation—your wife won't give you a divorce, your mother won't even hear of it. Think of what it's going to be like in *my* family when they find out the truth. They won't know what hit them."

Two deckhands approached with a wine bucket and a gigantic platter overflowing with fresh longans and lychees. Charlie popped open the bottle of Château d'Yquem and poured Astrid a glass.

"Michael loved Sauternes. It was one of the few things we both loved," Astrid said wistfully as she took a sip from her wineglass. "Of course, I learned to appreciate soccer, and he learned to appreciate four-ply toilet paper."

"But were you really that happy, Astrid?" Charlie asked. "I mean, it seems like you sacrificed so much more than he did. I still can't imagine you living in that little flat, smuggling your shopping into the spare bedroom like an addict."

"I *was* happy, Charlie. And more important, Cassian was happy. Now he's going to have to grow up a child of divorce, ping-ponging between two households. I've failed my son."

"You haven't failed him," Charlie scolded. "The way I see it, Michael was the one who abandoned ship. He just couldn't take the heat. As much of a coward as I think he is, I can also empathize a bit. Your family is pretty intimidating. They sure gave me a run for my money, and they won in the end, didn't they?"

"Well, you weren't the one who gave in. You stood up to my family and never let them get to you. I was the one who caved," Astrid said, expertly peeling a longan and popping the pearly fruit into her mouth.

"Still, it's far easier for a beautiful woman from an ordinary background to marry into a family like yours than for a man who doesn't come from any wealth or lineage. And Michael had the added disadvantage of being good-looking—the men in your family were probably jealous of him."

Astrid laughed. "Well, I thought he was up for the challenge. When I first met Michael, he didn't seem to care one bit about my money or my family. But in the end I was wrong. He did care. He cared too much." Astrid's voice cracked, and Charlie stretched out his arms to comfort her. Tears streamed down her face quietly, turning quickly into racking sobs as she leaned into his shoulder.

"I'm sorry, I'm sorry," she kept saying, embarrassed by her uncontrolled display. "I don't know why, but I just can't stop crying."

"Astrid, it's *me*. You don't have to keep your emotions in check around me. You've thrown vases and goldfish bowls at me, remember?" Charlie said, trying to lighten the mood. Astrid smiled fleetingly as the tears continued to flow. Charlie felt helpless and at the same time frustrated by the absurdity of the situation. His smoking-hot ex-fiancée was on a romantic Chinese junk with him, literally crying on his shoulder about another man. This was just his damn luck.

"You really love him, don't you?" Charlie said softly.

"I do. Of course I do," Astrid sobbed.

For a few hours, they sat quietly side by side, soaking in the sun and the salty spray as the junk floated along the calm waters of the South China Sea. They sailed past Lantau Island, Charlie bowing respectfully to the giant Buddha at its peak, and skirted past tiny picturesque islands like Aizhou and Sanmen, with their rugged outcroppings and hidden inlets.

All the while, Charlie's mind kept churning nonstop. He had coerced Astrid into coming on this afternoon sail because he wanted to make a confession. He wanted to tell her that he had never stopped loving her, not for one moment, and that his marriage one year after their breakup had been nothing but a mindless rebound. He had never truly loved Isabel, and their marriage was doomed from the start because of it. There were so many things Charlie wanted her to know, but he knew it was too late to tell them.

At least she had loved him once. At least he had four good years with the girl he had loved since he was fifteen, since the night he had watched her sing "Pass It On" on the beach during a church youth group outing. (His family had been Taoists, but his mother had forced all of them to attend First Methodist so they could mix with a ritzier crowd.) He could still remember the way the flickering bonfire made her long wavy hair shimmer in the most exquisite reds and golds, how her entire being glowed like Botticelli's *Venus* as she so sweetly sang:

> *It only takes a spark,*
> *to get the fire going.*
> *And soon all those around,*
> *can warm up in its glowing.*
> *That's how it is with God's love,*
> *once you've experienced it.*
> *You want to sing,*
> *it's fresh like spring,*
> *you want to Pass It On.*

"Can I make a suggestion, Astrid?" Charlie said as the junk made its way back to Repulse Bay to drop her off.

"What?" Astrid asked sleepily.

"When you get home tomorrow, do nothing. Just go back to your normal life. Don't make any announcements, and don't grant Michael a quick divorce."

"Why not?"

"I have a feeling Michael could have a change of heart."

"What makes you think that will happen?"

"Well, I'm a guy, and I know how guys think. At this point, Michael's played all his cards, he's gotten a huge load off his chest. There's something really cathartic about that, about owning up to your truth. Now, if you let him have some time to himself, I think you'll find that he might be receptive to a reconciliation a few months down the line."

Astrid was dubious. "Really? But he was so adamant about wanting a divorce."

"Think about it—Michael's deluded himself into thinking he's been trapped in an impossible marriage for the past five years. But a funny thing happens when men truly get a taste of freedom, especially when they're accustomed to married life. They begin to crave that domestic bliss again. They want to re-create it. Look, he told you the sex was still great. He told you he didn't blame you, aside from blowing too much money on clothes. My instinct tells me that if you just let him be, he will come back."

"Well, it's worth a try, isn't it?" Astrid said hopefully.

"It is. But you have to promise me two things: first, you need to live your life the way you want to, instead of how you think Michael would want you to. Move into one of your favorite houses, dress however it pleases you. I really feel that what ate into Michael was the way you spent all your time tiptoeing around him, trying to be someone you weren't. Your overcompensating for him only increased his feelings of inadequacy."

"Okay," Astrid said, trying to soak it all in.

"Second, promise me you won't grant him a divorce for at least one year, no matter how much he begs for it. Just stall him. Once you sign the papers, you lose the chance of him ever coming back," Charlie said.

"I promise."

As soon as Astrid had disembarked from the junk at Repulse Bay, Charlie made a phone call to Aaron Shek, the chief financial officer of Wu Microsystems.

"Aaron, how's our share price doing today?"

"We're up two percent."

"Great, great. Aaron, I want you to do me a special favor . . . I want you to look up a small digital firm based in Singapore called Cloud Nine Solutions."

"Cloud Nine . . ." Aaron began, keying the name into his computer. "Headquartered in Jurong?"

"Yes, that's the one. Aaron, I want you to acquire the company tomorrow. Start low, but I want you to end up offering at least fifteen million for it. Actually, how many partners are there?"

"I see two registered partners. Michael Teo and Adrian Balakrishnan."

"Okay, bid thirty million."

"Charlie, you can't be serious? The book value on that company is only—"

"No, I'm dead serious," Charlie cut in. "Start a fake bidding war between some of our subsidiaries if you have to. Now listen carefully. After the deal is done, I want you to vest Michael Teo, the founding partner, with class-A stock options, then I want you to bundle it with that Cupertino start-up we acquired last month and the software developer in Zhongguancun. Then, I want us to do an IPO on the Shanghai Stock Exchange next month."

"*Next month?*"

"Yes, it has to happen very quickly. Put the word out on the street, let your contacts at Bloomberg TV know about it, hell, drop a hint to Henry Blodget if you think it will help drive up the share price. But at the end of the day I want those class-A stock options to be worth *at least* $250 million. Keep it off the books, and set up a shell corporation in Liechtenstein if you have to. Just make sure there are no links back to me. Never, ever."

"Okay, you got it." Aaron was used to his boss's idiosyncratic requests.

"Thank you, Aaron. See you at CAA on Sunday with the kids."

The eighteenth-century Chinese junk pulled into Aberdeen Harbour just as the first evening lights began to turn on in the dense cityscape hugging the southern shore of Hong Kong Island. Charlie let out a deep sigh. If he didn't have a chance of getting Astrid back, he at least wanted to try to help her. He wanted her to find love again with her husband. He wanted to see the joy return to Astrid's face, that glow he had witnessed all those years ago at the bonfire on the beach. He wanted to pass it on.

18

Villa d'Oro

Peik Lin walked down the stairs carrying a Bottega Veneta tote. Behind her were two Indonesian maids bearing a pair of Goyard suitcases and a carry-on valise.

"You do realize that we're going to be there for one night? You look like you've packed enough for a monthlong safari," Rachel said incredulously.

"Oh please, a girl's gotta have options," Peik Lin said, tossing her hair comically.

They were about to embark on the trip to Shenzhen, where Rachel had arranged to meet her father, an inmate at Dongguan Prison. She had initially been reluctant to set foot on another private jet, but Peik Lin had prevailed upon her.

"Trust me, Rachel. We can do this the easy way or the hard way," Peik Lin said. "The hard way is to fly for four and a half hours on some third-rate airline and land in the clusterfuck that is Shenzhen Bao'an International Airport, where we can wait in a customs line for the rest of the day with thirty thousand of your closest friends—the vast majority of whom have never heard of antiperspirant and won't share the same concept of personal space as you do. Or, we can call up NetJets right now and fly on leather seats made from cows that have never seen barbed wire and drink Veuve Clicquot for the two and a half hours it takes to fly to Shenzhen, where upon landing, a young, fit customs officer will climb aboard our plane, stamp our passports, flirt with you because you're so pretty, and send us on our merry way. You know, flying private isn't always about showing off. Sometimes it can actually be for convenience and ease. But I'll defer to you. If you *really* want to go the chicken-bus route, I'm game."

This morning, however, with Rachel looking rather ashen-faced, Peik Lin began to wonder if the trip was a good idea so soon.

"You didn't get much sleep last night, did you?" Peik Lin observed.

"I didn't realize how much I'd miss having Nick next to me at night," Rachel said softly.

"His gorgeous, rock-hard body, you mean?" Peik Lin added with a wink. "Well, I'm sure he'd be happy to come over and climb back into bed with you in a nanosecond."

"No, no, that's not going to happen. I know it's over. It has to be," Rachel declared, her eyes moistening around the edges.

Peik Lin opened her mouth to say something, but then she stopped herself.

Rachel looked at her intently. "Just say it!"

Peik Lin put her tote bag down and perched on the velvet brocade settee in the entrance foyer. "I just think you need to give yourself some time before you make any final decisions about Nick. I mean, you're going through so much right now."

"It sounds like you're on his side," Rachel said.

"Rachel—what the fuck? I'm on *your* side! I want to see you happy, that's all."

Rachel said nothing for a moment. She sat down on the staircase and ran her fingers along the cold smooth marble. "I want to be happy, but every time I think about Nick, I just go right back to the most traumatic moment of my life."

Trump, the fattest of the three Pekingese, waddled into the foyer. Rachel picked up the dog and placed him on her lap. "I guess that's why I feel like I need to meet my father. I remember watching some talk show one night where adopted children finally got reunited with their birth parents. Every single one of these kids—all of them were adults at this point—talked about how they felt after meeting their birth parents. Even if they didn't get along, even if their parents were nothing like what they expected, all of them somehow felt more whole after the experience."

"Well, in less than four hours, you'll be sitting face-to-face with your father," Peik Lin said.

Rachel's face clouded over. "You know, I'm dreading the drive up to that place. *Dongguan Prison*. Even the name sounds ominous."

"I don't think they want it to sound like it's Canyon Ranch."

"It's supposed to be medium security, so I wonder if we'll actually be in the same room together, or whether I'll have to talk to him behind bars," Rachel said.

"Are you sure you want to do this? We really don't have to do this today, you know. I can just cancel the flight. It's not like your father's going anywhere," Peik Lin said.

"No, I want to go. I want to get this over with," Rachel said definitively. She ruffled the dog's golden fur for a moment and stood up, smoothing out her skirt.

They made their way to the front door, where the metallic-gold BMW, already loaded with their luggage, awaited. Rachel and Peik Lin got into the back, and the chauffeur pulled down the sloping driveway toward the gilded electronic gates of Villa d'Oro. Just as the gates were opening, an SUV suddenly pulled up in front of them.

"Who's the asshole blocking our way?" Peik Lin snapped.

Rachel looked out the windshield and saw a silver Land Rover with tinted windows. "Wait a minute . . ." she began, thinking she recognized the car. The driver's door opened, and Nick jumped out. Rachel sighed, wondering what kind of stunt he was trying to pull now. Was he going to insist on coming along to Shenzhen with them?

Nick approached the car and rapped on the back window.

Rachel lowered the window slightly. "Nick, we have a plane to catch," she said in frustration. "I appreciate that you want to help, but I really don't want you to go to China."

"I'm not going to China, Rachel. I'm bringing China to you," Nick said, flashing a smile.

"Whaaaat?" Rachel said, glancing at the Land Rover, half expecting a man in an orange jumpsuit and shackles to emerge. Instead, the passenger door opened and a woman in a pale orange trench-coat dress with pixie-cut black hair stepped out. It was her mother.

Rachel flung open her car door and jumped out hastily. "What are you doing here? When did you arrive?" she said defensively in Mandarin to her mother.

"I just landed. Nick told me what happened. I told him we had to stop you from going to China, but he said he wasn't going to get involved anymore. So I said I *had* to reach you before you tried to meet your father, and Nick chartered a private plane for me," Kerry explained.

"I wish he hadn't." Rachel moaned in dismay. *These rich people and their friggin' planes!*

"I'm glad he did. Nick has been so wonderful!" Kerry exclaimed.

"Great—why don't you throw him a parade or take him out for oysters? I'm on my way to Shenzhen right now. I need to meet my father."

"Please don't go!" Kerry tried to grab hold of Rachel's arm, but Rachel jerked back defensively.

"Because of you, I've had to wait twenty-nine years to meet my father. I'm not waiting another second!" Rachel shouted.

"Daughter, I know you didn't want to see me, but I needed to tell you this myself: *Zhou Fang Min is not your father.*"

"I'm not listening to you anymore, Mom. I'm tired of all the lies. I've read the articles about my kidnapping, and Mr. Goh's Chinese lawyers have already been in touch with my father. He's very eager to meet me." Rachel was adamant.

Kerry looked pleadingly into her daughter's eyes. "Please believe me—you don't want to meet him. Your father is not the man in Dongguan Prison. Your father is someone else, someone I truly loved."

"Oh great, now you're telling me I'm the *illegitimate daughter* of some other guy?" Rachel could feel the torrent of blood rushing into her head, and she felt as if she was back in that horrific drawing room in Cameron Highlands. Just when things were beginning to make sense to her, everything was turned upside down again. Rachel turned to Peik Lin and gave her a dazed look. "Could you ask your driver to step on his gas pedal and just run me over right now? Tell him to make it quick."

19

The Star Trek House

Daisy Foo phoned Eleanor in a panic, telling her to come quickly, but Eleanor still could not believe her eyes when she entered the living room of Carol Tai's mansion, the one everyone called the "Star Trek House." Sister Gracie, the Taiwan-born Houston-based Pentecostal preacher who had just flown in at Carol's request, circled around the lavishly appointed space as if in a trance, smashing up all the antique Chinese furniture and porcelain, while Carol and her husband sat in the middle of the room on the woven silk sofa, watching the destruction in a daze as two disciples of Sister Gracie's prayed over them. Following behind the diminutive preacher with tightly permed gray hair was a full brigade of servants, some helping to break the objects she pointed at with her rosewood walking stick, others frantically sweeping up all the debris and putting it into giant black garbage bags.

"False idols! Satanic objects! Leave this house of peace," Sister Gracie screamed, her voice echoing throughout the cavernous room. Priceless Ming vases were smashed, Qing dynasty scrolls were torn up, and gold-dipped Buddhas were toppled to the ground as Sister Gracie decreed every object bearing the depiction of an animal or a face to be satanic. Owls were satanic. Frogs were satanic. Grasshoppers were satanic. Lotus flowers, though not an animal and faceless, were also deemed satanic because of their association with Buddhist iconography. But there was none more evil than the devilish dragon.

"Do you know why tragedy has befallen this house? Do you know why your firstborn son, Bernard, has defied your wishes and run off to Vegas to marry some pregnant soap-opera harlot who pretends to be from Taiwan? It is because of these idols! Just look at the intricate lapis lazuli dragon on this imperial folding screen! Its evil ruby eyes have transfixed your son. You have surrounded him with symbols of sin every day of his life. What do you expect him to do but sin?"

"What utter nonsense is she talking? Bernard hasn't lived in this house for years," Lorena Lim whispered. But Carol was looking at Sister Gracie as if she were receiving a message from Jesus Christ himself, and she continued to allow the wholesale destruction of antiquities that would have made any museum curator weep.

"It's been like this for hours. They started in the *dato's* study," Daisy whispered. Eleanor jumped a little as Sister Gracie tipped over a Qianlong funerary urn next to her. "Those snakes on that urn! Those snakes are descended from the one in the Garden of Eden," Sister Gracie screeched.

"*Alamak*, Elle, Lorena, come help me rescue some things from Carol's bedroom before Sister Gracie gets in there. If she sees that ivory sculpture of Quan Yin, the goddess of mercy, she's going to start convulsing! That Quan Yin has been around since the twelfth century, but it will have no hope surviving this one," Daisy said furtively. The three of them backed slowly away from the living room and made a beeline for Carol's bedroom.

The ladies rushed about wrapping up any decorative objects that could possibly be at risk in towels and pillowcases and shoving them into their handbags and random shopping bags.

"Those jade parrots! Grab those jade parrots!" Daisy instructed.

"Is the water buffalo considered satanic?" Lorena wondered, holding up a delicate horn carving.

"Aiyah, don't stand there using eye power! Take everything! Put it all in your handbag! We can return everything to Carol once she comes to her senses," Daisy barked.

"I wish I'd used my Birkin and not my Kelly today," Lorena lamented as she tried to fit the water buffalo into her stiff leather handbag.

"Okay, my driver is parked just outside the kitchen door. Give me the first shopping bags and I will run them over to my car," Eleanor said. As she grabbed the first two shopping bags from Daisy, a maid entered Carol's bedroom.

Eleanor knew she had to get past the maid with her suspiciously bulging shopping bags. "Girlie, fetch me a glass of iced tea with lemon," she said in her most imperious tone.

"*Alamak*, Elle, it's me—Nadine!" Eleanor almost dropped her shopping bags in shock. Nadine was utterly unrecognizable. She was dressed in yoga sweats, and gone was the thick mask of makeup, the over-teased hair, and the ostentatious jewelry.

"Oh my God, Nadine, what happened to you? I thought you were one of the maids!" Eleanor exclaimed.

"Nadine, I love your new look! Aiyah, now I can see how Francesca used to look just like you, before her cheek implants," Daisy gushed.

Nadine smiled bleakly, plopping down on Carol's *Huanghuali* bed. "My father-in-law woke up from his coma, as you know. We were all so happy, and when they discharged him from the hospital, we drove him home and had a surprise party waiting for him. All the Shaws were there. But we forgot the old man had never been to the new house—we bought Leedon Road after he had gone into a coma. Old man threw a fit when he realized this was our new house. He said, 'Wah, who do you think you are, living in such a big mansion with so many cars and servants?' Then when he got inside and saw Francesca all dressed up, he started to choke. He started screaming that she looked like a prostitute from Geylang.* Aiyah, she was wearing haute couture for her grandpa! Is it her fault that hemlines are so short this season? The very next morning, he made his lawyers take back control of Shaw Foods. He kicked my poor Ronnie off the board, and he froze all the bank accounts, everything. Now he has ordered us to return every penny we've spent in the last six years, or he's threatening to disinherit all of us and give his whole fortune to the Shaw Foundation!"

"My goodness, Nadine. How are you managing?" Lorena asked, gravely concerned. Nadine was one of L'Orient Jewelry's biggest clients, and her sudden reversal of fortune would surely affect the quarterly numbers.

---

* Singapore's red-light district (sadly, not as picturesque as Amsterdam's).

"Well, you see my new look. For now, we are all trying to act *kwai kwai*. I mean, how many more years can that old man live? He'll have another stroke in no time. I'll be fine—I spent years living in that cramped shop house with him, remember? We put Leedon Road on the market, but the problem is Francesca. She doesn't want to move back to a small house again. It's so *malu* for her. She's really suffering. Francesca was always Grandpa's favorite, and now he's taken away her monthly allowance. How is she supposed to live on her lawyer's salary? Wandi Meggaharto and Parker Yeo have dropped her, and she's had to resign from every charitable board. She just can't afford the clothes for it anymore. She blames Ronnie and me. She comes into our bedroom every night and screams and screams at us. She thinks we should have pulled the plug on the old man when we had the chance. Can you imagine? I never realized my own daughter could ever say such a thing!"

"I'm sorry to say this, Nadine, but this is what happens when you try to give your children everything," Daisy sagely offered. "Look at what's happened with Bernard. From the time he was a small boy I already knew he was a disaster waiting to happen. The *dato'* spoiled him rotten, and never ever said no to him. And he thought he was being so clever, giving the boy that huge trust fund when he turned eighteen. Now look what's happened. They're getting Kitty Pong as a daughter-in-law. No amount of antique-smashing is going to change that."

Lorena giggled. "Poor Carol—she's always been such a good Christian, but now she has to deal with having a satanic Kitty in her life!" The ladies all laughed.

"Well, at least we succeeded in stopping that Rachel Chu from getting at Nicky," Nadine commented.

Eleanor shook her head sadly. "What's the use? My Nicky has stopped talking to me. I don't have a clue where he is—he's even broken off contact with his grandmother. I tried calling Astrid to find him, but she's missing too. *Sum toong, ah.* You love your children so much, you do everything to try to protect them, and they don't even appreciate it."

"Well, even if he doesn't want to see you right now, at least you succeeded in saving him from that girl," Lorena said comfortingly.

"Yes, but Nicky doesn't realize how much damage he's done to his relationship with his grandmother. I trained him to never, ever offend her, but he hurt her terribly in Cameron Highlands. You should have seen the old lady—she didn't speak once all the way back to Singapore. And take it from me, that woman never forgives. Now all the sacrifices I have made will have been for nothing," Eleanor said sadly, her voice cracking a little.

"What do you mean?" Nadine asked. "What sort of sacrifices did you make for Nicky?"

Eleanor sighed. "Aiyah, Nadine, my whole life has been spent protecting him within my husband's family, and positioning him to be the favorite grandson. I know my mother-in-law never truly approved of me, so I even got out of the way. I moved out of Tyersall Park so there wouldn't be two competing Mrs. Youngs. I always let her come first in Nicky's life, and because of this he's been closer to her. But I accepted that. It was for his own good. He deserves to be the heir to her fortune, the heir to Tyersall Park, but he no longer seems to care. He would rather be a bloody history professor. Hiyah, I always knew sending him to England would be a mistake. Why do we Chinese never learn? Every time we get mixed up with the West, everything falls apart."

Just then, Sister Gracie came walking down the lawn toward the bedroom pavilion with Carol and her husband trailing behind. She called out loudly, "Now, what demons lie in wait here? Exodus 20:3–6 says, 'You shall have no other gods before me. You shall not make for yourself a carved image, or any likeness of anything that is in heaven above, or that is in the earth beneath, or that is in the water under the earth. You shall not bow down to them or serve them, for I the Lord your God am a jealous God.'"

Daisy glanced at the other ladies and said urgently, "Everyone grab a shopping bag and run for the doors. Don't look at them, just keep moving!"

20

Villa d'Oro

SINGAPORE

Peik Lin sequestered Rachel and her mother in the library, shutting the boiserie doors behind her firmly. She then padded out to the terrace bar overlooking the pool and began mixing margaritas for herself and Nick. "I think we both deserve about a dozen of these, don't we?" she said, handing him a tall frosty glass.

Surrounded by bookshelves filled with gold-tooled leather volumes, Rachel perched on the cushioned bay-window seat and stared out at the rose garden angrily. All she wanted to do was get on that plane to China, but once again Nick had screwed things up. Kerry grabbed one of the dark green leather chairs by the reading desk and turned it around so she could sit facing her daughter. Even though Rachel wouldn't look at her, she took a deep breath and began the story she had flown halfway around the world to tell.

"Daughter, I have never told this story to anyone, and it is something I always intended to spare you from. I hope you will not judge me, and that you will listen with an open mind, an open heart.

"When I was seventeen, I fell in love with a man who was six years older. Yes, it was Zhou Fang Min. His family was from Xiamen, in Fujian Province. He was one of those 'Red Princelings' and he came from a rich family—at least, for that time period, they were considered rich. His father was the general manager of a state-owned construction company. He was well placed in the Communist Party, and one of his older brothers was a high-level party chief in Guang-dong Province. So the Zhous received the concession to build the new school in our village, and Fang Min was sent to oversee the construction. It was his summer job. Back then, I was in my final year of secondary school and working nights as a waitress in the only bar in our village, so that is how I met him. Now, up till this time I had spent my entire life in this small village outside of Zhuhai. I had never even left our province, so you can only imagine what it was like when this twenty-three-year-old man with slick black hair came into the bar, dressed in Western-style clothes—I remember his shirts were all Sergio Tacchini or Fred Perry, and he wore a gold Rolex. What's more, Fang Min had an expensive motorbike and chain-smoked Kent cigarettes smuggled into the country by one of his cousins, and he would brag to me about his family's big house and big Japanese car, and tell me tales of his holidays in Shanghai, Beijing, and Xi'an. I had never met a more handsome or sophisti-cated man, and I fell head over heels in love. Of course, back then, I had very long hair and fair skin, so Fang Min took an interest in me.

"Now, when my parents heard that this rich man was coming to the bar every night, taking an interest in me, they tried to put a stop to it. My parents were not like other parents—they did not care that he came from a rich family; they wanted me to concentrate on my studies so I could qualify for university. It was so hard to get into university in those days, especially if you were a girl, and that was my parents' sole dream—to have a child that got into university. But after so many years of being the perfect daughter and doing nothing but studying, I rebelled. Fang Min started taking me on his motorcycle in secret to Guangzhou, the biggest city in the province, and there I discovered a whole other world. I had no idea there was an entire class of people like Fang Min—the children of other high-ranking Communist Party members, who got to dine in special restaurants and shop in special stores. Fang Min treated me to expensive meals and expensive clothes. I became intoxicated by this world, and my parents noticed that, bit by bit, I was changing. When they found out he had taken me to Guangzhou, they forbid me to see him, which of course made me want to be with him even more. It was like Romeo and Juliet. I would sneak out of our flat late at night to meet him, get caught and punished, but a few days later I would do it again.

"Then, a few months later, when the construction project was finished and Fang Min was heading back to Xiamen, we made plans for me to run away with him. That's why I never finished my studies. I ran away to Xiamen, and we quickly got married. My parents were devastated, but I thought all my dreams had come true. Here I was living in a big house with his rich and important parents, getting to ride in a big Nissan sedan that had white curtains on the back windows. See, Rachel, you are not the only one who has experience dating a rich boy. But my dream quickly turned sour. I soon found out how awful his family was. His mother was one of these extremely traditional women, and she was a northerner, from Henan. So she was very snobbish, and she never let me forget that I was just a village girl who got very, very lucky because of my looks. At the same time, I was expected to perform a million and one daughter-in-law duties, like preparing tea for her every morning, reading the newspapers to her, and rubbing her shoulders and feet after dinner every night. I had gone from being a student to being a servant. Then the pressure started for me to get pregnant, but I was having trouble conceiving. So it made my mother-in-law very upset—she wanted a grandchild desperately. What use was a daughter-in-law if you didn't have a grandchild? Fang Min's parents became very displeased that I wasn't getting pregnant, and we started having big fights.

"I don't know how I managed it, but I convinced Fang Min to move us to our own apartment. And that's when things turned into a living nightmare. Without his parents under the same roof to check on him, my husband suddenly lost interest in me. He went out drinking and gambling every night and started seeing other women. It was as if he were still single, and he would come home late at night, completely drunk, and sometimes he wanted to have sex, but other times he just wanted to beat me up. It excited him. Then he would bring home other women to have sex in our bed, and he forced me to be with them. It was terrible."

Rachel shook her head in dismay, making eye contact with her mother for the first time. "I don't understand how you put up with that."

"Hiyah, I was only eighteen! I was so naïve and afraid of my worldly husband, and most of all I was too humiliated to tell my parents what a mistake I'd made. After all, I had run away and abandoned them in order to marry this rich boy, so I had to make the best of it. Now, right underneath our apartment lived this family with one son. His name was Kao Wei, and he was a year younger than me. My bedroom happened to be right over his, so he could hear everything that was happening every night. One night, Fang Min came home in a rage. I'm not sure what made him so angry on this night—maybe he lost some money gambling, maybe one of his girlfriends got mad at him. Anyway, he decided to take it out on me. He began to break all the furniture in the apartment, and when he broke a chair and started coming after me with the jagged chair leg, I fled the apartment. I was so afraid that in his drunken rage he would accidentally kill me. Kao Wei heard me leaving, so as I ran down the stairs, he opened his door and pulled me into his flat, while Fang Min ran outside of the building and began screaming in the street. That is how Kao Wei and I met.

"For the next few months, Kao Wei would comfort me after every bad fight and even help me devise tactics to avoid my husband. I would buy sleeping pills, crush them up, and put them into his wine so that he would fall asleep before he could get violent. I would invite his friends over for dinner and make them stay as late as possible, until he passed out drunk. Kao Wei even put a stronger lock on the toilet door so that it would be harder for Fang Min to break through. Slowly but surely, Kao Wei and I fell in love. He was my only friend in the building, in the whole city, actually. And yes, we started to have an affair. But then one day we were almost caught, and I forced myself to end it, for Kao Wei's sake, because I feared Fang Min would kill him if he ever found out. A few weeks later, I realized I was pregnant with you, and I knew Kao Wei was the father."

"Wait a minute. How did you know for sure he was the father?" Rachel asked, uncrossing her arms and leaning back against the window.

"Trust me, Rachel, I just knew."

"But how? This was back before DNA testing."

Kerry shifted in her chair awkwardly, searching for the right words to explain. "One of the reasons I had such a hard time getting pregnant was because Fang Min had peculiar habits, Rachel. Because of his drinking he had trouble getting erect, and when he *was* excited, he only liked to have a certain type of sex, and I knew I could not get pregnant that way."

"Oh . . . *oooh*," Rachel said, turning crimson when she realized what her mother meant.

"Anyway, you look so much like Kao Wei, there is no mistaking that he is your father. Kao Wei had beautiful, angular features like you do. And you have his refined lips."

"So if you were in love with Kao Wei, why didn't you just divorce Fang Min and marry Kao Wei? Why did you have to resort to kidnapping?" Rachel was leaning forward now with her chin in her hands, completely transfixed by her mother's harrowing tale.

"Let me finish the story, Rachel, and then you will understand. So here I was, eighteen years old, married to this violent drunkard, and pregnant with another man's child. I was so frightened that Fang Min would somehow realize the baby wasn't his, and he would kill Kao Wei and me, so I tried to hide my pregnancy for as long as possible. But my old-fashioned mother-in-law recognized all the telltale signs, and it was she who declared to me a few weeks later that she thought I looked pregnant. At first, I was terrified, but you know what? The most unexpected thing happened. My in-laws were overjoyed that at last they were having their first grandchild. My evil mother-in-law suddenly transformed into the most caring person you could possibly imagine. She insisted that I move back into the big house so that the servants could look after me properly. I felt so relieved, like I had been rescued from hell. Even though I didn't really need to, she forced me to stay in bed most of the time and made me drink these traditional brews all day long to boost the health of the baby. I had to take three types of ginseng every day, and eat young chicken in broth. I'm convinced this is why you were such a healthy baby, Rachel—you never got sick like other babies. No ear infections, no high fevers, nothing. At that time, there wasn't a sonogram machine in Xiamen yet, so my mother-in-law invited a famous fortune-teller over, who divined that I was going to have a boy, and that the boy was going to grow up to become a great politician. This made my in-laws even more excited. They hired a special nursemaid to take care of me, a girl who had natural double eyelids and big eyes, because my mother-in-law believed that if I stared at this girl all day, my child would come out with double eyelids and big eyes. That's what all the mothers in China wanted then—children with big, Western-style eyes. They painted a room bright blue and filled it up with baby furniture and all these boy clothes and toys. There were airplanes and train sets and toy soldiers—I had never seen so many toys in all my life.

"One night, my water broke and I went into labor. They rushed me to the hospital, and you were born a few hours later. It was an easy labor—I've always told you that—and at first I was worried they would see that you looked nothing like their son, but that turned out to be the least of my worries. You were a girl, and my in-laws were extremely shocked. They were outraged at the fortune-teller, but they were more outraged at me. I had failed them. I had failed to do my duty. Fang Min was also terribly upset, and if I hadn't been living with my in-laws, I'm sure he would have beaten me half to death. Now, because of China's one-child policy, all couples were banned from having a second child. By law, I could not have another, but my in-laws were desperate for a boy, a male heir who could carry on the family name. If we had lived in the countryside, they might have just abandoned or drowned the baby girl—don't look so shocked, Rachel, it happened all the time—but we were living in Xiamen and the Zhous were an important local family. People already knew that a baby girl had been born, and it would have been disgraceful for them to reject you. However, there was one loophole to the one-child rule: if your baby had a handicap, you were allowed to have another.

"I didn't know this, but even before I had come home from the hospital, my evil in-laws were already hatching a plan. My mother-in-law decided that the best thing to do was to pour acid in your eye—"

"WHAAAT?" Rachel shrieked.

Kerry swallowed hard, before continuing. "Yes, they wanted to blind you in one eye, and if they did this while you were a newborn, the cause of the blinding could look like it was just a birth defect."

"My God!" Rachel clasped her hand to her mouth in horror.

"So she began to devise a scheme with some of the older servants, who were very loyal to her, but the special maid they had hired to take care of me while I was pregnant did not share the same unwavering loyalty. We had become friends, and when she found out about their plan, she told me about it on the very day I arrived home from the hospital with you. I was so shocked—I could not believe anyone could think of harming you in this way, much less your own grandparents! I was beside myself with rage and still weak from childbirth, but I was determined that nobody was going to blind you, nobody was going to hurt you. You were my beautiful baby girl, the baby from the man who rescued me. The man I truly loved.

"So a couple of days later, in the middle of lunch, I excused myself to go to the toilet. I walked down the hallway toward the downstairs toilet, which was across from the servants' quarters, where you were being kept in a cot while the family ate. The servants were all having their lunch in the kitchen, so I went into their room, scooped you into my arms, and walked straight out the back door. I kept walking until I came to the bus stop, and I got on the next bus. I didn't know any of the bus routes or anything—I just wanted to get as far away from the Zhou house as possible. When I thought I was far enough, I got off the bus and found a phone to call Kao Wei. I told him I had just had a baby and was running away from my husband, and he came to the rescue immediately. He hired a taxi—in those days it was very expensive to hire one, but somehow he managed—and came to pick me up.

"All that time, he was already devising a plan to get me out of Xiamen. He knew that my in-laws would have alerted the police as soon as they discovered that the baby was missing, and police would be searching for a woman and her baby. So he insisted on coming with me so that we could pretend to be a couple. We bought two tickets on the six o'clock train, which was the busiest train, and we sat in the most crowded car, trying to blend in with all the other families. Thank goodness no police ever came on board the train. Kao Wei took me all the way to my home village in Guangdong Province, and made sure I was safely with my parents before he left. That was the kind of man he was. I will always be glad that your real father was the one who rescued us, and that he at least had the chance to spend a few days with you."

"But didn't he mind leaving me?" Rachel asked, her eyes welling up with tears.

"He didn't know you were his, Rachel."

Rachel looked at her mother in shock. "Why didn't you tell him?"

Kerry sighed. "Kao Wei was already far too mixed up in my problems—the problems of another man's wife. I didn't want to burden him with the knowledge that you were his child. I knew he was the type of man who would have wanted to do the honorable thing, that he would have wanted to take care of us somehow. But he had a bright future ahead of him. He was very smart and was doing well at school in science. I knew he would get into university, and I didn't want to ruin his future."

"You don't think he suspected he was my father?"

"I don't think so. He was eighteen, remember, and I think at that age, fatherhood is the last thing on a boy's mind. And besides, I was now a criminal, a kidnapper. So Kao Wei was worrying about us getting caught more than anything else. My awful husband and my in-laws used the situation to blame me for everything and plaster my name in all the newspapers. I don't think they really cared about you—they were glad the baby girl was out of their lives—but they wanted to punish me. Usually the police didn't get involved in family matters like this, but that politician uncle of Fang Min's put pressure on the police, and they came looking for me in my parents' village."

"What happened then?"

"Well, they put my poor mother and father under house arrest and subjected them to weeks of interrogation. Meanwhile, I was already in hiding. Your grandparents sent me to a distant cousin of theirs in Shenzhen, a Chu, and through her, the opportunity came up for me to bring you to America. A Chu cousin in California had heard about my situation—your uncle Walt—and he offered to fund our way to America. He was the one who sponsored us, and that is how I came to change your name and my name to Chu."

"What happened to your parents? My real grandparents? Are they still in Guangdong?" Rachel asked nervously, not sure she wanted to know the answer.

"No, they both died rather young—in their early sixties. The Zhou family used their influence to destroy your grandfather's career, and it destroyed his health, from what I know. I was never able to see them, because I never dared to return to China or to try to make contact with them. If you had flown to China this morning to meet Zhou Fang Min, I would not have dared to follow you. That's why when Nick found out about your China plans and told me, I flew straight to Singapore."

"And what happened to Kao Wei?"

Kerry's face clouded over. "I have no idea what happened to Kao Wei. For the first few years, I would send him letters and postcards from America as often as possible, from every town and city we lived in. I always used a secret name we had devised together, but I never got a single response. I don't know if my letters ever got to him."

"Aren't you curious to find him?" Rachel asked, her voice cracking with emotion.

"I've tried my hardest not to look back, daughter. When I got on that plane with you to come to America, I knew I had to leave my past behind."

Rachel turned to face the window, her chest heaving involuntarily. Kerry got up from her chair and walked toward Rachel slowly. She reached out to put her hand on her daughter's shoulder, but before she could, Rachel leaped up and embraced her mother. "Oh Mom," Rachel cried, "I'm so sorry. So sorry for everything . . . for all the terrible things I said to you on the phone."

"I know, Rachel."

"I never knew . . . I never could have imagined what you were forced to go through."

Kerry looked at her daughter affectionately, tears running down her cheeks. "I'm sorry I never told you the truth. I wanted so much never to burden you with my mistakes."

"Oh Mom," Rachel sobbed, clinging to her mother ever more tightly.

———

The sun was setting over Bukit Timah by the time Rachel walked out into the garden, arm in arm with her mother. Heading slowly toward the poolside bar, they made a detour the long way around the pool so that Kerry could admire all of the golden statues.

"It looks like mother and daughter have reconciled, don't you think?" Peik Lin said to Nick.

"Sure looks like it. I don't see any blood or torn clothing."

"There better not be. That's Lanvin Rachel's wearing. Cost me about seven K."

"Well, I'm glad I'm not the only one who's guilty of being extravagant with her. She can't blame it all on me anymore," Nick said.

"Let me share a secret with you, Nick. As much as a girl might protest, you can never go wrong buying her a designer dress or a killer pair of shoes."

"I'll try to remember that." Nick smiled. "Well, I think I'd better be off."

"Oh stop it, Nick. I'm sure Rachel would want to see you. And aren't you dying to know what they've been talking about all this time?"

Rachel and her mother approached the bar. "Peik Lin, you look so cute standing there behind the bar! Can you make me a Singapore Sling?" Kerry asked.

Peik Lin gave a slightly embarrassed smile. "Um, I don't know how to make that—I've never actually had one."

"What? Isn't it the most popular drink here?" Kerry said in surprise.

"Well, I guess if you're a tourist."

"I *am* a tourist!"

"Well, then, Mrs. Chu, why don't you let me take you out for a Singapore Sling?"

"Okay, why not?" Kerry said excitedly. She placed a hand on Nick's shoulder. "Are you coming, Nick?"

"Um, I don't know, Mrs. Chu . . ." Nick began, glancing nervously at Rachel.

Rachel hesitated for a moment before responding. "Come on, let's all go."

Nick's face lit up. "Really? I do know a good place we could go."

Soon the four of them were in Nick's car, approaching the island's most distinctive architectural landmark. "Wah, what an amazing building!" Kerry Chu said, gazing up in awe at the three soaring towers joined at the top by what appeared to be a huge park.

"That's where we're going. At the top is the world's highest man-made park—fifty-seven stories above ground," Nick said.

"You're not *seriously* taking us to the SkyBar at Marina Bay Sands?" Peik Lin grimaced.

"Why not?" Nick asked.

"I thought we'd be going to Raffles Hotel, where the Singapore Sling was invented."

"Raffles is too touristy."

"And this isn't? You'll see, it's going to be all Mainlanders and European tourists up there."

"Trust me, the bartender is brilliant," Nick declared authoritatively.

Ten minutes later, the four of them were sitting in a sleek white cabana in the middle of the two-and-a-half-acre terrace perched in the clouds. Samba music filled the air, and several feet away, an immense infinity pool spanned the length of the park.

"Cheers to Nick!" Rachel's mother declared. "Thank you for bringing us here."

"I'm so glad you like it, Mrs. Chu," Nick said, peering around at the ladies.

"Well, I have to admit, this Singapore Sling is better than I imagined," Peik Lin said, taking another sip of her frothy crimson drink.

"So you're not going to cringe the next time some *tourist* sitting next to you orders one?" Nick said with a wink.

"Depends on how they're dressed," Peik Lin retorted.

For a few moments, they sat savoring the view. Across the bay, the blue hour was settling in, and the crowd of skyscrapers lining the marina seemed to glisten in the balmy air. Nick turned toward Rachel, his eyes searching out hers. She hadn't spoken once since they left Peik Lin's house. Their eyes met for a flash of a moment, before Rachel turned away.

Nick jumped off his bar stool and walked down a few steps toward the infinity pool. As he strolled along the water's edge, a bold silhouette against the darkening sky, the women studied him in silence.

"He's a good man, that Nick," Kerry finally said to her daughter.

"I know," Rachel said quietly.

"I'm so glad he came to see me," Kerry said.

"Came to see you?" Rachel was confused.

"Of course. He showed up on my doorstep in Cupertino two days ago."

Rachel stared at her mother, her eyes widening in amazement. Then she jumped off her bar stool and made a beeline toward Nick. He turned to face her just as she approached. Rachel slowed her pace, turning to look at a couple of swimmers doing disciplined laps around the pool.

"Those swimmers look like they might fall right off the horizon," she said.

"They do, don't they?"

Rachel took a slight breath. "Thank you for bringing my mom here."

"No worries—she needed a good drink."

"To Singapore, I mean."

"Oh, it was the least I could do."

Rachel looked at Nick tenderly. "I can't believe you did this. I can't believe you went halfway around the world and back for me in two days. What ever possessed you to do such a crazy thing?"

Nick flashed his trademark grin. "Well, you can thank a little bird for that."

"A little bird?"

"Yes, a little blue jay that hates Damien Hirst."

At the bar, Kerry was nibbling the pineapple wedge from her third cocktail when Peik Lin whispered excitedly, "Mrs. Chu, don't turn around now, but I spy Nick giving Rachel a long, slow kiss!"

Kerry swiveled around joyously and sighed. "Aiyah, soooo romantic!"

"*Alamak, don't look!* I told you not to look!" Peik Lin scolded.

When Nick and Rachel came back, Kerry scrutinized Nick up and down for a moment and yanked at his rumpled linen shirt. "Aiyah, you've lost too much weight. Your cheeks are so sallow. Let me fatten you up a bit. Can we go to one of those outdoor food bazaars that Singapore is so famous for? I want to eat a hundred sticks of satay while I am here."

"Okay, let's all go to the Chinatown food market on Smith Street," Nick beamed.

"*Alamak*, Nick, Smith Street gets so crowded on Friday nights, and there's never any place to sit," Peik Lin complained. "Why don't we go to Gluttons Bay?"

"I *knew* you were going to suggest that. All you princesses love to go there!"

"No, no, I just happen to think they have the best satay," Peik Lin said defensively.

"Rubbish! Satay is the same wherever you go. I think Rachel's mum would find Smith Street to be more colorful and authentic," Nick argued.

"Authentic my foot, *lah*! If you really want authentic . . ." Peik Lin began.

Rachel glanced at her mother. "They can do all the arguing, we'll just sit back and eat."

"But why are they arguing so much over this?" Kerry asked, amazed.

Rachel rolled her eyes and smiled. "Let them be, Mom. Let them be. This is just how they all are."

Acknowledgments

In your inimitable and wonderful ways, you have each been instrumental in helping me bring this book to life. I am forever grateful to:

Deb Aaronson

Carol Brewer

Linda Casto

Deborah Davis

David Elliott

John Fontana

Simone Gers

Aaron Goldberg

Lara Harris

Philip Hu

Jenny Jackson

Jennifer Jenkins

Michael Korda

Mary Kwan

Jack Lee

Joanne Lim

Alexandra Machinist

Pia Massie

Robin Mina

David Sangalli

Lief Anne Stiles

Rosemary Yeap

Jackie Zirkman

A NOTE ABOUT THE AUTHOR

Kevin Kwan was born and raised in Singapore. He currently lives in Manhattan. *Crazy Rich Asians* is his first novel.

Visit Kevin Kwan at www.kevinkwanbooks.com.